Into the Light

Into the Light

A. G. Smith

Copyright © 2015 A. G. Smith
All rights reserved.

ISBN: 1514811197
ISBN 13: 9781514811191

"Some theories of the world's mysteries are incomprehensible."

"But that doesn't mean they're not true."

1

There was an eerie silence in the streets, on the morning of January 4th 1952. This was the time that I decided to make an appearance into this world, a day when the whole of South London England was covered in a thick white blanket of snow. Outside, all that could be heard was the crunching of frozen snow from the tyres of the occasional adventurous vehicle or the stomping of a few intrepid souls wrapped up like Eskimos not knowing whether their feet were on the pavement or the road.

As my mother already had had a child, my sister, two years previously, I had to be born at home and delivered by our family general practitioner. Dr. Brown. He was an elderly man, with a bald, liver-spotted head and thick, bushy eyebrows, which seemed to sit on the top rim of his spectacles. Luckily, his surgery wasn't far away and he had somehow managed to brave the weather conditions to get to my mother in time for my birth. That was after a frantic and laboured effort by my father, who called him from a nearby phone box.

Being born at home was quite normal in those days as midwives were a rare commodity and as only firstborns were usually afforded the luxury of being delivered in a hospital bed (unless, of course, there was a chance there might be complications). As she carried me, my mother had a normal pregnancy throughout, but just before my birth, she fainted and fell unconscious for approximately ten or fifteen seconds. She recovered quickly, though and after I was born, everything else went fine, although it was only later on in life that I would realise the significance of her fainting spell!

Apparently, I did not cry at birth, but instead had a smile on my face. That was until I received a whack on my bum to make sure my lungs got fully inflated. Obviously my mother had told me this story of my birth when I was older and I had not logged it into the fresh memory section of my brain. But what was strange was that, during my first year as a child, I remember a profound awareness, as if all the new surroundings and noises I heard were familiar to me. I didn't feel frightened or threatened in any way; I just had the feeling of somehow being safe and I seem to remember being totally content. I felt I wasn't in a scary world at all, although when I was in my pram, some of the unfamiliar faces that shadowed the light as they lurched toward me saying "goo, goo, goo," should have frightened me half to death; but no, I didn't react, nor was I in any way perturbed by the sights and sounds of the people I was encountering. I suppose the oddest thing of all is that I do actually remember thoughts and feelings from my very first year.

Four or so years passed and I was running around like every other toddler, playing with toy cars and getting into all sorts of mischief. The only time I would shed a tear was when I had fallen and hurt myself physically in some way, but I wasn't the kind of child who would cry just to get their own way. I didn't have any toddler friends, because up until then I hadn't had much contact with other children my age; the only time I might encounter them was maybe on a shopping trip with my mother. There was my sister of course, but she was in her own little dolly world, one which I couldn't relate to in the slightest.

As my mother had returned to work about a year after my birth and as my father was also out working most of the time, my grandparents, who lived on the ground floor of our small urban house, looked after my sister Linda and me. It was like that in England in the 1950's: the couple living downstairs in many dwellings were often the parents of one of the married pair living upstairs, if you can get your head round that. This meant that the older members of the family did not have to negotiate the staircase.

This arrangement was beneficial for all concerned as no one could afford child minders and the grandparents were mainly retired anyway, with not much to do all day. But the day had now come that I would have to go to a nursery school, alleviating my grandparents of my normal boyish, boisterous antics. That day I remember well.

In the morning, my mother got me up as usual and sat me on a cushion, which lay on top of a box on a chair up to the kitchen table. I don't know if high chairs were invented then, but I certainly didn't have one. She then scrunched up a block of something from a yellow box, put it in a bowl and added some cold milk for my breakfast. I enjoyed whatever it was along with a small cup of milky tea. Luckily, a makeshift bib, tied round my neck, prevented my pyjama top from getting constantly stained. After breakfast, I was lifted from my cushion and set on the table; my pyjamas were then removed and a damp flannel was rubbed over my face and then all over my body. I hated this, but after it was over, I enjoyed the warmth of the towel that had been draped over the back of a chair in front of the electric fire. It was a cold morning, I think it was April and that fire didn't seem to be warming the room much; my tiny teeth were chattering as my naked little body shivered. I was then dressed in freshly ironed underpants, a vest and a warm lumberjack shirt, followed by short grey trousers and a zigzag-patterned, sleeveless woollen jumper. My long, itchy woollen socks were put on and my shoes were rammed on my feet and laced. I think my shoes were getting too small for me, as the shape of my toes had started to become visible through the scuffed leather. Next came my favourite duffel coat, with the large, tubular wooden buttons and the hood that had to be folded at the front so I could see where I was going. That duffel coat was the gateway to all my superhero fantasies, because I would just do up the top button and wear it without putting my arms through the sleeves. I then became an instant caped crusader. For now, though, it was just to keep me warm.

I was all set to go, although I didn't know exactly where or how far and also what to expect when I reached this nursery place. I wasn't worried, though, as I had never encountered anything that I might be apprehensive about before.

Off we set, slamming the street door behind us, because it tended to get stuck in damp weather. My mother took my hand and we crossed the road. I never had permission to cross a road on my own and was always trusted to stay on the pavement when I played outside, even though then there was very little traffic about. We passed a row of houses on our right similar to ours, dodging an empty galvanized metal dustbin that had rolled onto the pavement; then, at apace, we crossed another road. I tripped but I was saved from grazing my knees on the rough tarmac by my mother's firm grip, but; my shoes got scuffed further for a few more paces till I became upright again. The houses this time on our right were prefabricated ones, like bungalows. These had been erected years ago as temporary accommodations because of bomb damage during World War 2. Although we hadn't travelled that far, my destination seemed to be a long way off for me and my short, little legs. Surprisingly, after a total of about five minutes, we reached the school.

Above the main gate, the words *boys* and *girls,* were carved into a dirty white stone which we then went through into a large, deserted playground. There were a couple of rubber balls there, which had come to rest over a drain grill. These had obviously been left there by the junior children who had already started their lessons inside and I could hear the throng of many children's voices coming from within this old Victorian building. As we made our way across the playground and approached its entrance, I saw chalk marks and carved initials etched into the soft red brickwork just outside. These etchings had likely been made by the present and probably lots of earlier generations of little hooligans but although these new sights and sounds were new to me, it all seemed very familiar for some reason.

We went up a flight of stone steps on the exterior, through a door and into a badly lit corridor. I remember seeing crates of small milk bottles stacked in the corner. The corridor was narrow and, on our left, was another flight of stairs going up to the next floor. This dark corridor and staircase surprisingly seemed a little scary, so I gripped my mother's hand tightly. From the top of the stairs, we turned right and were confronted by two large, heavy wooden doors with wired glass in their top sections. These swinging doors were both painted black and my mother struggled to push one open for us to enter into a large hall. In the hall, the wooden floor was highly polished and the high ceiling had lots of large hanging lights in a row, with white-enamelled metal shades. The three-sash corded windows of this hall were large, but each had many small panes of glass in them and on the walls between the windows, were two massive wooden climbing frames, with thick ropes hanging from the tops. These frames also had lots of horizontal wooden bars across them, like a ladder effect and I noticed the large hinges, with a big wheel attached at the bottom of the frame, which anchored them to the walls. The curved indentations on the polished floor suggested that the frames were pulled out and used quite often for children to climb. From within the hall, there were four or five accessible classrooms and we headed diagonally toward a small one located in the far corner. As my mother opened the door, a pleasant-looking lady greeted us; she was probably in her thirties and introduced herself as Miss Healey, my new nursery teacher.

"Good morning Mrs. Seer. I presume this young man is Terry," said the lady, cordially.

Miss Healey was slim and very tall. She had brown shoulder length hair and wore black, thick-rimmed glasses. She was also wearing an obnoxious perfume, which seemed to fill the room and made me feel a bit sick. After a brief chat with her, my mother then said to me,

"I'll see you later then Terry. Be good for Miss Healey."

She then started to leave.

I think my mother thought I would be OK to be left under the supervision of Miss Healey, as I had almost always adapted to new sights, situations and people without a care. She was soon to learn different. Before the heavy classroom door closed, I managed to squeeze through the gap and chase her into the hall, screaming with all my might and begging for her not to leave me. I'm sure all the other children in the adjacent classrooms must have heard. It must have taken a good fifteen minutes for my mother to finally convince me she would return in a few hours, before she could pry my tiny fingers from her skirt and lead me back into the classroom. It wasn't the new surroundings or the other children that concerned me; it was only the thought I might never see my mother again. It turned out I could handle new places and situations but could not easily handle my emotions.

Although obviously upset at my mother's departure, this fact did not explain why my moment of terror at her leaving didn't result from the sight of twenty unfamiliar boys and girls, as well as a giant person named Miss Healey, towering over me. Reluctantly I wiped my sore, red eyes and the springy mucous from my nose on the sleeve of my duffel coat and sat down on one of the chairs. Miss Healey asked me to take my coat off, but I refused because I wanted to be ready for my mother when she returned.

After that horrible day had passed and after the realisation had dawned on me that my mother would return to fetch me each day, I soon came to terms with my new situation.

But Miss Healey would soon discover that I wasn't exactly the same as the rest of the children in her charge.

The classroom I was in consisted of ten low-level tables pushed together lengthways into two rows of five. Two small wooden chairs sat beneath each table. Miss Healey had a similar type table and chair at the front of the class, only hers were full-size versions. The walls were painted brown about four feet high up to the center of the wall and then green further up to the ceiling. A large map of the world, held on by white sticky tape, rose high up on the wall behind Miss Healey's desk and there were pictures painted by children, stuck on with the same tape, lining the walls. I had never seen pictures of houses with green smoke coming from the chimney or blue-stick people with no feet and spiky hair before! I had designated my own seat at a table on the row furthest from Miss Healey. The perfume wasn't as strong there and I had a large cast-iron radiator behind me. I loved the warmth that radiator would kick out. Audrey Higgins, who shared my table, had lots of freckles on her nose and always looked as if her clothes and long ginger hair had never been washed. She also smelled of stale urine, so there was no way I could get away from the pongs in that room.

After a week or so had passed, I had settled into my new environment surprisingly well. I enjoyed modelling plasticine and painting pictures and Miss Healey often commented on how well I had picked up the alphabet and the basic math she taught. In her eyes at that time I was a model student, as I was attentive and eager to learn, but this attentiveness was all about to change.

One day in the classroom, I saw something in the corner of my eye move from an empty space in front of me. I instantly felt a cold tingle from my neck and down my back. I had never experienced this feeling before, but once at home I had heard my grandmother say that she had felt a cold tingle in this same way. She then commented that she felt as if someone had just walked over her grave. Obviously I didn't know what she meant, but I likened my cold tingle to hers.

These glimpses of things then occurred quite often and I couldn't understand why the other kids didn't see something too. Consequently, they laughed at me when I kept turning my head sharply, as if afflicted by some nervous tick.

As the days went by, these glimpses turned into strange moving blobs (now in full view), but it was like I was looking at them through a thick, opaque window.

Gradually the images seem to evolve into what looked like people because I could see the outline of a body form, with a head, two arms and two legs. It was as if there were more people in the classroom than there actually were. I knew no one else saw them because the rest of the children just carried on with what they were doing and Miss Healey would raise her voice to me to tell me to stop staring into space. But it was difficult for me to concentrate with busy apparitions moving about the room and seemingly passing through solid objects with ease. Although vague at first, these wispy forms became a little more defined as each day went by. They were definitely shaped like people, although seemingly unclothed and colourless. If I had not been so young, I probably would have instantly thought I was seeing ghosts, but I had never heard of ghosts before and no one knew of Halloween and what it entailed—at least, not in England in those days.

My fascination with these spectral-type beings—and therefore my lack of attention and participation—resulted in a stern reprimand from Miss Healey. Prior to that, I could tell she was getting more and more agitated with me. Finally after class one day, Miss. Healey, asked my mother to stay behind for a while. It was obviously about my attention deficit.

Later that afternoon when we had returned home, my mother questioned me as to why I kept staring into space instead of participating along with the other children. I decided there and then not to tell and just said I didn't know and would try to pay more attention in the future. I felt I was already in trouble and because no one else could see what I could, I feared that I wouldn't be believed and would get into further hot water for lying.

My parents were loving toward me but fairly strict about certain things such as telling the truth. I realised then I should try to ignore my visions as much as possible, but not paying attention to them was not going to be easy, because an intense curiosity about these apparitions burned in my mind constantly. From then on I had to do my utmost to act like the other kids and disregard any spectral distractions. After some time, I think I learned to do this quite well, but it became apparent these apparitions were not planning to go away.

At a tender age, a child doesn't usually question whether he or she is any different from other children of the same age, but, due to my visions, I started to discover that I had something else unusual going on inside my head. I found that sometimes when Miss Healey spoke, I seemed to know exactly what she was going to say. This did not always happen, but sometimes I could finish some of her sentences in my thoughts before she completed them. This strange occurrence also happened at home with my family members. I found it strange as some of the words spoken by them were words I had never heard of before and also didn't know the meaning of. For the same reason, as my visions increased and because I thought no one else could do this, I thought I'd better not say anything, so I didn't let on to anyone. I must admit though, I did enjoy this amusing ability.

Within the same school building and at seven years old, I graduated from my nursery schooling and infant classes and was now at my primary school stage. This time there was a set curriculum, which included the three *R*s: reading, writing and arithmetic. I'll never understand the logic of naming these subjects the three *R*s when writing begins with a *W* and arithmetic an *A*. My English and form teacher was the notorious Miss Steggle, known by and feared by all the children in the school—and also feared by some of the staff as well, I think. She was a small, wrinkled woman, who, I thought, must be 105 years old. She had a bellowing, shouting voice, which could be heard over the entire school. I actually found her to be OK but made sure not to antagonise her in any way. My limited ability—predicting some of her words in my head—did help a little with her demanding lessons, as well as spelling and compiling sentences, but it didn't make me top of the class, although I wasn't at the bottom either. I was, however, one of her privileged few who worked in her class as a milk monitor. I gave out the milk, to each pupil in the class, one small bottle each day that contained about a third of a pint. These were the bottles that the milkman stacked in crates every morning in **that** dim corridor. I even got paid for my efforts, thrupence a week. That was three pennies in the old Sterling currency and just over a penny in today's decimal money.

You may not think it was that much, but I could buy a lot of small sweets for that amount back then. I also had the bonus of drinking some extra milk from the unopened bottles that were left over.

Apart from English, there were also other lessons with different teachers. Mr. Philips was my maths master. I didn't like him much, but again my predictive ability helped me in learning all the set times tables, although I couldn't understand why we were taught all the tables up to twelve, after which we'd jump straight to the sixteen tables. What was wrong with the thirteen, fourteen and fifteen time's tables? History was a bit of a bonus as a lot of that was taught strangely somehow I seemed to already know, as if I'd been taught it before. I hated religious education and I could not see the point of teaching baseless or unsubstantiated dogmas or events. Science was OK I suppose, but it did not give me any insight into my visions and even now I haven't got the hang of what colour litmus paper tests for acid or alkaline. One lesson I really enjoyed though was physical education. I finally got to climb up those two large wooden frames in the hall that I had first seen with my mother before starting nursery school. The final lesson that was compulsory was art. This lesson was great as the art teacher was a real pushover and even when paper airplanes were flying all over the room, he would never raise his voice or chastise us in any way.

Through those primary school years, I was gradually gaining knowledge from various sources about general life and the myths that went with them, such as those stories and legends about ghosts, for instance. It seemed that most children and a good few adults were absolutely terrified of ghosts if they believed they existed. I thought that if my visions were indeed ghosts, then I certainly wasn't afraid of them as they had never hurt me in any way.

There was something I did realise about my sightings though; the school building had two levels and some of my lessons were up **those** stairs and through **that** dark corridor to get to the top floor. On that level, for some reason, my visions of the beings were fewer. To my logic, that meant I must be seeing some sort of community down below on the ground, just as you might expect to see more people moving about at ground level on the street than you would on an upstairs level.

I also noticed something very odd on my way home from school one day. It was an incident that helped verify that my visions had some basis in reality.

A dog without an owner was trotting away quite happily on the pavement when I saw it walk straight through one of my spectral sightings. Instantly the dog bolted with its tail between its legs, as if being stung by a bee. I surmised that either one of two things had happened: either the dog had been stung by a bee, or it had experienced the same cold tingling sensation that both my grandmother and myself had experienced. If the latter was the case, then, to me that absolutely proved my visions were not a product of my imagination and that they actually did exist. As my general knowledge grew each day, I felt determined to get answers. I decided I would investigate all avenues to get to the truth.

My four-year stint passed at my primary school and I had taken the eleven plus examination to determine what kind of secondary school I would attend. Needless to say, I failed the exam, so a grammar school was out of the question. Still living at the same house, I was attending my new school, a secondary comprehensive, which was a couple of miles away.

For my twelfth birthday, my parents had bought me a brand new bike. I already had a bike, but it was a small second hand one, which was going a bit rusty and the handlebars and saddle were at full adjustment. This new bike was a shiny black and white model, with gears and racing handlebars and because this new school had a bike shed, I could ride this magnificent machine there to show it off to my schoolmates.

On my way home from school after just two days of commuting, I decided to stop at a confectionery shop. I parked the bike at the kerb and went in. You never heard of bikes being stolen in the early sixties, so it did not cross my mind that it might be. When I came out of the shop, my bike was still there, but, to my horror, a lorry had backed up, knocked the bike over and crushed the front wheel.

I was utterly devastated and shouted all kinds of abuses at the driver, who was still sitting in his cab, not realising what he had done. He finally saw me ranting at him and, after getting out of his vehicle, managed to calm me down enough to explain that his insurance would pay to have the bike repaired. He then wrote down his insurance numbers on a piece of scrap paper, vehicle registration and phone number of the firm he worked for. I was then to give this to my father for him to sort out. All I could think of as I dragged my one good wheeled bike home was that even if my bike was repaired, it would never be that brand new sleek racing machine again. The next day and for about a month after, I had to walk to and from school, as I had already given my old rusty bike away.

I suppose it's some kind of juvenile human nature that when telling other kids about your misfortune, you get laughed at more often than you receive sympathy. Needless to say, I did get over all the laughs and jokes at my expense and with the return of my repaired bike, I continued using it as my school transport, but treating it with reverence no more. But hey, it was 1964. The Beatles and Rolling Stones were on the music scene and all the girls were wearing miniskirts. It was a new era and people had started casting off their Victorian and post-war inhibitions. It was also an exciting time because the boys and girls of my comprehensive school were getting a less strict, new style of education.

The school building itself was more modern than my primary one and was constructed mainly of metal framework and glass. The school uniform dress code also meant that I had to wear long trousers all the time. At last, no more frozen kneecaps and my legs would finally be warm on cold days. I hated short trousers and although I was born in winter, I really didn't like being cold. My secondary school also excited me because I knew that I would be having more advanced science and biology lessons, lessons that might give me a better understanding of how to make sense of the unusual things I had seen. Up until now my theories were all based on my limited understanding of the world with no real scientific facts to back them up. This all made me hope for some revelations.

My form teacher, Mr. Williams, was also the person who gave the science and biology lessons. He was an average-looking man in his forties, going a bit bald and who wore the standard national health glasses of that time, the ones that had thin, brown round wire frames. He also wore the same tweed jacket and brown corduroy trousers every single day and at break time in the playground, he would smoke a droopy pipe, like Sherlock Holmes.

There were about forty pupils in all of the classes, so that meant that no one really got any special attention when they did not understand something, except for the teacher's pets of course, of which I was not one. Generally the lessons were a bit boring, but in science, I did learn a few basic things, like magnetic fields and electricity. Once Mr. Williams made us all stand in a circle and hold hands. He then joined the circle by giving the student on either side of him a wire to hold while he held a car dynamo. He then spun the core of the dynamo, giving everyone one hell of a shock. Not many of us thought it was funny, but he certainly did, the sadistic bastard.

Dissecting frogs in biology wasn't much fun either. I just kept wondering why thirty-odd poor little frogs had to die, just so we understood the nature of their anatomy. Why did we need the experience of cutting them up when we could have looked at one already dissected by the teacher.

What I did find interesting in these classes, though, was finding out about the brain and how it works and how it produces tiny electrical impulses called alpha, beta, gamma, theta and delta waves. The brain's complexities really had me thinking. This new kind of information opened up new theories for me to explore and revealed new possibilities that might help in my quest to find answers. I speculated brainwaves were thoughts that could be turned into signals and possibly transmitted. Could it be that my strange psychic ability was the result of me being an intermittent receiver of someone else's electromagnetic oscillations? Not really! I had to make sense of these things in layperson's terms and I still couldn't get my head round electromagnetic oscillations anyway.

My new knowledge was helpful but too confusing at times, but basically I understood that a person only really uses about a sixth of their brain capacity and therefore no one really knows what the brain is capable of. It turned out that, during my four years at that secondary school and not missing a single class of any of the sciences there was only that one subject that intrigued me—the brain and how it works. I didn't know at the time, but I was definitely on the right track.

Although wanting to soak up as much knowledge as possible to help me find answers, my main interest at that time, to be honest, was girls. I liked nothing better than to snog as many girls as possible, with the occasional fumble; at different times of course, behind the bike shed. That seemed to be every boy's prime directive and in that respect I was no different from anybody else. Although my visions remained during those years, I just wanted to be a normal teenager and have fun with the rest of the lads. I had a few girlfriends and lots of boy mates and we were always involved in some sort of mischief or antics. Sometimes one of us would pay to get into a cinema, while the rest of us would run around the back to the exit door. When the film started and the lights fell in the theatre, the one who paid would then open the exit door and we'd all rush in. I enjoyed my school years but they did seem to whizz by. I had acquired some knowledge though, that was to help my theories progress a little closer to the truth and that would help me find out what made me different.

My psychic ability didn't really increase much, although I had tried to force it a few times but that didn't seem to work. Occasionally, though, I would know when the telephone was about to ring or when there was someone at the door before she or he knocked, but I somehow knew that this intuitive ability was always going to be a spontaneous thing and not something I could contrive. I had to come to terms with the fact I wasn't going to be any kind of superhero with special powers, but I also knew that no one that I had met could do what I could or see what I could see.

At fifteen years of age, I left school without any academic qualifications and, like most boys of my age in that era; I too believed the only course open to me was to learn a manual skill. A few years previously, my father had started his own plastering business, a move which ultimately led to my apprenticeship in his firm. It was to be a rude awakening to the real world, getting up at six in the morning and not getting home until between seven or eight in the evening. It was not my idea of fun at all. By this time, my dad's business was doing well, so my parents decided to move from our South London home to a semidetached house in Surrey. I didn't like the suburbs one bit as all my friends were in London. Our new neighbours were OK I suppose, but they were a little too high brow and snooty compared to what I was used to.

My plastering tuition, working on building sites and getting filthy dirty every single day, turned out to be very demanding. The only good thing was that I learned to drive a dumper truck. The truck had the same controls as a car and, as I was on private land, my being under age didn't matter. Sometimes I'd see one of those beings and intentionally head straight for it. I knew instinctively I would pass right through it and not do it any harm, but I did it because it was a way of venting my frustration about not knowing what or who it was.

Four years had passed and I was now nineteen. I had finished my apprenticeship and was very competent, probably because I had genetically inherited some of my father's plastering skills. My sister, who was now twenty-one, had left home and got married at nineteen to Martin. He was a nice enough fellow but I didn't quite gel with him for some inexplicable reason. They now had a child of their own and were living in their own house, so I was now feeling the urge to move out of our parent's house and get a place of my own. I had passed my driving test the first time a year earlier and I think driving that dumper truck gave me a bit of an edge, so now that I was getting a full plaster's wage, I managed to put a down payment on an old banger. This car enabled me to drive back and forth to my old area of London to visit my one remaining friend Jeff from my school days.

Together, Jeff and I would go to our favourite pub to play darts and barbilliards. But although he was my best friend, I never ever told him about my visions or my sporadic psychic experiences. My link with the past didn't last long, though, as he announced he was going to join the army. I never saw or heard from him ever again for some reason.

So now it was time to up sticks from my parents and Surrey and get myself a place back in the South London area, where I felt more comfortable. I managed to get a converted flat on the top floor of an old three-storey Victorian house. I wanted somewhere fairly high up, as I knew there would be fewer sightings of my psychic enigmas. The flat had a small kitchenette, a reasonably sized lounge and a slightly cramped but adequate bedroom. It suited me perfectly and of an evening I would look out over the rooftops of the smaller buildings and watch the busy nightlife below. I rarely saw the spectral beings when it was dark unless they were in close proximity or a street lamp may have illuminated them. This place was a great respite for me, as it allowed me to see the world as others do for a change. Although out of sight, my visions of the spectral apparitions were never out of mind, as that nagging question haunted me to know exactly what I was seeing and why.

Life and work went on in its monotonous way, until one particular Friday I had to go to a building site in Putney, also a borough of South London. My task was to plaster the ceiling of a stair well. I had rigged a scaffold similar to many others I had done in the past and started the job. This particular day I didn't realise that my movements on the scaffold boards were causing them to inch off one of the supporting ladders. A few minutes later, the entire scaffold collapsed and I had fallen down onto the concrete staircase with an almighty-sounding crash. There is often a saying that when banging your head you see stars. I saw those stars all right, but that wasn't the only thing. In close proximity were two of the beings I had seen all my life, but this time it was obvious that they saw me.

2

Although still dazed, the beings features were now fully defined. They had large, black, almond-shaped eyes and greyish faces, which had a look of astonishment, as if they could not believe what they were seeing. Then one of them said to me in a frantic voice.

"You can't see us, it's impossible." They both then scurried away leaving me numb from my fall. After a few minutes the realisation of my accident came into focus and I got up from the floor. Luckily, I had no broken bones, but I was badly bruised and I had a splitting headache. I then began to doubt what I had seen and heard and wondered whether it was just all down to the bang on my head.

The rest of that day I tried to make sense of the incident. Had it now become a two way vision between me and these beings? Was it a one off experience? Or maybe it didn't happen at all and it was just the bang on the head. But the being spoke to me in English. That inferred that they were aware of human existence and that they knew enough about us to be able to speak in our language. It was hard to make sense of all this. I would have to consider everything to come up with a logical explanation.

That evening, at home in my flat, I decided to try to piece together the whole incident and try to make sense of what had happened. Assuming that the vision was in fact based on some reality and not a hallucination, what did I now know? I sat down and began to write down my thoughts on a notepad.

Even only in a vague way, I had always seen these beings, but they had never responded in a way that suggested they could see me. Yet I now know that even if they could not see me, they were aware of human existence.

The beings that spoke, suggested in their tone that some sort of barrier should have been in place to prevent either one of us seeing each other.

Speaking English meant its species had to have been aware of humans and our culture, so they have probably been around a long time.

I had finally seen the beings close up and fairly clearly, even if it was for a brief moment. They resembled very closely what the general consensus depicted as aliens, especially the ones that supposedly crashed at Roswell and were taken to Area 51, so it was a good assumption that they could indeed be aliens.

Did my minor psychic ability have anything to do with my visions?

My head was buzzing trying to come up with a logical, feasible explanation for what I had written on my notepad. I convinced myself within the first few minutes; going by what I thought of my conclusions, that aliens had invaded Earth at some stage but had not been successful, so they left. The aliens that I saw were left behind, but had found some way of hiding themselves with some sort of invisible force field. Finally, because my mother fainted just before my birth, I had been starved of oxygen briefly, which triggered a psychic ability to see through that invisible field.

After my initial conclusion of what I thought must be true, I ripped the page from my note pad, crunched it up and threw it on the floor. I realised that what I had come up with was a load of speculative sci-fi nonsense, which you might read in a comic book. The truth was I could not make sense of any of my experiences and the knowledge I now had was nowhere near enough information for a reasonable and logical assumption.

I was glad to get to bed and go to sleep that night, as my head was not only pounding from the fall but was throbbing from umpteen, ever-changing scenarios of what might be the truth.

Saturday, the day after, I woke and my physical headache had finally gone. It was the weekend and I didn't have to go to work. I needed to get provisions for the coming week, so I washed, renewed the sticking plasters to my minor injuries and put on some clean clothes. Then, off I went to my local high street shops. I had a list of things in my head of what I needed to get, mainly twelve pints of milk and ready meals, which I could just bung in the oven for twenty minutes.

The milk was a vast amount for one person I know, but I had acquired a taste for it in my early school days. And since I didn't drink any alcohol on a regular basis, I drank milk by the gallon. After purchasing my meagre rations for the week, I called into the jewellers to have a new battery put into my watch. Then, I started to head back home, passing one of those cancer research charity shops that sold second hand things. I don't know why, but I decided to go back and have a look inside. I was somehow drawn to the second hand book section and, scanning my way through, I came across one hardback title called, *The Brain and ESP* (Extra Sensory Perception), written by an Oxford college professor. Named Dr Anton Serebral with umpteen letters attributed to him. I decided to purchase it for the astounding price of thirty pence. To be honest I couldn't wait to get back to my flat, sit down with a cup of coffee and stick my nose into the book's contents.

The book was about case studies of people that had, or claimed to have had, extra ordinary mind abilities. These studies included telekinesis, mind reading and accounts of uncanny reincarnation knowledge. It even dealt with alien abduction experiences. Each chapter of the book dealt with cases from each of these subjects. The telekinesis chapter did not relate to me at all, but the mind reading chapter made me realise that what I could do intermittently—namely, my occasional psychic intuitions and visions—might be something quite common in humans. What it did not tell me is why everyone doesn't have this ability. The reincarnation section was interesting, as it made me think it could explain why sometimes I had a sense of already visiting a place or why I saw some things I had never seen before as familiar. The alien abduction chapter was a real eye opener; so many people were convinced that they had been abducted. On top of this, abductees experiences of the aliens seemed to all have similarities in their accounts of the events. These people's descriptions of the beings were nearly all the same and these descriptions resembled the beings in my encounter. Many also said that they had been taken on board a craft and were experimented on. Each also reported that the beings had probed them in some way.

Somehow all the things I was reading about seemed to tie together and relate to me in some way, except that I was absolutely sure that I had never been abducted and had certainly never seen a UFO. The author also added as a footnote that some autism could not be explained psychologically or medically. Some people diagnosed as autistic, for example, have the ability to do fantastic equations in their head or can record memories instantly (i.e., a photographic memory). Others are endowed with an ability to draw in detail what they had seen for just a few seconds. But many of these people were missing a normal perception of basic human traits. I knew I did not come under this autistic category, but it still made me think that this too was connected to me in some way.

All this new information was just too much for my brain to handle and I just felt like I wanted to shut my eyes and have no thoughts on the subject whatsoever. I needed a short break away from the city's hustle and bustle and somewhere quiet and open, without the noise of traffic, of people and of alien-type forms that only I could see. Tomorrow was Sunday and I decided that I was going to drive out into the countryside somewhere to find a deserted grass field and just relax.

Sunday's weather forecast was not great, although it was June 24. The sky was a bit dull with a few dark clouds overhead, but I thought I would take the chance that it wouldn't rain. I packed a couple of sandwiches, made myself a flask of coffee and set off in my car out of the city. After driving about an hour, I managed to find a nice, quiet spot and parked just off road in a country lane. Walking across a ploughed field, I found myself in a large grassy area and laid out a waterproof sheet, as it had rained the night before and I knew the ground would still be a bit damp. I sat on the ground sheet and was now in a nice tranquil setting. I wanted to empty my brain of all related thoughts of the disposition that had tormented me all my life. I want to be free of sights that I didn't have a tangible explanation for and all the scenarios that went with them. I lay down and closed my eyes.

Less than ten minutes had passed when I felt a drop of water on my face. I opened my eyes to see the sky had gone from a dull grey to black. Then an almighty clap of thunder rang out that seemed to pulsate all through the ground. Disappointedly, I got up quickly and gathered my things together, roughly folding my ground sheet. It was apparent that this was not going to be a light shower. Dressed only in jeans and a T-shirt, I was not prepared for a deluge. A flash of lightning appeared in the sky, as if the entire universe had cracked, followed by a blast of thunder directly after. In a matter of seconds, the heavens completely opened up and I was soaked, after managing only a few yards of my escape. The storm was obviously directly overhead, so all I could do was run as fast as I could, back in the direction of my car, which was at least eight hundred yards away in the nearby lane. I only managed about a hundred yards when a searing pain shook my entire body, and I felt as if I had been hit on the head with a concrete block. I had been stuck by a lightning bolt and my body crumpled onto the wet grass. At that moment I felt, saw and thought nothing, as if I had never existed.

When I started to come around, I could not tell if I had been out cold for a few seconds or a year. My body was pulsating with excruciating pain in every joint and muscle. Gradually, I began to open my eyes but saw nothing except a blinding white light, just a few yards away. Then the light vanished for a few seconds; a moment later, it reappeared. Although still hazy and barely open, my eyes were beginning to focus on two figures, silhouetted within the light. As my brain started to half function my immediate thought was that I must be either dead or dying and that the two figures were deceased relatives beckoning me into the light—to enter paradise or somewhere similar. I had read this at some stage in the past so I was now convinced that it must be true.

Somehow I realised that I was still breathing, if only barely, but I also accepted the inevitability of my demise. But I was far too weak to move, so how was I to enter this light?

Suddenly, the two figures I had seen, emerged from the brilliance and although my eyes were still glazed, I could see that they were both about six-feet tall. Each of these forms grabbed one of my arms and then dragged me from where I lay into the radiant light. At that point my consciousness completely gave out and everything went black.

I had never thought about being dead before, but it was logical to assume that when it happens, there are no thoughts, no consciousness. But my brain was beginning to work again and my consciousness returning. Slowly, I was having lucid thoughts, so surely I could not be dead. With my eyes still closed, I was feeling muscular sensations running through my body and my brain and senses determined I must be lying down. I ached all over, but hey! I remembered being struck by lightning and I thought it was a miracle I had even survived.

Gradually with my eyes remaining shut, I started piecing together the events I could vaguely recall just prior to my blackout. The two six-foot figures were certainly not relatives of mine. They had dragged me into the light with what seemed like brute force. There was no serenity about it, so what in the world had happened to me?

Now fully aware that I was indeed still alive, I began to open my eyes with a chilling apprehension. I was prostrate, facing a pastel blue-coloured wall. With my eyes now fully open, I wondered how long I had been unconscious for, so I instinctively looked at my watch. The digital screen was blank, as if the battery was dead. I thought that was odd, as I had only just had a new battery put in it. I then looked down to see what I was lying on. It looked like water that was suspended in the air a couple of feet from the floor, without being encased. The wetness was firm enough to take my weight with no penetration. Shuffling my body around to face the other direction and putting my feet on the floor, I held my breath with trepidation, but with relief, I found I was quite alone. I was in an oblong-shaped room, which was about eighteen-feet long by about twelve-feet wide. The ceiling was white and about ten-feet high and had a kind of short hairy texture to it. All the walls were pastel blue but seemed ultra-smooth.

Being a plasterer, I would often notice degrees of smoothness and was able to estimate quite accurately the room's dimensions. The floor was very curious, because it was not a textile but more like a firm but slightly spongy light green plastic. None of it had a joint to be seen anywhere. There were no windows in this room, but somehow it had an even amount of adequate brightness, all without the aid of light fittings. A door was centralised on the wall to my right, but it lacked a handle or hinges. What was most amazing was the furniture, which only consisted of a coffee table–type rectangle, a sofa-shaped seat about six-feet long and the bed I had been lying on, all of which was made from this watery-looking substance. I could feel a slight breeze of fresh air but had no clue from where it originated. On the table, there was a silver coloured, plastic-looking jug, filled with water and a matching beaker. There was also a bowl made of the same material, which had small cubes stacked inside what looked like pieces of fudge.

I poured and drank some of the water as my mouth and throat was dry, like the thirst you feel after a medical operation. I also tried one of the cubes from the bowl and yes, it tasted like chicken.

Realising the fact I was in confinement and who ever brought me here was not from my era. I began to speculate as to where I was and exactly what had happened after my electrocution. I was still wearing the same clothes, so years could not have passed or they would have rotted or, at the very least, smelled bad. Nor were my clothes even singed from the lightning. My best conclusion was that I had somehow been transported into the future or was on a spaceship of some kind. My futuristic new surroundings would back up both those theories—or had I just read too many of those sci-fi comic books as a child?

Just as I started to relax my bewildered mind and aching body, the sliding door opened with a rush of air and a swooshing sound. As I looked at the opened doorway, I felt my eyes bulge, as I took a sharp intake of breath. It seemed like an eternity passed. Yet it was only a split second before three figures, one by one, entered the room, after which the door closed behind them.

With my breath firmly stuck in my lungs, my mouth open and with my eyes unblinking, I told my brain these forms were definitely not human. A flash recollection of the beings I had always seen and the images of the Roswell aliens combined in my mind to assess what I was actually looking at. Two of the beings were about six-feet tall and the other, about five-feet five. The smaller one faced me and immediately said, "You are quite safe and are in no danger," in a way as if it knew I would be alarmed and as if it wanted to pacify me as soon as possible. My lungs slowly started to deflate, as the three beings sat down onto the watery sofa with the shorter one between the larger two. I could not stop my eyes from scanning their bodies, as my brain tried to make sense of what was sitting before me.

They were quite thin and their skin had a smooth blue-grey colour all over, except for their eyes, hands and feet. They did not appear to be wearing clothes—only what looked like a utility belt around their waists. There were no signs of genitals. Their heads were enlarged from the brow up with large, black almond-shaped eyes, which only seemed to blink once about every thirty seconds. They had small noses and definitive lips were missing from their tiny mouths. I saw no ears visible on them. I noticed their hands were distinctly different from humans, with each having three long, bony fingers and a thumb, which had what looked to be tiny sucker pads on their tips. Their feet were unshod, human-like in shape and they only had two large toes. I assumed the three beings I was looking at were male but only because the one who spoke in English sounded male. It was apparent from their postures that the smaller being was some sort of official; the other two were his body guards, or something. The official began to speak again.

"My name is Theron and I represent the high council of our race. Our species are called Terrans and we are of the planet Earth."

Confused, I immediately thought: How was this possible, that they were from Earth?

"We evolved on this planet millions of years ago, when the solar system was still not fully defined," Theron continued. "I suppose the nearest species in your world you could liken us to are reptiles, except we have traits of mammals within us. With our rapid evolution, we quickly gained intelligence and established our cities and technology. We can live for a thousand years but can only reproduce once in every ten. Unlike humans, our brain and body functions work purely by chemical changes and although we breathe air to oxygenate our bodies, we have no need of blood. Clothing is also not required, as our skin acts as a shield against extreme heat or cold; therefore our body temperature is always stable. I am giving you this information to help you understand and realise the biological differences between our species. By me informing you of this, I hope you might trust whatever I tell you to be the truth."

I was flabbergasted, but I was warming to this creature. He was obviously very intelligent and knew by telling me about his species I would feel a bit more at ease. I started feeling the courage to ask questions, but before I could, the creature spoke again.

"You were careless to be struck by lightning and to save your life we had to make the decision to bring you here. I think you should try to rest for now and I will return in a quarter day. If you require anything, one of my assistants will be on the other side of the door for your safety and our security. By what name may I call you?"

"My name is Terry," I replied, without hesitation.

Saying no more, the three beings stood up and the door opened with another swooshing sound. Then, they filed out of the room with the door closing swiftly behind them. Now alone again, I tried to come to terms with what had just happened; a million questions were spiralling out of control in my head. I had just had an encounter with what the world perceives as aliens, so how was it, although my adrenaline was at maximum, I also had that feeling of being safe as I did when I was very young? Nothing made much sense, but I was still aching all over from my ordeal, so I had to lie back down on my floating mattress and get more rest.

I must have eventually fallen asleep through fatigue. I awoke a while later feeling slightly better.

With no watch as reference or windows to see out, I had no idea how long I had slept for, or what time or even day it was. I poured a beaker full of water from the jug and swallowed a couple of gulps. It was still cool and fresh, so either I hadn't slept long, or while I slept, it had been refreshed. It wasn't long before the events prior to my sleep flooded back to my memory and all the questions I had wanted to ask returned to addle my brain. I felt more relaxed, though and was somehow looking forward with anticipation to the return of Theron. To my own amazement, I did not feel threatened or frightened by this being.

Needing to stretch my legs, I got up and started to walk around the room feeling the wall's texture on my right hand side as I moved; it was indeed ultra-smooth. I hadn't noticed it before, but when I looked at the ceiling, I could see the tiny bristles moving, as if there was air flowing through them. These pores must be how the room was ventilated. As I reached the far side of the room opposite my sleeping place, the entire wall, as if by some magic, turned into a vast heavily tinted window and I stepped back, startled. Although the glass was darkened, I could now see an entire city, made of streets and tall buildings and I realised I was about four stories high.

Down below in the streets were the Terrans, going about their business at what seemed to be a leisurely pace. On the roads and even in the air, vehicles without wheels and wings were moving about or hovering. I now knew definitely I was not on some kind of spaceship, but how could this be Earth? I couldn't hear any sound from the outside, so I assumed the room was soundproofed in some way and when I looked at the buildings opposite, they too had large, tinted windows, so I could not see into the rooms. Just then as I peered out, I heard the door swoosh and open again. Turning swiftly around, I saw Theron, this time alone; though I wasn't positive it was him. Apart from size, I could not really distinguish one Terran from another. He asked me to sit on my sleeping place again and as I started to comply and took a few steps away from the window, it turned back into a solid looking wall again. I sat down where I had laid and Theron touched the corner of the watery mattress.

It immediately altered its shape and became a comfortable chair with arm rests. Somehow all thoughts of anxiety and any remaining thoughts of fear had left me and now all I wanted was answers to all my questions. Theron, as if he knew this, said, "All your questions will be answered as long as you are patient, but first I must explain a few things. You are not a prisoner but you are the first human to enter our realm. As it would be if one of us were to be in your community, fear and lack of tolerance are the same. For this reason I cannot allow you to be seen by the rest of our species. The only reason you are here is the fact that somehow when you had a fall recently, you were able to see into our world. We knew we would have to investigate the reason for this at first opportunity. The lightning provided that opportunity. All of our species know of human existence, but only very few of us have come into contact with them and if so, it is only ever in your realm. There are two reasons you were brought here. One is because you would have died if we had not intervened and the second is that we need to know how you were able to see us before this time."

I folded my arms, filled my cheeks with air and slowly blew out as I thought about what Theron had just said. Then I replied, "From an early age I have always seen vague figures, which I now know to be your people. It was only that time when I banged my head that I saw you more clearly. As to why I have been able to see you, I don't know."

Theron replied, "Then that is to be determined. I know you have a thousand questions, but if you will allow me, I will tell and show you our history. This will probably give you answers to most things and may shed light on your visions of us."

Looking at this greatly intelligent creature I felt a sense of mutual trust and friendship developing. I had not noticed before, but there were a series of black dots just below his shoulder on the left side of his chest. I surmised that this must be an indication of rank within his government. Also in what would have been his pubic area, I noticed a fold of skin, barely visible but like a small inverted kangaroo's pouch, so I speculated to myself: "That's where he keeps it!"

From his utility belt, Theron pulled out a black device, as small as a matchbox and a silver coloured ring, which he put on the end of his index finger on his left hand. He then put the device on the table and it immediately projected a three dimensional image in front of the adjacent wall. The image was of a brightly lit landscape, unlike anything I had ever seen before, but it was so vivid I felt as if I was part of it. There was dense vegetation and huge lakes everywhere, as the camera angles panned and gave aerial views of the landscape. Indigenous sounds, intentionally turned down but still audible, played in the background.

Theron began a narration of all the video images I would be shown: "This was how our world looked after our evolution had taken place. There were no predators, as the environment could only be tolerated by certain plant life and minor derivatives of our species. It was millions of years ago when the Solar System had not completely stabilised and the Earth's ozone layer was incomplete. As our intelligence progressed, we built machines and our power source was mainly gamma rays from the Sun. Gamma rays are a good source of power but would kill most life forms; our bodies have evolved to tolerate them."

He twitched his finger with the silver ring on the tip and another video scene was projected. This was what looked like a commonly reported shape of a UFO.

"As we progressed, transportation devices were needed," continued Theron, "so we developed a craft that was capable of negotiating any terrain. We found by projecting a layer of magnetism and magnetising our craft with the same polarity, we would travel in the opposite direction. We could then travel in any direction, at any height, wherever we made that projection. Somewhat like your Maglev machines. Wherever the track is laid, the vehicle, utilizing a magnetic force, would be propelled along it. The only difference is the magnetic force of our craft is localised and intensified to give us greater speed and this, of course, makes them completely silent."

This was mind blowing! I was looking at a real flying saucer, apparently hovering and then zooming off into the sky at fantastic speeds, then returning and landing about six inches off the ground with total stability and with complete silence.

No wonder all the UFO sighting reports have always said that the crafts that were seen travelled at an unbelievable velocity and had no engine noise. I envisioned that this type of engine would be the answer to the world's fossil fuel depletion it would revolutionise everything. But this also meant that the Terrans must visit my world quite often, due to the amount of sightings that are reported each year. I started thinking about how they could do this and more importantly, why they did it.

Images of the Terran cities, with various shapes and sizes of their vehicles followed and I gulped some water from the beaker in anticipation of what was to come next. Theron led with a short narration before each scene was shown.

"As time went on, the ozone layer was becoming denser, which meant our power source from gamma radiation was becoming more difficult to obtain," he continued. "Another form of power was needed and our scientists now had the task of finding it. Using quantum physics, our scientists determined that here on Earth there must be an alternate dimension, a mirror equivalent to our own. It was found to be correct, this was your world. We discovered that, with our technology, we could open portals, gates into your world, wherever we would choose. The experiments for this were at first not completely successful.

"We have an area, which we now call the Delta Rift and our first attempt to open a portal was done there, as it was a less populated area of our world. We were not fully able at that time to predict the full outcome of our tests when we opened the portal. The predicted ten- metre hole escalated into a vast area, hundreds of miles wide, so we had to shut it down and try to seal it quickly, as both our worlds were in danger of imploding into each other. Although we managed to localise and stabilise the portal, we could not close it fully and even today we cannot go near that area, as any craft or being that enters the rift would not return. It is a kind of void between dimensions, a black hole. On your side it was the same. You now call the area, the Devils Triangle or the Bermuda Triangle. I must remind you that all this was done before your species had even evolved and before all life on your world was still of a basic form. In the recent past, a couple of hundred years ago, your world has lost many vessels into the Delta Rift, both from the sea and from the air. We have attempted to turn many of those vessels away from the danger, but most of the captains of those crafts, believing our intentions to be hostile, have attacked us.

"Our inter-world personnel have strict instructions not to have direct verbal communications with humans and to keep visual sightings of us to a minimum because the confirmed knowledge of our Earthly existence could have catastrophic implications for the well-being of our species. So, you see, for those reasons, our attempts to save the vessels were mainly in vain. For now, it is best that your race believe us to be extraterrestrial."

My jaw dropping open was becoming a bit of a habit now and the thoughts going through my head were changing by the second. I was now privy to one of the world's greatest mysteries and each time Theron spoke, another revelation would come to light. I also thought of what he had said about the two species' interaction and fleetingly thought that I would have a price to pay for this knowledge. Although I was becoming slightly aware for my safety, I couldn't help trusting this creature. His intelligence and mannerisms were reassuring in some way and anyway my brain seemed to thirst for the information I was receiving.

In eager anticipation, I asked Theron to continue and he did so.

"When life on your world had transformed from sea to land creatures, there were many varieties of huge beasts."

Theron's finger twitched and I was now looking at, as if transported into, a prehistoric world, with huge dinosaurs roaming through vast areas of jungle-like vegetation. I could see active volcanic mountains set against the red-tinged sky in the distance.

"Having at that time the safe technology to enter your realm," Theron continued, "we then started to look for the power source that would replace our diminishing supplies of gamma radiation. We detected and realised that some of the creatures of your world had brains that emitted alpha, beta, gamma, delta and theta waves. These brainwaves have a certain kind of electrical output, which our brains do not have and which are also not present anywhere in our realm. Obviously we would need to conduct many experiments and tests to establish if there might be a way to utilise this resource."

Just then, an angry-looking Tyrannosaurus Rex came toward us on the video screen; it was terrifyingly huge and looked as if it could swallow a cow whole. As it rapidly neared, I cowered back in my seat, only for the camera angle to rise above it about twenty feet.

For a moment, I had forgotten the scenes must have been taken from a camera mounted on the Terran craft. I must have audibly blown air from my mouth with relief because Theron looked round at me with a slight smile on his face. The T. Rex looked up opening its massive jaws wide, and streams of saliva dripped from its numerous large teeth as it gave out a thunderous roar. It was difficult for me to come to terms with the fact that I was not actually in this Jurassic land, as the film footage quality was so defined it only lacked smell.

I realised then that no other modern day human had seen what prehistoric times on Earth were actually like and anything else I was about to see from this technology was also unique to me; it gave me an overwhelming feeling of exhilaration..

The craft that I felt I was inside must have now been hovering about twenty-five feet from the ground in an open, grassy area when a Pterodactyl glided in front of us at roughly the same height. As it passed, a circle of bright light flashed, like a camera aperture opening and two differently shaped craft appeared within the light instantly. The brilliantly lit hole lasted for only a split second, then closed and disappeared without a trace. Now hovering in front of us was a tubular-type ship and a more disc-like shaped craft. After a few seconds, a voice, which seemed to be in my proximity, spoke in a language I had never heard before. It uttered a couple of sentences and immediately all three craft set off in a triangular formation, across the sky, heading for a range of volcanic mountains.

"At this point a group of your ancestors have been detected," said Theron "and we are heading to that area."

Within about thirty seconds, these crafts must have travelled a hundred miles and were now landing one by one on a small, flat grassy area at the foot of what looked like a huge mountain. At the bottom of the mountain, I saw cave entrances visible.

From the side of the tubular craft, I could see a panel open, like a flap, which was used as a ramp for two Terrans emerging from the craft. They were carrying between them what looked like an aluminium coloured chest about two-feet square by about a foot deep. They laid the chest on the ground, opened it and brought out an odd-shaped instrument that looked a bit like a portable television aerial but with more gizmos fixed to it. I wondered what was to come next when Theron halted the images.

"Before I continue, I must ask you to remember, what you are seeing are scenes taken a **million** years ago by **my** ancestors, when little was known of your world or your species," said Theron. "You may find some of the scenes harrowing or even barbaric, but at that time all that our scientists knew was that we had to assess the potential of an alternative form of power. The life forms we would need to experiment on were primitive and, to us, unintelligent. "He paused and then asked: "Do you still wish me to continue?"

My immediate thought was that this was going to get bloodthirsty. But then I recalled back in my school days, I had to dissect a frog and I thought to myself, "What little difference is there?" And so I replied to Theron, "I understand the necessity of what your scientists had to do and I am aware that it might be distasteful. Please continue."

In truth, I have never been squeamish when watching operations on the television and also never when I had cut myself badly at work. So the sight of flesh being cut up or organs being removed would have no effect on my stomach. Theron then continued the recording. A group of about six half-human, half-ape-like people emerged from a cave and started throwing large stones at the two Terrans. One of the Terrans must have activated the device from the chest because it emitted a loud, pulsating humming sound. Instantly, the cave dwellers fell to the ground motionless.

From the other disc-like craft, two more Terrans disembarked, each carrying what looked like rolled-up exercise mats. They went over to the stunned or dead Troglodytes, unrolled their mats and pushed a male and a female from the group onto each mat. Astonishingly, without effort, the mats levitated to about three feet from the ground and they were then pushed with ease through thin air, back and into the tubular craft.

The next camera sequence was then taken from the inside of the tubular ship. It showed the two specimens on silver-coloured metal tables. These cave dwellers were, I thought, obviously dead, as there was absolutely no sign of any life or movement. With the cave dwellers skulls surgically opened, the two surgeons systematically removed and dissected sections of the two specimen's brains, examining them intricately and talking to each other as they continued.

I did not feel as if these cave people were human, more like apes, although I knew they were probably human ancestors. I also felt that what had been done to them was not barbaric, as they did not suffer and were not subjected to pain in any way.

I said to Theron, "But what of the rest of the group?" I thought, had they been needlessly left to rot or eaten by animals?"

"I am sorry," Theron replied, "but I do not have that information. Many experiments were done in this way to hundreds of species in your realm at that time, but we found that it was the species that you have just seen that had the most advanced brains and the greatest output potential of the power source we were seeking. Obtaining and maximising this resource would be a greater challenge. Our scientists realised that the humanoid brain basically has two outputs: electrical emissions and the radio like waves, which are both the result of thought. The more complex human thoughts are, the more memories the human brain stores. This storage leads to greater electrical output. This meant we would need the human race to become more intelligent to maximise this resource and this could only be done by an evolutionary process. Our scientists knew we would have the time for this to occur, as our life-spans are much greater than yours and the new power resource would only be needed in our distant future.

"But to speed the process, we decided the best way to help your species develop was by selecting individuals of your kind who could assimilate new ideas slightly in advance of that era's technology. For instance, during your ancient Egyptian period, we would select the wife of a builder, architect, or mathematician who was pregnant with a child and just before the birth, we would transmit advanced data to the brain of the foetus. The foetus would have already acquired a certain amount of natural skills from the father's genes, but with the added enhancement, he or she would have much greater skills than the father in adulthood."

The projected video scenes had now changed to ancient Egypt and I was now looking at a vast building site, with thousands of people and half-built cities, pyramids and monuments.

"At no time," Theron stressed, "did we influence the natural cultures of your race, although sometimes we found them to be barbaric at the treatment of their own kind."

As new scenes filled my vision on the screen, I saw mind boggling, huge stone structures and thousands of slave labourers working in a hot, dusty environment. They were cutting large stones with hand tools and hundreds of people were physically moving them into position with ropes and pulleys.

The narration continued as the views moved from one area to another.

"During these early eras, we were not overly concerned if our crafts were sighted, as human flight was far off into the future and conflict with humans would not be an issue. We knew that sometimes we had been seen, but we were interpreted as gods and we were even recorded as such in early human drawings. Unfortunately, the enhancement of intelligence to specific members of your race had an adverse side effect within your different cultures. We regret this, but were unable to do anything about it. Religions sprang up all over your world in different continents, exalting certain humans as gods simply because of their higher knowledge. Stories were told by the lesser intelligent which escalated and included untruths of their own unusual abilities. This has led to many wars of your kind in the past and even now in the present. We still do not understand why humans want to believe in and worship something or someone that cannot and has never been corroborated."

It's funny, but I, too, have never understood why so many people want to believe in something or someone that could not have possibly existed without any form of tangible evidence. Sometimes the problem escalates to the point of slaughtering each other in the name of that belief. It doesn't make any sense! It was only a couple of hundred years ago when women were put to death because people naively believed them to be witches.

It seemed as if I had been sitting and watching the scenes with Theron for hours and I think that he had noticed my restlessness. Inadvertently I must have looked at my blank watch because he said, "When you entered our world, your timepiece was drained of its power."

He then asked me to hold my wrist out to look at my watch and, by touching it with the silver ring on his index finger, it sprang into life. It read 4:32 p.m. on Monday, the twenty-fifth of June.

"Is this the correct time?" I asked, without even thinking the time might be different in his world.

"Yes," Theron replied. "I set your timepiece to the correct time for your world and ours. The timeline on both our worlds is parallel."

This meant I had been here for over twenty four hours. I know it may sound stupid, but my immediate thought was whether my car was OK. Quickly dismissing that thought, I realised that I hadn't even been to the toilet since I left home yesterday. Now that I was thinking about it, I was bursting to go. There did not seem to be a bathroom in this room and I could not even imagine Theron's toilet habits. I just had to ask!

"Theron, is there somewhere I could go to the toilet?" I asked, hoping that the Terrans had that kind of facility.

To my relief he replied, "Of course there is. You have not fully explored this room, have you? While you were recovering, we adapted this room as much as possible for your needs. The temperature has been adjusted to suit your comfort; the window has been heavily tinted to protect your eyes from the exterior brightness and the place for washing and body waste has been altered accordingly. As you walk along the wall to your left, the wash place will become apparent. Inside, you will see a gel seat; sit on the seat and do what you must. The seat will take care of the rest. There is also what you call a shower. Step inside and move the wall lever either to the left or to the right. Moving the lever to the left will give you a water shower and moving it to the right will give you a sonic shower. Both methods will have the same results. If you wish to wash your clothes, remove them from your body and put them within the shower, setting the lever to sonic. The usages of the objects within this room are for you to discover. Do not be apprehensive to try them out. I will leave you for now and return in a few hours."

After saying this, Theron stopped the film show and left the room. I had to find this bathroom quickly. It seemed that I had been sitting in one position for so long my legs and back ached when I stood up, but I had to find this concealed room. I took four steps along the left hand wall toward the window when zap! Just like the window, the entrance to this bathroom opened up. I went inside this average to large size bathroom and found the all-important seat Theron had mentioned.

I think you can imagine the relief, so I don't need to go into too much detail, except to say the seat was similar to the bed I had been sleeping on except a little softer. When I got up, there was no trace of anything. The seat must have absorbed everything and left me clean and dry at the same time. What a revolution! No pipes, no paper and no odours whatsoever.

My next thought was to try the shower. I disrobed completely, stepped in and found the lever on the wall. Do I move it to the right or the left? I opted of course for the right, the sonic shower. I immediately felt a tingling sensation all over my body and what I can only describe as a blast of warm air from all sides. Although it felt strange, it was also exhilarating and I felt really refreshed. After about thirty seconds the lever had returned to the middle position and it was all over. There was a three-tier rail inside the shower, which swung out from the wall. I hung all my clothes on this, put my shoes on the floor and moved the lever to sonic again. After another thirty seconds, my clothes felt and even smelled clean; no water was used, so they were dry I put them back on.

It didn't take me long to find what I thought must be a teeth cleaning gizmo. It was a catapult shape, without the rubber bands of course, but it also resembled the metal thing that dentists take dental impressions with. I carefully inserted it into my mouth with the curved shape covering my top teeth. Instantly I felt another tingle in my gums. Fearing I may get an electric shock, I quickly pulled it out. To my amazement my teeth had become a perfect white colour and felt unbelievably clean and refreshed. I inverted the tool and applied it to the bottom teeth and the result after the tingle was the same.

This was a great gadget, but I didn't even know that Terrans had teeth, as their mouths seemed so tiny and I had only ever seen Theron give half a smile. But like a toothbrush, I hoped this gadget was new, or at least had a new mouth piece! Luckily there was a mirror attached to the wall but no evidence of a comb anywhere. There was nothing I could shave with, but that would be understandable as the Terrans were hairless. So for now my fingers would have to do the job of a comb and I would just have to forego shaving. Thoroughly clean and refreshed, I stepped out of the shower room and zap! The wall was reinstated.

I had a lot to think about after my film show session with Theron, so I sat down again on my morphing bed and closed my eyes. It felt like I had been handed lots of jigsaw puzzle pieces that had to be laid down in the correct order in order to make sense of some of my world's mysteries and my own personal life.

I now knew that the human race was not the most advanced and dominant species of planet Earth and that all through our evolution, the Terrans had steered the path for our progression. I also knew, intentionally or not, they were probably responsible for the majority of religions that, although they had brought many people solace, had also been the cause of wars throughout history. My continued thoughts were that many people would not have been lost if the Terrans had not breached the dimensional barrier and created the anomaly of the Bermuda triangle. So despite good intentions, I asked myself: Were the Terrans in fact a threat to the human race?

It also occurred to me at that time that my brain must have been tampered with in my foetal stage and that somehow this was the cause of my visions. All these things were negative, but I couldn't help thinking that we would still be in the dark ages if the Terrans hadn't intervened and that even without the Terrans, there would always be people willing to believe in a higher entity, or some sort of physical god. For me personally, the visions throughout my life were more of a nuisance than anything else, an unwelcomed distraction, so I felt comfortable enough to raise questions about myself with Theron.

During all my contradictions and analyses of thoughts, I had unknowingly fallen asleep, but I was awakened again by the swooshing sound of the door. I looked at my watch and found I had been asleep for about three hours; it was now 8:00 p.m. Theron had entered the room bearing gifts, a bowl of assorted fruits, a bottle of full cream milk and a packet of chocolate digestive biscuits. I was very pleased to see these items as water and bland chicken cubes were a bit boring in terms of taste. These items were obviously not from his world, but I thanked him and asked how he managed to get them.

"I had instructed one of our crews visiting your realm to acquire edible items that humans usually find pleasant to eat," Theron replied, "but with a special request for the fresh milk as I knew this item would be agreeable to you."

The reply didn't exactly answer my question, but I was not about to give Theron the third degree for the method of acquisition. I wondered though how he knew that I liked to drink milk and put the question to him a minute later.

"When you were first brought here unconscious, we quickly scanned your brain for damage and some of your traits were revealed to us," said Theron. "I would like to give your brain a further full scan to determine how in the past you have managed to see my people. I believe that you would like to know the answer yourself. Since we last met, I have been checking our records and found that you were indeed a candidate for our enhancement program in early 1952. Your foetal brain was given information to assist you in becoming a mechanical technician of great standing."

"Well, that didn't quite work, did it?"

"We are fascinated with the human brain. It is much more complex in its workings than ours. We can absorb information and store it quickly. That is why every Terran at an early age is taught every known Earth language. Ergo, it is the reason I am able to talk and understand English with you. The human brain, however, decides of its own accord whether to absorb or reject certain information. It also has the capacity to achieve paranormal and miraculous feats, although as yet only very few of you have the use of that certain part of your brain. The human race has not stopped evolving and in thousands of years to come, human beings will all be able to achieve great things."

"When do you want me to have the scan?" I asked. "And will it hurt or affect me in some way?"

"No, it will not hurt or damage you in any way and I would like you to have the scan tomorrow. I will leave you for now to enjoy the food I have brought and after you have slept tonight, I will return in the morning."

With that Theron left the room.

The biscuits Theron had brought tasted great and after six or seven of them, I washed them down with a beaker of cool milk. It's amazing how a few biscuits can fill you up so quickly. Now I had to mull over what I had learned from Theron and I wondered just how many important people in my world had undergone the Terrans' enhancement program.

I have often thought about what makes someone suddenly think of something like sending pictures through thin air—to the point of actually making it possible. Normal people just don't come up with that sort of thing. Atom splitting is something too. How do you find an atom in the first place, let alone split it. These things are not what I would call a normal train of thought, yet no one ever thinks of questioning the very thoughts that go on inside these people's heads.

I suppose, if they did, the questioner would be deemed ignorant. I always imagined that I could probably come up with some fantastic idea, like making a light beam bend round corners, but I would not have a clue how to go about it, let alone how to make it work. There was also the issue of what happens to the people when the enhancement does not go as expected, like with me. Maybe I was just lucky that it didn't have too adverse an effect, but others may not have been so lucky. The most important thing of all was the method the Terrans use to extract the power source they needed from human brains. The worrying thing was that they would have to kill us for it.

It seemed that every single time I got a little more information, my mind reached different conclusions. I still had not got all the answers and the frustration was becoming unbearable. To be honest I was getting a bit fed up now from being kept in that room. Although the room was pleasant enough, I really wanted some fresh air.

Pacifying myself a little by remembering I was lucky to be alive, I got up and went over to the window. As before, it revealed itself, as I approached. Although now night time, the streets were all fully and overly lit. Judging by the Terrans' large black eyes, I supposed the species was used to the brightness and probably needed it.

I looked up above the buildings and saw the stars of the night sky. They looked exactly how it does in my world, which started making me feel a bit homesick. So much had changed for me in a mere thirty-six hours and it was hard to face up to this new reality. I was beginning to wish it really was all just a dream.

I hadn't felt physically tired the night before, but I must have eventually fallen asleep through sheer mind fatigue. It was now a new day and I wondered what new revelations it would bring. I could really have done with a nice strong cup of coffee, but I had a banana from the fruit that I had been given. I had already finished off the rest of the milk for breakfast. On this day, I felt determined that I would ask Theron for a change of scenery.

I knew, though, at first I would have to undergo this brain scan I had been asked to participate in and although a little apprehensive, I thought that it might just give me more important answers.

My watch read 9:15 a.m. on Tuesday, the twenty-sixth of June and I began to wonder if my family or anyone who knew me had realised I was missing. Again, I thought about my car and hoped it was all right. Just as I got up to stretch my legs, the door opened. Theron entered with another Terran who was slightly smaller than him and said, "This is the technician who will be performing your scan this morning."

With a gentle feminine voice, the Terran technician said, "Good morning, Terry. I am Madri, I hope you slept well and have positive thoughts for your scan today. You can be assured that you are in no danger and will be conscious throughout. The scan will probably take about thirty minutes. Do you think you are now ready?"

This Terran was obviously female, although I couldn't see much physical difference. Her mouth had a suggestion of a smile and her voice had a soothing reassurance about it.

I replied, "I am as ready as ever I could be."

I wasn't sure if my reply actually made sense, but I'm certain she got my drift. I still fleetingly wondered if this scan would be my demise and this was how the Terrans would extract what they needed from my brain. On the other hand, surely they could have easily killed me at any time to get what they required. Anyway, I thought, my brain wouldn't power much, so I asked myself why go through an elaborate farce to get it. I decided to feel deep down that I could trust what they said to be true.

Theron led the way out of the room with myself and Madri following. We did not have to go far, just a few yards down a corridor and into a similar-sized room to the one that I had already occupied.

The room was quite sparse really, except for a dentist-shaped chair made from the watery gel stuff. There was also what looked like a large television screen in front of the chair and a small table at the side, with a bowl-shaped helmet and three or four gizmos beside it.

It seemed obvious these Terrans did not go for anything that wasn't completely functional as the place had no décor, as such and very sedate colours. I noticed this when I had been watching scenes of the Terran cities and crafts: there were no markings or colours to distinguish or denote anything.

Madri said, "Would you please sit in the chair for me, Terry?"

I gingerly complied.

"Try to relax; there really is nothing to worry about," she said.

She then handed me the helmet and asked me to put it on. It fitted quite snug and I could see beforehand that it was double lined, as if all the workings were within it. There was no sign of any circuitry on the outside.

Madri spoke again. "When we start, you will see on the screen in front of you images from your past. We will quickly scan those images and your thoughts and you will regress all the way back to your foetal awareness stage. There should be nothing there to alarm you, as you have already lived every second. Are you ready to begin?"

I gave a tentative nod; she then picked up one of the instruments. The gizmo was about the size of a pack of playing cards and had a screen and dials on its face.

Now you may think this is a classic alien abduction and mind probing scenario, but then again you must ask yourself why you've probably heard all this before. The answer might just be because it is a fact and it **has** happened before.

How do we know there haven't been many others that have experienced this very same thing, but they were probably in a Terran ship within the boundaries of our dimension? Perhaps it could be that many people have been disbelieved, just because of the idea of being probed by aliens is unbelievable and absurd.

I nodded my head again to indicate I was ready. Instantly images started to appear on the screen in front of me and I could feel or maybe imagine a slight but sharp vibrating sensation in my forehead. After about thirty seconds, the images stopped, as if the video was paused. On the screen was an image of the two Terrans I had seen when I had fallen off the scaffolding recently. The image was through my eyes, so I was looking at the scene exactly as I had seen it before.

"You recognise these images, do you not?" Madri said.

"Yes," I replied.

She continued. "My instrument tells me that your brain waves had peaked at this incident and a combination of alpha, beta, gamma, delta and theta waves were all present for a few moments. This is very rare, as a combination of all five brain waves do not usually occur. The human brain at your stage of evolution only transmits a combination of two or three different waves at any one time, depending on your moods or tasks you are performing. The combination of all five is the probable reason you managed to see our kind. Let us proceed."

The pictures, as seen by me from my past, started whizzing along in reverse. It was far too fast for me to depict times and places, but I was aware of all the events that I was seeing.

I was looking at a recording of my entire life. I suppose most of my life was uneventful and of no interest to Madri and Theron, as the next paused image was of my time in the nursery class.

"At this stage of your brain's development," Madri said, "all five brain waves had started to interact, which means there was an over activity compared to others of your age. This must have been the start of your visions of us."

I said, "Are you saying that the reason I was able to see into your dimension was because of the way my brain was functioning and nothing else?"

Madri replied, "Yes. The human brain usually only ever emits the five main brainwaves waves when…"

Theron interrupted quickly, stopping what Madri was about to say. "We will deal with that answer at a later stage. Please continue with the regression Madri."

I should have insisted that Madri finish what she was going to say but for some reason, I kept quiet.

My images restarted on the screen and quickly stopped again. This image seemed blank and grey and only slight movements of the environment I was in were noticeable. Peering at the gadget she was holding, Madri paused for a few moments and then said, "You are within your mother's womb and it is at this point you are receiving projected information from us. The data we sent you was of a technological nature, but your brain function at this time is of an unusually receptive degree. The data was a combination of our technologies and of a past human technician, who had not yet reached his full potential before his death. His previous personal traits and memories should have been filtered out to the degree that you could only receive his technical abilities and not the knowledge of his existence."

I asked, "Do you think that this could possibly be the reason I felt at home with my surroundings after birth. Also, is this the reason why I had the feeling that new sights and sounds were familiar to me when I was young?"

Madri replied, "Yes, there is a strong likelihood of this."

"We have projected information to many thousands of humans over the past few thousand years," Theron said. "Occasionally we would enter your world and bring them aboard one of our science vessels to assess their progress. Not all of them respond well to the input and unfortunately some human brains have an input defence. Although their brains are not damaged, their perception of the world differs. Some of these people your society call autistic. In truth these humans have brilliant minds but are unable to combine their extraordinary abilities with everyday tasks or rationale. The human brain has endless capabilities and that is why we are so fascinated with your race. There are some humans that can see what you would call ghosts. Their brains have an ability to synchronise with transmitted thought waves, emitted by individuals while living but received after their death. It is also possible for a human brain to project an image of their living body, which is then interpreted and received long after they have died. Human thought waves, once emitted, are present all the time, like radio waves, until they are received by another receptive human."

Theron then had a small conversation with Madri in their Terran language. Turning back toward me, he said, "Your brain, it seems, has received and accepted all the information that was transmitted to you and has also managed to filter in deleted memories of its donor. Although you have this data within you, your individuality does not support its use. Your brain has the most brilliant potential and, according to Madri's findings, you should be able to read the minds of others or perform supernatural feats, such as levitation or telekinesis. It is like you are a forerunner for human brain evolution, because no other human we have come across has ever had the capability you possess. It is a pity that your mind has chosen to only use a fraction of its potential. Maybe nature is intentionally subduing your progression."

That explanation had left me a bit speechless. According to Theron, I should have turned out to be one of the world's super brains instead of a plasterer from South London.

Madri switched off the screen and announced that the scanning session was over. She then said to me "It appears we have discovered the reason for your ability to see us though the dimension barrier. It is now up to you and Theron to discuss the implications of this knowledge."

With that thought, I instinctively took off the helmet, got up from the chair and Theron led me back to my room, leaving Madri with the scanning equipment.

I sat on my familiar chair and Theron said he would leave me to think about my new found knowledge of myself. He also said he would bring in some more food and drink on his return.

Only a few days ago I was a normal person in a normal world, except for the fact I could see things others couldn't and now and again read other people's thoughts. There might be something in the saying, "ignorance is bliss," because now I had a whole new set of things to think about to macerate my mind. Obviously if all this new information was true, I wanted to exploit my so-called abilities, but I doubted somehow this would ever happen.

For now, the main thing I had to think of was what Madri had said about the implications of their scan findings. Did this new knowledge about me affect my situation in any way, for me and for the Terrans? Just as I did before, when I wanted time to relax and reflect, I needed to get out in the fresh air and into an open space somewhere, only this time without being struck by lightning. I decided to ask for this outing on Theron's return.

About half an hour later, Theron returned as he had said, clutching another packet of biscuits and a large bottle of cola. Although grateful, I just had to speak to him about what instantly came to mind. "You do realise that I cannot exist on this kind of food and drink for any long period of time."

Theron replied, "I do realise this, but as yet this is all my inter-dimensional crews could procure."

I asked, "Where are you getting these things from?"

He replied, "You must realise that we try to minimise entering your realm. Usually we do this under the cover of darkness and from isolated places. Your world has entered the technological phase where remote cameras are present, so it is becoming more and more difficult for us to be undetected. There is a small provision provider construction in a place you know as Wales. It is in a quiet isolated place in the countryside. Although it appears it does not have many visitors, the owner keeps open twenty-four hours a day. He has an assistant, a young teenage boy who manages the establishment when the owner is not there. From a hidden vantage point our crew can see this young boy who very often just falls asleep through boredom. We are able to enter the premises when this happens and acquire what we can. We realise that this is basically theft, but we have not the means to leave anything in return as payment. We have to risk our craft and personnel being seen during this covert operation and in recent decades we know our crafts have been seen and reported. But because this area has a small population, it is worth the risk of our detection."

I hoped I didn't seem ungrateful by my comment about the type of food Theron was supplying, because it was now obvious that the Terrans had gone to great lengths just to cater to my familiar tastes. Although bland, their chicken tasting cubes were not that bad. I thanked Theron for his efforts and went on to broach the subject of my internment.

I said to Theron, "You have given me a lot to think about with the results of my scan. Whenever I have a lot on my mind, I like to isolate myself somewhere in the open air. I find it easier to get my thoughts in order. Is it possible for me to get out of this room and into the open countryside for a while?"

He replied, "I had anticipated that at some stage this room would feel more like a prison to you and I have prepared for this event, as best I can. The atmospheric radiation outside this building will not be congenial to your body, unprotected. Although the air quality is what you are used to, the sun's rays and glare would be too extreme. We have fabricated a suit, protective eye covers and a solution to apply to your face and hands, which will give you a few hours on the outside. Unfortunately this is the best we can offer."

With a touch of his utility belt, a Terran, one of the larger ones, entered the room carrying what looked like the items Theron had just described. He had a stern look in his eyes, as he put them onto the table and left the room without saying a word.

Theron remarked, "I am sorry for the coldness of my assistant. There are very few of my people that know of your existence here and not all of them regard it as a good thing."

I told Theron that I quite understood and then asked him if I should put the suit on.

He replied, "You will need to completely disrobe before putting the suit on. Once you have done this I will explain the other protective measures."

I took the suit into the shower and stripped off. The suit was a blue-grey colour, much like the colour of the Terran's skin and it felt silky to the touch. In fact, I found it quite sensual, as I pulled this one piece garment on. Its design was much like a diving wet suit, although it had no zipper and slid on easily. Once on, it felt a very snug fit. All that was left exposed were my feet, hands and head, so I returned to Theron for the rest of the protection.

He said that my own footwear would be adequate and produced a small silvery bowl, about the size of half a teacup, filled with a grey coloured salve, much like petroleum jelly. I was to apply this salve to my face, hands and feet before putting my shoes on.

This ointment wasn't sticky, nor did it feel wet in any way, but it absorbed into my skin instantly, without any discomfort. Apart from the eye protectors, I was ready and in quiet anticipation of my jaunt.

Theron said, "You will not need the eye protection until we arrive at our destination. My personal craft is waiting at the rear of this building, but to enter it, we will need to put a covering over your body, to protect your eyes and to conceal your being from the general Terran population."

We left the room and I could feel my heart beat start to quicken. A short distance down the corridor was an open lift that Theron entered and I followed. A split second later, we were on the ground floor and facing what I assumed was the door to the exterior. The mean-looking Terran was there, holding a silver blanket, which I guessed was to go over my head for the outside.

Theron said, "Are you ready?"

With a nod from me, the sheet was draped over my head and I was ushered forward about twenty paces, up a ramp and into Theron's ship. I heard the ramp door shut with a sudden, ambient silence you get when an aircraft door shuts before takeoff. I could now emerge from under my covering.

I could tell, by the interior, the craft was a kind of arrowhead shape, with oblong- shaped tinted windows at the sides and front. At the front end was a control panel covered in different coloured lights and dials and at the centre of the panel was a pad with the shape of a three-fingered hand on it.

Theron said that the windows were one way, which meant no one from the outside could see in. There were two seats at the front end, again made of the gel material and long bench seats by the side windows. Cabinet panels seemed to be attached to the walls everywhere there wasn't a window. The inside area of the craft suggested it was about the size of a four-seater plane, but it felt very roomy as all the gadgetry was neatly tucked away.

"This is my private vessel," Theron said. "Like you, whenever I have an important decision to make, I find solace in the open terrain and I have a certain place I go to, which I would like you to see."

Theron sat at the control panel and beckoned me to sit beside him. With his left hand placed on the control pad, the craft gently started to rise from the ground.

Apart from a vague hum it emitted, the craft was virtually silent. I looked down on the Terran city, as we rose vertically about fifty feet and then at an incredible speed we zoomed away. I couldn't understand why I didn't feel any backward movement or even g-force, as we sped off so quickly. Neither I, nor Theron were wearing any seatbelts or restraints of any kind, yet inside the craft it was like we were not moving at all. I looked around the vessel in awe, as I had never been in any form of transport that I could compare to this wondrous machine.

High above this alien landscape I could see marvellous, sleek shape buildings, as we passed over various cities. The open landscape was incredible, too. Vast green forests and blue and green open plains of thick, dense grass seemed to dominate the uninhabited areas of land. On the horizon, the glare of the sun reflected on huge mountains, as if placed there to fill in blank spaces.

Theron spoke, saying, "Like your world, our land masses have the same continents but our oceans consist of freshwater; ergo, we would never be without water to drink or land that could not be cultivated."

My immediate thought was that the Terrans have everything going for them: long life, technology, harmony and an abundance of food and water. Was this the ideal and perfect equilibrium that was Nature's design in this world? Surely there must be some sort of defect or natural disaster that occurred in this place, I thought. If there was, I haven't been made aware of it yet.

I could see that the craft was gradually losing height, which meant we were getting close to our destination. I eagerly peered from the windows to see what sort of area Theron was taking me to. At very low altitude, we passed over a lush green forest of plant life with a small river running through it, then came to land in an open area of grass.

"We have arrived," Theron said. "It is time for you to place the eye protectors on."

These eye pieces were much like the shape and dark density of the Terran's eyes, but I hadn't got a clue how to put them on as they had no straps or visible means to attach them. I looked at Theron for guidance.

"Just place them over your eyes and they will adhere themselves," he said.

Sure enough, these things just grabbed on over my eyes like limpets, but without any discomfort. Why was I surprised? I asked myself. As Theron rose from his seat, the door in the side of the craft started to open with a short sucking sound and then the door formed a shallow ramp to the ground outside. I noticed Theron open one of the smaller wall cabinets and take out a handful of what looked like those edible cubes I was given when I first arrived. I thought he must be a bit peckish after the flight, but I also thought it was odd that he hadn't asked if I had wanted any.

Theron led the way, as we both emerged from the ship. At last, I was out in the open air, even though I was covered all over with protective elements. Although quite hot, the gentle breeze felt good on my face and, taking a few paces away from the ship, I stopped and scanned the area with my tinted eye-pieces. Theron walked up and stood beside me and said, "The special place of mine is not far away, over there, just beyond that vegetation."

He pointed in the direction of a large area of green and blue leafy plant life about twenty-five yards away. We started to head in that direction when suddenly a huge lizard creature emerged from the undergrowth. It started bounding toward us at top speed. Its body must have been fifteen-feet long, with an approximately six foot long tail, making it enormous. I completely froze as this blue and grey creature got nearer. To my amazement, Theron just kept walking in the creature's direction.

"Habya Grizel," he shouted, as this huge beast approached him. I was totally stunned when I saw this monstrous creature wrap its long, thin tongue all around Theron's face and neck and seemed to lurch up and down with excitement.

Theron then fed the creature with the cubes he had brought from the ship.

"This is Grizel," he said. "He has been a companion of mine for many years now, when I come here to contemplate matters. He is completely harm-less, so please don't be afraid."

Theron handed me a couple of the food cubes and said, "Give him this food and you will also be his friend for life."

Cautiously, I stretched out my hand and offered the creature one of the cubes and thought I might lose my entire arm as its massive head neared. Delicately it took the food from my hand with the tips of its mouth, as if knowing one false move could separate my hand from my arm. This huge creature was a gentle giant and seemed to understand that a missed placed swing of its head or tail could easily hurt Theron or me.

"Grizel is of the Onabi species," Theron explained. "As are all the crea-tures in my world, he is an herbivore, so you have no need to fear any of them."

I gave Grizel the other cube and stroked its head, as you would do a horse. Although slightly rough to the touch its hairless skin had a spongy quality about it, which wasn't at all unpleasant. I now felt completely at ease and rubbed my hands over its head and neck and Grizel responded with a wet tongue lashing all over my face. The sensation was a bit gooey perhaps, but nonetheless I felt I had made a new friend.

Realising that there was no more food to be had, Grizel scurried off, leaving Theron and me to continue on to his special place. With Theron leading the way, he parted some tall plants and beckoned me with a crook of his finger to pass through. It led me into a rocky area and I could hear the gentle sound of trickling water. He then pushed his way through a narrow opening between two large rocks and alarmingly gave out a hurtful cry. Theron had gashed his right hip, just below the waist and his grey inner flesh was clearly visible.

"Are you all right?" I exclaimed.

"Yes," he said. "Do not worry. Although we feel pain, we can quickly heal ourselves."

I looked at the bloodless wound and, within less than a minute, the gash had started to heal. In two minutes there was nothing to be seen of the wound at all, not even a scar.

"Let us continue," Theron said. "But please be careful not to injure yourself as I did."

Having safely passed between the jagged rocks, we then had a slight incline of more rocks to negotiate to reach a smooth plateau. On the small plateau, Theron sat down.

"We have arrived," he announced.

This place overlooked a small stream and was surrounded by vegetation. All you could hear was the gentle rippling of the water splashing against the sides of the river banks. It was absolutely perfect for some serious meditation. I sat down next to Theron with my legs outstretched, supporting my back with my elbows.

"I can see why you enjoy coming here," I remarked.

"Yes, it is idyllic," Theron replied. "But I have brought you here because there are some important things I need to tell you."

I thought, this sounds ominous.

Theron began to speak with a serious tone in his voice. "You have obviously been wondering how we extract the electrical power of human thought waves and why I stopped Madri telling you what happens when the combined, alpha, beta, gamma, delta and theta waves are present at the same time in human brains and therefore ready for us to collect. It is at the point of a human's natural death that all five waves occupy their brain. As you know, we have been studying human brains ever since the beginning of your evolution. We have found that, at a certain point of your development, a human brain only emitted the combined waves at the point of death, but then an amazing thing happened: together the waves resonated at a particular frequency which opened a portal into our world, purely by nature's design. Seconds before death, a portal would appear to that human as a blinding light and with the portal open, the light allowed them to see into our world. Their consciousness would then leave their body and pass through; the portal would then close.

"All we have done is to set up stations to collect and store this brainpower before dissipation into our world. So you see: nature itself has provided us with the power source we required. Also, from the stored brain waves, we can extract particular information to help us enhance future generations of humans. So you see, Terrans are really a natural part of a human's life cycle, making sure the human life force has not been lost forever."

"So the myth is true," I said. "When we die, a blinding light does appear and naturally we are meant to enter it. But you said the portal opens during a human's natural death. What if a human dies unnaturally, such as by an accident or by violence?"

Theron replied, "When this happens there are two scenarios depending on the circumstances. Either the consciousness will open the portal and it will pass through as in a natural death, or only a partial opening will appear. In this instance a human's life force will be trapped between the two worlds—in limbo, so to speak. This particular consciousness has to wait for another person's portal to open. It can then decide whether to come through to our dimension or to return to your world as what you would call a ghost or a spectre."

"So ghosts do exist," I said.

"Yes," Theron replied. "But they can only appear to other humans who can receive their brain patterns. That is why not everyone can see them."

It took a little while for this information to sink in, but when it did, I realised it all made complete sense.

I said to Theron, "I have to admit: it did cross my mind that for you to use our brain waves, you would have to kill us first."

"Kill you!" he said, with indignation. "Humans to the majority of the Terran race are gods. Not in the sense that we worship you but in the realisation that the human brain is far superior to ours. As I have said before, our brains are of a different structure to yours. Yes, we are far more intelligent than humans, but our intelligence is only capable of absorbing information and expanding our technologies.

"However the human brain will be capable of fantastic mental feats in the future, but, at this stage of your development, humans are only just starting to acquire supernatural capabilities. When the time comes that the human race has lost its greed and violent tendencies, we will make ourselves known to you. However before that happens, our elders have prophesised that the day will come when a human with great powers will be able to walk among us, without the need of protection. This event will herald the beginning of interaction between our species and hopefully will bring about harmonious acceptance of each other."

I was speechless and had almost forgotten the reason I had come to this place with Theron.

It seemed what I had learned about myself after the scan was totally insignificant anyway. I couldn't exactly zap myself with new supernatural abilities, even if I did have that potential. After a pause of a minute or two, Theron spoke again, saying, "There is one last thing I must tell you."

I sensed a hesitation in his voice and sat upright to look him in the face while he spoke.

"Our calculations," said Theron, "tell us that it is almost impossible for you to return to your world."

My jaw dropped slightly as I digested the thought that I might never return home.

"You said 'almost impossible,'" I uttered. "What exactly does that mean?"

"It is nature's design that once your consciousness has passed through the dimension barrier, you can never return. I have had my scientists working on a solution to this problem, but to no avail. Even with all the protective devices we can produce, we cannot protect your brain matter. Diagnostic simulated tests can only reveal that you have less than a three-percent chance of survival. Even within our craft, there is no protection from the forces that only our bodies and brains can endure."

Silence fell as I turned my gaze from Theron's face, skyward. My thoughts fell immediately to my family and life as it used to be. I even thought about that damn car of mine again.

Still without another word spoken, I shifted my position and lay on my stomach, with my head hanging over the edge of the rock plateau, looking down approximately six feet to the stream below. A handful of light blue fish, going upstream, were swimming past. Even the sight of their strange, part reptilian form didn't shake my mind from the numb feeling I was experiencing. Suddenly, I felt my eyes bulge within my protective eye pieces. As I peered into the crystal clear water, my reflection started to materialise. My hair had turned completely white. I quickly turned to Theron and said with alarm, "What's happening? My hair!"

Theron replied, almost calmly, "Yes, we must return. The atmosphere is taking its toll on you. Do not worry though: your hair will return to normal once we are within the walls of your room, but we must leave immediately."

With that reply, I felt a slight panic but without outwardly showing it to Theron.

We calmly got up and started making our way back to his craft and soon we were on our way back to my confines.

I'm sure Theron hit the gas going back as it seemed a lot shorter distance than going. When we arrived, one of the larger Terrans was there ready to usher us into the building.

I had to don the silver sheet over my head once again for protection against the atmosphere before fully emerging from the ship—but I expected that.

Once inside Theron and I made our way back to my room and I managed to pop the eye pieces off on the way. After this, I headed straight for the shower room to get out of the protective suit. The suit hadn't been uncomfortable, but I was glad to get it off, have a shower and put my own loose-fitting clothes back on.

Once dressed, I looked in the mirror and saw that my hair had already started to change from pure white to a tint of brown, so I was confident my natural hair colour was returning. As I came out of the wash room, I watched the wall zap back into place; then I saw Theron sitting on the sofa seat, looking pensive.

As I sat in my usual position, he said, "I had put off, as long as possible, telling you of the dilemma we face with your future, but you would have had to be aware of it sooner or later."

I had no words to say to Theron as a reply.

While I was taking a shower, one of the Terrans must have entered the room with some more fast food that I had been getting accustomed to. They were only snack items, but I was glad of them anyway.

With an almost rueful tone, Theron said, "I will leave you now so you can relax for a while and ponder on the unfortunate information I have given you."

"OK," I replied. "And thank you for the food and your honesty."

With that he left the room and I began to think of my disposition and think to myself, "What the hell am I going to do now?"

I don't remember doing so, but I had chomped my way through five packets of crisps and half a pack of cheese crackers. My mind was oblivious to everything except the thought I may never return home.

After I had sat for a time, I began to think back on all the new things I had learned about my world and myself. I had always wanted to know what the images were that I was seeing every day of my life and why I was the only one to see them. Also, I had learned that it wasn't just intuitive that I was able to sometimes know what people were going to say. The disclosed mysteries of the world, such as the Bermuda triangle, gave me a real buzz, knowing I was the only human with the answers. But what good were all these revelations if I was stuck in this dimension? I thought very deeply and realised that, even if I was back in my world, I could never tell anyone of what I had learned. It would mean revealing the existence of the Terrans, which would have devastating consequences for both civilisations.

The real question was whether I take the very slim chance I might survive and return to my world, or whether I stay here for the rest of my life and eat junk food, especially crackers that were three months out of date! Here I had to be a recluse with only a mere handful of the Terrans knowing I existed within their world. Although Theron and I had become good friends, I knew I must be a real headache for him by keeping me fed, amused and assured that none of his general species would find out about me. There could only be one answer. I must take the chance and return to my own world. I would tell Theron and discuss it with him on his return.

About an hour passed before Theron returned to my room and in that elapsed time, my primary thoughts were mainly of my mortality. Sitting opposite me again, Theron's eyes were downward, as if he didn't want to make eye contact, but after a short while he said, "Now that you know the whole truth about yourself and your human cycle, would you like for me to share your thoughts?"

It took a few seconds for my reply, as I was trying to snap out of my despondency.

"It's a lot to take in," I said. "To find out that the human soul or consciousness is dissolved into this world upon death and that you, the Terrans, are apparently made by nature's design, the disposers of a lifetime of human thoughts and memories. Please don't misinterpret what I have just said to be a negative thing; in a way I'm glad you are the keeper of souls. It is better that our accumulated thoughts and memories are put to good use when we die rather than for them to just fade into nothingness."

Theron replied, "Many humans need to believe there is a life after death and to know the factual truth might be devastating for them. If it has been decided that someone has something to offer the human race, I'd say that there is life after death, when we can use their thought waves to enhance the minds of future humans, they do, in a way, live on. Whatever way, human consciousness is recycled, as we see nature has intended. But what are your thoughts on being marooned in our world?"

I gave a submissive sigh.

"I believe that you are a good and hospitable race of people," I said. "And I thank you for saving my life, but I cannot stay here. I think you know that my world is where I belong and that I could never survive here physically or mentally. If I stayed, I would always be confined to solitude, apart from visits by you and I could not exist on the limited resource of food that you could obtain for me. I am very grateful, but I think I must try to return to my world no matter what the odds of my survival."

Theron said, "I understand and predicted that you would wish to return even knowing that you would probably not survive. We can open a portal at the exact location you entered, but we cannot offer you any protection against the forces you will encounter."

"Are you going to erase my memory or something, on the chance that I might survive?" I asked.

Theron replied, with a half smile, "Although we have projected ideas and thoughts into many thousands of humans, we have never taken memories or thoughts away. Even if we did have that ability, we would not erase your thoughts. I believe you understand what is at stake and because of that, you would not talk of things you have learned."

He then asked, "When do you wish to attempt the transition?"

Maybe it was the exposure to the atmosphere or just an overload of things to assimilate, but I felt really tired and it was getting late in the day and I needed to sleep, so I gave an immediate reply without really thinking. "Tomorrow if that is OK."

"Then I will make all the arrangements and hope you have a good night's rest," he said.

Theron then stood up and left the room.

When Theron had gone, I realised that, due to my fatigue, I had really made a rash decision as to when I should attempt the return to my reality. After all, it was more than likely to end my life, but like most young people, I had probably always thought I was immortal and nothing adverse would happen if I took a risk. But this time the real sense that death was awaiting me was firmly fixed in my mind. The only solace I could find is that I had survived the portal once, why not again, even though Theron had basically said that nature had let me enter his world but would not let me return to mine?

That night I eventually dropped off to sleep, not thinking about anything that I had experience in the Terran world but only of my family and life in mine. Oh and the well-being of my bloody car!

3

I awoke the next morning about 7:00 a.m. It was Sunday, July 1st. I had been in the Terran world a whole week, but it felt much longer. I got up and went over to the window wall when Zap; it revealed what was going on outside. Silent flying machines were dotted about the sky, with some hovering and others just zooming about. The streets I suppose were an average level of busy, although none of the Terrans actually raced about or moved at any great pace. Although I had become accustomed to this sort of panorama, I knew deep down that all this was alien to me and I would give anything to peer out of my own flat's window again and look upon the chimney-covered rooftops and the hustle and bustle of human urban life. Maybe this was the day.

I had not fixed a specific time to try to return but knew, with Theron's efficiency and fore-thought, the time would be at its optimal. A final sprucing up was needed, so I hit the shower room for the last time. After sonic washing myself and my clothes, I emerged spic and span for the big event. It's strange: I did not have any fear in my mind, considering what I was about to attempt, but I was apprehensive not knowing what to expect. I think I was excited also, or were these feelings just my nervous adrenaline that was making my heart beat faster?

They were the kind of feelings that you get just after you are strapped in for a rollercoaster ride and you wished you had gone on the spinning tea cups instead. Anyway, there was no going back now. I ate a few out-of-date biscuits and drank some weird tasting fruit punch that I had left over, so this meagre meal was to be my last breakfast here. I only hoped it wasn't to be my last ever.

There were a few gentle taps on the room door, which was strange as Theron had never used that sort of etiquette before. He usually just entered as if it was the normal thing to do.

I called out, "Come in."

Theron opened the door and entered. "I have made all the arrangements," he said, as he sat opposite me. "I have scheduled everything to take place at 3:00 p.m. today. This may depend on the observations of my crew on their off world craft who will be at a great height over the designated area at the exact place from where you entered. This is to make sure that there are no other humans in the vicinity when we open the portal. Two of my people will be at your side to give you physical support as you go through. This is because you will not escape the effects of this endeavour, as I think you know. You also know we cannot provide you with any kind of protection as we have no technology that would make any difference to your chances. Please be aware Terry, that whatever happens, we cannot bring you back again and your chances of survival are slim. My people will have to return once you are through the portal no matter what your condition."

As an addendum, Theron said, "It will not be too late to cancel up until the time just before you begin to enter the portal but once you have started there is no coming back. Do you still wish to proceed?"

"Yes, I must do this," I replied, determinedly.

"Then on behalf of the Terran Council and from me as a friend, I hope you will succeed."

I had about seven hours to kill before the big event, so I asked Theron if he knew of any more of Earth's mysteries or unaccountable things that might be within my dimension.

"So you are interested in the unexplained," he said.

"Yes," I replied. "Anything that hasn't been documented or established as fact in my world."

"Now let me think for a moment, what information might be of interest to you." Theron's eyes looked up at the ceiling as his left hand lightly squeezed his tiny chin. "We have found evidence that alien life forms had visited Earth in your realm millions of years ago, before even we evolved and when the beginnings of human life were just microbes. Soon after we had the ability to enter your world, metallic objects were found within your African continent. It was obvious to us that the visitors must have been from a distant galaxy, looking to settle or to just investigate, but the climate to them was probably not agreeable, so we believe they just moved on to another world. Is that the kind of information you are seeking?"

"Yes, that's great," I replied. "That proves there is intelligent life on other planets."

Theron continued, saying, "Many of human Earth's mysteries can be explained if speculation is not based purely on logic. The more humans understand about the forces that are within our world and in both dimensions, the more mysteries will be solved. There is one enigma that we know exists in your realm, which we cannot explain and only speculate about. When our Solar system was formed and the very fabric of our universe had been established. There were isolated pieces of unstable matter trapped within it. Although unable to eliminate this matter, natural force fields formed to contain it. These fields are like invisible bubbles that trap the energy that defy all laws of nature or physics. Sometimes they are static to a particular area and sometimes they move their location. They are various sizes of energy mass that, when living things or solid objects are caught within them, they don't behave as they should. For example, a solid rock might act weightless and move its position, or a living thing might age ten years in an instant. It has been witnessed by us that a whole village and its occupants were sent back in time fifty years and then returned to the present the next day. Yes, even the timeline had been disrupted. When these anomalies have moved away, things usually return to normal, but there have been times when the force has relocated them, such as, animals and solid masses have merged, leaving the organic embedded in solid rock. Luckily throughout your world these anomalies are of a very small number—at least, we think they are. We can detect them with our instruments, as blank atmospheric readings and we know to stay well clear of them."

That rendition was another first from Theron, which again left me with a dropped jaw, but it could probably explain a good few old and new legends.

Summing up, Theron said, "I do not think there is any more knowledge of your world I can give you, but I hope it has enlightened you to some extent."

A mere seven days ago, I was ignorant, along with every other human being, about most of the age-old, inexplicable things people have strived to rationalise without reaching any tangible explanations. I was now the sole human possessor of this knowledge. In my head, I tried to go through all the things I had learned since my time with Theron and my thoughts were the following:

Another dimension does exist.

The Terrans actually caused the creation of the Bermuda Triangle, which is a rift between the two dimensions.

The Terrans themselves, thought to be aliens, were actually the first intelligent beings to evolve on Earth.

UFOs—seen, documented and photographed throughout time—were not alien but in fact Terran craft able to move between dimensions.

Masterminds, such as Einstein, have heightened intelligence due to selected brain input by the Terrans.

Intelligent beings do inhabit other planets and have the technology for space travel.

Ancient civilisations were given enhancements from the Terrans, in order to help human advancement.

Unstable matter that Theron describe helps explain some legends and impossible scenarios.

Ghosts and spectres can and do exist.

Paranormal abilities are real, albeit minor ones like my own; sporadic mind reading.

Perhaps the biggest of all of these insights was that humans do have a soul or at least a life force energy which automatically opens a dimensional portal at the point of death and then the image of that person in spirit form passes through it and therefore goes into the light.

I was beginning to think that I was not meant to know all these things and this knowledge was only to be a brief revelation for me. My chances of surviving the move back into my world only bolstered the thought all this information would never see the light of day and I would not live to tell the tale. I could tell by Theron's demeanour that he felt ill at ease, so it seemed obvious to me that he valued our friendship and knew whatever the outcome of today, our friendship would be lost forever. Either I would die, or I would never come into contact with him again. I suppose I felt the same really. This highly intelligent, skinny little being had made a big impact on me as a good and caring friend and as a great ambassador for his race. Deep down though, I knew the people of my world had a hell of a long way to go before accepting Terrans for integration.

Theron started speaking with enthusiasm, as if diversion was needed. "We have a few hours. Would you like to go for a flight in my craft?"

With a slight smile on my face, I replied, "Not really. It would mean I would have to put that suit on again and balm my face and hands. Besides, I don't want to return home with grey hair, do I?"

I detected a sigh as Theron's eyes lowered toward the floor. A full minute must have passed in total silence before either of us said anything.

"I know," I said, lightening the mood. "I would really like to see more footage of my ancestors. Have you any scenes from the Mayan era or the pioneering days of North America?"

"I believe I do," he said, perking up.

Theron took out his projector gadget from his belt and placed it on the table. Then with the silver ring on his finger, he whizzed through footage at fantastic speed, stopping it on a Mayan city, bustling with people. I wondered how he knew when to stop at the exact place on this gadget, but I didn't really feel like asking.

Hours passed and I had again witnessed actual scenes from the Mayan dynasty and a few confrontations between the Native American Indians and the early settlers. The clarity of the scenes were remarkable considering, as I previously explained, they were either shot from high in the air or miles away from the actual event, so the Terrans would not be seen. Photographers in my world would kill for a Terran zoom lens.

Although totally fascinated, I had intermittently been looking at my watch throughout this elapse of time. It was now 2:15 p.m. and Theron knew it was time to shut the film show down.

"I thought you would like some refreshments," he said, pressing a certain point on his belt. After thirty or so seconds, I heard the familiar whooshing sound of the door and Madri entered the room clutching a tray of various items of my usual fast food.

"Hello, Terry," Madri said.

At first meetings with the Terran people I found it difficult to tell them apart, but I could definitely recognise Madri and now distinguish the difference between other Terrans I had met since. I welcomed Madri saying, "Hello, Madri, how are you? I hope some of the data you collected from my scan was of benefit in some way."

"I am well, thank you," she replied. "And the scan certainly was of interest to us. We have not encountered any human before that has your unique brain waves; therefore, your scan has been recorded for future analysis. You will also be remembered in our archives as the first human ever to enter our realm and live through the transition. The council wishes you every success for your return."

As she spoke, she put on the table a bottle of milk, a packet of milk chocolate biscuits and some various snacks in small bags. The Terrans had obviously gone out of their way to obtain items that they knew I would enjoy.

Opening the milk bottle, I asked, "Would both of you like to share the food with me?"

"Unfortunately, we cannot," replied Theron. "Our digestion would not tolerate such foods. We can only eat vegetarian based meals and drink plain water."

"Oh well," I said. "I had better have some of this myself then, as time is marching on."

I ate a few of those biscuits and a packet of crisps. Then I drank a few large gulps of milk and as I put the bottle down, I looked at my watch. It was now 2:35 p.m. I looked at Theron and he looked back, he then nodded, saying, "Yes, it is time."

The three of us then stood up. I could swear I saw a tear emerge from one of Madri's eyes, but I'm not sure if that was even possible. The door opened and Theron and I headed through it, leaving Madri behind, saying in a soft voice, "Good-bye, Terry and good luck."

I looked back at her and smiled. Theron and I then went down that familiar route to the backdoor, where two of the taller Terrans were waiting. With the silver sheet then placed over my head, we all boarded Theron's craft. After the door closed, the taller Terrans sat opposite each other on either side of the craft, while Theron sat at the front controls with me beside him.

"Are you sure you want to do this?" Theron asked.

"Yes," I replied. "There is no going back now."

"Then we will proceed," he answered. "It will take us approximately eight minutes to reach the location."

With Theron's left hand on the control pad, the craft gracefully lifted high off the ground, turning about forty-five degrees to our right in the process. Then gradually the craft increased speed to an amazing velocity. I was looking out at the Terran landscape and cities for the last time and I felt a certain sense of privilege and achievement. I felt privilege because I had seen and been made aware of mysteries and passed events no other living human could possibly have witnessed or know about. I felt achievement because I had finally got all the answers to questions about myself that I had always craved. The only thing was, could I return to my former life with this knowledge by surviving the short but potentially fatal journey?

During that eight-minute flight, no conversation was made between any of us. It seemed a really solemn atmosphere as if no one knew quite what to say. I didn't expect any words from the larger Terrans anyway as they gave the impression they were military and were only there to follow orders, but Theron hadn't uttered a sound or moved his gaze from the ships controls.

The craft came to rest in an open area and I could see through the window that we were a couple of miles away, on the outskirts of a city. It was now just a few minutes to 3:00 p.m. Theron turned to me and said, "Well, Terry, this is it. It has been a great honour to have met you and I hope that our friendship has meant as much to you as it has to me. I have just received word from my crew that all is clear on the other side so we are now ready to proceed. Are you ready?"

"I am ready," I replied. "And it has been an honour for me too, meeting you and your race. I really hope that someday both our species will be able to interact freely, because only good can come of it."

Theron gave that little half smile that I had seen before when he was pleased. "I believe the best way to do this is for you to keep your eyes closed at all times as the brightness may damage them. You will need to walk in reverse, which might protect your face and fool the force field into believing you are not trying to enter again back from the totality of death. My associates will escort you through; each one will hold one of your arms to prevent you from stumbling and to help guide you. Remember, no matter what happens, once you are on the other side, my assistants will have to return immediately. Are you clear on this?"

"Yes," I said.

"Then good-bye, Terry. I wish you life and good fortune."

With a vacuum release sound, the door of the craft opened to form a ramp. I closed my eyes and the two Terrans escorted me down the ramp and onto the ground. I turned around in the direction of the craft and felt each of the larger Terrans take one of my arms.

I didn't hear anything but felt a kind of sucking sensation behind me, then a blast of air pushing me forward toward the ship. I supposed that this was the portal's effects as it opened. Unexpectedly, one of my Terran escorts whispered in my ear, "Good luck," as I tentatively started walking in reverse, feeling their firm grip on my arms as support. Suddenly, I felt an intense pressure all over, as if I was being pulled through a dense rubber hole, which was far too small for my body. Through my eyelids, I could also see a great burst of light, which was followed by an excruciating pain in my head. Then for a few seconds, everything went quiet and I no longer felt the Terran's grip. I opened my eyes to see the blue-tinged portal I had just come through close firmly shut, leaving no trace of itself.

A few seconds later, a multicoloured tinged portal opened in the same place and I am sure I could see Theron and the other two Terrans on the other side. A weird sensation came over me, as if the portal was beckoning me back into the light and I somehow knew that this was nature's death call. But apart from aching all over and a massive headache, I was not in a state of dying, so there was no way I was going to be drawn into it. Then, as if the portal conceded defeat, it closed with a silent zap.

I had somehow cheated death itself and returned to my own world alive and free and this exhilaration overcame all of my aches and pains. The most major thing I could think of now was: Where did I park my car?

Although covered in bird droppings, my car was exactly where I had left it and I was astounded to find it started on the first try. I couldn't wait to get back home, have a nice cup of coffee and lie down in my own bed.

I arrived home in the early evening to find my letters strewn all over the hall floor together with the usual pile of junk mail advertising pizzas, Chinese and India Take-away foods. Going through my letters as I walked upstairs, I saw that a muddy shoe had stepped on one of my letters. It was probably done by one of my neighbours in the other flats of the house. The muddy print had blotted out the *ce* from my first name, Terrance and my eyes then began to widen as my brain analysed what I was seeing. With the missing *ce***,** it read, Mr. Terran Seer**.**

All this time, I hadn't realised that my name was actually linked to my destiny. Even the fact that my name should have been spelled Terrence with an *e* instead of an *a,* was the result of some twit spelling my name wrong on my birth certificate. This surely was no coincidence.

After entering my flat I breathed a big sigh of relief. I was home at last. I felt very fatigued and I likened my tiredness to coming back from an arduous journey. In a sense, I **actually** had!

Coffee was next on the agenda, but the pong and green, hairy sludge in the half bottle of milk in the fridge meant I had to go out again briefly to get some fresh. I really didn't feel like doing so, but my craving for a caffeine infusion gave me the strength to go. On my return, I finally got to down a large mug of strong coffee and the thoughts in my head were starting to make sense of the experience I had just endured. The enormity of it all was overwhelming. I had just returned after a week in another dimension and although not leaving this planet, I had still been in an alien world and survived the transition back.

Although grateful to be alive, I couldn't help wondering **how** I survived, as Theron only predicted a slim chance of my surviving the transition. Surely, there must have been a missing factor in the calculations the Terrans ran that would have given me much better odds, but they didn't seem to be a race that wasn't precise in everything they did. I also realised that the blue-tinged portal I came back through was a manufactured one by the Terrans, but the multicoloured one was of a natural source and maybe my own death gateway. If I was truly back safe and secure, why did I feel compelled to return to enter that light? My quest for answers before meeting the Terrans had been fulfilled, but now it seemed they had been replaced by new questions. It was all too much to think about and sleeping in my own bed was a welcomed prospect. I wasn't up to contacting anyone yet, but knew I would have to phone my family the next day to offer them some sort of explanation as to where I had been for the past week.

It was Sunday morning. I awoke to the birds outside whistling away on this bright, sunny day. All that had happened to me during the past week felt as if it was all a dream. Although bleary eyed, I saw I had forgotten to put the milk back in the fridge last night and left it, minus the silver-foil cap, on the kitchen's work surface. I knew the leftover bread from a week previous wouldn't exactly make good toast, so I thought I would have some cereal instead. As I got my yellow-boxed cereal out of an overhead cupboard and put it on the work surface, I accidentally knocked over the milk bottle and it rolled to the edge of the surface to fall onto the floor. When something like that happens, usually your natural instincts kick in and in a split second you make a grab for it. This time it was different! Although my mind made that split second decision, my hands remained still and instead, as the bottle rolled over the edge, it froze in mid-air. It was as if the event slowed down into separate video frames until time stopped completely. Although the milk still poured out of the bottle and all over the floor, the bottle remained suspended without any means of support.

I immediately realised that I had used some sort of mind power to stop the bottle falling and then I remembered that Madri had told me my brain had the potential to do this stuff. Grabbing the bottle quickly in case I lost concentration, I was relieved to find there was just enough milk left for one cup of coffee.

Once I had cleaned up the spilt milk and sat on my sofa with my coffee, I started to look around the room in excitement, to see what other objects there were that I could attempt to move with my mind. I selected a plastic cup that had the words, "World's greatest plonker. Happy eighteenth birthday," written on it. Gathering a bit of dust, it was sitting on a shelf in the corner of the room. I concentrated hard to raise the cup into the air. Of course, nothing happened, but maybe I was trying too hard, so I relaxed and closed my eyes with the thought of the cup lifting itself up from the shelf. With great expectation, I gradually opened one eye to see if it was working. Nothing! The dust hadn't even been disturbed.

With that, I came to the conclusion that it must have been just a fluke experience and would probably never happen again.

In a disappointed mood, I thought I had better get dressed and go down to the shops for some fresh supplies. When I returned, I would shave off my week old beard growth and make that apologetic phone call I needed to make to my dad for my absence.

On this lovely, sunny Sunday morning, there weren't many people about. In fact, there was only one other person, coming toward me as I sauntered along the pavement heading for my local *sell almost anything* shop. The woman, who was heavily pregnant, was also carrying a full bag of shopping in each hand. I immediately thought to myself that she shouldn't be carrying all that stuff in her condition and just as I thought this, I saw her ankle twist beneath her, as she stepped on a loose-paving slab. I was about five paces too far away to grab her before she fell, but to my amazement, my new ability happened again. I froze her as she started to fall forward toward the ground. This gave me enough time to make up those five paces and grab her a split second later, then I felt the weight of her body on my arms.

"Oh, thank you," she said. "I felt my foot twist and thought I would fall over. But how did you reach me in time? You must have moved very fast to catch me."

"No, I must have been closer than you thought," I replied. "Are you OK now?"

"Yes," she said. "Thanks to you."

After I saw the woman safely on her way, I carried on walking towards the shop and felt that feel-good factor, which made me feel a bit smug.

This feeling, I thought, arose in me for two reasons.

One was that I managed to stop a pregnant woman from falling and possibly hurting herself and her unborn child. The second, I now knew that not only was my telekinetic power still there, but it had worked on something living.

I finally reached my local shop and I was greeted with that familiar Punjabi accent as I entered.

"Hello Terry, How are you? Haven't seen you around lately? Are you growing a beard, or have you been eating a cat?"

"Oh very funny Mr. Patel. No, I've been on holiday for a week and I forgot to take my electric shaver with me"

"Was the holiday nice?" he asked.

"Out of this world," I replied, quietly chuckling to myself.

After exchanging a round of words, asking how each other's families were etc, I collected and paid for all the necessities I needed and headed off back home, all the time thinking about my new found ability. I somehow knew that I would find a way of controlling it, so I could use it at will.

My father, who was also my boss, wasn't too pleased with me when I phoned him to say I had been too ill to go to work last week.

He said that I should have phoned to let him know, but I managed to smooth things over, although he said that I should also take another week off, which would then be my annual two-week summer holiday. I hadn't really planned a holiday, but another week off work suited me just fine.

With that dreaded phone call out of the way, I made myself a couple of pieces of toast fully charged with marmalade and a coffee to wash it all down. Then as I washed my sticky hands, I pondered how I managed to stop that milk bottle dropping and the pregnant woman from falling over. It then occurred to me that what I had actually done was not telekinesis, as I hadn't actually moved anything. What I was actually doing was freezing an object in time and I couldn't think of a name for that. Nevertheless, I thought time freezing objects and telekinesis must go together somehow.

Sitting in my living room, I decided I was going to try and move something with my mind again anyway. I closed my eyes and concentrated to move that plastic cup I had tried before. After a good few minutes, I stood up and went over to the cup on the shelf. Amazing! The cup seemed to have more dust on it than before, but I still hadn't moved it. It seemed moving things about with my mind was not my thing, at least for now anyway.

The knowledge that I had acquired in the past week was mind blowing and my thoughts returned to thinking about Theron and the Terrans. As my line of thought came to the portal through which I had entered the other dimension, I felt a sudden gust of air within the room. Then almost immediately a portal opened about eight feet from where I was standing. It was about six-feet high by about four-foot wide, oval in shape with a multi- coloured tint to its outer edges. The core light it produced was blinding and I had to mask it with my forearm; somehow I had made it open with my thoughts. Gradually by squinting and moving my forearm up and down a little, I managed to look inside.

The view wasn't clear but I could tell, from the position I was looking from, it was a good few feet off the ground. I had obviously managed to open the gateway by combining my alpha, beta, theta and delta brain waves and because I was in my flat a few stories up, I assumed I was looking at the equivalent place in Theron's world. Then this eerie feeling saturated my body and I felt like I was being drawn into the light. The feeling was so powerful I really had to fight to resist the urge. I had read something in the past about how some people suffer from a kind of vertigo where, when they are confronted with being high up; let's say a roof; although they are terrified of heights, they have an overwhelming urge to jump off. This feeling I supposed was exactly like that, but I somehow knew that, if I entered the light, it would be at my peril, so I came to the conclusion that nature was still trying to exterminate me. Determinedly, I shut off my portal-related thoughts and started to think of something unrelated; thankfully, the portal snapped closed without any trace. With relief, I sat down exhausted, but with a cold, clammy sweat all over my body. That was an experience I did not want to repeat any time in the near future.

I had been back only a day and new things had started happening to me that I could not quite understand, but at least this time, I had the knowledge to make sense of them. So far, since being back, I had not seen the blurred images I had gotten used to; of the Terrans going about their business. Hopefully now, that was a thing of the past.

Now recovered from my latest ordeal and feeling much better, I told myself it was a beautiful sunny day and that I was on holiday. I decided I would jump into my car and go down to the coast and maybe have a meal out. And that's exactly what I did.

I stopped off to fill my car with petrol at a local garage. Then I was on my way heading south for the coast. This was in the early seventies when petrol was affordable and also when the roads were drivable; it was a time when ten cars waiting in a line were considered a traffic jam.

With my car fully tanked, I tore down the motorway flat out at about sixty-five miles per hour (most cars then, especially mine, wouldn't go any faster without overheating or the fan belt snapping). Anyway my old banger got me to the coast and as I cruised along the front of Hastings seaside town, I could see the pebbled beach, packed with holidaymakers sitting in row upon row of striped, multicoloured deckchairs. The sea was its usual dirty grey colour, but the sky was a beautiful blue. I got lucky and managed to park in a nearby side street, none of which had any yellow lines back then. Getting out of the car, the warm sun hit me square in the face and luckily I had remembered to bring my sunglasses. With all the privileged knowledge I had acquired the past week and with the supernatural ability I had exercised, I had a sort of superior air about me. I had never felt like that before and I wasn't sure if I really liked it.

Anyway, onward and upward, I was heading for the pier. I had been to this place before and knew that this old Victorian cast iron and wood pier had large rooms, full of fruit machines, or colloquially (one armed bandits). Cafés and all sorts of curious booths like madam Zazar, the fortune teller was dotted about the length of the boardwalk.

Coming here with my parents as a child, I never forgot how scared I was as I walked along the wooden slats of the pier's boardwalk because I could see I was high up above the pebbles and the sea directly below. The gaps between the boards were probably only an inch wide but when you are small, you still think that you might fall straight through them. It's funny, but as I started walking onto those timber slats, I still had that same feeling.

I finally arrived at the far end of that pier, where a half-dozen men had their fishing rods leaned up against the white painted, ornate wrought iron railings of the pier. Although I had seen people fishing here before, I had never actually seen anyone catch anything, so I thought I would linger for a while just in case I saw a miraculous event of a fish being caught. After fifteen minutes or so I gave up.

The sea breeze was nice though, gently blowing my hair and cooling my face. What should I do next? After a minute or so, I decided to try out my luck on the penny-fruit machines, so I ambled my way back to a large hall, packed with holidaymakers, with their children who were all running about and making lots of noise.

To my horror, I realised that all the machines were now a minimum of sixpence to play. I had forgotten that in February, Great Britain had changed to decimal coinage and instead of getting twelve nice, chunky feeling copper pennies for our shillings; we were now only getting ten. That meant that the old trusty half a Shilling or sixpenny piece was now only worth two-and-a-half new pence. It was so confusing for us back then, but in real terms it meant everything was much more expensive. Depressed that I knew I could not afford to lose too much money on these cash guzzlers, I located a machine that I thought looked interesting.

The fruit machine was a silvery metal one with a bust of a laughing clown located centrally on its front and just below the bust was a glass panel, crammed full of sixpenny pieces; this was obviously the jackpot. To win the jackpot after pulling the handle, the centre lines of the three reels had to read "tic-tac-toe." Reluctantly, I fed my first sixpence into the slot of the machine, pulled the handle and watched as the three reels spun showing various fruit symbols as they whizzed round. The reels each stopped with a loud click, one after another. Looking at the stationary reels I knew I was not going to win anything with two apples and a pear. I wondered whether I should continue as I couldn't afford to keep feeding this machine my hard-earned cash. Oh well. Since I was here now, I would make my limit fifty pence, which to me was still half of a pound note sterling, considering I only earned about eighteen pounds a week).

I put my second coin into the machine and pulled the handle. Click, click, click went the machine. There were cherries on all three reels! I had won six sixpences, which dropped out into the tray below. I felt a mild adrenaline rush and was now eager to try again. Having inserted my third sixpence into the slot of the machine and pulled its handle, I peered intensely at the reels, as they spun round. *Click* went the machine and the first reel was *tic. Click,* it went again and the second went *tac. Click*, the third went *toe.* With a loud tinny sound, the jackpot compartment released its booty and all the coins fell into the tray below. Quickly scooping up the coins, I counted the amount as I dropped each coin into my pocket. I had won eight pounds, which was nearly half a week's worth of wages.

Excitedly, I looked around for another machine that I could apply my magic to. I came across an electronic machine that had a push button instead of a handle. The symbols listed on the winning chart were similar to the last machine except the jackpot line this time was three bars. I was on a high and knew the adrenaline was pumping so I quickly inserted a sixpence into the slot and pressed the start button. Again I peered intently at the reel's window, as one by one it revealed the outcome of the spin. Each of the three reels had stopped on a bar, another jackpot win and this time amounting to ten pounds. I had won my wages for a week in less than five minutes.

It suddenly dawned on me that the reason I could stop a bottle dropping, save someone from falling and make a fruit machine stop on the jackpot must have something to do with some sort of adrenaline rush, a sudden burst of energy when I needed to think or act quickly. At least I thought it was probably the trigger.

With both front pockets of my jeans bulging with sixpences, I waddled over to an old, scruffy-looking woman who gave out change for the machines; she had her arms folded and was sitting behind a raised counter. The woman looked about seventy-five, had matted grey fuzzy, shoulder-length hair and was wearing a dirty food-stained red cardigan, with holes in the sleeves. I emptied each pocket of coins onto her counter and she said in an old quivering cockney voice, “Who’s been a lucky boy, then?”

She then unfolded her arms, lowered her head and started to count up my winnings. “Eighteen pounds one and six---no wait, sorry. Eighteen pounds seven-and-a-half new pence. Bloody decimal! I’ll never get the ang of it.”

She then handed me three five-pound notes, three one-pound notes and the three remaining sixpences, saying, “Good on yer, boy, about time somebody won something on those blinking machines.”

She was obviously not the owner.

I felt great and moderately rich, so I was now off to find a nice café, off the pier and on the other side of the promenade, to have a nice fish dinner. Isn’t it funny how, when most people visit the seaside, fish is their usual choice of menu? I suppose it’s because you would assume it must be freshly caught from the sea. Anyway, I thought a nice piece of Rock salmon fish would go down just fine, coupled with plenty of chips, salt and vinegar.

As I strolled back along the pier with my hands in my pocket and with a smug smile on my face, my mind kept going over my wins on the fruit machines. I hadn’t really won anything before, but I remembered the jackpot wins were not really luck as I had stopped the machines on the winning symbols with my mind. I didn’t feel guilty, though; those machines had probably been rigged not to pay out much anyway, so I felt getting a bit back wasn’t really a crime. Dodging an overturned ice cream cone which had half melted and was gradually sinking through the timber slats of the pier floor, I eventually arrived at the sea-front’s promenade.

I looked across the road to the shops and cafés to see if there was an establishment to suit my needs. One blue fronted café caught my eye, The Blue Anchor. That place sounded like the place I wanted to get the meal I was looking forward to, so darting between the traffic, I made my way across the road.

On entering this café, I could see it was reasonably clean and as I sat down at a table I looked at what other people had on their plates. Mostly fish, of course, but a couple of people had sausages and eggs; everyone had chips. The waitress came over to me and handed me a menu. She was a stunningly attractive girl, with long natural-looking blond hair and about my age, but what I noticed the most about her was her glowing, emerald-green eyes.

She said, with a slight Welsh accent, "Let me know when you are ready to order."

I smiled, nodded and coyly buried my face in the menu. My instantaneous thought was wow! She is gorgeous, but apart from her, let me see what I fancied from the menu. I could see that Rock salmon, with chips of course, were available, so I looked up to beckon the waitress over to me. Our eyes met; she smiled and made her way over to my table.

"You want Rock salmon and chips don't you?" she asked.

"Yes, how did you know that?" I replied.

"Don't know," she said. "It just came into my head."

She wrote the order down on her little notepad and disappeared into the rear of the café. That was weird, I thought. Is she some sort of mind reader? A few minutes later she emerged from the multicoloured plastic strips, which replaced the door of the kitchen and came over to my table carrying a cup of coffee. It had entered my mind that I would like a cup of coffee while I waited for my dinner, but I was so bowled over by her appearance I had forgotten to ask for it.

"How did you know I wanted a cup of coffee?" I asked.

"I thought you ordered it," she said.

"Oh! Did I?" I replied, knowing full well I hadn't. "Well, that's good. I wanted one anyway."

Again she smiled and disappeared into the back. Was this girl reading my mind, or was I unknowingly transmitting my thoughts to her? I couldn't quite get this because in the past I was always the one reading other people's thoughts, not the other way around. I would have to try a little experiment. When she brings my meal up, I'll think of tomato ketchup and see if she mentions it, I thought to myself. Ten minutes had passed and I had finished my coffee when she emerged from the café's kitchen carrying my dinner on an oval-shaped plate. As she neared the table, I thought of tomato ketchup and she said, "There's salt, pepper, vinegar and tomato ketchup at the side of you, but let me know if there's anything else you need."

I felt a bit silly because I was so wrapped up with the thought she could mind read, I hadn't even noticed the tomato ketchup was already on the table right next to me. That little experiment told me nothing. I thanked her for my food and started to tuck in. I couldn't remember the last time I had Rock salmon and chips and with loads of salt, vinegar and ketchup. The meal went down lovely, but another coffee to finish off the meal, I decided, would be a great cap on the meal. I felt a definite attraction between myself and the waitress, as all through the meal our eyes would meet, while she busily attended to other customers.

When I had finished my meal she came over to remove my empty plate and asked if I wanted another coffee. *She did it again.* She knew that I wanted another coffee, or was it that she just asks everyone this question? I just did not know. When the second coffee came, I asked her what time she finished work and she said she finished at 6:00 p.m., so I asked her if she would like to go out with me then. I didn't think she would, because she was so attractive and must have had lots of men scrambling for her attention, but surprisingly she agreed. She carried on working, while I slowly sipped my coffee till it was gone and when she noticed my empty cup, she presented me with the bill. I paid her and of course added a generous tip.

Then I said, "I'll wait for you outside at six, then shall I…oh and by the way, my name is Terry."

"I'm Diane," she said. "See you at six."

With that I got up, smiled and touched her hand as I made my way to the door. Once outside I looked at my watch to see how long I would have to wait to see her again.

I had an hour and a half to kill, so what was I going to do till then? I know, I thought. I would have to make sure I had enough money to take this girl out, so I'll go to the amusement arcades, dotted along the promenade.

My adrenaline levels were high with the thought of having a date with Diane, so there shouldn't have been a problem winning a bit more cash. This time I wouldn't go for jackpots, just nice little even amount to boost my wallet a bit.

I had no problem in making those machines stop on winning symbols and I had increased the cash in my wallet by another fifteen pounds. It was closing in on six o'clock, so I made my way back to the café and as I arrived, Diane was just coming out.

"Hi ya," I said. "Anywhere special you would like to go?"

She replied, "I wouldn't mind going to the cinema to see *"On Her Majesty's Secret Service"* last year's James Bond film. They're showing it again and I missed it the first time round."

"OK, great. I missed it first time round too."

It felt so natural when we instinctively held hands as we set off for the cinema.

Following her directions and after catering to all her confectionary needs at the cinema's kiosk, we managed to get a nice couple of seats in the back row. During the film we became closer and closer, not just bodily but we somehow felt at ease with each other, which led to the occasional eye-to-eye contact, followed by a long drawn out kiss.

When the film had ended at around 9:00 p.m., we emerged from the cinema acting as if we had known each other for years. With my arm around her shoulders and hers round my waist, we headed for a vacant bench on the promenade. It was a warm evening with a nice, gentle breeze, which made her golden hair lift from her shoulders now and again and I couldn't believe how lucky I was to be with her. Sitting centrally on a bench to avoid the seagull droppings at the ends, we cuddled up and looked over the sea. The rippling waves, making a nice background sound, consistently lapped against the pebbled beach, as the stones were dragged back with the waves' ebb. We obviously hadn't done much talking in the cinema, so now was the time to find out as much as I could about her.

"Do you live in this town?" I asked.

"No," she replied. "I live in South London. I'm on a break from my studies. My aunt and uncle own that café and I came down to help out and earn some extra money by working for them."

"That's strange. I live in South London, too." I said.

After further probing, it turned out that Diane's surname was Smith and she lived with her parents about a mile away from my flat. She was twenty-one years old and was training to be a medical doctor. She had left school at sixteen and went straight into a doctors' training college; she said her aim was to become a paediatrician. Wow! Brains and beauty, I thought. Diane then asked several questions about me and I gave her the rundown of my surname, background and the boring work I did. I had already noticed a slight Welsh accent in her voice, so I said, "You don't come from London originally, do you?"

"You noticed my accent then. No, I originally came from Shropshire, but we moved to London when I was ten years old."

"Why did you move?" I asked, for added conversation and wanting to know everything about her.

"If I tell you, promise you won't laugh or anything."

Feeling intrigued, I replied, "I promise."

Her monologue that followed left me stunned.

"When I was nine, I was playing in a nearby field with some friends. It was a wheat field, I think and the crop was taller than all of us. We were playing hide and seek, which wasn't that difficult considering the height of the wheat. Anyway, somehow I got completely separated from my friends. I couldn't find my way out of the field for what seemed like hours and I got tired and fell asleep. When I woke up, I found myself in some sort of airplane, lying on a silver table, which had a clear jelly like surface. Although the plane wasn't moving, I knew I was high up in the air. For a brief moment I swear I saw two aliens with me in this plane, you know, like the ones that supposed to have crashed at Roswell. Then I must have passed out because, the next thing I knew, I was back in the field with my dad towering over me saying, 'Everyone has been looking for you for hours. You should have known better than to come into a field with a high crop.' He then picked me up and carried me home. It was strange where he found me, though, because all the wheat had been flattened down into a perfect circle about fifteen feet in diameter and I was in the dead centre. I should have kept quiet about what had happened to me, but I told my parents and my school friends. From then on, I was a laughing stock and the kids at school mocked and made fun of me all the time. It got so bad that I was dreading going to school and was crying every single day. Eventually the only solution was to move. My dad had better work prospects south anyway, so that's why we moved to London."

I was totally gob-smacked because I was pretty sure that I knew what she had just told me had actually happened—but how could I tell her I knew she was telling the truth because of my own experience?

"You don't believe me, do you?" she said.

"Oh, I totally believe you," I replied in a serious voice.

I was now trying to join up the dots by asking her how she knew what I had wanted when I came into the café.

"Since I was very little," she replied. "Now and again, I would know what people were going to say before they actually said it. It wouldn't happen all the time, but my family would say jokingly I must be psychic or something and it was all down to my mum passing out for a few seconds just before I was born."

I found this answer incredible because I really couldn't tell if it was just a fantastic coincidence meeting Diane or had the Terrans interfered with a higher percentage of the world's population than I had originally thought. Gently pulling Diane closer to me, I said, "Now I want you to believe me, just in case you think I am making it up for your benefit. The knowing what people are going to say and the fact your mum passed out just before you were born is exactly what happened to me."

She smiled and I could see there was disbelief in her facial expression.

"No, seriously," I said.

Her smile gradually faded, as she saw I meant what I said. Then I continued. "My mother did actually pass out for a few seconds just before I was born and from an early age, I have been able to finish people's sentences or know what they were going to say. Their words came into my head, even when I didn't know some of the words or knew what they meant."

"That's exactly like me," she said.

I couldn't believe I had found someone that I could relate to as much as Diane; nor could I get over how intelligent and beautiful she was. The realisation of our similarities inspired a long, intimate kiss. It was like we had been destined to meet.

After a period of not speaking at all and just cuddling up with the occasional kiss, we decided we should get up from the bench and walk in the direction of the café by taking a stroll along the beach.

After trundling our way over the mounds of pebbles, losing half a pace with each step as the stones gave way, we came to the wet sandy area at the sea's edge. The waves were now gently lapping on each flow of movement and ebbing back toward us with hardly a sound. Hugging each other just enough not to hinder our walking, we strolled off at a snail's pace heading toward the underside of the pier, about a quarter of a mile away. It was obvious we both wanted to make the moment and indeed the evening last as long as we possibly could.

It was getting late as we neared the pier and with a quick glance, I looked at my watch.

"Your aunt and uncle won't be worrying where you are, will they?" I asked.

"No," she replied. "I told them that I might be late back."

"Oh, that's all right then," I said, breathing an inner sigh of relief.

We walked back up onto the pebbles a little bit and sat down with the pier directly above us. It was a bit darker here, shading us a little from the glare of the promenade's lights.

"I have really enjoyed this evening, Diane," I said, "and hope that you will want to see me again."

"Don't be silly," she replied. "Of course I want to see you again."

"When do you come back to London?"

"I'm due to come back this Tuesday."

I then told her that I had the rest of the week off work and asked her if she would come to my flat on the Wednesday, about 10:00 a.m. She agreed, so I told her my address. I didn't have a pen with me and nor she, but she said not to worry, she had a great memory and would not forget. That's one thing we didn't have in common, a great memory.

"There are a lot of things I want to talk to you about," I said.

"That sounds ominous."

"Not really," I said, "but you might find it interesting."

"I'm looking forward to it already." She replied with a smile.

Now and again, there was a creaking coming from the pier, which interrupted the stillness as we lay side by side on the pebbles, holding each other's hands. I assumed it was the movement of the cast iron structure rubbing against the weathered timbers as the evening started to cool down. The pier closed at eleven, so I knew, with the lack of movement from above, that it must have been well past that time.

There was no way I was going to look at my watch this time and give Diane the totally wrong impression. I wanted the evening to last forever.

"I really don't want to," Diane finally said, "but I had better get back to my aunt's place. I have got to be up early tomorrow for work."

It sounds ridiculous, but that little statement from Diane gave me a kind of instant depression. Without showing my reluctance, I said, "I suppose we had better go then."

I stood up from the pebbles and offered Diane my hand to help her stand. As I gave a little extra yank, she ended up in my arms, tight to my body and that uninterrupted manoeuvre ended with a long, lingering kiss. Our lips slightly stuck together when they finally parted, with both of us peering into each other's eyes; it was obvious we wanted that moment to last forever.

Finally one of us had to come back to Earth, so Diane broke the mood by saying, "Race you to the promenade."

With the displaced pebbles rolling over my feet, she ran off up the beach. By the time I had caught up, she had made it there laughing and panting at the same time.

After we had both caught our breath, we held hands, crossed the road and made our way to The Blue Anchor, where her aunt and uncle lived above the café.

"I'll see you on Wednesday then," I said.

"Yes," she replied. "And don't worry: I will write your address down as soon as I get inside."

I kissed her again and hesitantly said, "Bye then."

With that beautiful smile, she replied, "Go!"

After gently pushing me away, she entered the café and closed the door behind her.

I felt absolutely deflated and was missing her almost immediately, but I had a long drive home, so I made my way back to my car, reliving the past few hours with every step.

It was about 1:30 a.m. as I started to drive back to London on the almost empty roads. I must have been on autopilot or something as I had been thinking about the evening with Diane all the way home. Before I knew it, I arrived outside my flat, not remembering any part of the journey. As I got out of my car, the stillness of this Monday morning was only disturbed by my car door shutting with a clonk and the sound of my keys hitting the pavement as I accidently dropped them. I looked around feeling guilty that I may have woken someone, but I heard no shouts of complaint.

As I looked up into the sky at the twinkling stars, I sucked in a long deep breath of air through my nostrils and then closed my eyes with a wide, smug smile on my face. I felt that the world was a perfect place and I was so very grateful that I was in it. This time very quietly, I opened the main door to my building and once inside closed it also with minimal sound. Then with the occasional creek, I crept up the stairs to my flat at the top. My stealth finished once I was inside. A nice cup of coffee was required, so that I could sit down and go over again and again the events of the previous evening.

I couldn't believe my incredible luck at meeting Diane and as I started to think about the chain of events that I had been through the past few days, there was a zapping sound in the air, as a portal appeared over by my window. A cold sweat came over me as I had the same intense feeling of being drawn into the bright light. I knew I was cured of seeing the vague Terran forms, but now I had a much bigger problem: nature was trying to reclaim my existence. I closed my eyes quickly and tried to focus my brain on something entirely unconnected. The thought that I must get my car cleaned of all the bird droppings came into my head and I meticulously went over, step by step, how I would clean it. I started at the roof and worked my way down to the side panels and wheels. After a few minutes I slowly opened my eyes and the portal had vanished. **Why** was this happening? I asked myself. Life had just become more important to me than ever before and I didn't want this burden of having to focus my thoughts in order to subdue the portal's intense magnetic pull.

I began feeling the effects of the long day and a sapped brain, so I went to bed and quickly fell asleep.

I woke about 11:30 a.m. that day and instantly thought of the great night I had had with Diane. Bleary eyed, I tipped some breakfast cereal into a bowl and added some milk. With my eyes barely open, I sat on my sofa spilling some milk from the bowl into my lap. Slurping each mouthful with a bit more care, I started to wonder what day it was. After the cereal and a strong coffee my eyes began to focus. Thoughts of preparation for Diane's visit on Wednesday were foremost in my mind. A shower would wake me up to give me a clear head for the tasks I wanted to achieve during the rest of the day.

Like yesterday it was a very pleasant sunny day and the first thing I did was wash the bird droppings and muck off my car. Even with the rust patches on it, my car's light blue colour started to look quite smart. The next thing I did was go to the supermarket on my local high street to get provisions, although I had no clue of the foods Diane would prefer.

I know I thought, pasta, everyone likes pasta I think! Oh well, Spaghetti, some tinned Bolognese and some ready meals would give her a varied choice.

I finished shopping and I arrived back at my flat, loaded down with everything I thought Diane might like, even a packet of chocolate biscuits, which I made sure were in date. The two bags of groceries I was carrying had left red marks on the palm side of my fingers when I finally set them down on my kitchen worktops. I felt sure I had covered most of the angles of what Diane's tastes might be. With my cupboards and fridge now fully stocked, I slumped down on my sofa to relieve my fatigue. I smiled to myself and felt kind of satisfied as I looked around the room, until it finally dawned on me how untidy, dirty and dusty everything was. The flat needed a really good cleaning. I decided that was going to be my job for tomorrow, so my place wouldn't have too much time to get messed up again before Wednesday. The rest of the day, I tried to go over all the things I wanted to tell Diane and I wasn't sure just how much detail I should go into with her, as she may think I'm absolutely barmy. The thing I was mostly concerned about, though, was telling Diane about the portals and what they meant to a person if seen. Would she totally freak out, or would she realise that Nature itself has made a certain provision for the death of a human brain? I came to the conclusion that if this is the woman who would ultimately be my soul mate, then she would understand the mechanics of the human life cycle. But the fact that she had already had an unpleasant encounter with the Terrans led me to believe she might not look upon them as friends, as I did. I suppose I just had to play it by ear, although I felt that I wanted to tell her everything.

After a good sleep that night, I woke up Tuesday morning feeling refreshed and, with breakfast and a shower done, I started the cleaning task ahead me. It was about time I changed the bed sheets anyway, as I realised they smelt a bit of stale sweat. Luckily I had a spare set of sheets my mother had given me when I first moved into the flat; they were new and still in their packaging so the dirty ones went straight into the washing machine.

As my flat was on the top floor, I had an eaves cupboard where the roof sloped down. It was just high enough to keep my vacuum cleaner in and an assortment of cleaning materials. Even the cleaning stuff itself was dusty and I had to wipe over the vacuum before I could think of using it. My bedroom wasn't that big, so dragging my double bed out didn't happen too often. In fact I don't remember ever doing it. With a series of shunts backward and forward, I finally managed to manoeuvre it enough to access the hidden section of floor beneath. Wow! My blue patterned carpet had a perfect oblong-shaped layer of grey dust except for a couple of bumps, which turned out to be odd missing socks. I also uncovered some loose change, as my vacuum cleaner rattled and spat them back out. I fitted a fresh bag when I started and although the vacuum was red hot, it managed to do the whole flat without blowing up.

Now for the dusting! I never quite understood why you should vacuum and then dust and not the other way round. My mother had said it was because dust flies about and settles everywhere when you vacuum. Surely the dust goes back on the floor after dusting, I thought. To me it was one of life's mysteries, but I bowed down to her expert opinion by vacuuming first. I then dusted and polished everything in sight with a lemon-scented aerosol. Although well out of date, it left the flat smelling nice and fresh. I cleaned the windows with ease on the inside, but the outside proved to be a bit more difficult. As the centre sash window had always been hard to open I gave it a sharp yank, which nearly broke the glass. This then allowed me to sit perilously on the crumbling stone sill.

I had put my water bucket inside on a small occasional table to the side of my legs, so that I could rinse my cloth without getting back inside. After a stretch, I managed to clean all of the exterior glass, but without thinking I rested one hand behind me to launch myself off the sill to get back inside. A piece of stone the size of a tennis ball broke off the sill and in a split second I feared it might hit a passerby. I must have also thought in that split second to freeze it, because once inside I turned around to see the piece of stone fixed in mid-air, between the sill and the pavement.

As I could see there were no pedestrians in sight, I released with my mind the stone to see it plummet to the street leaving a chalky white mark on the pavement where it bounced then came to rest in the kerb. I felt I was beginning to have total control of my ability as I had performed this little miracle without even seeing the subject matter. Smugly, I shut the window to inspect the clean glass now glistening with the incoming sunlight.

After all the cleaning was done I flopped on my sofa, as if I had just come home from a hard day's work. I felt the satisfying knowledge that my flat was now respectable and acceptably clean.

Wednesday, the big day, had finally arrived and I woke up to an instant excitement. I showered, had breakfast and made the bed with alarming gusto, as usually I take a bit of time to crank up in the mornings. It was now 9:50 a.m. and I had just enough time to scan the flat for minor imperfections or embarrassing things left out, like smelly socks or dirty underpants. Everything was perfect; the sun was shining and everything was all in order. I just had to clean my teeth again for the third time.

My digital watch was blank again because the battery had been drained when I came through the portal on my return. So I had to rely on a battery clock pinned to the wall with an oversized nail, which hung over the mantelpiece of the boarded up fireplace. The second hand was on its last revolution to reach ten o'clock!

I'm sure we've all done this as I did—eagerly looked at the clock for something or someone to arrive at a certain time and as soon as the second hand passes that time, we were instantly disappointed. Ten o'clock passed, then five past, then ten past and then twenty-five past and dejectedly I thought she's not coming.

But at twenty-eight minutes past ten, my doorbell rang and I flew down the stairs and opened the main door. Diane was standing there, panting with a smile on her face and looking quite flushed. Her hair was all pulled back into a ponytail and the sun glistened on the sweat on her forehead.

"Sorry I'm late," she said. "The bus broke down on the way here and I had to run the rest of the way."

Without even answering, I lurched forward and hugged her tightly.

"Whoa! You missed me then," she said. "Bet you thought I wasn't coming?"

After a well and over-timed hug I replied.

"Of course I missed you and yes I thought you had ditched me."

"No chance of that," she said. "Are we going in then?"

"Yes, of course." I replied.

Shutting the entrance door behind us, I told Diane to go up the stairs to the very top. I followed close behind. Once inside we embraced with a long, lingering kiss, holding each other as tight as possible. Strangely a kind of shock wave went through my entire body.

"Did you feel that?" I said.

"Yes," she replied. "It was like a mini-earthquake, wasn't it?"

I have heard somewhere that sometimes when people make love they feel the earth move; this felt as if the earth moved alright and all we were doing was kissing.

Enthusiastically, Diane scanned my flat with interest.

She then said, “Not bad is it, nice and airy?”

I was in no mood to discuss my flat because seeing Diane again was too overwhelming. How could I have missed someone so much after meeting them just once before? It was obvious to me I was very much in love with this girl and my emotions quickly spread to her. Hand in hand, we instinctively made our way to the bedroom and of course the inevitable happened.

We had now fully bonded and both of us knew that we were a perfect match for each other. It seemed like hours that we just lay there, naked in each other’s arms, not saying anything, just savouring the moment.

It was now about one o’clock and with renewed energy, I jumped up from the bed and started getting dressed.

“I’m starving,” I said. “Fancy something to eat.”

“I wouldn’t mind a ham sandwich,” she replied, “with mustard pickle on it.”

I was so glad that I got some fresh ham in when I went shopping, but it was funny how I also enjoyed a ham sandwich with mustard pickle on; it seemed that we also liked eating the same things.

“Coming right up,” I said.

As I started to make the sandwiches, I couldn’t stop myself looking through the open bedroom door where Diane was getting dressed. She had set her hair free from the ponytail as we undressed to make love and now her long golden tresses gently floated with every movement she made. She looked absolutely stunning and I just could not believe that she found me the least bit attractive. I suppose I wasn’t that bad looking, but I was no Robert Wagner or Roger Moore.

I finished making the sandwiches about the same time as Diane emerged from the bedroom. I told her to sit on the sofa. I then shunted my coffee table up close to her legs with my shin and placed both the sandwiches on it on separate plates, side by side.

"Thanks," she said and started to tuck in.

I sat next to her and began to demolish my sandwich at about the same rate as her. We both looked at each other and chuckled as we ate because we knew those sandwiches were being consumed at an alarming rate, as if we hadn't eaten for a week.

As Diane finished eating she said, "Boy that was good," as she wiped her mouth with the paper napkin I had placed in front of her plate. She had actually beaten me eating that sandwich by a good thirty seconds before I wiped some mustard pickle from my chin with my napkin.

"Yeah, that was nice," I said. "Now do you fancy a coffee to wash it down?"

"Ooo, yes please."

"Instant OK?"

"Yes, fine. With a splash of milk and one sugar please."

After making the coffees, I sat down again next to Diane placing the cups with saucers in front of us. She then said, "When we were sitting under the pier the other night, you said that you had things to talk to me about. I like a bit of mystery and intrigue. What were they?"

I had a feeling that Diane wouldn't freak out by what I wanted to say, so I decided there and then to tell her everything. I started obviously with my childhood, how I could anticipate what people were going to say and how I saw many sightings of the vague figures. I went on to describe the incident where I fell off the scaffolding and saw the Terrans in their true form.

"Those are the aliens I saw when I was little," she said with alarm.

"Well, yes," I replied. "But they are not really aliens."

"What do you mean, not aliens?"

"All will become clearer as I go on."

I continued my story up till the time I was struck by lightning when Diane intervened and said, "Not many people could survive being struck by lightning in those circumstances."

I responded by saying, "I don't think I should have survived, but then something unbelievable happened. As my body hovered between life and death, my blurred vision saw a blinding light in front of me, with two silhouetted figures in the centre then everything went blank. I don't know how long I was out for, but I woke up in a strange room."

"So what happened next?" she said, with an element of excitement and anticipation in her voice.

"Are you sure you are ready for this?"

"Yes, yes, go on."

"Well, it turned out that the creatures you think of as aliens had brought me through a kind of gate into their world, another dimension."

"*You're joking*," she said with a fixed stare into my eyes.

"No, I'm deadly serious. The beings are actually called Terrans and they live on this planet in this other dimension. They have been here since before the human race had ever evolved."

"*Bloody hell*! Oops! Scuse my French."

"The Terrans are a good race of people and have dedicated their lives to the progression and welfare of the human race, simply because they believe the human brain has the potential and they say our brains will in time be far superior to their own brains. Although they were not geared for it, they took good care of me, until I recovered fully from the lightning strike. They also told me that no human before me had ever entered their world and that is because nature has intended it that way."

"I don't understand. What do you mean; Nature has intended it that way?" Diane spoke with puzzlement.

"OK," I said. "I am going to tell you everything, but promise you won't say anything until I have finished."

"Ooo! OK, I promise."

I then proceeded to tell her about how the Terrans constructed a machine to be able to enter our dimension and why they needed to do so. I went on to explain the Terrans found that, during human brain development, our brains acquired the natural ability to open portals into the Terran world. Now I was getting to the crunch!

"You must have heard the stories of people having near death experiences and saying that they saw a bright light with their dead relatives on the other side," I said.

"Yes, of course. But they are just myths made by people not in control of their minds at the time."

"No, they are not myths, but they are misconceptions. What's really happening is, when we are taking our last breaths before death, the different waves that our brain emits merge together. This turns out to be a natural occurrence at the point of death, but it's also a trigger to open the portal into the Terran dimension. The dying person is the only person who is able to see this portal and the fuzzy visions on the other side are not long dead relatives but the Terrans themselves. It's only the dying person's brain waves, their amassed experiences and thoughts, or even their so-called soul, that actually enters the portal. In other words, our life's history enters into the Terran world to be either recycled by them as a power source or stored to be used as an enhancement to future generations of humans. You and I both have been enhanced by the Terrans just before we were born."

Diane said, "So that's the reason both our mothers passed out."

"Yes and when you were small, the Terrans took you on board one of their crafts just to monitor your brain's progress."

Diane reached for her coffee that was by now probably stone cold and downed it with one swallow. She returned her cup to the saucer and pensively looked down into her lap. I could literally see her brain working overtime to assess and analyse what I had just told her. While she was silent and thinking, I downed my coffee in one gulp, as it, too, was now stone cold.

Diane emerged from her thought stupor by saying, "I always thought that there must be something after death, but I really didn't think that we just got recycled in some way."

"Fraid so, but some of us do get to live on inside the minds of future generations. We both have dead people's thoughts, memories, or data in our brains somewhere. Now I've got to make you promise that no one must ever know about this: it would have a devastating effect on religions and everything."

"I promise," she said. "But how did you get back into our dimension?"

"About a week after I recovered, I realised that I could not survive in the Terran world. The climate was inhospitable and the food I was given was only from what the Terrans could pilfer from their missions into our dimension, so I made a conscious decision that I must try to come back, although the Terrans had told me I probably wouldn't survive the transition. They reopened a portal for me and, as you can see, I did survive and not only that, I don't see the Terran's' vague forms wherever I go anymore and I have developed a special supernatural power."

"Wow! What is it?" Diane asked.

"It seems that either when my adrenaline levels are high or when something happens spontaneously, I can freeze an object or a person. So the event doesn't happen. Like, if someone is falling over, I can stop them before they hit the ground."

I could see Diane went into that thinking mode again, but without warning and in an instant, she reached for her empty cup and threw it across the room and I instinctively froze it in midair. She then just sat there, with her mouth open.

"You didn't believe me, did you?" I said.

"No, I believed you," she replied. "I just wanted to see it for myself."

She stood up and went over to the cup suspended in the air, looking at it from all angles before plucking it from the air into her grasp. She then came back over to me, put the cup back onto the saucer, threw her arms around my neck and planted a massive kiss on my lips. After the kiss she said, "Terry, *you are amazing*."

The kiss and compliment of course made me smile, but then I knew I had to tell her the rest. Noticing my slight change of mood, she said.

"What's the matter?"

"There is a downside to all this."

"You're not dying or something are you?" she said, hastily. "I've only just found you; I couldn't bear to lose you now."

"No, I'm not dying, but since I came back, a portal has opened again a couple of times and when I see it, I feel drawn to go in, as if Nature is telling me I should have died when I was struck by lightning and that it wants to reclaim me. It's like it's trying to put right an imbalance. I seem to know that if I was to enter the portal, I would certainly die.

"If a portal was to open when you're with me," I continued, "you wouldn't be able to see it, only me. So if all of a sudden you see me cower and shut my eyes, it will mean I am trying to shut the portal out of my mind, to make it go away."

"I understand," she said. "But don't worry we'll fight this thing together."

No sooner than Diane had finished speaking, a portal opened by the window. Diane saw my reaction and immediately knew what was happening. She grabbed my arm to reassure me that I was safe with her; then, she unexpectedly shouted out, "I can see it too!"

Strangely this time, I didn't feel the urge to go into the light and I soon realised why. From within the blue-tinged light, a figure emerged; it was Theron.

With a slow, loud voice, Diane said, "OH-MY- GOD," as Theron entered my living room.

"Hello, Terry," Theron said, in his calm, unshakeable manner.

I had previously explained to Diane how the Terrans could speak English and all known human languages.

"What are *you* doing here?" I said.

"Our monitoring stations have been reporting uncommon activity of portals opening and closing with no data or energy coming through. This is very rare as it only happens occasionally when humans come back from the brink of death. As it is my job to investigate abnormal activity, I deducted that it must have something to do with you and that you had survived the return transition. I am glad to see you are alive and well, but who is this female?"

I replied, "This is Diane. She was also one of your enhancement programs and I just know she has a similar brain function to me."

"I am sensing there is indeed a strong connection between you both," Theron said.

Gripping my arm, Diane, who still had her mouth open, was still in a state of shock and I could feel a bruise forming with the pressure she was exerting on it. I said to Theron, "I don't know why my portal keeps appearing. I can only assume that Nature wants to reclaim me."

"This *is* an unusual situation," Theron said. "I will ask Madri to try to find out if there is a way to prevent it from reoccurring. In the meantime, try to be strong and not let the urge to enter the portal overpower you."

He then addressed Diane. "It is a pleasure to meet you Diane and I trust you know the importance of keeping your new found knowledge between you and Terry alone."

Speaking to us both, he then said, "We will no doubt be in contact again."

With that, he turned and again entered his portal, with it zapping shut behind him without a trace.

Diane remained silent for a little while. She was obviously still mesmerised by the event. I asked her, "Are you all right?"

Still shaken, she replied, "I…I, just met an alien. I mean a Terran."

"Yes," I said. "What did you think of Theron?"

"I don't know yet, I haven't quite taken it all in."

"I think I had better make you another coffee and a strong one this time."

The strong coffee did the trick, but it was quite a time before Diane was *compos mentis* again, seeing Theron had really unnerved her.

I said to her, "Did you find Theron threatening in any way?"

"No, I suppose not," she replied, as she gradually relaxed her tensed muscles. "It was only the fact I wasn't expecting it. I think I'm all right now."

She thought for a bit longer and said, "But he sounded more like an English gentleman than an alien. Sorry, Terry, than a Terran, but what would you call him if not an alien?"

"To me, Diane, he's a good friend."

"OK then, from now on, if I see him again, I'll call him by his name and I promise I won't freeze up on you, how's that?"

"Great," I replied.

I could see Diane was in thought again for a little while before she said, "I thought you said I wouldn't be able to see the portal. How come I could?"

"That is because the portal you saw was a manufactured one. The Terrans tinge their portals blue because they mainly use them to enter our world in their crafts high in the sky. The blue blends in, so they are less likely to be seen. A natural portal is multicoloured around the outside and only the person who is dying can see it."

Diane then said, "Then I don't really want to see one of those, do I?"

"Not really," I replied, with a smile.

I put my arm around her to reassure her that all was OK. It had been an eventful day, one which I doubt she would never forget.

"Well, now that you know everything about me, do you still want to be with me?" I asked.

"Don't be daft," she replied. "I knew from the very first time we met that we belonged together."

"Me, too," I replied.

Diane and I agreed we would be careful not to talk about the portal event, just in case it provoked a sighting of *another one*, so for the rest of the day we got to know each other better, if you know what I mean?. Then afterward I drove her home and we said we would see each other the next day.

On Thursday I picked her up in my car from her house and we spent the day having a picnic by the River Thames near Putney. All day we talked about things from our pasts and laughed a lot about the silliest things. I suppose, at the back of my mind, I had the dread that a portal would conjure itself up from nowhere, but I think I did pretty well to subdue it.

On Friday we spent the whole day in my flat, just being with each other, making love and generally bonding closer together.

Saturday was going to be a big day for me, which inevitability meant that Diane was going to introduce me to her parents. We agreed that I would come to her house about two in the afternoon. This would give me ample time to spruce myself up and time for her mother to prepare for the occasion. I arrived bang on two o'clock, not just to make a good impression but also to be punctual (I have always been a bit of a stickler for being on time).

Diane's house was a mid-terraced building, which was probably built in the thirties. There was a small front garden with a tiny patch of lawn and a flower bed in a crescent shape around the front bay window. I could tell that her parents must be clean, tidy people by the neat, well-kept appearance of the house. There was a single step going up to the glossy blue-painted front door, with a doorbell on the frame just opposite the lock. With a deep inhalation of breath, I nervously pushed the bell button. Before the *dong* of the *ding-dong* had a chance to sound, Diane opened the door. I was nearly sucked in by the vacuum.

"Saw you coming through the curtains," she said with excitement. "Come in."

She gave me a big, wet kiss, shut the door and then grabbed my arm with both hands. Then, she led me a few paces from the hall into the front lounge where Mr. and Mrs. Smith were each sitting in their respective armchairs.

"This is Terry!" Diane exclaimed.

"Pleased to meet you both," I said, nervously.

Mr. Smith stood up and stretched his arm across a wooden coffee table to offer his hand for me to shake, which I enthusiastically and over quickly responded to. Mrs. Smith just gave me a big, beaming smile.

"Sit down, lad." Mr. Smith gestured to the sofa in front of the bay window. I sat down on the sofa and Diane sat next to me, still holding my arm and smugly smiling. I don't know why but Diane's familiarity toward me made me feel a little embarrassed.

Mrs. Smith arose from her chair and, in that atoned Welsh accent, said, "Everyone for tea then?"

A chorus of *yes pleases* rang out by all three of us almost immediately, so Mrs. Smith escaped the lounge and went into the kitchen.

"I hear you're a plasterer," Mr. Smith said, in a less prominent accent than his wife's.

"Yes, sir," I replied, not knowing how formal to be.

"Call me Jim," he said. "We don't stand on ceremony in this house. Glad to hear you've got a trade then, can't go wrong with a trade!"

After a bit of banter between us, I found out Jim was a mechanic and worked for a nearby firm repairing cars and trucks. I was beginning to feel a bit less nervous as we talked about his work and my old banger of a car. About ten minutes passed, after which a rattling sound was heard as Mrs. Smith entered the room carrying a tray of cups, saucers, spoons and a plate full of small cakes, precariously balanced on the top.

"Here, let me help you," Diane said, as she leapt up from the sofa. Then with the cups and saucers arranged and corresponding to our seating positions, Mrs. Smith returned to the kitchen and brought back a large teapot.

"Those cakes look nice, Mrs. Smith," I remarked.

"Call her Lottie," Jim piped up.

"I baked them myself," Lottie said with a small amount of pride in her voice.

After a pause and looking straight at me, Lottie said, "Diane does nothing but talk about you all the time, but next week though she is going to have to knuckle down when she starts work in the casualty department at St. Gregory's Hospital in Tooting as part of her doctor training."

I looked at Diane and said, "You never told me that."

"No, I *was* saving it as a surprise."

"Oops! Sorry, love," Lottie said to Diane apologetically.

We all got on very well with all things considered and at about six o'clock, I thought I was ready to go and not outstay my welcome, so I announced I was going to go. "Well, it was very nice meeting you both and I hope we can get together again sometime."

Diane said to her parents that she was coming back with me to my flat and that I was not to worry: she would have dinner with me and be home by about 11:00 p.m.

"Look after her, lad," Jim said. "She may be twenty-one, but she's still our little girl."

Red with embarrassment and her eyes glaring wide open, Diane said, "Da-ad."

It only took about ten minutes to drive back from Diane's house to my flat and in no time we were cuddled up on my sofa.

"Why didn't you tell me about working at St. Gregory's Hospital?" I asked her.

"I was saving it to the very last minute as I wanted us to be together for as long as possible without the thought that I'm not going to be able to see you much. I will be working long hours and sometimes through the night. Plus I will be studying in-between."

"I realise that now and I've got to start work again on Monday as well. We will just have to keep in touch by phone and see each other whenever possible. I'm worried though, that you might meet some dashing young doctor and forget all about me."

"I promise you, Terry. That is not going to happen." She said this indignantly.

We had one of my shop-bought ready meals for dinner that night and just enjoyed each other's company till about 10:45 p.m. I then drove her home. We agreed that we would spend Sunday afternoon together and that she should walk to my flat and be there about one o'clock. I gave her a spare key, so that she could let herself in. Then after a long, goodnight kiss outside her front door, we said goodnight.

Sunday morning came and it was another pleasant day. I got busy making the bed and throwing loads of dirty clothes in the washing machine, so that the flat was clean and tidy for Diane's visit. I knew I wasn't going to see much of Diane once she started work in the hospital and I was bit down about the prospect.

One o'clock arrived and a couple of minutes later Diane opened the door to my flat.

"Oh! No," she bellowed out.

Diane had found me gripping the arms of the sofa with both arms outstretched and my head facing down between them. The knuckles of my hands were white with the pressure I was exerting and I was also making a dull moaning sound. She raced over and crouched down in front of me and put her hands on mine. Turning her head sideways, she could now also see my portal over by the window.

"It's all right now, Terry. I'm here. Try to focus on me." She put her head as near to mine as she could.

"My head feels as if it's going to explode," I said.

Again she said forcibly, "Focus your thoughts on me."

After a couple more minutes the portal closed and I started to recover. With my eyes still shut, I started to slowly raise my head and felt Diane's warm breath on my face. Gradually opening my eyes, I said, "Wow, that hurt. I've not found it as bad as that before. It was as if the portal was upping its game to get me into it."

"Well, it's gone now," Diane said.

"I hope Theron can come up with something soon," I said. "I don't think I can take many more of those episodes."

My head pain eased off a bit and I started to feel partially normal again.

"Sorry, Diane, that wasn't very nice for you, was it?" I said, praying the incident wouldn't damage our relationship.

"Stop worrying about me," she replied. "We are in this together and I'm sure Theron will come up with a solution soon."

After Diane saw that I had come to my senses a bit more, she said, "Do you know that I saw your portal too? Although the inner part was very bright, the outside of it was very beautiful."

I replied with concern, "You didn't feel the urge to enter it, did you?"

"No, I didn't get any feeling like that. I didn't see it straight away, only after I touched your hands, but even when I briefly let go of you, I could still see it."

"It must have something to do with our brains being in tune then."

"It must be," she replied.

I didn't feel much like going out after that incident, so we spent the rest of that day just talking, mainly about our future together. If I survived, that is.

Diane said that after six months of her hospital stint, she would get three weeks off, which was meant to be for revision, but she indicated we could spend some more time together then. I said that would be OK, but the only way we would do it was if she brought her work revision to my flat to do. There was no way I was going to be responsible for Diane flunking exams because she hadn't put the work in. She smiled and agreed. As far as the portal incidents was concerned, I assured her I would be able to handle it by tying myself to the sofa, if need be.

I could tell she was concerned, but she realised there wasn't much more that could be done about it. We would keep in touch by phone though and at any real opportunity, meet up.

4

I returned to work the following week feeling very depressed knowing that I wouldn't see Diane for a time, even though she had phoned me from the hospital a couple of evenings to make sure that I was all right.

It was on that Friday when I was working on the outside scaffold of a new build block of flats. I was rendering brickwork panels using sand and cement. The flats were ten stories high and, during the course of the week, I had worked my way down to the seventh floor. It was about half past eleven in the morning when I heard a clattering above me and, in the wink of an eye; I saw a workmate fall past me on the outside of the scaffolding. In a flash I looked over the scaffold and just managed to freeze and release him as he hit a pile of sand. This I did hoping I had done enough to break his fall before the impact.

A group of workers on the ground quickly surrounded him, which made it difficult for me to see if he had survived. After a few minutes, the workers stood back and one of them was helping the injured man to his feet. From what I could see, the man must have broken his arm or something similar, as he was clutching it with his other hand. I thought that at least he was not dead after falling eight floors. After about ten minutes, an ambulance arrived to take him to hospital and work on the site gradually went back to normal.

At lunch time in our makeshift canteen, I heard a couple of the workmen talking about the man's accident. One said to the other, "God knows how Bert survived that fall. He should really be dead."

"I know," said the second man. "That sand had a load of loose bricks in it. Even if the sand was clean, he should have broken his back from that height. Lucky bugger is what he is, to get away with just a dislocated shoulder."

I smiled a smug little smile, as it was now confirmed that I had made a difference to the outcome of Bert's fall.

That evening Diane phoned me from the hospital to check on how I was and to tell me that I'm in her thoughts all the time and as a by-the-way, she said, "A man from a building site came into the casualty department that day with a dislocated shoulder from falling eight stories. Can you imagine how lucky he was?"

"Christ! He was lucky, wasn't he?" I replied to her.

"You be careful when you're up scaffolds, won't you, Terry?"

"You can bet on that," I replied.

Changing the subject, she then said, "I've got to work all this weekend. I don't mind. Sometimes it's interesting, but a lot of the time it's boring. Anyway, no pain, no gain, I suppose."

Hastily she then had to sign off.

"Sorry Terry, got to go now. Love you very much."

"Love you more than you can imagine," I replied. Then the connection was broken.

I'm glad that I didn't work Saturdays, especially this one, as I was not in a good mood at all. I was missing Diane too much and her not being with me was hard to bear. I suppose at least at work I could occupy my mind with something else, but even then it was hard to concentrate. Today all I was going to do is take a trip to the high street to get a bit of shopping and a new battery for my watch. It was now beginning to bug me that I was always looking around for someone or something to tell me what time it was.

I had just got back from the shops that Saturday at about a quarter past eleven when the phone rang. It was my father asking me to go over to my parent's house, as there was something he wanted to tell me. When I asked what it was, he wouldn't discuss it on the phone and by the tone of his voice, it sounded quite serious. I immediately got in my car and headed for their house, which was at Tolworth, in the county of Surrey. Normally it was about half an-hour drive, but it took me longer because of the Saturday traffic. I arrived at my parent's semi-detached suburban house just after twelve. I parked in the road and walked up the small driveway past my father's car. As I reached the front door, my father opened it without me having to knock.

"Come in, Terry," he said with a serious look on his face.

He led me into the lounge and told me to sit down on one of the armchairs.

"Where's Mum?" I asked.

"This is why I called you over. She has been taken into hospital and I'm afraid it's not looking good. They've discovered she has cancer and it's very aggressive and advanced."

"Oh no," I said, as tears started to fill my eyes. "I must see her. Where has she been taken?"

"St. Gregory's in Tooting."

With a kind of panic in my voice, I said, "Come on, let's go now."

"All right, but we go in my car." My dad said.

With that and in just a few minutes we were on our way to the hospital.

On the way to the hospital, I asked, "How long have they known about the cancer?"

"She had tests done about two weeks ago, as she started to complain about pains in her stomach and feeling sick.

The results came back yesterday and our GP phoned and said I should take her to the hospital this morning and that they will be expecting her. They didn't tell us what the problem actually was until she was admitted to the ward. It was like being hit with a sledge hammer. I can't even let your sister know because she's on holiday in Spain and I haven't got a contact number."

As we reached the hospital and parked the car, I tried to compose myself by making sure I had no tears in my eyes for when I saw my mother. My father led me from the car park into the hospital and through a long corridor to where the elevators were. We went up in the lift to the third floor, then through another corridor to a pair of large swinging doors with *St. Agnes Ward* in large letters over the top. Once through the door, that common hospital disinfectant smell made my nose tingle and bolstered my thoughts that people were only here for a serious reason. Moving about half way down the mixed ward, we came to my mother's bed. I expected to see her ashen face and generally on death's door but no: she was sitting up in bed, reading a magazine.

"Hello, Mum, what's been going on?" I asked.

"Hello, love," she replied. "Doctors tell me I've got cancer, but I don't feel that bad."

I asked, "How long have you been having the pains in your stomach?"

"Oh, about six months I suppose."

Trying to stop my facial muscles contorting into a devastated look, I said, "And you only went to the doctors a couple of weeks ago. I don't know." I ended my sentence with a *tut tut* sound.

Cancer at that time, I think, was not fully understood and the treatment for it was purely experimental.

With this in mind and knowing there was no cure, it seemed that my world was caving in on me, because I had been told my mother had a fatal illness and I was apart from my soul-mate, Diane.

My father and I spent about two hours with my mother and by that time it was obvious she was getting tired. We both kissed her on the cheek in turn and told her we would be back tomorrow to see how she was doing. Finally I asked her if she would like anything brought in.

She replied, "I wouldn't mind a couple more magazines I've read this one twice. Oh and a bottle of blackcurrant cordial, you know, the one you mix with water."

My dad said that he would see to that.

Waving good-bye to her all the way as I walked down the corridor to the swinging doors, my emotions started to kick in. Noticing my distress, my dad said,

"She's in good hands, son. Try not to worry."

As we descended down the elevator, my father and I agreed to go in to visit my mum at separate times, so she would have family around her as much as possible. When reaching the ground floor, the lift opened and, in front of me, I came face to face with Diane, with a stethoscope around her neck.

"What are you doing here?" she said in dismay.

"Diane," I said with surprise.

We instinctively kissed.

"Here, steady on, son," my father said.

Up till now, I hadn't seemed to get the chance to tell my parents about Diane.

"This is Diane, my girlfriend," I said to my father. "We've been seeing each other for a couple of weeks now."

"Hello, Mr. Seer, I'm pleased to meet you."

"And it's nice to meet you, too. Call me Harry."

Then Diane asked, "Why are you here, Terry?"

I told Diane that my mother had been admitted to Agnes ward.

"That's a cancer ward," she said. "I hope it's nothing too serious."

She could see by my face that I didn't think the problem to be a minor one, so I told her all the details and added, "I'll be back here to visit Mum tomorrow, about two o'clock."

"Well, when you get here, come and find me in casualty and I'll come up to the ward with you," said Diane.

I could see my dad was getting a little agitated at not being part of our conversation, so I said to Diane, "I'll see you tomorrow then, about two."

We kissed again and said good-bye.

As we were walking to the car park, my dad said, "You're a dark horse, dating a doctor."

"She's only a trainee at the moment, Dad, but I do love her. We seem to have a lot in common."

I obviously wasn't going to go into any more detail than that and luckily my father didn't ask.

After my father had driven us back to his house, I said, "I might see you tomorrow then." As our arrangement was that he would visit my mother from twelve to two and I said I would be there from two onward.

He replied by saying, "OK then, son, drive safely." And with that I got in my car and drove back to my flat.

Back at the flat I sat down on a chair at my dinner table. I placed my elbows on the table with the palms of my hands against my cheeks, repeatedly thinking about my mother's mortality. It was fairly rare to hear that someone had cancer in the seventies. Of course the condition was there, but

I knew the disease was sometimes misdiagnosed as something far less invasive, so I still held out some hope. Nevertheless, the news that my mother had it was devastating.

I suppose it wasn't *that* big a coincidence when I bumped into Diane as I came out of the lift; after all she was working there. Nonetheless, it is a large hospital and she could have been anywhere at that precise moment. I started to think it wasn't just a chance encounter because the meeting provided an opportunity for Diane to meet my parents.

The next day, at 2:00 p.m., I walked into the hospital's casualty department to seek out Diane. The department wasn't that busy; there were only about ten or so patients waiting to be seen and I could see Diane through a gap in a half-drawn curtain of a cubicle. She noticed me also and silently mouthed, "Won't be a minute," and a few minutes later she appeared and came over to where I was standing.

"Sorry about that," she said. "I was just finishing dressing some stitches; I put in a young boy's leg."

"Don't apologise" I replied. "I shouldn't be taking you away from your work anyway. Really though, if you are needed or busy, I can go up on my own."

Diane replied, "No way. I want to meet your mum and at times like these we should be together."

Diane had already arranged with her mentor doctor to get a half hour or so off, so she could come with me to visit my mother. I think the doctor thought the meeting might be beneficial for Diane in some way, to help her deal with distressed relatives and so forth.

We arrived at my mum's bedside about 2:10 p.m. to find her just stirring from a nap and I thought she might be a bit groggy from medication.

"Hello, Mum, how are you feeling?" I asked.

"Not too bad, Terry," she replied, with her eyes half open.

Seeing Diane in her white coat and stethoscope round her neck, she said to me, "Oh no, not another examination, I only had one about half an hour ago, when your dad was here."

"No, Mum," I said. "This is Diane. She's my girlfriend and she is training to be a doctor here in this hospital. At the moment she is working in the casualty department."

My mother's face changed from a grimace to a big grin as she said, "Ooo, it'd be nice to have a doctor in the family."

My face flushed red with embarrassment. I said, "Mu-um."

Then I apologised to Diane for my mother's comment. Diane told me not to be daft as she stepped forward, held my mother's hand and said, "I am very pleased to finally meet you, Mrs. Seer."

"Call me Rose," my mother said.

Diane was still holding her hand when my mother said, "Do you know? I can feel a tingling sensation all over my body and suddenly I feel much better."

Diane and I looked at each other in surprise and I came around the side of the bed where she was standing and held Diane's other hand. As soon as I touched Diane's hand, my mother exclaimed, "Ooo, I feel wonderful. The pain's gone and I feel as fit as a fiddle. You two must have just worked some magic on me, or something."

Smiling and then looking at her watch, Diane said, "I'm sorry Rose, but I must get back to work. I'll come and see you again, as soon as I get the chance, so we can have a long chat about this son of yours. Wish you better, bye."

"Bye bye," my mother replied. "Don't work too hard."

Diane let go of my mother's hand but held on to mine, dragging me away from my mother's bedside. Out of my mother's earshot, Diane whispered in my ear, "We've got to talk! I finish about 8:00 p.m. tonight and I'll come round to the flat."

A little mystified, I said, "OK, I'll see you around 8:45 p.m. then."

The 45 minutes would probably give her enough time to change her clothes from work and travel to my flat.

We kissed good-bye and Diane disappeared through the ward doors. As I returned to my mother's bedside, I was mulling over the slight intensity of Diane's words and what she meant by "We've got to talk."

My mother was now in a very happy mood and said, "Diane is a lovely girl. It was a stroke of luck finding her, Terry."

"Yes," I replied, "I love her very much, but you seem to be a lot better all of a sudden. They must be giving you some good medication."

"I haven't had any medication yet, unless you count a couple of painkillers that seem to make me sleepy. All the doctors seem to do at the moment is push and press my stomach about, but I'm going down for an x-ray this afternoon, so they can find out the size of the tumour. Then they will know how to treat it. But since you and Diane came in, I feel great, no pain or discomfort at all."

"It must be those pain killers then."

"No. It was seeing you and Diane together: you make a perfect couple."

Just then a porter turned up, pushing a wheelchair. "Come on then Mrs. Seer, time for your x-ray."

I helped my mother out of bed and then helped her put on her dressing gown, which had been hanging high on a hook above her bedside cabinet.

"I don't need any help to sit in that thing," she said, pointing to the wheelchair. As she sat into the chair unaided, I kissed her on the cheek and said, "Hope it all goes well, Mum. I'll be back in the morning to see how you're doing, OK?"

She smiled and said good-bye and then the porter pushed her off down the corridor.

Driving back home, I kept thinking about that strange tingling sensation I felt when I touched Diane's hand and sort of knew it was the reason why she wanted to talk to me.

About 9:50 p.m. that evening, I heard Diane's footsteps coming up the stairs to my flat. As she had her own keys, she had let herself in the main entrance, but I anticipated her arrival at the flat's door and opened it as she reached the top step. She flung her arms around my neck and kissed me, I could tell she was tired but was excited at the same time.

"Make me a coffee please, Terry. I've got something fantastic to tell you."

Although I was bursting to know what was making her so excited, I just told her to sit down on the sofa, while I made the coffee.

After putting the hot cups on the coffee table and sitting down next to her, I said, "Now, what's this all about?"

She took a sip of coffee, then took a calming intake of breath and said, "I've got two things to tell you, but I don't know which to tell you first."

"God, you're not pregnant are you?" I said.

"No, silly."

"Then what?"

With an air of delight, Diane began. "Right, this is back to front but I think you should know this first."

I took a quick swig of coffee in an effort to reduce any shocking news.

"Your mum doesn't have cancer and not only that, there's not a thing wrong with her. She doesn't even have arthritis anymore."

"What! How do you know this?" I asked.

"I had a chance at around five o'clock to go up to the ward to see her again. Her doctor was with her and I explained I was a student doctor currently working in casualty. He was looking at an x-ray photo of her from all different angles in one hand and scratching his head with the other. Finally he said, 'Well, Mrs. Seer, from this x-ray, you have absolutely nothing wrong with you. I don't quite understand this as it was I who first examined you and at that time you most certainly had a large-sized growth in your stomach.'

"He pondered for a bit then said, 'I think we will keep you in overnight though, just to be on the safe side.' With that he went off and left your mum and me alone. Your mum was so happy that she called me over to her to give her a hug. She then said, 'Isn't it great Diane? I feel wonderful and even the arthritis in my hands seemed to have healed themselves.'"

Astounded, I said to Diane, "Bloody hell, that's marvellous, but how?"

She answered, "That's the other thing I wanted to tell you. Since I have been working in casualty, on more than a few occasions people have remarked, as I dressed their wounds, that they felt a tingling sensation when I touched them and also that any pain they were feeling felt much less. I just thought that it must be a bit of static electricity coming from my nylon apron and told them the same. Now I'm pretty sure because of your mother's recovery, that it isn't static."

"What then?" I asked with puzzlement.

Diane answered, "Since I have been with you I've felt different, more alive if you like. It's as if something has rubbed off from you to me and I think it's to do with you going into the other dimension and coming back. When I held your mother's hand, I felt a force running through me, a kind of healing power, but then you touched my hand and it seemed to get much stronger. I feel sure that, together, we can cure people of anything."

"Wow, that's some assumption."

"Yes," Diane replied. "And you and I are going to put it to the test!"

Diane wouldn't tell me that evening what she meant by putting it to the test, but we did do a bit of catching up with our relationship and afterward I drove her home.

In the car outside her house, Diane said that she would be working at the hospital from 10:00 a.m. to 10:00 p.m. tomorrow, a twelve-hour stint, but she wanted me to meet her in the hospital car park at 9:15 p.m. When I asked her why 9:15 p.m. instead of 10:00 p.m., all she said was, "You'll see, trust me!"

I was gradually learning that Diane had a maverick quality about her and I must admit I liked it.

Sunday came and it was quite a nice day. It was even nicer when my father phoned me about 11:00 a.m. to tell me he was off to the hospital to pick up my mother.

You could tell by his voice that he was overjoyed when the hospital had phoned him to say that she was in absolute perfect health, although they couldn't really explain why. I said that it was really great news and would be over to see her about 3:00 p.m.

I arrived at my parent's house, as I said I would at 3:00 p.m. and was greeted by my mother on the doorstep.

"Isn't it great news, Terry," she said, as she ushered me through into the lounge where my dad was sitting in his usual chair. After being urged for me to quickly sit down, she said, "They couldn't find a thing wrong with me and my stomach doesn't hurt anymore."

"That's marvellous, Mum."

"I'm sure it had something to do with you and Diane."

"Don't be daft, Mum; they probably diagnosed you wrong in the first place."

"But how do you explain that even my arthritis has vanished and it all seemed to happen when you and Diane were together at my bedside?"

"I can't really answer that one, Mum, but all I know is that you're not ill anymore and that's what matters and what has a bloke got to do round here to get a cup of tea."I said lamely trying to change the subject.

My dad then piped up.

"Still, it is some kind of miracle."

Full of beans, my mum left the room to go and make the tea.

With a lowered voice, my dad said, "The hospital wants to check her again in a month's time, just to make sure the cancer hasn't come back. Now come on son, what really happened when you and Diane visited your mum, because she's full of it? She's convinced that you and Diane cured her."

With all my fingers and toes mentally crossed I replied.

"Honest, Dad, I haven't got a clue,. "But you do hear of cases where people are ill and are suddenly cured for no apparent reason. I'm just glad it happened to Mum."

My dad's eyes squinted as he looked at me, as if to determine whether I was actually telling him the truth; then, he seemed to relent and believe what I had told him. Then, he said, "To change the subject, Terry, I am afraid I've got some other news you may not want to hear."

"Oh yes, what's that then?"

"I'm going to sell the business. Now that your mother has had that scare, I think it's high time that I retired, so your mum and me can go and get a bungalow somewhere with a nice garden, out in the country. Only thing is it will mean you will be out of a job unless the new owner wants to keep you on."

"Don't worry about me, Dad. I can get a job anywhere; they're always looking for plasterers. It's about time you retired. You and Mum deserve to have it easy for a change."

Just after that my mum came into the lounge with a tray of tea. I think she must have overheard our conversation from the kitchen, as she said to my father, "You've told him then."

"About Dad retiring and you moving to the country," I said. "I think it's a great idea. Maybe it's time for you both to put your feet up and take it easy from now on."

"Are you sure you'll be OK, though, Terry?" she asked.

"Mum, I'm a big boy now. Besides, I've got Diane now so she will keep me on the straight and narrow."

Luckily for me, the subject of my mum's amazing recovery was overshadowed by what kind of house they will be looking for, its location. And everything else connected with their retirement. I was pleased for them but selfishly hoped they wouldn't move too far away.

After about an hour and a half, I announced that I was on the move and said my good-byes. I wanted to get back to my flat to tidy up a bit, have something to eat and generally try to make sense of yesterday's events. I also thought about the impact of my parents moving would have on me as they had always been close enough for me to go to if I had any problems to sort out.

It was getting near the time to go and meet Diane at the hospital so I locked the flat up and got in my car. I don't know why I was so obsessive about time, but I always tried to judge my journeys to arrive bang on the time agreed. This time was no exception: I arrived at the hospital car park at about 9:13 p.m.

The large car park was dimly lit and virtually empty, as I pulled into a space closest to the hospital building, which was about a hundred and fifty yards away. Through the darkness I could see a white figure come out of the hospital entrance and head my way. As the figure got closer, I could see it was Diane in her hospital coat, carrying something white that was rolled up under her arm. I got out of my car to greet her and she gave me a quick kiss and then hastily said, "Hello, Terry, right on time as usual; I knew you wouldn't let me down."

She then unrolled what she was carrying and said, "Quick, put this on."

It was a hospital coat similar to what she was wearing, except the plastic pin badge on it read, "Gabrielle Stone, student doctor." I put the coat on, although it seemed to be about two sizes too small.

"What's going on?" I said.

"No time to explain, but everything will become clear."

With that she grabbed my hand to follow her to the hospital building. It soon became obvious that she was going to try and pass me off as a doctor.

"Gabrielle Stone!" I said, pointing to the badge.

"Yes," she said. "It's Lucky that the name Gabrielle can also be a man, isn't it?"

I didn't reply. As we neared and then entered the hospital, it felt eerie, because it was very quiet with no one about.

"If we see a security guard or anyone else, act like a doctor."

"How do you act like a doctor?"

"Just walk upright with confidence," she said, as she dragged me to where the elevators were. She pressed the call button and immediately one of the two lifts opened. Yanking me in, she then pressed the second floor button.

"What is going on?" I said.

"You'll see," Diane replied, in a forceful but low voice. "Now be quiet."

When the lift opened, she gestured me to follow her close behind and then stopped at a corner. Holding me back behind her, she furtively poked her head around the corner.

"All clear," she whispered.

We turned the corner and were facing a pair of large double doors, which had a section of wired glass in each. Above the doors, it read, "St. Nicholas: Ward for Children."

Peering through one of the panes Diane again said, "All clear, come on."

Once through the doors, we were in stealth mode, almost on tiptoe, as we passed rooms with closed doors to our left and right. The ward, with very subdued light, was very quiet, but I could hear little whimpering sounds now and again. Diane stopped at another corner with a brighter light shining in from the unseen area. I noticed a sign hanging from the corridor ceiling with an arrow pointing to this area which read, Reception Area. Diane poked her head round the corner and back in a flash. She then looked at me, put her index finger vertically up to her lips and raised her eyebrows. She then repeated the quick glance and gestured me to follow her, tiptoeing across the more brightly lit area to the next section of corridor. I followed close behind and turned my head to look at whom or what we were hiding from. It was a lone nurse, sitting at a desk with her back to us, with one of those white enamel desk lights shining on her paperwork amid the dimness. We were now in the corridor where the actual children's ward was to our left and I could see small beds and cots dotted all around this larger area.

"We have to be quick," Diane whispered. "The other nurse is on her break and will be back soon."

With that, Diane grabbed my hand and pulled me over to a small bed, with a boy sleeping in it. The lad was probably about eight-years old. Holding my hand, Diane touched the boy's forehead with her other hand. I felt the tingling sensation for about twenty seconds before it desisted and luckily the boy did not wake up. She then moved us to a cot where a small girl was also sleeping. She could have only been about three or four.

Again, holding my hand, she touched the girl's forehead with the other. Just as the tingling died down, the little girl woke up and looked as if she was beginning to cry. Diane stroked her hair and whispered, "Shush, go back to sleep now."

Amazingly the little girl did just that.

"We're done," Diane said, in a low voice. "Let's go."

We reversed our previous route as silently as possible and then pushed our way through the main ward doors into the corridor. As we turned the corner to the lifts, we passed the other ward nurse coming back from her break. She glanced at us fleetingly, but I don't think she suspected anything and luckily we managed to jump into the lift, which the nurse had used; just before the doors closed. Exiting the lift on the ground floor and going through the entrance corridor to the main exit, a security guard was walking toward us.

Oh god! I thought. *We're in trouble now.*

The guard looked at us, then smiled and spoke.

"Good night, doctors, mind how you go."

"Ni-ight," we replied, simultaneously.

We exited the building and on the outside our pace quickened. It then developed into a full sprint with both of us laughing all the way back to where

I had parked my car. Once inside the car, we sat for a few minutes to get our breath back, then I said, "So that's what it was all about."

"Yes," she replied. "Those two children are both seriously ill and I just had to see if we could cure them. Now all we have to do is wait."

"It was a bit risky though, but I've got to admit, it was a buzz," I said. "What would we have done if we had been rumbled?"

"I thought of that. My adrenaline level was through the roof doing that, so I bet yours was too. If that nurse doing her paperwork had turned round, I knew instinctively you would have frozen her."

"You're gorgeous and intelligent, aren't you?"

"You don't *have* to flatter me to get me into your bed you know. Now come on; drive us to the flat. I already rang my parents to say I was spending the night at your place."

That remark put an even bigger smile on my face, so without hesitation I started the car and drove off.

Back at the flat we relived our covert mission and Diane couldn't stop laughing at how I looked in the doctor's coat that was two sizes too small. She said she would return the coat to its owner in the morning and would tell Gabrielle Stone that she took it home accidentally, thinking it was hers. She also said it was going to be at least three days to a week before we would know if our escapade was a success, as the children's doctors would not take things at face value without running extensive tests.

It was getting late and although Diane had a later start in the casualty department in the morning, we decided to go to bed.

I could never understand why people get dressed up to go to bed, so for as long as I could remember, except when I was very small, I've always slept in the buff. Diane was of the same opinion, I'm glad to say!

About 2:30 a.m. I awoke with a really bad headache and, gradually opening my eyes, I could see that damned portal had opened a few yards from the bed. The pull of the portal seemed to be greater than ever and I unknowingly grabbed Diane's arm.

She awoke immediately and saw the portal over by the bedroom door, with its blinding light filling the room.

"Focus, Terry," she said. "Focus on something good."

She prised my fingers from her arm and got out of bed.

"What are you doing?" I shouted. "Don't go near that thing."

"Trust me," she replied, sternly.

Slowly walking toward the portal, Diane's beautiful naked body was silhouetted and her perfect form provided a partial screen from the blinding light. As she got closer she raised her right hand with the palm facing forward. Stopping inches from the portal's entrance, she then moved the flat of her hand to touch the anomaly. As her hand met the portals boundary, in a flash, it disappeared. I was still in a lot of pain from the headache, but I could only think about Diane's safety.

"Are you all right?" I asked, with immediate concern.

"Yes, I'm OK," she replied.

"You took a hell of a risk," I said.

"Not really," she replied. "Logically the portal believes that your body should be dead after the lightning strike and only keeps appearing to resolve the issue of your soul. It was a calculated guess that it didn't want my soul, as I have never died. The portal vanished when I touched it because I wasn't the entity it wanted."

"You sure have got some brains in that head of yours," I said.

"Yep," she replied. "And if I can shut the portal once, I can do it again. So there is going to be no argument. I'm moving in. I know I can't protect you twenty-four seven, but at least if the portal appears and I'm here, I can close it."

There was no way I was going to argue. It suited me just fine to have Diane around and although my male pride was hurt a little by being protected by a woman, I also realised she was my saviour—at least until Theron could come up with a more permanent solution.

We didn't get much sleep that night after the portal incident, but we did discuss some logistics of Diane moving in. We decided that she would make the move this coming Friday but would have to make arrangements first to alter her shifts. I would also have to phone my father to tell him about our decision. And I would need to make up some story that it would be cost effective for Diane to stay at my flat and therefore that I would need the day off to help her move in. Our main problem was Diane's parents and how they would react to her leaving home to live with me. Financially it was going to be tight as Diane had hardly any income, just a small grant, which was subsidised by her parents, but we were convinced that we could manage somehow.

On Monday evening, I rang my father with my news and asked him for Friday off work. He thought it was great, as he had never liked the idea that I was all alone in the flat and he agreed that I should have Friday off to help Diane with her move. He also said that he had put his business on the market that day and would now be waiting for a prospective buyer. At the end of our phone conversation, he added something a bit worrying, as a by-the-way sort of statement. He said that my mother's arthritis had returned.

Diane rang me that evening to tell me about her parent's reaction to the move. Apparently it was not easy to convince them she was doing the right thing, but they eventually agreed that she was old enough to make her own decisions. They also said that they thought I was a nice fellow and that I would take good care of her. Little did they know that it was Diane who was going to be taking care of me! Diane also said that she had managed to get Friday and Saturday off, so it was all systems go. I didn't tell Diane on the phone about my mother's arthritis returning, just in case that worrying thought was with her all week and distracted her from her job, as I knew it would me.

Friday came and I was released from my mundane work on the building site. I had said to Diane I would be at her parent's house at about 9:00 a.m. and of course I arrived on time.

I was greeted with a hug and a kiss from Diane on the front step, but as I entered the house, avoiding suitcases with piles of clothes stacked on top, I could see by Diane's parent's faces that they were not overjoyed to see me.

"Morning," I said to her parents, both standing by the kitchen door with their arms folded.

Grudgingly, Diane's father replied in a serious voice, "Morning Terry, I hope you two are sure you're doing the right thing."

"Don't worry, Jim," I said. "We're not teenagers and we really have discussed all the pros and cons. Also, you must know by now how much we love each other."

Even though technically I was still a teenager, I didn't really regard myself as one.

"I suppose so," Jim replied.

Diane's mother unfolded her arms and gave me a relenting smile, after hearing my remark about loving each other.

"Come on then," Jim said. "I'd better give you a hand with all this stuff, but there's no way this lot is going to fit in your car all at once. I reckon you've got at least three trips."

Sure enough, it took three trips to move everything Diane wanted to take with her and by the time we had finished, my flat's living room floor was totally covered in her stuff.

During the past week, I was preparing for Diane's stay by clearing out a lot of junk I had accumulated over the years and I managed to free up four out of five drawers of a second chest of drawers I had. I also managed to make space in the one drawer I used most in my wardrobe. Most of my junk and excess clothing I stuck in plastic bags and put them in the cupboard under the eaves where the vacuum cleaner lived. I could tell the vacuum cleaner wasn't very happy about having to lie on its back and share the space, as its tools kept trying to escape as I forced the cupboard door shut.

With all the effort to produce as much space as possible, I realised, with all that Diane had brought with her, we needed another wardrobe, which would have to go in the living room.

After a long day, Diane had managed to stow about half of her clothes in the spaces I had provided. She had stacked the other half on the dining table and chairs. They would have to remain there until we had acquired another wardrobe from somewhere.

That night, totally knackered, we had a pizza take-away for dinner and we sat on the sofa and ate straight from the box on our laps. After, with a nice cup of coffee to round it off, we had a chance to talk.

Diane said, "Guess what? There's a rumour going round the hospital staff that a woman in her fifties was admitted with stomach cancer and left a day later completely cured. Ring any bells? There's also another one going around that a couple of the kids in the children's ward seem to have been cured of their illnesses, too. No one has confirmed the rumours yet, but I think it worked: we cured them."

"That's great news, but I'm going to hold off on celebrating as yet because my dad has told me my mum's arthritis has returned."

"Oh no!" Diane replied, with disbelief. "I can't believe it didn't work. There has got to be a logical explanation."

"Well, we will just have to wait for a few weeks until my mum has gone back for her check-up to see if she really has been cured of the cancer. I think we'd better not try curing anyone else yet until we know for sure."

Diane agreed and said, "You poor thing, you must be worried sick again, but I'm sure she will be OK. I just know it!"

Agreeing not to talk about the issue any more that night, our conversation went on to our new venture: living together.

"Tomorrow we'll go out and look for a cheap wardrobe for you to put the rest of your things in," I told her.

Diane replied, as she pointed to the window.

"Yes and we are also going to get a new pair of curtains for that window over there. Those curtains are disgusting."

I really hadn't noticed how dismally bad the curtains were. I think if they were washed, they would probably fall to bits, so I agreed we would buy a new pair. I could see Diane was going to take charge of things in the flat and I actually welcomed it as I had no idea about décor or design. I just knew Diane was going to change things for the better.

On Saturday morning, we both woke up about nine o'clock. It had been a long previous day and it was fortunate that neither of us had to go to work. After a quick breakfast of cereal, we washed and dressed, laughing as we got in each other's way in the bathroom. We were both enjoying this new experience of being a couple.

At about 10:00 a.m., we set off in the car to Wimbledon. Wimbledon wasn't a massive shopping area, but I knew I had seen a few second hand furniture places there and I also knew of a large drapery shop. Having parked the car, I believed our mission was clear: I wanted to acquire one second hand wardrobe, which was capable of accommodating Diane's extensive range of clothes and shoes and a pair of new curtains, which, unlike my current ones, didn't look as if they came from the haunted house. Luckily I had the frame of mind to measure both items before we left the flat and I hadn't forgotten to bring my measuring tape.

First off was the curtains and in the drapery shop Diane was in her element. I just stood back and said nothing except to remind Diane of the drop and width measurements and of course that we were on a tight budget. Diane made up her mind and I thought fifteen pounds wasn't too bad for her selection. That was one item down and one to go. Coming out of the drapers and onto the pavement, we came directly in line with a little old lady, hobbling toward us. Her severe dowager's hump made her head face downward, so to avoid her, we veered to her left, but she veered the same way, you know, when you step one way and the person facing you goes exactly the same way. This happened about three times on the trot. After the third direction change, the old lady stood still and with effort looked up and then scanning our bodies, her eyes widened with intrigue.

"Are you brother and sister?" she said with great interest.

"No, we are partners," Diane replied.

"Why?" I said.

She replied, "Because I can see a great colourful aura all around you both. It sometimes happens with blood relatives, but even that is very rare. If you are not blood related, then you are two very special people sharing a very special gift."

Diane and I just looked at each other.

"I am a medium," the old lady continued. "And have seen many things in my years, some ghostly and some very strange from the living, but I have only ever met one other person who had a smaller, less colourful aura than yours and he had the power to read others thoughts. Do you know what powers you both possess?"

"No, sorry, we don't know what you mean," I replied.

"I think you do," she said knowingly. "But I don't blame you for keeping it a secret. Use your gifts wisely."

With that, she continued on her way. Diane and I both looked at each other with our mouths wide open, saying nothing, until in the same instant, our dumbfounded faces cracked and we started laughing.

"Come on," I said. "We've got a wardrobe to buy."

After a few disappointing used furniture places, we eventually found a second hand shop, which had a wardrobe sitting in the corner, gathering dust. It was made of pine and, on inspection and measurement, was perfect for our needs. It was quite tall and, on opening the two doors with its brass latch and key, it revealed a set of four large drawers and a hanging bar. The shop owner wanted thirty pounds for it, but with bartering confidence, I managed to get the price down to twenty-five, which included delivery at around 11:00 a.m. on Sunday the next day. I thought to myself, *Right, job done. Let's go.* I was one of those men that regarded shopping as a chore and once the mission was complete, I just wanted to go. But it was different now; Diane said we were going to need some groceries and provisions for the week. I had never really had a set regime for getting my groceries because I always just got them when I ran out. I could see that I was going to have to get used to a completely new way of doing things.

Loaded down with groceries and the curtains, we started to make our way back to the car, but on turning a corner, we were confronted by a snarling Alsatian dog. It had obviously escaped its owner, as its leash was lying on the pavement still attached to its collar. The dog seemed to be making a firm stand not to let us pass. Fearing that it might go for us, I slowly put the bags I was carrying onto the pavement in readiness to freeze its attack. Diane also put down the bags she was carrying.

"What's all this, then?" Diane said to the snarling beast and then she started to walk toward it.

I was totally primed to freeze that dog at a moment's notice but surprisingly as Diane neared the animal; it whimpered and lay on its back. Diane rubbed her hands lightly over the dog's stomach.

"What's the matter boy?" she said. And as if the dog could understand her, it gave out a few more whimpers. Just at that moment an out-of-breath man of about thirty years old came running up.

"Are you OK?" he said to Diane, grabbing the dog's leash. "He didn't bite you or anything, did he? He's usually quite friendly, but just lately he's been pulling at his lead and snarling at everyone. He's a strong dog and yanked the lead out of my hand."

"No, he didn't hurt us," said Diane. "He's a pussycat really, but you might want to take him to the vet. I think he's got something wrong with his stomach."

"How do you know that?" the man asked.

"Let's just say he told me so," Diane replied.

"Well, thanks for catching him," the man said. "I'll take your advice and get to the vet as soon as I can, to get him checked out."

With that the man led the dog off.

"That was a bit scary," I said to Diane. "How did you know the dog wasn't going to attack you?"

"I didn't know really. I could just sense the dog was in pain and wanted me to know about it."

"Well, let's hope the man takes your advice."

We eventually reached my car and with relief put all the shopping into the boot. It was about 2:00 p.m. and I was starting to feel a bit hungry, so I started to say to Diane.

"Shall we—"

She stopped me mid-sentence. "I know what you're going to say. You want us to go and have a meal at that Wimpey burger bar that we passed just down the road, don't you?"

"So you *can* still read my mind then!" I said.

"Only sometimes." She replied.

"Well, after, we can pick up that bunch of flowers you want then."

Diane nudged me in the ribs and said, "So, *you* can read my mind too!"

Giving her a smug smile, I replied, "Only sometimes."

We had our burger and chips lavished with tomato ketchup and afterward made our way to a florist, so that Diane could pick out a moderately priced bunch of flowers. We then made our way back to the car holding hands, with both of us feeling very content that we were together.

Back at the flat and after putting all the groceries away in their respective storage places, we set about removing the old curtains from the living room windows. I took a pile of Diane's clothes off one of the dining chairs and put them on the sofa, so I could use the chair to reach the curtain hooks. The old curtains were filthy and basically falling to bits. They had been left there by the previous tenant, so God knows how old they were. Diane threw them straight into the bin and then unpacked the new sky blue curtains she had bought and we both sat on the sofa with a curtain each, threading the plastic hooks into the top hems.

"You haven't done this before, have you Terry?" she said.

"No," I replied. "Why?"

"You've put all the hooks in upside down. Let me do that and you go and give the curtain rail a wipe over."

With that I got up and dampened a cloth under the kitchen tap. Then standing precariously on a chair, I proceeded to wipe the plastic rail. Instead of moving the chair along as I wiped each section, I stretched across and the chair toppled beneath my feet. Thud was the sound of my body as it hit the floor. Dazed and winded, the next thing I saw was Diane cradling my head.

"Are you all right?" she said.

"I think so," I replied. "My back hurts though."

Lifting my T-shirt, Diane examined my back.

"I don't think you've broken anything," she said. "But you're going to have a nasty bruise there. Come on, get up and sit on the sofa and I'll make you a nice sweet cup of coffee and I think I'll have one too."

I gingerly got up from the floor, feeling a sharp pain in my back, then I managed to make my way over to the sofa, but as I went to sit, I accidently knocked a pile of Diane's clothes onto the floor. I stooped to pick them up.

"Oh, oh," I cried, placing my hands on my back where the stabbing pain was.

"Don't worry about those," Diane said. "I'll pick them up. You just rest."

Diane brought the drinks over and put them on the coffee table.

"Thanks," I uttered painfully.

Thinking for a few seconds, I said to Diane, "Hang on. How come we can cure people, yet we can't cure ourselves?"

"That's a point. I suppose it just doesn't work that way."

After we had finished our coffees, Diane hung the curtains herself, being extra careful not to overstretch but I gave a watchful eye and ready to freeze her if she did. With delight Diane dismounted the chair and said, "Now, don't they brighten the place up?"

"Very nice," I painfully replied.

"Right," she said. "Now for the flowers. Where do you keep the vases?"

"Vases," I replied. "I haven't got any vases."

Diane stood aghast with her hands on her hips looking at me with disbelief. Then after a long incredulous look, she said, "You *must* have *something* I can use?"

"Sorry," I replied, with no answer to give.

Diane went hunting around the flat for a good five minutes, but to no avail. Then I heard her rummaging around in my wardrobe in the bedroom. After a few minutes, she emerged from the bedroom with one of my wellington boots that I sometimes used for work. Saying nothing, she put water into the wellington from the kitchen tap, put the flowers into it and stood it on top of the television, which was on a small cabinet over in the corner of the room. She stood back to admire the flowers, then looked at me. As what happened quite often between us, we simultaneously both burst into a fit of laughter.

The rest of that evening we spent cuddled up on the sofa watching the TV, with the occasional groan from me when I altered my position, since the bruise was now maturing on my back.

Diane had an early start at work the next morning, so that night about eleven we went to bed and set the alarm clock for 6:00 a.m., as she had to be at the hospital by 7:00 a.m.

The next day I got up at the same time as Diane, as I said I would drive her to work. The bruise on my back had fully flourished into a yellow and black mass, but it didn't hurt as much.

It was a nice Sunday morning. The sun was up and pleasantly warm, considering it was early. There were hardly any cars on the road, so it only took ten minutes for us to reach the hospital. I kissed her good-bye and told her I hoped she would have a nice day and as she got out of the car, she asked if I could please pick her up at 7:00 p.m.

I replied, "On the dot," then drove off heading back to the flat.

I stopped off on the way home at Mr. Patel's shop, to get a newspaper to read, while I was having breakfast. As I entered the shop I could see Mr. Patel had a leather strap on his right wrist and it was unusual to see his wife helping him out.

"Hello, Terry, how are you?" Mr. Patel said.

I replied, "I'm OK thanks, and you?"

"Oh, not so good I'm afraid," he replied. "I have sprained my wrist and Gitta, my wife is having to help me stack shelves and so forth. She isn't that good also as her asthma has been bad lately."

Gitta was just coming out of a door opening from the rear of the shop, wearing a bright red sari with gold flecks sewn into it, with a piece of the same material covering her head like a scarf or a veil. Her back was noticeably bent, as if she had a problem with her spine.

"Hello, Mrs. Patel," I said.

I knew Mrs. Patel didn't speak much English, but she smiled back at me, acknowledging my greeting.

I then said to Mr. Patel, "I just want a newspaper please."

Picking up a Sunday tabloid, I noticed a stack of *South London Press* local newspapers on one side of the counter.

The front page headline read, "Miracles at Local Hospital." Intrigued, I bought both the tabloid and the local paper, bid the Patel's a nice day and drove the rest of the way back to the flat.

Back at the flat, I couldn't wait to read about the headline in the local paper.

The story reported that there were unconfirmed reports that a middle-aged woman with stomach cancer, a child with leukaemia and another child with multiple sclerosis had somehow been miraculously cured at St. Gregory's Hospital in Tooting. Doctors at the hospital were baffled as to what caused their complete recoveries. *Wow*, I thought. *It seems that our little covert mission worked on those children. I must show Diane this paper when she gets home tonight.* Little did I know that Diane already knew about the story the moment she arrived at the casualty department.

Having flicked through the rest of the local rag and the tabloid, I decided to have some breakfast and after preparing the space in the corner of the living room, ready for the wardrobe to arrive. By 11:30 a.m., I had the flat pretty tidy, having made the bed and dusted and vacuumed everywhere. The wardrobe had still not arrived and I was just about to phone the second hand furniture shop when the flat's bell rang. With anticipation, I hurried down the stairs to the main door. A middle-aged man, about 5ft 6 inches tall wearing a flat-brimmed cap, was standing in the middle of the pavement.

"Got a wardrobe for you guv!" he said in a broad cockney accent and pointing to his very rusty white van.

"Where's it going?" he asked.

I stood to one side, so he could see the staircase at the end of the entrance hall and said, "Up the top, mate, I'm afraid."

He put one hand on his hip and with the other hand lifted his cap and scratched the few remaining hairs on his head and said, "Oh blimey, just my luck."

Putting the door on the latch and propping it open with a battered phone book, which had been in the hall for months; I followed the man to the back of the van. Having opened the van doors I could see the wardrobe lying in the middle, flat on its back, with other smaller pieces of old furniture all around it. Having bruised my back the previous day, I knew I was going to suffer.

Between us, we managed to manoeuvre the wardrobe out of the van, across the pavement, through the hall and to the foot of the stairs. With a lot of swearing being uttered after every second step by the both of us, we finally got it up the stairs, through my front door and into my living room. Then, after the wardrobe was put in its permanent resting place, we both just stood there, panting with our hands on our slightly bent knees and heads facing the floor. Totally knackered and after a few minutes to regain my breath, I asked the man if he fancied a cup of tea.

"No, thanks, mate," he said, still gulping for air. "I've got to deliver the other lot yet."

I gave the man a pound note and thanked him for his efforts. He graciously touched the brim of his cap and said, "Cheers, mate." Then, he returned to his van.

My back by now was killing me, but I sat on the sofa admiring the pine beast and thought Diane would be pleased now she had somewhere to put all her clothes, which were piled up on the dining table and chairs.

About 1:00 p.m., I had some lunch and the rest of the afternoon rested my back by watching a *Magnificent Seven* cowboy film on the television, occasionally laughing to myself, seeing the Wellington boot with flowers in, above the TV screen.

It was about a quarter to seven when I decided I'd better go and pick Diane up from work, so I got into my car and set off. When I reached the hospital, I found an unusual amount of cars in the car park and a lot of people coming and going.

It was a couple of minutes to 7:00 p.m., so I sat in the car as usual waiting for Diane to appear. By twenty past seven, Diane was still nowhere to be seen, so I decided to go and look for her.

Reaching the casualty department, I was confronted with what seemed like a hundred people outside, all obviously trying to get in. I spotted Diane at the entrance and pushed my way through the people to get to her. They were not very pleased about it shouting,

"Oi, you! Wait your turn."

I ignored them and finally reached Diane.

"Oh, Terry," she said. "All these people have read an item in a local paper and think they will all be miraculously cured here. The hospital put me on the door to assess their ailments, to see if they have a real emergency before I can let them in. It's a nightmare."

There wasn't a triage in those days, as people only used to turn up only in a real life-or-death emergency or if they had cut themselves badly or broken a bone. I could see Diane had a real job on her hands as the waiting room inside was also jam packed.

"I'll stay with you," I said, as I could see that some of the people were getting aggressive.

A member of staff came out with a large makeshift sign, which read, "Non-emergencies will **not** be treated or admitted. Please do not waste your time and ours."

He placed it as high as he could reach and with a hammer and a single nail, fixed it on the wall to one side of the entrance doors. Diane and I hoped it would do the trick.

With Diane assessing people's ailments and I, acting as if I had some sort of authority in the matter, it was a good couple of hours before the crowd of people eventually subsided.

"What have we done?" Diane said.

"Hopefully we've cured an adult and two children of ailments that probably would have killed them, that's what," I replied.

"But we can't go through this every day," she said.

"I think it won't be too long before people realise that by coming here, they won't be miraculously cured," I said.

Just then an ambulance sped up to the entrance door, with its lights flashing and siren blazing. The ambulance driver jumped out and opened the backdoors of the vehicle. Inside, another crewman was tending to an old man lying on a stretcher, with an oxygen mask on his face. Together the two men lifted the stretcher onto a trolley brought out by a nurse. Diane grabbed my hand and pulled me over to the old man and put her hand on his head, while the two crew men were busy getting an oxygen cylinder safely stowed underneath the trolley. Diane and I both felt the tingling sensation for a few seconds before it subsided. A few seconds later, the old man was wheeled into the department with Diane and the nurse close behind. I waited outside. After about ten minutes, Diane emerged from the building.

"What's happening?" I said.

"They told me my shift ended three hours ago and told me to go home," she replied.

"What was wrong with the old man?" I asked.

"Heart attack. Come on, let's go."

It was obvious Diane had had a tough day and was very tired, as she nodded off on the ten-minute drive to the flat.

Back at the flat, I asked Diane if she was hungry and she said she managed to grab a sandwich at about 3:00 p.m. and all she wanted to do is go to bed. Poor Diane was dead on her feet and as she sat on the end of the bed with her eyes shut and head to one side, I helped her off with her shoes and clothes, then virtually dragged her so her head met the pillow. I then threw the duvet over her and kissed her goodnight. Diane was so tired when we eventually got back to the flat that she hadn't even noticed the new, or should I say old, addition to our furniture.

I myself had only had a sandwich at lunchtime that day, so I decided to make myself beans on toast. I sat on the sofa with my plate of beans on toast on my lap and pondered the events of the day, occasionally foraging for the odd bean that had fallen off my fork down the side of the sofa. Eventually I decided I'd better go to bed as I had to go to work the next morning. Quietly slipping into bed next to Diane, I could hear her gentle inhale and exhale of breath, but she didn't move a muscle as I pulled my side of the duvet over me.

The next day I woke up about 7:30 a.m. I was pretty good at getting up without an alarm on a workday, like I had some sort of inner built-in clock that probably came from my punctuality. I washed and dressed and made my sandwiches and flask for my lunch break and by 8:00 a.m. was ready to leave. Diane was still sleeping soundly, but I thought I had better wake her before I left. I crouched down by her side of the bed and gently shook her saying,

"Wake up sleepy head, time to get up."

She slowly opened her eyes, yawned and said, "What time is it?"

"Eight o'clock," I replied.

"Eight o'clock," she repeated, jerking her head up from the pillow with panic. "I'm supposed to be at the hospital at eight."

"Listen," I said. "You did at least three hours overtime last night. I don't think they can say much if you are an hour or so late."

"Suppose your right," she said. "But I'd better get up now anyway. Are you off to work?"

"Yes," I replied.

"What time do you finish today?" I asked.

"Six, I think. Yes, it is six today."

"I'll meet you in the car park about six then."

After a long kiss, I told her to have a nice day and not to rush about. I also said, "Love you," as I shut the flat door behind me and went to work.

Plastering is a very strenuous job and you tend to use all your muscles to do it. Although I hated all the preparation and physical strength putting the plaster on the wall, I did occasionally have a certain satisfaction seeing the finished article. I still found it generally boring, though and this day was no different from the rest, apart from the fact my back felt grossly overexerted and was still hurting me from the fall I had had on Saturday. I was so relieved when finally it was time to go home.

I met Diane in the hospital car park about 6:05 p.m. and we drove back to the flat. We had both had another tiring day, so after I made us both a coffee, we slumped on the sofa.

"How did it go today?" I asked.

"Thank God there weren't so many people today," she replied. "I think they have got the message now, that they will only be treated if there is a real emergency."

"What happened with that old man who came in by ambulance last night?" I asked.

"He died."

"But I thought we saved him."

"So did I. Something must have gone wrong, but there has got to be an explanation for it not to have worked."

"We'll have to try and figure it out," I said.

After resting up for a while, Diane threw something together in the kitchen, which we sat up to the table to eat. This morning, she must have finally noticed the wardrobe and had put her clothes in it after I had left because the table and chairs were clear and usable again.

After our dinner we started to try and work out why we were not able to cure everyone we intentionally tried to. On a piece of paper, we listed all the people we had tried to help, their sex, age and ailments.

On the surface, it seemed that it was only the older people we couldn't cure, but that left my mother's cancer and I didn't want to consider that her cancer would return. Diane could tell I was worried about our findings and told me not to jump to any conclusions and that we would just have to wait until my mother went back to the hospital for her check-up. Until that time, we agreed that if an opportunity came up to try to cure someone, especially an older person, we must try it and assess the outcome. I suddenly remembered that the last time I saw the shop keeper Mr. Patel; he had a sprained wrist, so I suggested to Diane that we go to his shop tomorrow evening from work and see if we could heal his sprain. Diane agreed we should try it.

The following evening I picked Diane up about 7:00 p.m. and we stopped off at Mr. Patel's shop on the way home. As we entered his shop holding hands, I was greeted by Mr. Patel in the usual way, with the added, "And who is this beautiful young lady, Terry?"

"This is my girlfriend, Diane, Mr. Patel. She works as a trainee doctor in the casualty department at St. Gregory's Hospital."

"Pleased to meet you, Mr. Patel," Diane said. "What have you done to your wrist?"

"Oh, I have sprained it picking up some heavy boxes. Now my doctor is telling me it will take about two weeks to heal up."

"Can I have a look at it?" Diane said.

"Of course, why not? It is always good to get a second opinion."

Mr. Patel then unbuckled his leather wrist strap and rested his arm on a pile of newspapers, which were on top of the counter, so that Diane could inspect his wrist.

With her left hand behind her back holding my hand, she held and then turned over Mr. Patel's hand with her right.

"Ooo, that is tingling," Mr. Patel said.

"That's just the nerves in your wrist," Diane stated. "It looks to me as if your wrist will heal up much quicker than two weeks, but be careful not to lift anything heavy for at least a couple of days."

As he put the strap back on his wrist, he said, "Well, I hope you are right. I am having to have my wife help me and it is not good for her to lift heavy things."

A few seconds later, Mr. Patel's wife emerged carrying an opened, shallow cardboard box of tinned food, which she put on the floor by a set of shelves. We noticed, after putting the box on the floor, she couldn't straighten her back properly.

"Miss Diane, this is my wife Gitta," Mr. Patel said. He went on to tell Gitta in Punjabi about who Diane was and where she worked. Because Gitta didn't speak much English, she just smiled at Diane and nodded. Still holding my hand with her left, Diane dragged me over to Gitta, who seemed a little breathless.

"Oh, what lovely bangles, can I see?" Diane said, with enthusiasm.

Diane then held Gitta's hand, as you would with a handshake and lowered her head, as if to get a better look at the bangles on Gitta's wrist. I think Diane overdid the inspection a bit, but I suppose she just wanted to make sure our curing process had long enough to take effect. Gitta must have felt the tingling sensation but didn't comment or react physically in any way. After telling Gitta how beautiful her jewellery was, Diane announced, "Well, we must be off now I'm afraid, but can we have a pint of milk and a packet of chocolate digestive biscuits, please?"

Mr. Patel gathered the items, put them in a plastic bag and handed them to me over the counter. After paying for the items, we all said our good-byes and then we left the shop. When we got back in my car to drive home, I said to Diane, "I don't think they suspected anything, do you?"

"No, but you will have to go back in the shop tomorrow to see if it worked on them. Gitta has osteoporosis and by the sound of it asthma. It will be interesting to see if her back is any straighter and her breathing is any different."

Back at the flat, I put the oven on to warm up for our staple diet, pizza, which we had left in the fridge as our dinner for that evening. Diane flopped on the sofa, stretched out her arms and yawned. Looking toward the coffee table, Diane said, "What's this?"

On the table was a piece of thin opaque plastic-type material, which was folded in half. I sat down next to Diane, picked up the material and unfolded it. It had writing on it, with slightly embossed black letters. It read as follows:

> THERON HAS ENTERED TODAY.
> MADRI BELIEVES SHE HAS FOUND A
> SOLUTION TO YOUR LIFE EXTINCTION PORTAL.
> WE WILL ENTER HERE TOMORROW AT
> 10 P.M. TO SPEAK.

"That's good news, Terry, at last you could be free of that thing," said Diane.

"I suppose so," I replied. "But I wonder just what they've got planned?"

"Whatever it is, it has got to be better than you going through all that pain when the portal appears. I know what, though! I'm not looking forward to seeing those creatures. Theron was pleasant enough, but he is a bit scary. I'm wondering what this Madri will look like."

"There's not much difference between them," I said.

As I came to the end of my sentence, I put the note from Theron back onto the coffee table.

"Look!" Diane said.

The note seemed to be melting and within a few seconds it had completely turned into a little pool of water.

"Wow! That was cool," Diane said.

"I'm not surprised really," I replied. "I think Theron would be very careful not to leave anything from his world on this."

The next day I arrived back at the flat from work about 6:00 p.m. After having a quick wash and brush up and then a change of clothes, I made my way to Mr. Patel's shop. I didn't have to collect Diane from the hospital till 8:00 p.m., so I knew I would have enough time to check up on the results of our little experiment.

Mr. Patel's shop wasn't that large and with all the various kinds of things he sold, it didn't leave much floor space for customers. As I pushed open the door, I almost barged into a rather fat lady who took up most of the limited space. Mr. Patel was just putting the items she had purchased into two large plastic bags and then for the lady to leave, I had to ram myself up against a rack of shelves. Having closed the door behind her, I now had an opportunity to talk to him.

Mr. Patel's name was Sanjay, but isn't it strange how some people you feel you can call them by their first name, while some you feel it's more appropriate to use their title? It didn't seem right somehow to use his first name, so I never did.

"Hello Terry," he said, still wearing his wrist strap.

Thinking his wrist had not healed, I replied, "How's the wrist?"

"Oh! Much, much better, but I'm keeping the strap on though, just in case."

I asked, "Is Gitta OK?"

"Why do you ask?" he replied, with surprise.

Thinking quickly, I said, "Oh, I thought she had a bit of breathing trouble when Diane and I came in yesterday."

"Yes, that was probably her asthma. Funny, though, come to think of it, I haven't heard her wheezing today. She should be back from the Cash and Carry soon. I will have to ask her. Anyway, what are you wanting today, Terry?"

"Just a packet of ham and a jar of mustard pickle, please."

I didn't really need anything from Mr. Patel's shop, but I had to buy something or he would have been curious to know why I only came in to ask about his wife. After I had paid for my items and left, I thought I'd wait around outside for a little while at a short distance away, to see if Gitta would drive up from the cash and carry. Sure enough, after about five minutes, Gitta arrived and I watched as she got out of the estate car and went to the rear tailgate. As she hobbled along, I could see there was definitely no change in the condition of her back; her dowagers hump was still clearly visible.

Back at the flat, I began to tidy up a little—well, I didn't want Theron and Madri to think Diane and I were slobs! Then time seemed to move quickly and I found myself having to rush to be on time for 8:00 p.m. to pick Diane up from the hospital; needless to say I made it with a couple of minutes to spare. On the way home we decided to stop off and get fish and chips for our dinner, as we both didn't fancy cooking anything.

As we sat up to the table for our meal, I began to tell Diane about the Patels. I told her that I was quite sure that Mr. Patel's wrist was healed and I thought that Mrs. Patel's asthma was also, but her spine curvature had definitely remained the same. Diane said that after our meal, we should make a chart, with all the information we knew, of all the healings and see if we could assess what exactly was happening.

I didn't enjoy the meal much as the batter on the cod I had was far too thick and the chips were big enough to wedge under a door to stop it shutting. This fish meal didn't have a patch on the one I had in Diane's uncle's place, even though Diane had served it on both occasions.

After the meal we both sat on the sofa as usual with our coffees on the coffee table in front of us. Diane had a notepad and pen and started to make a chart, listing the information we had. I was glad to have something to occupy my mind as the thought of what was to come when Theron emerged, quite frankly was scaring the shit out me.

The Chart:

Name	Age	Condition	Cured
Rose	55	Cancer	yes/?
Rose	55	Arthritis	no
Boy	8	Leukaemia	yes
Girl	4	Multiple Sclerosis	yes
Old man	85	Heart attack	no
Mr. Patel	64ish	Sprained wrist	yes
Gitta	60ish	Spine curvature	no
Gitta	60ish	Asthma	yes/?

"This is what we know so far Terry," Diane said. "Although we have got a couple of question marks, we have to assume those ones have been cured."

"I hope you're right," I said.

"Now, can we see a pattern" Diane asked?

"I can't see any pattern there." I replied.

"Well," Diane said, "if we eliminate the two youngest ones because they were cured, that would suggest it is to do with age."

"OK," I replied hesitantly.

"Now let's look at the older ones ailments. Cancer, sprained wrist and Asthma have nothing to do with age, but arthritis, heart attack and spine curvature are. On the surface, it seems we can't cure age-related ailments but anything unrelated to age, we can."

"Do you think that's the answer then?" I said.

"I think it is," Diane replied.

Looking at my watch it was getting close to 10:00 p.m. I was beginning to sweat a little and Diane, realising the time, became a bit anxious, too.

"Oh God, I'm not looking forward to this, Terry," she said.

"Me neither," I replied. Not because I felt like Diane, uncomfortable with the sight of the Terrans, but because of the lack of knowledge about what Madri had come up with to free me of my deathly portal.

The hour had come and with a blast of intense light, a portal opened over by the window. Theron emerged first, with Madri following close behind, both wearing their customary utility belts and nothing else. After they had stepped clear of the portal, it closed leaving no trace.

"Hello to you both," Theron said. "May I introduce Madri to you, Diane?"

Madri spoke. "I am pleased to meet you, Diane."

Diane remained silent, with a forced smile on her face.

"What is that delightful aroma?" Theron said.

"Fish and chips," I replied.

"Oh, your sustenance," Theron said, repeatedly sniffing the air.

"Yes," I said.

I went over to the dining table and pulled out a couple of chairs and gestured for Theron and Madri to sit down. I could tell they didn't find them comfortable but after a wriggle or two, they got settled. Madri then began to speak.

"As I think you know, Terry, I have been doing extensive tests and by using simulations, I have tried to find an answer to your portal problem. Theron and I have also had to convince the Terran council that it was our duty to help you in any way we could. To do this we have had to break our most fundamental rule, 'no human contact in your world.'

"I believe I have managed to come up with a solution, but there may be side effects that I cannot foresee. It is up to you if you are willing to attempt what I have prepared. I would say this though: if you do nothing, my simulations suggest that the portal will become increasingly stronger each time it appears. Eventually you will not be able to resist and upon touching the portal, your body will instantly become extinct and your life force will enter our world forever. When Earth was formed, nature had to find its equilibrium and if it is altered in any way, it will be relentless in rectifying the imbalance."

I then said, "The last time the portal appeared, Diane touched it and she wasn't hurt and it disappeared. Why is that?"

Madri replied, "That is because it was not Diane's portal. She had not died nor was it her time to die. The portal didn't want her and it closed to protect her from harm, but Diane will not always be there to close it for you."

"OK," I said, "I'm sitting down. Go for it."

"Does that mean you want me to explain the procedure?" Madri said.

"Yes," I replied.

Madri began to explain, saying, "Do you remember when I ran that scan of your brain in our world, Terry?"

I nodded and Madri continued.

"Well, I recorded every thought that you had ever had from birth. I have used those thoughts and managed to incorporate them into a transmittable wave that the portal should accept. When the portal opens, I intend transmitting those stored thought waves, thus tricking the portal that your life's cycle and death sequence has been completed."

Diane was sitting next to me on the sofa intensely listening; she was as stiff as a board, with her eyes and mouth wide open.

"So that's all there is to it?" I said.

"Not quite," Madri replied. "In order for this procedure to work, you will have to die first."

"Die!" I said.

"Yes," Madri replied.

"Your heart must stop functioning while the transmission is taking place."

Diane came out of her trance and said, "You mean you are going to stop Terry's heart, but how do you intend to get it going again?"

From a pocket in Madri's utility belt, she produced a small object about as big as a matchbox and shaped like a ladybird. Then she said, "This object has the technology within to stop a human heart and to restart it again as long as the procedure lasts no longer than two minutes. Initially Terry, you must try to open the portal with your mind, we will then stop your heart, transmit, then revive you. If you are unable to open the portal, then we will have to stop your heart first and hope the portal realises you as deceased. Now it is up to you if you wish to proceed."

Diane grabbed my arm and said, "It's too risky, Terry. Suppose they can't get your heart going again?"

I answered Diane by saying, "If I don't take the risk, the portal will eventually draw me in. I can't see that I have got much choice."

With tears starting to seep from her eyes, Diane reluctantly agreed.

"Well, there's no point in dragging this thing out, let's do it." I said.

"First you must take your shirt off and lay flat on the floor," Madri said.

Having complied with the request, I then asked, "What's next?"

"I am now going to put this instrument upon your chest over your heart."

Madri placed the ladybird-shaped gizmo in position. It was sticky and felt a little cold.

"Now you must concentrate, Terry, to evoke the portal," Madri said.

I closed my eyes and tried to think of nothing except the portal.

It must have taken a good ten minutes as I concentrated and as I did so, everyone else virtually held their breath in deadly silence before I realised this portal was not going to appear on demand. I finally relented and said to Madri,

"It's not going to work this way is it? I think we will have to go for plan B."

"No, Terry, it's too dangerous," Diane shouted.

"It's the only way," I said.

Madri came over to me and, with her long and pointed index finger, touched the device on my chest. I felt a powerful compression for a few seconds then, I totally blacked out.

Obviously I did not die, but Diane told me of the chain of events after my black out, while I recovered on the floor.

She said, "I came over to you, Terry and checked your pulse. There wasn't any. Knowing you only had two minutes I watched the second hand of the clock on the wall. A minute and fifty seconds elapsed before the portal appeared. Madri sent your recorded brainwaves into the portal, but it took at least ten seconds before it closed. She then tried to revive you repeatedly, but the device didn't start your heart again."

Madri continued relating the chain of events: "Diane pushed me out of the way, made a fist and hit your heart using her fist as a hammer. Your heart started to beat again, but you were not breathing. She then put a cushion beneath your shoulders. With your head turned back, she pinched your nose, put her lips to yours and blew into your mouth a few times. You then started to breath for yourself."

"So that is why my chest hurts so much," I said.

"Yes, Terry," Madri replied. "You owe your life to Diane's quick thinking and expertise."

Diane helped me to my feet and I thanked her in the only way I knew by giving her a big hug and long, loving kiss. Then I turned to Madri, who was now back sitting next to Theron and said, "Do you think it worked?"

Madri replied, "I believe the portal now recognises you as deceased and will not appear to you again, but remember, Terry, I have no way of knowing if there will be side effects."

"I understand," I replied.

With all that had happened, Diane now seemed to be totally at ease with the presence of the Terrans. So much so in fact, she began to ask Madri some personal questions.

"Is Theron your husband?" she asked.

I butted in and said, "Of course he isn't."

"Well, in fact, Terry, Madri is my mate, which I suppose is the same as humans have wives," said Theron. "We have been together for many years."

I was stunned. "You didn't tell me Madri was your wife, sorry your mate," I said.

"There wasn't the need to tell you," Theron said.

Diane then asked if they had any children.

Madri replied, "Yes, we have a very young male offspring, named Zecron."

"How old is he?" Diane asked.

"Forty-two years," Madri replied.

Diane looked at me dumbstruck and seeing this I said to Madri, "I suppose that **is** very young considering your people's life span is a thousand years."

Madri and Theron both smiled, then Theron said, "We must leave you now and we will probably never see each other again."

I thanked Theron and Madri for all they had done for me. They had pretty much saved my life twice. Diane also gratefully thanked them.

"Live long and may your lives be fulfilling," Theron said.

He then took another small device from a pocket in his belt, held it at arm's length and a blue-tinged portal opened immediately.

"Just before we go." Madri said, pointing to the Wellington boot. "Is that a usual receptacle for flowers?"

"No," Diane said, with a chuckle. "We didn't have anything else."

With that final word, Theron and Madri walked into and through the portal. It then zapped shut behind them.

Being resurrected is a tiring business and Diane also felt quite exhausted, but at least my chest wasn't hurting anymore, so we decided it was a good idea to go to bed.

Cuddling up tightly facing each other, I said to Diane.

"Where did you learn that trick you used to restart my heart?"

"I read about it in a medical magazine, apparently the technique is being used more and more worldwide."

"Well, I'm not complaining, even though I've got a hell of a bruise on my chest."

"Madri said that there might be side effects from what was done tonight. I hope it hasn't affected your ability to help me heal people."

"We will have to try and put it to the test and also see if I am still able to freeze things."

We kissed each other and fell asleep in each other's arms. Although I was unaware of any side effects at the time, I would in the future realise that there would be, and they weren't necessarily good!

5

The next day we woke up to find that my inner alarm clock malfunctioned and we had both overslept. With all that went on the previous night, neither of us set the alarm clock and as we both had to go to work, a certain panic set in. Diane got in the shower first and then while she was getting dressed, I had my shower. I had just stepped out of the shower dripping wet when she came into the bathroom, gave me a quick kiss, said good-bye and then zoomed out of the flat to catch her bus for work. I hated being late for anything so facing the bathroom mirror, I cleaned my teeth like the piston of a steam train. In my haste I went to grab the drinking glass on the shelf below the mirror when I accidentally knocked it off. As quick as a flash, I managed to freeze it in mid-air. *Phew*, I thought to myself, *at least I have still got that ability.*

The bathroom mirror had started to clear of steam and as it did so, I noticed that the bruise on my chest had completely gone. I could only think that Diane hadn't hit me as hard as I thought last night. Still in panic mode though, I got dressed, left the flat and screeched away with a tyre spin in my car. Luckily by the time I reached the building site, I was only half an hour late and the foreman of the site had been held up in traffic himself, so he didn't say anything to me.

During the day in my mindless job, I thought about how lucky I was. I should have died on two occasions, but here I was with a beautiful, intelligent girlfriend, a flat that I could call home and an ability to help and heal others. What more could I want?

Greed seems to overcome us all at some point or another in our lives and I started to think of how much better it would be if I had lots of money. I could buy Diane and me a nice house with a garden, get a new car and or better still, help pay all Diane's tuition costs, since at the moment her dad was footing all her bills.

I wouldn't have to work on a dirty, dusty building site anymore either. It wasn't just all about me, though: I wanted to make life a little easier for those around me, but I didn't realise at the time that those thoughts, which were not going away soon, were the seed of a desire that would begin to grow inside my mind.

A month had passed from the time my mother had been discharged from hospital and it was now the day she had to go for her follow-up examination. My Dad was taking her to St. Gregory's for an 11:00 a.m. appointment and I had asked him to phone me that evening to let me know the results. I had been worried all day that the outcome was not going to be good, which would also mean that Diane and I had not permanently cured her.

That evening Diane and I were watching TV when the phone rang. We looked at each other, both with worry written all over our faces. I picked up the receiver and Diane dashed over to the TV to turn the sound right down.

"Hello, Terry," my dad said.

Diane put her ear to the side of the receiver near to mine.

"All clear," he said. "No cancer cells whatsoever."

"That's great news," I said with relief.

With a big grin on her face, Diane moved away from the phone.

"Just a thought, Dad," I said. "How is her arthritis?"

"Oh, that's just as bad as it ever was, but who cares? Arthritis is manageable and isn't exactly life threatening, is it?"

"No, I suppose you're right," I said. "Give her all our love, won't you?"

"I will, Terry," he said. "Bye for now."

Putting the receiver down, I punched the air and bellowed, "*Yes!*"

Diane said, "Do you see, Terry? Your mum's cancer was cured because it wasn't age related, but her arthritis **is** age related and that's why she has still got it."

I replied, "Do you know? I think you're right."

Diane then said, "I've just realised something else. When we first met, I told you that I had a good memory."

"Yes," I said, wondering what she was going to say next.

"Well, I remember when I first touched your mother's hand. She said she felt a tingling. You have touched your mother's hand since you came back from Theron's world. Did she feel a tingling with you?"

"No, she didn't," I replied.

"Also when you met my father for the first time, you shook his hand. He would have said if he had felt a tingling, but he didn't."

"That's right," I said.

"Now, while I have been working in the casualty department, I have been told by patients that they were feeling a tingling sensation when I treated them."

"Yes, I remember you said that," I replied. "But what are you getting at?"

"Don't you see? It's *me* who has the healing touch and you just seem to boost it somehow. Now what that really means is that I can cure people, but not instantly, but when you hold my hand and I touch someone, they are cured virtually straight away."

I suppose I must have looked a bit bewildered trying to keep up with Diane's revelations because she said, "I know this is a little confusing but bear with me. It all boils down to the fact we've been going about curing people the wrong way. If people are instantly cured, they and others are alarmed and start to speculate the reason for it. But if it was just me who touched them, they would still be cured but at a slower rate and therefore would not become suspicious in any way. I will only need you to back me up and hold my hand if the cure we needed to give was an emergency, if they couldn't survive the time it takes for my curing power to work."

"Oh, now I understand," I said.

What Diane had said all seemed to make sense and if it was indeed the case that Diane was the healer and I was just the supercharger, then it would make it so much easier to help people without arousing suspicion. Just as I pondered on that thought, the phone rang again. I picked up the receiver to the sound of my sister's sobbing voice.

"Oh, Terry," she said, "Steven is ill and has been taken to Greenford Hospital."

Steven was her two-year-old son.

"What's wrong with him?" I asked.

"The doctor thinks he has meningitis," she bawled.

"Have you told Mum and Dad?" I said.

"Yes," she replied. "I have just got off the phone to them. Dad told me that mum has been given the all clear, which is great, but now this. What am I going to do?"

Linda, my sister, up till now had not met Diane, but she had heard all about her from our parents.

I said to her, "Don't worry, he will be OK. Diane and I will go to the hospital tomorrow to find out exactly what is happening."

After replacing the receiver, I related the news of my sister's son to Diane and she agreed we would go to Greenford hospital the next day.

Luckily the next day was Saturday and Diane and I both didn't have to work. After having a quick breakfast, Diane and I set off in my car to where my nephew had been taken. We arrived at the hospital about 9:00 a.m.

Greenford hospital was very large and modern compared to St. Gregory's in Tooting and after parking the car, we entered through the main lobby of the building. There was a large reception and information desk, which was manned by three people. Behind them on the wall was a large, clearly marked sign showing the directions to all the departments and wards, but just to make sure we knew where to go, I asked one of the receptionists where Steven had been taken, as he had been admitted as an emergency. Having been told that he was on a children's ward on the fourth floor, we headed straight for the lifts. There were a set of four lifts with a lot of people waiting for one to reach the ground floor. Two of the lift doors seemed to open simultaneously and, within a few seconds, all who were waiting got in. The lifts were quite large, I suppose, so they could accommodate bed trolleys. After a few people pressed the buttons in our lift for the floors they wanted, I pressed for the fourth. With Diane to my right, we were standing at the rear of the lift holding hands when a Down's syndrome boy of about twelve years old stood in front of Diane and held out his hand for her to shake. Diane immediately reciprocated.

"I'm David and I am very pleased to meet you," he said, continually shaking Diane's hand and not letting go.

"And I am Diane and I am very pleased to meet you too," she said.

The boy's mother spoke up and said, "David, give the lady her hand back. Sorry about that. He doesn't mean any harm."

"There's no harm done," Diane said. "He's a lovely, friendly boy. That's all."

The lift doors opened on the fourth floor and the boy and his mother got out along with us. The boy continued talking to Diane outside the lift.

"We are going to see my little sister," he said. "She's not very well."

"Oh, I'm sorry to hear that," Diane replied. "But I'm sure the hospital will make her better."

With that, we all headed for the children's ward and as we did so, I couldn't help wondering if something miraculous might happen, since Diane and I were holding hands and she was shaking the boy's hand at the same time.

We passed through a couple of corridors and finally made it into the correct section of the children's ward. As we entered the tiny area, we found there were just six beds—three on one side of the room and three on the other. I saw my sister next to the middle bed on the right hand side and she immediately saw me. As Diane and I approached, Linda said with obvious anxiety, "Hello, Terry thanks for coming."

Little Steven was lying asleep in one of those small, cream coloured, enamelled, tubular metal beds with detachable rails on either side. He had a saline drip going into his tiny arm from a plastic bag suspended from a hook on a stand. His breathing seemed to be quite fast and he looked very sweaty.

"Hello, Linda," Diane said, offering her hand to shake.

Linda said, "Oh, sorry, Diane, I didn't mean to ignore you. Mum has told me quite a bit about you."

As Linda's hand touched Diane's, Linda recoiled back.

"Ooo, that tingled," she said.

"Oh, sorry," Diane replied. "I think I must have picked up a bit of static from the lift."

Thinking no more about it, Linda said, "I hear you are training to be a paediatrician. Can you have a look at Steven and tell me honestly what you think? The doctors here are not telling me much."

Diane first looked at Steven's chart hanging at the foot of the bed, then went to Steven, held his hand and inspected his arms and face. Still holding Steven's hand with her other hand, she pulled back the sheets to look at his chest area.

She then said, "There are the signs that look like meningitis Linda, but I don't think he has got that. The rash on his body to me looks as if he has come into contact with something he is allergic to. I really think he will be starting to feel fine in about twenty-four hours, once his body deals with the problem naturally."

"God, I hope you're right," Linda said, enthusiastically.

Diane then said to Linda.

"But don't forget: I have not qualified as a doctor yet and I am only giving you my opinion."

Linda replied, "I know Diane, but you have at least given me a bit of hope that he will be all right."

I knew that even if Steven did have meningitis, Diane had held his hand long enough for her healing to take effect. After Diane backed away from Steven, Linda went close to him and stroked back his mousey brown hair from his forehead and gently wiped away the sweat with a tissue. At this point I looked over and saw the Down's syndrome boy and his mother next to the bed of a little girl, who was about four years of age. The boy, seeing me look at him, gestured at me to come over to him. I tapped Diane on the shoulder and with my eyes coaxed her to look in the direction of the boy.

"Won't be a minute," I said to Linda. "We met that little lad in the lift and he wants us to go over to him."

"OK," Linda replied.

Diane and I responded to the lad's gesturing hand.

"This is my little sister; she's not well," the boy said.

The little girl looked as if she was asleep, but her mother; with a very worried look on her face, said, "She had a fit and has been like this for two days. The doctors say she's in a coma and don't quite know what to do yet."

The little girl had lots of coloured wires with small, round pads stuck to her head; all the wires were linked to a machine on a trolley at the side of her bed and a drip was going into her arm, like Steven's.

"Do you mind if I take a look?" Diane said.

"Are you a doctor then?" she asked.

"Not quite, but I'm training to be a paediatrician."

"Well, it can't do any harm then," the mother said. "Go ahead."

Diane held the little girl's hand and, with her other hand, put her fingers on the side of the girl's neck.

"I think she is going to be all right," said Diane. "She is breathing for herself OK and her heart beat is quite strong."

"Do you really think so?" the mother said.

"Yes, I do," Diane replied. "I'd say it won't be too long before she wakes up and wants an ice cream, as if nothing had ever happened."

"Thanks," the mother said. "At least I can think there's a chance she'll be OK. It's more than the doctors have said."

As we started to turn away, Diane put her hand on the mothers shoulder and said, "Try not to worry. She will be all right."

With a big smile of his face, David, the little girl's brother, said to Diane, "Thank you for mending my sister."Diane, looking down at him, just smiled and briefly put her hand on his head.

As we walked away from the little girl's hospital bed, Diane could see Linda was absorbed in giving Steven a lot of attention. There were no other relatives or nurses about and Diane decided to look at the charts of the remaining four children in the ward. I went over and stood behind Linda to block her view of Diane in case she turned around. Standing still, I scanned around to make sure that no one was taking any notice of Diane as she went and looked at each chart, one by one. Three of the four children were asleep and the other was sitting up in his little bed cage, busily playing with some plastic bricks. She didn't touch any of the first three children except the fourth, a small girl asleep. Diane held her hand and I could see she was in her curing mode. After a short while, Diane came back over to where I was standing behind Linda.

"By the way, where's Martin?" I said to Linda.

Martin was Linda's husband.

"Oh, he's at work, but he is coming in later to see Steven and take me home," she replied.

"Are you sure you are going to be OK till then?" I said.

"Yes, I'll be all right," she replied.

"Well, we are off then," I said.

Linda then said, "Thanks for coming and it was very nice to meet you at last, Diane."

Diane replied, "Don't worry, Linda. Steven will be fine."

Linda was still obviously very upset, so she just nodded, swallowed and said, "Take care."

As a last thought, I said to Linda, "Keep us informed about Steven, won't you?"

"I will," she replied.

As we started to make our way out, a nurse passed us in the corridor, walking in the direction of the ward and just after she passed us, we heard a loud voice shout, "Nurse, come quick. She's waking up."

We left the hospital building and headed back to the car park and as we reached the car, Diane said, "That was a good job done."

I replied, "It certainly was."

We got into the car but before I turned the ignition key, I had to ask Diane something that was bugging me.

"There's something I don't understand," I said.

"When we were in the lift going up to the ward, the Down's boy—"

Diane interrupted, saying, "You mean David."

"Yes, David," I said. "Well, he shook your hand and I was holding yours. How come it didn't have any affect?"

"You still haven't quite got it yet Terry, have you?"

"Got what?" I replied.

Diane began to explain her meaning.

"Look at it this way. We know that Nature itself is the creator of all things and its prime directive is to create those things and people as perfect as possible from conception. Sometimes things go wrong, but in a mysterious way somehow, we have been given the power to correct some of those errors. It is predetermined that a human's life cycle starts as a baby, matures, gets old and dies, leaving room for the next generation.

"The reason why we can't cure age-related illnesses is because it is a natural part of the human cycle. The reason why we can cure children and other people's non-age-related ailments is because they are not part of that natural cycle. Children shouldn't have things go wrong with their bodies, not until they have matured and started to decline with age."

I said, "I get that, but what about David?"

Diane replied, "The reason that our powers didn't affect David is because there is nothing wrong with him. He is as perfect as Nature intended him to be and there's something else too: he *knew* that we could cure his sister. I don't know how, but maybe he has the gift to see our auras, or something."

Feeling as if I had been reprimanded for being ignorant, I kissed Diane and said with a smile, "I wish I had your brains."

She replied also smiling, "You're OK just as you are Terry."

"Oh, just one other thing," I said. "Why did you only cure one of those four tots in the ward?"

She replied, "Because the one I cured could not have survived and the other three had illnesses that, going by their charts, the medication would cure them. We can't use our power to cure everyone; it would cause too much suspicion. We must only cure the ones we encounter in desperate need; I think that's the way Nature has intended us to do it."

With Diane's words of wisdom now firmly established in my head, I started the car and began to drive back home. On the way, we stopped off at a local bakery to pick up a French stick for our lunch. We hadn't eaten anything since breakfast and we were getting quite hungry.

In the flat, I cut the French stick in half and then along the two lengths and buttered all four open sides. It suddenly occurred to me that I used to have something as a child for my lunch, which I hadn't had for years. I started to say to Diane, "Do you know what I really fancy to eat?"

Diane interrupted, "Don't tell me; cream of tomato soup with vinegar in it."

"You're doing it again, aren't you? Like when we first met," I said.

She replied, "Vinegar in tomato soup, though, sounds gross."

"No, trust me," I replied. "Then you dip the buttered bread into the soup and eat it that way. It's magic."

"OK, I'll try it," she said.

I got a tin of tomato soup out of the cupboard and began to open it with my old can opener—you know, the metal ones that you squeeze to pierce the tin before turning the key thingy to go round the lid cutting the can. Half way round the can, the key sheared off, leaving me with nothing to open the rest of the lid.

Haven't we all done it? I got a knife out of the cutlery draw and started to cut the lid off the rest of the can. The knife slipped of course and I gashed my other hand that was holding the can and blood started to spurt everywhere. Hearing me yell with pain, Diane rushed over to me and asked what I had done. Without touching me, she looked at the cut.

"I'll get something to put on that," she said, heading for the bathroom cabinet. She was only gone for about half a minute, then she returned with some sticking plasters. While she was gone for those thirty seconds, I was holding the gash together to try to stem the flow of blood.

"Let me see," she said.

I gradually released the pressure I was exerting on the cut and took my hand away. There was absolutely nothing there except the stains of blood from when I had initially bled. The gash on my hand had completely healed leaving no trace, not even a scar. Diane and I looked at each other in amazement.

"You can self-heal, Terry!" she exclaimed.

I thought for a bit and said, "I wonder if it's one of the side effects that Madri was talking about when she closed the portal for me."

"It must be," Diane replied. "I noticed cuts on your hands from work before Madri did her thing and they didn't heal up for days."

With an element of delight, I said, "Well, I don't mind if *this* is the side effect."

I didn't know at that time, but this wasn't the only side effect I had. Another would show itself in the near future, one that wasn't so good!

Although the can wasn't fully open, I somehow managed to bend the lid back enough to pour the soup into a saucepan and when it was hot enough, I put it in some bowls. We then both sat at the table with our buttered bread, the vinegar bottle and spoons all ready to eat the soup. The malt vinegar was in one of those bottles that you had to shake, so it would come out through the small hole in the top.

"Now watch this," I said to Diane.

I shook the bottle so streams of vinegar went into my soup and it was clearly visible, as it lay as streaks in the red, creamy broth. Then I stirred it up with my spoon, dunked the buttered bread into it and began to eat, leaving a buttery red and yellow residue all around my mouth and chin. After the first delectable mouthful and swallow, I said to Diane,

"Now you try it."

Diane copied the ritual exactly as I did and with soup dripping from her chin, she said, "Wow! That **is** nice! **Messy!** But nice!"

After our lunch and a coffee to wash it down, we were so bloated that we decided to lie on the bed. Inevitably we fell asleep. The next thing we knew the phone was ringing and Diane jumped up and went into the living room to answer the call. Still a bit sleepy, I just lay there, gradually coming to my senses. Diane must have been on the phone a good ten minutes before she came back into the bedroom; the call was obviously for her so I didn't feel the need to get up.

"That was my dad," she said. "He's was made redundant last week and has been putting off telling me."

I said, "Surely he should easily be able to get another job though, with his qualifications."

"Yes, he should," she replied. "But he's been trying all week now and can't find anything. He said if he can't find any work soon, he won't be able to carry on supporting me. If that happens, what am I going to do?"

"Don't worry," I said. "We will manage on our own somehow."

It was OK me saying to Diane it would be all right. The living expenses I could manage, but there were course fees and umpteen other things Diane needed in order to complete her training. These things started to go round in my head and I wondered how the hell I could afford them.

Another week passed and Diane's six-week stint in the casualty department was up. It was on that Friday evening that Diane said to me:

"Terry, now that I have finished at the hospital and there's not a lot of the summer left, do you mind if we go to Hastings tomorrow for the weekend, to see my aunt and uncle? I'd like them to meet you properly and I wanted a little break before I continue with my course work. It would only cost the petrol money, because we can stay at their place and because they will insist on feeding us."

"OK," I replied. "But you had better give them a call first to confirm if it will be all right for us to visit."

"I'll do it right now then," she replied.

I was sorting out a few things in the bedroom when after about half an hour, Diane finally put the receiver down and came into the bedroom and said, "My aunt said that they would be pleased to see us tomorrow and is looking forward to meeting you."

"That's all right then," I replied. "Let's leave early in the morning by about 7:00 a.m., so we can get there by about 8:30 a.m."

"Great," Diane replied.

We got up nice and early that Saturday morning and I checked the weather report from the radio, which said it was going to be a fine warm day. Packing the bare essentials into the car, we were nearly ready for the off when Diane said, "Hang on a minute, Terry. Have you packed your swimming trunks?"

"No," I replied. "Where are we going to swim?"

Diane replied, "In the sea, of course. I like swimming in the sea."

"You're joking," I said. "The water's freezing."

"Don't be a woosey. It'll be warm enough." She replied.

Reluctantly, I sorted through my bedroom drawers and came across my Speedos. I just hoped they'd still fit as I hadn't been swimming since I was about sixteen. Finally with two large holdalls of clothes and toiletries, we set off for Hastings.

The journey down to the coast usually took about an hour and a half, but as we had left early, we arrived at Diane's aunt and uncle's place about twenty past eight. Diane told me to drive around the back of the restaurant as there was a courtyard there where we could park the car. I hadn't really explored Hastings before and was quite surprised to find at the rear of the restaurants and shops there was a little cobbled street, which was just wide enough for my car. Having driven down it about half way, I pulled into the restaurant's small courtyard and parked. As we got out, Diane's aunt and uncle came out of their backdoor to greet us. Her uncle was a tall, thin man with greying hair. Her aunt was a lot shorter than him and was quite rounded in appearance. Both were wearing aprons and they looked as if they were both in their late fifties.

"Hiya," Diane said to them.

Her uncle came toward me, offering his hand to shake as he said to Diane, "So this is the lad you met in our restaurant."

"I'm Terry, pleased to meet you," I said.

"Call me Bob," he replied, with a big smile.

As she stepped back a pace to let her aunt through to me, Diane said, "And this is my aunt, Sally."

I chuckled a bit in my head. *Aunt Sally,* I thought as I bent down to kiss her on the cheek.

"Hello, Terry," she said. "I've heard a lot about you."

I replied, "All good I hope."

With all the greeting formalities over with, Diane and I got our holdalls out of the car and went through the open rear door, straight into the restaurant's kitchen. We were closely followed by Bob and Sally. Diane then led me up four narrow flights of stairs that looked and felt as if they had come out of a haunted house. The stairs, leaning to one side, had apparently shifted over the years and creaked like crazy.

Finally at the top of the house, we came to an attic room.

"This is the room I stay in when I visit," Diane said.

The room was quite small, with blackened wooden beams to support the sloping roof. The floor was also leaning to one side quite a lot and you had the feeling you were going to topple over as you walked on it. There were two single beds pushed against opposite walls and an old oak dressing table with a mirror in front of the small, single-sash window facing the front and overlooking the sea. The room was a bit dingy really, but it was clean, so I wasn't complaining as it suited us for just one night.

After unpacking our things and pushing the two single beds together, we went back down the stairs and into the kitchen where Bob and Sally had lots of pots and pans boiling away on a large, old-fashioned multi-burner cooker. In the middle of the room, there was an old pine table, on which Sally placed a couple of plates, each loaded up with a full English breakfast.

"Come on, tuck in," she said.

I wasn't used to eating a large breakfast, but I felt as if I had to comply so as not to offend anyone. The restaurant opened at 10:00 a.m., so Diane and I wanted to be out before things started to become busy. So after the huge breakfast, Diane said, "Come on, let's go up to the cliffs."

I felt as if I could do with walking that breakfast off, so I readily agreed.

We came out of the front of the restaurant, turned left and headed to where the road ended and the beach stopped at the base of the cliffs. This was where all the fishing boats were dry docked and leaning to one side on the steep pebbles. Across from the fishing boats was a large brown and cream coloured railed lift car at the foot of the cliffs. For a small amount of money, it took us up and gave us a fantastic view of the whole town, as it ascended.

When the lift reached the top, the doors opened to a vast grassed area with a serpentine trodden path, about six feet away from the contours of the unfenced cliff edge. With the sun glaring down on us from a cloudless, blue sky, we walked hand in hand along the path for about a quarter of a mile, until we came across a small copse higher up on the grassy expanse. We decided to sit on the grass just in front of the trees and take in the warm sunshine and the ozone-filled air. As I started to lie back, I could swear, from the corner of my eye, I saw a portal flash open and close in the sky. It may have been just a trick of the light, or there again it might have been one of the Terran ships slipping back into their own dimension. Whatever it was, it was there and gone in a flash and was not worth telling Diane about.

"This is the life," Diane said, as we both lay flat on our backs.

"Yes," I replied. "It's a pity summer didn't last all year round. I dread the cold of winter."

"You really don't like being cold, do you, Terry?" Diane said.

"No, I don't," I replied. "I suppose it's because when I was small, I went to bed with big heavy coats over the top of my blankets to keep me warm. We only had coal or a feeble electric fire back then and you couldn't leave either of them burning all night. Those coats nearly crushed me, but it was either that or freeze."

Diane said, "Well, we've got gas fires now and you have got me to keep you warm at night."

I smiled and leaned over to kiss her when I spotted a cream-coloured butterfly with black dots resting on her arm.

"Have you seen that butterfly?" I said, pointing to her arm.

"Yes, it has been there for a couple of minutes now" she replied.

As she finished speaking another butterfly landed next to the first. Then after about thirty seconds, one by one, ten of fifteen different coloured butterfly were fluttering all around her.

I remarked, "I've never seen anything like that before."

She replied, "It's never happened before, Terry. It must be the deodorant I'm using."

With a big grin on my face, I replied, "It's amazing! You must have been a fairy princess in a former life and now you are the queen of the butterflies."

"Ha! Ha!" Diane said sarcastically, as she sat up and gently tapped me on my arm and as she made that movement, the chorus of butterflies dispersed.

"Come on. Let's go down to the beach," she said, as she stood up.

I followed suit and Diane put her arm around my waist and I put my arm around her shoulders. Then, we leisurely ambled back to the cliff's lift. Those butterflies seemed to flutter above our heads all the way back, something which I thought to be very strange!

As we got out of the lift at the bottom, we headed toward the beach, passing between the fishing boats and avoiding the heavy rusty chains and thick ropes that secured them to large, wooden, sea beaten posts, which were driven deep into the sand beneath the pebbles. A white froth residue was left behind as the flowing tide crept onto the short expanse of sand at the water's edge and there was a line of seaweed, which moved backward and forward with the sea's movement. As we walked just a few feet away from the water's edge, we left our footprints in the spongy, wet sand, which then disappeared with the next ebb of seawater. Passing beneath the pier as we strolled, I noticed the beach had started to fill up with holidaymakers with their deck chairs springing up everywhere. We finally arrived directly opposite Bob and Sally's restaurant, so we made our way up the beach to the promenade and to the kerb of the busy road. Carefully crossing, we entered the half-full restaurant and went straight through the opening of the coloured plastic strips into the kitchen.

"Hiya, Uncle," Diane said. "We are just going up to get changed for the beach. Is that OK?"

"Course it is, love," Bob replied, as he flipped over a piece of fish in a huge, blackened frying pan. Sally was just coming down the stairs, with a fresh box of serviettes to put on the tables and she must have heard what Diane had said to Bob.

"You going for a swim?" she said, addressing Diane.

"Yes," Diane replied.

Sally then said with concern in her voice, "Be careful in that water, won't you? And don't swim out too far." Obviously she knew what Diane was like and knew she had a bit of a cavalier attitude toward her own safety.

We continued upstairs and got changed for the beach. Diane put on a lemon yellow bikini, which didn't leave much for the imagination, but she looked absolutely stunning, with her long blonde hair loosely trailing down her back. Her flip-flop sandals, with yellow and white daisies on the tops, completed her attire. I donned my blue Speedo trunks, which were a little on the tight side as I must have had them for a good few years and had now put on a bit more weight. On my feet I had to wear my day trainers, as I didn't own any kind of sandal.

Taking a couple of large towels from the airing cupboard in the bathroom, Diane said, "Right, that's it we're all set. Let's go."

With our towels rolled up under our arms, we came down the stairs through the restaurant and onto the pavement facing the busy road. Every time I crossed that road, I thought that it really needed a pedestrian crossing, but after managing to dart between passing cars, we reached the promenade on the other side, then went straight onto the beach. With the pebbles giving way beneath our feet with every step, Diane held my hand as we negotiated our way around the basking holidaymakers. We finally stopped at the top of the first ridge of pebbles, about ten feet from the water's edge and laid our towels down onto the hard, bumpy surface.

"Come on," Diane said.

In a flash, she ran from our base camp, straight into the sea's crashing waves and started swimming out into deeper water.

"Hang on!" I shouted.

Although the sun was fairly hot, I knew that the sea was freezing cold and I wasn't about to leap into it without testing it with my big toe. Diane was already bobbing up and down about twenty feet from the shore, shouting.

"Come on in, you big sissy."

Even being egged on by Diane's taunts was not going to make me take a leap of faith.

That water was bloody freezing and it was going to take a fair bit of psyching up for me to enter it, so I stood at the water's edge, letting the tail end of the advancing waves just roll over my toes, while swinging my arms about, as if I was limbering up. I suppose I wasn't fooling anyone as it was probably obvious to my onlookers, including Diane, that I was just fearful of taking the plunge.

After a good few minutes, I had ventured into the sea up to my calves and I didn't know whether I had become accustomed to the water temperature or my lower extremities had just gone numb—but all the time I had Diane in my sights. She had stopped swimming and was now standing on the seabed, seemingly looking around the immediate vicinity of her body.

"Come and have a look at this," she shouted with a *must see* tone to her voice.

I was a little worried and that was enough to spur me on to fully enter the icy wetness. After diving in, I quickly overcame the temperature shock and swam out to Diane's location. The depth of water came up to about the height of Diane's waist.

"Look," she said, indicating by pointing with a moving finger. There was a fish about six inches long, seemingly swimming in a complete circle around her. Then another appeared and another and after a few minutes, there seem to be about fifty fish all swimming around her.

I was a couple of feet away from Diane and to complete the fish's circuit, they were all passing right in front of me.

"That's strange," I said.

"Yeah, it's never happened before," Diane replied, as she stroked the fish as they swam bye.

"They're not biting you, are they?" I said, with concern.

She replied, "Not at all, they just seem to want to be near to me."

After a few minutes of watching these fish form a moving ring around Diane, I was starting to feel my fingers, as well as my legs, go numb, so I said, "Sorry Diane, my blood must be a lot thinner than yours and I'm really cold. I'm going back to the towels. Are you coming?"

She replied, "You go. I'll come back in a minute after having a little swim."

With that I swam rapidly back to the beach and painfully trod those hard pebbles as fast as I could to wrap a towel round my upper body. I could see that Diane was enjoying herself with her new fishy friends and somehow I knew there was no need to worry.

Five or so minutes passed when my body had finished visibly shaking and the rattle of my chattering teeth was no longer audible. I finished drying myself off and let the sun do the rest to bring my body temperature back to normal. Diane had been swimming to the left and right of me during this time and had kept about the same distance out, so I was glad that she had always been in my field of vision, but I was relieved that she was now on her way back to me.

As she came out of the water and neared me, I threw her the other towel and then she purposely shook her dripping hair all over my nicely warmed body.

"That was great," she said. "You didn't last long, though."

"No, sorry," I replied. "I just can't stand being cold."

"What about those fish, though?" she said.

"I've never seen anything like it. You must have some sort of affinity with living things.

First the butterflies, and now the fish. Maybe one of your ancestors was the pied piper," I remarked, jokingly.

Suffering another sprinkling of cold water from Diane's hair as she threw it back, I sat down on my towel and laying her towel next to mine, she sat beside me.

"Seriously, Terry, all these strange things that are happening with me only started when I met you. I feel very lucky."

"Whoa!" I said. "I'm the lucky one having met you. I love you very much and don't know what I would do without you now."

Diane smiled and kissed me hard on the lips, then said, "You'll never be without me, Terry."

Hearing those words from Diane certainly warmed me right up and I remember thinking life couldn't be more perfect. After a few more minutes, she said, "I'm feeling a bit hungry now after than swim. Shall we go back now?

"OK," I replied. "But we had better not have fish, or your friends out there in the sea might want to eat you next time."

We put our damp towels around our waists and with effort, hand in hand; we made our way up the pebbles to the promenade and to the edge of the busy road. I held Diane's hand tightly as I scanned for a safe gap between the traffic. A large blue and white coach was coming along on our side of the road, so I wanted to wait for it to pass before I could get a better view for when to cross.

As it approached, a thirtyish looking man in a red T-shirt and shorts brushed my arm and ran past us into the road; supposedly, he thought he would have enough time to reach the other side, but this wasn't the case.

Bang! The sound of the coach hitting the man echoed out. The driver immediately stopped and got out of his coach shouting, "He ran out in front of me. I didn't have time to brake."

All the traffic and pedestrians alike stood completely still and a ghostly silence fell over the entire area. The accident happened so fast I had no time to freeze the man in his tracks before he attempted to cross. Pulling at my hand, Diane said with urgency,

"Come on, Terry, we must help him."

Diane lunged forward, but I pulled her backward and threw both my arms around her body.

"Look, it's too late," I said forcibly.

As we looked at the man crumpled in the middle of the road, an opaque replica of himself arose from his body and stood over his lifeless corpse. The man's effigy seemed to look directly at us when a rainbow-tinged portal opened a few feet in front of him. Slowly his spirit started to move toward it. Just before his ghostly form entered, he once again looked back in our direction, as if he knew we were the only ones that could see his final presence in this life and then as soon as he entered, it zapped shut. Diane turned her body towards mine and began to cry floods of tears.

"We can't save everyone," I said.

Slowly the eerie silence began to develop into a host of voices all talking at once and the sound of an ambulance siren became louder. With all traffic at a standstill, I ushered Diane across the road and into the restaurant, passing her aunt and uncle standing outside the door. Still cradling Diane sobbing in my arms, I pushed passed some of the diners, who stood in the gangway looking out the door and then we headed upstairs to our room.

Diane was really upset by what we had witnessed and it upset me too, seeing her cry like that. Once in our room and sitting on one of the beds, I put my arm around her and said, "Come on, Diane, please stop crying. I hate to see you like this."

Sobbingly, she replied, "I've never seen anyone die before, especially like that. Even the old man at the hospital who had a heart attack, I wasn't present at his death. I suppose I just thought that I could cure or save anyone around me, except of course if they died of old age, but that man was too young to die. Why the hell did he dash into a busy road like that?"

"Who knows why people do such stupid things," I said. "But it happens. We will never know the reason why, but we've just got to accept it. At least we know there are people we can save."

Wiping the tears from her puffy red eyes, Diane replied, "You're right, Terry. There are people we can save and I'm supposed to become a doctor. It just wouldn't do for me to break down like this every time someone died on me, would it? I'm glad I've got you to make me see sense. I'm going to be stronger in future and not get so emotional, I promise."

I handed Diane a clean handkerchief from a pocket in my jeans, which I had left on the bed after getting changed for the beach. She blew hard into it leaving plenty of...Well I suppose you'd call it, wet snot.

"Come on," I said. "Let's have something to eat, get showered and dressed and go out for the night. We're wasting time, sitting up here moping."

Diane nodded in agreement.

We had a light meal at the table in the restaurant's kitchen and Diane was feeling much better. After our shower, I put on a clean white shirt, blue-flared trousers and a pair of black platform shoes, which made me look at least an inch taller than I actually was.

Diane wore a scarlet red blouse, a matching miniskirt and red high heeled shoes. Wearing her red outfit, she looked really hot, so much so, I wouldn't have been surprised if she had caught fire.

It was still light outside, but the sun was beginning to go down.

"I know," Diane said. "Let's go to The "*Sundowner.*"

"What's that?" I said, thinking of the coincidence.

"It's a discotheque," Diane replied. "It's about a quarter of a mile along the main road. It used to be a cinema called the Roxy until a couple of years back. It's only a couple of pounds to get in. You'll like it."

"What are we waiting for then?" I asked.

Although the sun was setting, the evening still seemed to be fairly warm, so neither of us decided to wear anything else except what we had changed into after we ate. After telling Diane's aunt and uncle where we were headed, we came out of the restaurant's main door. Everything seemed to have gone back to normal outside. People were going about their business in all directions and the traffic was back to its usual manic racetrack. All that was left of the man's horrific death was a couple of shovels of blood-stained sand which was now spread thin and had a multitude of tyre tread marks embedded into it. Having reverently passed that spot, we walked hand in hand and to the disco place Diane had mentioned. As we arrived at the discotheque, I noticed that this large building stood detached from its neighbours and had narrow, dark alleyways on either side. Presumably these alleys must have been the exits from the cinema that it once was. After joining the queue from the pavement and up the steps, we finally reached the ticket office, where we got our wrists stamped with an invisible mark. We then went through two large doors into the main disco area. It was quite dark inside except for the flashing coloured lights that seemed to flash to the beat of the music.

There was also a white strobe light that would bring on a fit to anyone photo sensitive and a constant ultraviolet light, which made my white shirt look as if I was in an advert for washing powder. I also noticed that this light showed up the invisible stamp on our wrists with the word *Sundowner* imprinted on them. We managed to navigate our way across the packed dance floor and find a table and a couple of seats in a far corner of this once ornate auditorium. I asked Diane what she would like to drink and she said she wanted an orange juice. Diane was like me and didn't drink alcohol, so I left her to guard my seat while I headed for the bar to get our soft drinks. Understandably the bar was also packed and it took me a good ten minutes to get Diane's juice and my usual Coca-Cola, with no ice.

Heading back to our little nook and dodging my way around the dancers, while desperately trying not to spill the drinks in the not so sturdy plastic cups, I saw that there was someone sitting next to Diane in my seat. As I neared our table, the flashing lights revealed a man of about twenty-five years of age and as Diane saw me, she immediately said, in a stressed way, "I've told this man that I am with you, but he won't go away."

Looking straight at the man, I said, "Sorry, mate, but she is with me and you're in my seat."

The man then stood up, stepped forward and put his face close to mine. He was about six foot three inches tall and built like one of those outside places with a toilet in them; his breath smelled the same. In a threatening way, he replied, "Why don't you push off, squirt? Can't you see the lady would rather be with me than you?"

I suppose it had to happen sooner or later; Diane was a good-looking woman and was bound to attract other men.

"Look, mate," I said, quite calmly. "We have come here to have a night out. We don't want any trouble. Please just go."

Taking a swig from his pint of beer, he replied, "I thought I just asked you to push off, didn't I?"

With his pint in one hand, he went to shove me with the other, but somehow I instinctively knew the shove was coming and I immediately froze him. Calmly I put our drinks on the table and then tilted the pint of beer in his hand, so the contents soaked the front of his trousers. For him, time hadn't stopped, but the few seconds he was motionless allowed me to put the situation in my favour. Afterward, I quickly released the freeze.

"Seems like you've wet yourself," I said. "What girl is going to want a bloke who can't hold his drink?"

Realising he was holding his tilted glass toward his soaked trousers, he said, "I don't know how you did it, but I know you did this to me. I'm going to get you for that."

With that threat, he went off, walking distinctly bowed legged.

I regained my seat next to Diane and she started laughing. I chuckled along.

"That was quick thinking," she said.

"Yes," I replied. "He won't want to spend the rest of the night with wet trousers, will he?"

We soon forgot about the incident, as we sipped our expensive soft drinks and laughed a lot at some of the weird dance moves people were doing, although I couldn't dance to save my life. After some lively tunes, the disc jockey played "Theme from a Summer Place" by Percy Faith. It was an instrumental, mainly composed of violins and the tempo created the mood for a slow dance.

"Come on, Terry," Diane said, jumping up and dragging me onto the dance floor. "This is my favourite tune."

As I said, I was no dancer, but I could shift my weight from one leg to the other for a slow one like any other and with Diane's arms around my neck and my arms around her waist, we held each other as close as we could.

I don't think we actually moved from the same spot, but we managed to sway our way all through that tune, with the occasional loving kiss, of course, to capture the moment. Although it was Diane's favourite tune, it turned out to be a ploy by her to get me onto the dance floor for the rest of that evening. I was in no doubt that there was another couple sitting down somewhere taking the rise out of me, but after that first dance, I didn't really care.

We ended up having a great evening and, at about 1:30 a.m., we decided we had better get back to the restaurant. The cool air hit our partly sweaty bodies coming down the steps outside the disco club and as we turned left from the main entrance and started to walk, we huddled together for warmth.

Now this is strange! When I was young, I was always taught, as a protective courtesy to women, to walk on the pavement on the nearest side to the road when walking with a female. This was to guard her from any vehicles that came too close to the kerb. In this instance, when we came out of the disco club, Diane was the one nearest to the road and I didn't instinctively change position. It turned out that it was fortunate that I didn't because as we passed the dark exit alleyway of the disco, the man who had his trousers soaked jumped out at us, with a raging look on his face and brandishing a knife.

"I said I'd get you," he said, as he lunged toward me thrusting the knife forward. It all seemed to happen very quickly and the knife slashed my left arm, as I put it up in defence and the blood immediately soaked the sleeve of my white shirt. Diane screamed, but as she did I froze the man in his tracks, fearing that Diane might get hurt. While the man was static, I disarmed him and threw the knife far down the alley. Then, probably because I was so angry, I punched him squarely in his face and his nose splattered and bled instantly. The punch had released him from my freezing influence and he landed in a heap on the floor, clutching his nose. Half sobbing as the blood streamed between his fingers and down his shirt, he said, "You've broken by dose."

I replied indignantly, "You asked for it, mate."

With concern for me, Diane said, "Let me take a look at your arm Terry" and pulled back the blooded sleeve of my shirt. Although the knife had cut me pretty deeply, there wasn't a mark to be seen. Diane looked up at me with an open mouth, which then turned to a beaming smile.

"Come on, let's get back," I said.

Diane got close to me cuddling my blooded, sleeved arm with both her arms as we continued on our way.

Having crept back into the darkened restaurant and quietly up the stairs to our room, we got undressed and although we had basically been on our feet all night, we still found the energy to make love. Soon after that, of course, feeling totally exhausted, we both fell asleep.

It was about 10:30 a.m. the next morning when there was a loud rap on our door with Sally's voice shouting, "Are you two going to lie in bed all day? There's breakfast downstairs if you want it."

As we both smartly sat up in bed startled by Sally's wake-up call, we looked at each other and quietly laughed. That is when a warming thought came over me: we were being treated like a married couple by Diane's family and to me that felt good.

We had our breakfast and decided to take a final walk along the beach before we packed up our things to head back home. We had decided to leave Hastings in the early afternoon so as not to get caught up in a possible traffic jam on the way back to London. After tidying our room and separating the single beds again, we loaded all our things into the car. I suppose I hadn't seen much of Sally and Bob during our stay, but I really felt that they were now part of my family and our thanks and good-byes to them, from my point of view, seemed much closer and warmer than when we had arrived.

The drive back to London went well, with no major hold ups and we got back to the flat by late afternoon. Having parked the car and lugged our hold-alls up the stairs, I sat on the sofa with the fingers of my hands linked behind my head and reflected on the events of the previous day, while Diane made us some coffee. While thinking, I was oblivious to what was around me, but then suddenly I looked at the flowers in the Wellington boot, sitting on the television.

"When did you get fresh flowers, Diane?" I asked.

"I haven't," she replied.

"You mean they are the same ones you bought six weeks ago?"

"Yes," she said.

I hadn't noticed before, but those cut flowers had not wilted once in those six weeks. I wondered if it was my smelly-welly that was keeping them alive or if something had been added to our water supply, but the obvious answer was that every time Diane took them out of the Wellington boot to change the water, her touch had revived them. To me that was more proof of her affinity with all living things and her healing capabilities.

My wonderment of Diane's capabilities was interrupted by the phone ringing. It was my sister, Linda. She gave me the good news that Steven, my nephew, was now at home and completely healthy again, but she also wanted to speak to Diane. Diane had just put the coffees down onto the table by the sofa, so I gestured her to the phone by holding out the receiver in her direction. As I handed her the receiver, I whispered with my hand over the mouthpiece, "Linda wants to speak to you."

I was a little puzzled that Linda wanted to speak to Diane, as she had only met her that one time, but I sat on the sofa with my ears pricked, as I began to drink my coffee.

About five minutes passed before Diane finally put the receiver down and all I could overhear during the conversation was Diane saying lots of *yeahs, rights*, *OKs* and finally *thanks*. I asked, "What was all that about?"

With a smile Diane said, "Mind your own business."

I replied, "Come on, I'm intrigued."

Diane relented. “Your sister said that I must have been right about Steven having an allergic reaction to something, although the doctor at the hospital said that he had been ninety-nine percent sure he had meningitis. She told him what I had said about it being an allergic reaction and although sceptical, he ran allergy tests. None of the tests showed up anything, of course, but he conceded and said that’s what it must have been. He also said that I would make a good doctor if I, being a mere student, could make a correct diagnosis like that. Linda also thanked me for my support at the hospital and said that you are one lucky sod to have met me.”

I replied, “Well, she’s not wrong about that.”

We finished our coffees and Diane went to wash the cups up. I felt rather smug as I thought about the way I could self-heal and that even if I couldn’t, Diane could probably keep me alive like those flowers that didn’t wilt in the Wellington boot. But then it struck me: Diane was now the most precious person in my life, but who would heal her if something happened? Maybe she could self-heal, but then again, maybe she couldn’t!

I now felt as if I must be diligent at all times to make sure she would not get into any situation where she might get harmed, especially as I knew that she could be a bit reckless with her own safety.

The following Tuesday evening, after our trip to Hastings, my father rang me to say that he had finally sold the business and that the new owners did not need me, as they had their own work team. That meant at the end of the week I would be out of a job, but my Dad did say that he could manage to give me two-thousand pounds severance pay out of the deal, which should give me enough money to tide me over till I got another job. That was quite a lot of money in those days, but I knew it wasn’t going to last forever.

6

I thought it was going to be a good idea Diane and I both being at home together every day, but it wasn't really an ideal situation. After a couple of weeks of Diane being totally engrossed in her studies and me pottering about doing housework and looking through the newspapers every day to find another job, I felt my presence was distracting her and I was uncomfortable about being idle all day with no income.

One day, totally bored silly, I was sitting on the sofa looking at my eighteenth birthday gift, the plastic cup, the one I had tried to levitate with my mind when I first found out I could freeze things. I don't know why, but for some reason I again thought of the cup rising from the shelf. At first, it wobbled from side to side, then to my amazement it lifted off the shelf a couple of inches. Diane could not see this as she was sitting at the dining table, with her back to me and facing the window, oblivious to anything not related to her studying.

With my mind, I played around with the cup, moving it through the air in all directions and then finally sitting it back down to its original position. My freezing powers had now evolved into full telekinesis. I tried other objects and found no difficulty raising and moving them about at will. Although I was ecstatic as I thought of the possibilities my new found ability could bring, I still did not want to disturb Diane's intense concentration. A couple of minutes passed after I had finished testing my new skill when Diane turned toward me and said, "Terry, would you please pass me that book on the top of the pile at the side of the wardrobe?"

I said, "OK," as she turned her back to me again. This was a great opportunity for me to show Diane what I could now do.

With my mind, I made the book she had asked for rise from the top of the pile.

I then skilfully floated it across the room and stopped it in mid-air near to her left shoulder, in a position that was similar to me handing it to her from behind. As she briefly looked round to take the book and saying "thanks" as she did, she almost jumped out of her seat.

"Ooo, w-what's going on?" she said, as she looked at me sitting on the sofa, bursting with laughter.

"Magic," I replied.

"How long have you been able to do that?" she said with amazement.

"About five minutes," I said.

She stood up from her chair, walked over and sat next to me on the sofa. "That could come in very useful," she said. "Show me more."

"What shall I try?" I said.

"Try something heavy," she replied.

She then stood up, faced me and said, "Try me."

"I'm not sure about that," I replied. "I've only just found out that I can do it. What if I drop you or something?"

"If you can levitate me, Terry, I know that you wouldn't drop me."

There it was again—Diane's disregard for her own safety—so if I could lift her from the floor with my mind, I would make sure it wasn't going to be too high.

"Stand back a bit then," I said.

Diane stood about six feet away from me.

"Are you ready?"

"Yep, go for it," she said.

I visualised Diane's body arising from the floor about six inches and to both our amazement, up she went as steady as a rock.

"This is like flying!" she exclaimed.

Not pushing my luck too far, I gently lowered her back to the floor. Once her feet made a touchdown, she ran over to me, gave me a big kiss and said, "That was fantastic. Do you think that was another side effect of when Madri closed the portal for you?"

"No," I replied. "When Madri first gave me a brain scan on Terran, she said that I should be capable of powers like that, but she didn't know why I couldn't use them. With all that's happened and meeting you, it must have triggered something inside my brain."

I gave Diane a hug and said, "Now all I've got to do is figure out how we can use it to our advantage."

"I do love you, Terry," she said warmly.

I replied jokingly, "Now get back to work, you slacker."

While Diane resumed her work and I looked through the papers for jobs without success, my mind went back to the time I thought about being rich and not having to worry about money. In my mind, I gradually formulated a plan—the only trouble was would Diane go for it?

One evening when Diane was taking a break from book worming, we were sitting on the sofa watching a program on the television. The program was just finishing and I had it in my mind to run my idea of getting lots of money by her after it had ended.

"I've got an idea that I want to tell you about. It's about money," I said, with a slight hesitance in my voice.

"OK, go on then." she replied, squinting a little.

"Right," I said.

"Do you remember when we first met and we went to see that Bond film?"

"Yes," she replied.

I continued. "Well, I won the money to pay for it on the fruit machines. The only thing is..." I hesitated slightly. "Well, I suppose I cheated a bit. Well, that's not quite true either: I cheated a lot."

"How did you manage that?" she said, a bit taken back.

"I froze the barrels of the machines to stop on winning symbols. Do you think I was dishonest?"

"Of course, you were dishonest," she said. "Let's go back to the seaside and do it again. The owners of those machines earn a fortune without having to do a thing and nine times out of ten; they fix the machines, so that no one ever wins anything decent on them. It doesn't bother me one little bit how you won."

I replied, "If you feel that way about it, I'm going to tell you what I have in mind."

Deep down I knew Diane wouldn't feel any less of me if I told her the truth about my winnings: as I had said before, that maverick element was definitely in her.

I continued, saying, "Right, are you sitting comfortably? Then I'll begin. No interruptions until I have completely finished though, OK!"

"OK!" she repeated.

"Facts: your dad has lost his job and cannot afford to support you anymore. I am also out of work, but my dad is giving me two-thousand pounds severance pay. Paying the rent for the flat, general living costs and the money needed to complete your training; that two-thousand pounds isn't going to last long. Now, this is a bit of a gamble, literally, but this is what I propose: you and I use a big chunk of that money to go to Las Vegas for a week."

Diane's eyes started to bulge, followed by a concerned expression on her face, but she didn't speak.

I continued. "We stay in a cheap hotel and go round all the casinos to find the ones we feel comfortable about. I'll explain what I mean if you agree to what I say. I want you to play on the roulette wheels and if it all works out OK, we will never have to worry about money ever again. Also, this is the best bit: if all goes well and we are financially OK, I'd like us to get married when we get back. Right, you can speak now."

Diane said, "Did you just ask me to marry you, Terry?"

"Yes, of course, I did. I love you to bits and I want you to be my wife, but with **my** job, even if I find one, there's no way I can give us a good start together."

"Well, it's a funny proposal, but yes, I want to marry you too," she said.

I smiled then said, "But what about all the other stuff though. What do you think?"

She pondered then said, "How is it that I have got to do the gambling?"

"Because I'm not old enough," I replied. "You have got to be twenty-one to gamble in America."

As she paused again for a little while, I could literally see her brain ticking.

"Let's do it," she said. "I've always wanted to go to Las Vegas. Hold on though! I haven't got a passport. I've never been abroad before."

"Neither have I," I replied. "But don't worry about that. I'll get everything sorted out."

Diane then exclaimed, with a joyous shout, followed by a big beautiful grin, "Yes! We're going to Vegas!"

Now that Diane had agreed to my plan, the next hurdle would be to tell our parents. I'd also need to come up with a believable explanation to them as to why we were going to take the trip. We decided that the following Sunday, we would visit my parents in the morning and Diane's in the afternoon, to get our explanations for going to Vegas over with all in one day. We were both dreading it as lying didn't come easy to either of us, but nevertheless we phoned our respective parents to let them know we would be visiting them and hoped our explanation would be met with some approval.

That Sunday we arrived at my parent's house late morning and as usual my mother opened the front door as we got out of the car. As always, if she knew someone was visiting, my mother would be looking out for them from behind the curtains in the lounge. Diane went in front of me, as I was locking the car.

"Hello, you two. It's lovely to see you," Mum said, overjoyed.

"Hello, Rose, you are looking well," Diane replied, offering my mum a bunch of flowers we had bought on the way over. As usual, we were ushered into the lounge where my father was sitting in his armchair. Diane and I sat on the sofa next to each other.

"Have you come to pick up your cheque?" my dad said.

"Well, yes, but that isn't the only reason we are here. We wanted to see how you and Mum were getting on," I replied.

"I'll put the kettle on," Mum said, smelling the flowers as she made her way to the kitchen.

In the corner of the room was a polished wooden bureau, with a flap that came open to form a writing desk. For as long as I could remember, my dad had always had that bureau, which he kept his important papers in and from which he did all the bookwork from for his business. He stood up from his armchair, went over to the bureau, opened the flap and from the inside he took out a cheque that he had previously made out to me.

"There you go, son. Don't spend it all at once, will you?" he said, handing me the cheque then reseating himself.

"Thanks, Dad," I replied.

Just then, my mother entered the room with a tray of cups, sugar, milk and a teapot with a woollen cosy on it.

"Blimey, that was quick," I said.

I'm sure my mother must have pre-boiled the kettle just before we arrived.

"How's the studying going, Diane?" my mother said as she started pouring the tea into the cups.

Diane replied, "Oh, not bad. There's a lot to get through, though."

My mother then said, "Isn't it great news about Steven? The paediatric consultant Mr. Williams seemed very impressed with your diagnosis of him; and how good is that offering you a job at Great Ormond Street hospital when you qualify." (That hospital was the most notable children's hospital in England.) I looked straight at Diane. She hadn't told me that bit of information when she informed me what Linda had said to her on the phone, but I didn't let on to my parents that I didn't know.

Diane replied to my mum, "Yes, I'm glad that Steven is all right now. Linda must have really been worried."

After sipping a drop of my hot tea, I said, "Sorry to change the subject, but there's something we have to tell you."

My mum's face lit up. "Diane, you're not pregnant are you?"

"No, Mum," I replied.

Funny how that is the first thing that comes into people's heads when a young couple says, "We've got something to tell you."

Taking a deeper breath than usual, I continued, "You know I've been trying for weeks to get another job. Well, jobs are just not about in London at the moment, but I've seen an advertisement for English plasterers in Las Vegas and they are paying really good money. Work is available on a hotel casino called the Union Plaza, so Diane and I are going over there to check it out. I know it will cost us a lot of money to do it, but to be honest I think it is worth the gamble and besides Diane could do with a holiday away from all that studying. If nothing becomes of it, well at least I would have tried. We will only be gone a week, but if I do manage to get work there, Diane will return home by herself. You've always told me, Dad, 'You've got to speculate to accumulate.' Isn't that so?" I added at a rate of knots so that I couldn't be interrupted.

After taking a moment to digest my hastened monologue, my dad replied, "You're right Terry, I have always said that. I think it's a bit risky though, but you go for it son, and have a bloody good time while you're at it. Good for you."

My mum couldn't believe her ears that my father was actually agreeing with what I had said and quite frankly I couldn't believe it either, but she could see that the idea of the trip had been finalised between my father and I, so she offered no criticism, which I was very relieved about.

"Oh and by the way," I said, "I have asked Diane to marry me and she has said yes."

My mother's expression changed from mild concern to jubilation. "Why didn't you tell us that news first? It's much more important than any job you're going for. It's wonderful news," she said as she came over to Diane and me kissing us both in turn on our cheek.

"You two were made for each other," she concluded.

My dad then said, after staring at us for a moment. "We've got some news, too. In three weeks' time, we will be moving. We've bought a bungalow, not in the countryside as we originally intended, but on the coast."

I said, "Don't tell me, let me guess, Hastings!"

"What's wrong with Hastings?" my dad sternly remarked. "And how did you know anyway? We haven't told anyone yet, not even your sister."

With a little chuckle, Diane spoke, "There's nothing wrong with Hastings, Harry. It's just a coincidence, that's all. I have an aunt and uncle who own a fish restaurant there and it is also where Terry and I met."

My mother then said, "Then that makes it all the more reason to move there then. I knew it would be the right decision."

There was a short interlude while everyone seemed to drink their tea all at the same time and while I was finishing mine, I thought how strange it was that as we go through life, coincidences keep cropping up. We tend to think of them just as events that connect, but I'm not sure if that is really what they are. Could it be that these events are predetermined right from the time we are born? This might be the reason why ancient Greeks and Romans believed that humans were just pawns in a game that were played by the gods and human destiny was just part of their stratagem. All I really knew was that the coincidences in my life just lately seemed to be occurring more and more often.

"Oh, I just thought," I said. "As we are planning to go to Las Vegas in three weeks' time, we won't be around to help you move."

"Oh, don't worry about that," my father said. "The removal firm will take care of everything. We had better give you our new address and phone number though for when you get back."

With that, my mother went over to the bureau, pulled down the flap and produced a piece of paper with the address and phone number of their new abode. She then came over and gave it to me, which I then put in my pocket as I stood up.

"We had better be off now," I said. "We are going over to Diane's parent's place now, to tell them our news."

"OK, then," my mum said. "But you two keep in touch and mind how you go."

"We will, Mum and thanks for that cheque dad," I said, as Diane and I made our way toward the door.

"Bye, then!" Diane said. "See you again soon."

We left my mum waving from the doorstep as we drove off and headed for Diane's parent's house and on the journey I said to Diane, "How come you didn't tell me that the consultant had offered you a job when you qualify?"

Diane replied, "I didn't tell you because the job offer was based on a lie. I told Linda that Steven was probably allergic to something, when I knew full well he had meningitis. I just *knew* I could cure him, so I had to come up with something that was at least feasible. The consultant thinks I must have been correct about the allergy as Steven recovered quickly and without any side effects. I couldn't consider the job offer on that basis."

"But the fact is you did diagnose Steven correctly. You knew he had meningitis and if you hadn't been able to cure him that would have been your diagnosis."

"Yes," Diane replied. "But I wouldn't have told Linda that. How would you feel if someone who was not qualified told you your son has probably got a serious life threatening illness?"

"Yes, I suppose you're right, as always," I said. "But you should at least think about the job."

When we drove up to Diane's parent's house, I parked up and switched off the engine. Then, without saying a word, we looked at each other as if to say, "One down, one to go!" Somehow we had got away with our fabricated reason for going to Vegas with my parents, but we both wondered if we were going to do the same with Diane's.

Grabbing a second bunch of flowers from the back seat of the car, we made our way to the front door and Diane, still having her key, opened it and shouted out, "Hello, people. It's me and Terry."

Diane's mother emerged from the lounge into the hall and said, "Lovely to see you both. Come on in and sit down."

As we went into the lounge and sat beside each other on the sofa, Diane said to her mother, "Where's Dad?"

"Oh, he's in the garden. I'll give him a shout. Do you want something to drink?" she replied, as she lingered by the lounge door awaiting our answers.

"We wouldn't mind a coffee please," Diane said, speaking for both of us.

Diane's mother left the room to make the coffees and call her husband Jim from the garden.

I said to Diane, "You did it again. You read my mind and knew I'd prefer a coffee."

"Yes," she replied. "But I've got a confession to make. You know I told you I could only read your mind sometimes."

"Yes."

"Well, that isn't exactly true. Sometimes what you are thinking just pops into my head, but if I concentrate, I can read your mind whenever I want."

"Why didn't you tell me that before?"

"Because I thought you might not want to be with a person who could deprive you of all your personal and private thoughts."

"Why are you telling me now?" I asked.

"I'm telling you now because you might have second thoughts about marrying me if you knew I can know everything and anything you might think about." She said nervously.

I replied, "I'll never have secrets from you. I love you too much and I don't care that you can read my mind, as long as you don't concentrate that often that is," I said jokingly. "Besides, that's great. It will make things all the more easier in Vegas."

Just then Lottie, Diane's mother, closely followed by Jim, came into the room with a tray of four coffee cups.

"Hello, you two. Nice to see you. How are you getting on?" Jim said.

"Not bad," I replied, "although I'm finding it tough to get a job now that my father has sold his business. Have you had any luck?"

Jim replied, "I can't find anything either: the work just isn't out there. It seems everyone is feeling the pinch."

I said, "There is a job that I am going to try for though."

Diane quickly butted in. "We have got something to tell you first," she said, remembering what my mother had said about how some news is more important than any job. "Terry has asked me to marry him and I have said *yes*."

"That's wonderful news, isn't it Jim?" Lottie said with delight.

Unconvincingly Jim replied, "Yes, I suppose so."

Diane then said, with a determined tone to her voice, "I know what you're thinking, Dad. Terry and I haven't known each other that long, but you must realise we have been living together and know we are right for each other even though we only met this year."

"I suppose you're right," Jim said. "Even I think I've known Terry for much longer."

Directing his speech toward me, he continued, "It does seem that you're the right person for Diane Terry. I know you love her and will look after her."

"Believe me, Jim," I said. "Diane will always be the biggest priority in my life and I will make sure she will always be safe and happy."

"Well, that's settled then," Lottie said with relief.

"Have you decided when you're getting married?" she asked.

"Not yet, Mum," Diane replied. "We have got to get financially settled before we can plan a wedding."

Drinking half way down my coffee cup, I decided that Diane's comment was my cue to tell them about the Vegas trip and as Jim and Lottie took a gulp of coffee at the same time, I said,

"Talking of finance, that's another reason why we are here."

Assuming I was going to ask to borrow some money from him, Jim nearly choked on his coffee.

I continued. "I have seen an advertisement for "British Plasterers Wanted" for a company working on the refurbishment of a casino/ hotel in Las Vegas. I have decided that Diane and I will go out there to check it out."

Lottie said, "Won't that cost a lot of money in air fares and things?"

"Yes," I replied. "I will have to dip into my savings quite a bit, but I have got a feeling it will be worth it."

Jim asked, "Why are you going to the extra expense of taking Diane with you?"

I replied, "Because to be honest, Diane could do with a break from all her studying and if I am going to have the experience of going there, I want Diane to share that experience with me. It might be a once in a lifetime thing."

Jim then said, "As long as you think it will be worth it Terry, then good luck to you. When are you thinking of going?"

"In about three weeks time, after I have got everything arranged—tickets, passports and things."

"Wow, Las Vegas in America, who'd have thought?" Lottie said. "But don't get hooked on gambling though, will you?" she added.

Diane replied, "No, Mum, we're not that daft."

It seemed as though we had pulled it off and now both of our parents had accepted the fact that we had made up our minds to go. All that was left to do now was make the arrangements.

Three weeks passed and within those weeks, I had managed to book our airline tickets and sort out our visas and passports.

We both had our photographs taken for the passports in one of those photo booth machines. They were black and white pictures back then and I had never known anyone whom those machine photos actually flattered except now, of course, Diane. My photo made me look like a villain from a Charlie Chaplin silent movie, while she looked like a Disney princess.

Diane had never held a bank account before, as she had always been reliant on her parents, so we opened a joint account with the cheque from my dad and the remaining money I had saved over the last few years. I also withdrew enough money in dollar bills that I thought we would probably need. In preparation of our trip, I asked Diane to include in her packing, her very best glamorous clothes and jewellery. These would be essential to create the right impression in the casinos.

We were both very excited when the big day had finally arrived and we were now in the departure lounge at London Airport awaiting our first ever flight. I had booked our flights with TWA (Trans World Airlines), the first stage of which would be to New York followed by a connecting flight to Las Vegas. The airport was fairly busy and there were people going in all directions, toting their handheld cases. (Wheeled ones hadn't quite caught on yet.) Outside one of the few internal airport shops, I saw a sign that said they sold electrical adapters for use in America and as I had an electric shaver, I thought it was a good idea to buy one.

With lots of time to kill waiting for our flight to be called, all we could do was sit and people watch. The occasional flight crew passed and Diane remarked how smart they looked in their uniforms. Even a porter pulling a large trolley full of cases looked smart in his tight red waistcoat and grey trousers, with a red line going down the sides. For some reason, probably boredom, I got fixated on this porter, as he headed for a corner of the lounge where he started unloading cases onto a large, low metal platform. There was another man on the other side of the platform who was checking the labels on the cases and putting them into separate stacks on his side of the counter.

I said to Diane, "Watch this!"

As the porter lifted one of the large, obviously heavy cases from the trolley, with my mind I lifted the case with him. Of course to him it appeared to be very light and he nearly threw it completely over the other side of the platform. Scratching his head for a moment in disbelief of his own strength, he then started to pick up a much smaller case. Again with my mind, I found I could put a downward pressure on the small case. This had the effect of seeming much heavier than it could possibly be and he struggled just to be able to remove it from the trolley. Diane gently slapped me on my arm and said in a low voice, "Stop it, Terry, you'll give the poor man a heart attack."

I gave a little laugh and released the pressure on the small case, just as the porter gave a final heave to put it on the platform. The case hardly touched the platform but zoomed over and hit the other man on his leg. He was literally hopping mad and Diane and I couldn't contain our laughter. We laughed so much our stomachs hurt and our eyes were red and wet with the tears. Unfortunately we attracted attention to ourselves and were given stern looks from other waiting passengers.

I couldn't really understand why back in the seventies, people took the whole business of airports and flying so solemnly, as if you must be on your best behaviour at all times. Also everyone seemed to be dressed up in their Sunday best clothes, the men in suits and ties and women in long dresses and high-heeled shoes. I also saw one older woman wearing white-laced gloves. Diane and I just dressed casual, as it seemed logical that you needed to be wearing something comfortable if you are going to be sitting on an airplane for eight or nine hours.

The TWA flight boarding call to New York finally came over the Tannoy system and we and the other passengers were led onto the tarmac to board the Boeing 707 up some very steep aluminium stairs.

Our boarding passes were taken by the stewardess as we entered the plane and I can't quite remember and I might be wrong, but I'm sure we were not even given specific seat numbers, so we just sat in the seats that took our fancy. Anyway whether we had seat numbers or not, we ended up sitting on the right side of the plane, with me by the window looking out over the wing and Diane next to me. After the plane was boarded by all its passengers and we put our seat belts on, the captain announced we were about to depart. This was a whole new experience for us both as we had never even been in a plane before, except my experience in the Terran craft of course, but this was nothing like that. The engines were started and we slowly began to move, as the engines whirled into a high-pitched crescendo. After taxiing to the runway, we were finally ready for takeoff. Diane grabbed hold of my arm tightly and, nodding my head slightly, I looked at her and whispered, "It'll be all right."

With a sudden roar of the engines, our bodies were forced into the back our seats and the plane hurtled down the bumpy runway. Then it pitched about thirty-five degrees and we were in the air. As I looked through the porthole, I watched the houses and cars on the ground getting smaller and smaller and although my stomach did roll a bit, like when you are on a rollercoaster, I felt exhilarated and loved every minute, as we flew through and then above the clouds. Diane's grip on my arm was gradually becoming less intense and by the time the plane had levelled out and started to cruise, we both felt very at ease. The seatbelt signs above our heads went out and you could hear all through the aircraft the clicking of seat belts being undone. We were on our way!

After about an hour into the flight, the stewardesses brought round alcoholic and soft drinks to everyone and after that a miniature meal. I couldn't help but notice how slim and sexy the stewardesses looked, in their tight uniforms and stockings with seams up the back, but I wasn't about to let Diane catch me looking.

Again, I couldn't believe how the rest of the passengers were dressed, as they ate their meals with a serviette tucked into their starched collars and lacy-necked dresses.

With the meal over and the empty food cartons removed, we settled back into our seats for the long, long flight. Diane fell asleep with her head on my shoulder, while I looked out of the window at the clear, cloudless sky.

Suddenly the sun glinted on a metallic object, which was probably a couple of miles away to our right. It was travelling at incredible speed, at the same height to us but in the opposite direction. I immediately thought it could be one of the Terran crafts, but as it hurtled nearer and paralleled us, I could see it was just another plane. As the two planes passed each other, its velocity and our speed combined meant we passed each other at about nine-hundred miles per hour, a walk in the park for a Terran ship. From that point on, looking out over the empty sky became boring and gradually our early morning wake up and the time spent at the airport was getting to me. And at that point, I must have fallen asleep, just like Diane had.

It must have been about six hours into the flight when we were awakened by the aircraft being buffeted around and it felt like we were going over rocks, but it was the plane rapidly losing, then gaining height. We were going through an Atlantic storm and hitting lots of turbulence. The captain told everyone, including the cabin crew, to put our seatbelts on and said not to be alarmed as he was going to climb above it. I wondered what the paper bags were for in the seat pockets in front of us and I could see there was quite a few people using them. Although Diane looked a bit worried, I convinced her it was nothing to fret about and fortunately neither of us needed to use those paper bags. Just as he had said, the captain steered the plane above the storm, the buffeting stopped and we continued to cruise at a greater height.

For the most part, the flight was long and boring, but as it was our first time in a plane, I think we both enjoyed the experience. After finally landing in New York, Diane and I were both relieved to get out of the plane and get the feeling back in our legs. The next step was to go through immigration. I hadn't realised that as New York was the first port of call, even though we were travelling on another flight to a different state, we had to go through passport control. It took us a good half an hour to reach the front of the queue, where we were confronted by a stern-looking, heavily built American official, sitting in a booth mainly consisting of glass. He was wearing a gold coloured metal badge on his dark, blue shirt, with brightly coloured badges sewn each side at the top of his arms. His thick, black leather belt around his waist revealed a menacingly holstered pistol. From behind his desk he gestured for Diane and me to give him our brand new passports. As he flicked through the empty pages, he said in a direct, "no nonsense" kind of way, "You haven't travelled much, have you?"

"No, first time," I replied, wondering if there was a problem.

After a few minutes of him saying absolutely nothing and us quaking in our boots, he thumped a red rubber stamp in each of our passports and as he handed them back to us, his stoic face changed to a smile as he said, "Welcome to the United States of America."

With relief that our documents were all in order, we hurriedly left passport control and headed to retrieve our cases.

Diane said, "That was a bit of an ordeal, I hope we don't have to go through that again in Las Vegas."

I replied confidently, "No, we won't have to now. We are officially in America."

The next stage was to get our cases to another part of the airport and check in for the flight to Vegas. We had a couple of hours before we were due to leave and found the departure lounge in good time.

As we sat once again waiting for our boarding announcement, not for any particular reason I asked Diane if she was OK.

She replied, "I'm excited, but I will be glad when we finally get there."

"Yeah me too," I said.

Where we were sitting there was another row of seats opposite and facing us, about fifteen feet away. The end two seats were taken up by a man and a woman in their early thirties. Next to the end seat, a girl of about eight years old was sitting in a wheelchair wrapped in a blanket from her neck to her feet. The girl obviously had some sort of disorder but with the blanket virtually covering her whole body, it was impossible to see exactly what it was. From beneath the blanket a tiny hand emerged and gave a little wave in our direction. The hand was accompanied by a smile, which had two missing front teeth.

"She's waving at us," Diane said.

"I know," I replied.

Without saying any more, we both knew our mission was to help this child somehow and the opportunity soon presented itself. The mother of this little girl stood up from her seat, said something to her husband and then went off. We could see she was carrying some sort of make-up bag and hair brush as we watched her disappear along a corridor into the ladies toilets. The man had seen his daughter wave to us, so he wasn't alarmed in any way when we came over to him.

Diane then said to the little girl, "Hello and who have we got here? Are you a princess in disguise?"

The man smiled and seemed grateful that we had taken an interest in his daughter.

"My name is Lori," the little girl said.

Just at that moment a message came over the announcement system for a Mr. Clark to go to the check in desk.

"That's me!" the girl's father said, with an American accent. "Would you mind keeping an eye on Lori while I see what they want? It's typical that they call me just as my wife leaves us to go and freshen up."

"No, we don't mind keeping an eye on her, you go," Diane said.

"Thanks, I'll only be just over there." He pointed to the desk about twenty-five feet away. As he left we knew it was our perfect opportunity to try and help this girl.

"Are you angels?" Lori said.

"Why do you say that?" Diane replied.

"Because I know you are here to help me," she said.

"Well, we will just have to see about that," Diane replied.

As the little girl spoke, her blanket slipped and fell down to her feet, revealing a twisted malformed little torso. She was clutching a small teddy bear, which she held close to her body. A lump immediately entered my throat and my vision blurred from the tears which started to form in my eyes, as I saw the girl's pretty yellow dress was occupied by her disfigured little body.

Diane looked at Lori's body and said, "So you have scoliosis of the spine. Am I right?"

Lori replied, "Yes, but I can't say that word. Mommy and Daddy are taking me to Canada, where my aunt lives, because she says there is a good hospital there that might be able to help me."

"Well, let me tell you something, Lori," Diane said. "A powerful wizard has sent us here to try to help you. Are you ready?"

"Yes, please," Lori replied, eagerly.

Diane held Lori's hand and I held Diane's other. A warm tingling sensation was felt by all three of us, which lasted about twenty-five seconds.

"Ooo, I feel all tingly," Lori said.

Diane and I witnessed Lori's body gradually contort into a normal form and Lori showed no signs of any pain or discomfort during the morph. As soon as it was over, Diane pulled Lori's blanket back up to her neck and wrapped it behind her so it wouldn't fall down again.

"How do you feel now Lori?" Diane said.

"I feel all mended," Lori replied.

Diane then said, "You know that this must be our secret and you mustn't tell anyone we helped you. Also I know you want to get out of that chair now, but you have to wait until you see us start to go toward that door over there." Diane pointed toward the door we would have to go through to board our plane. "Will you promise us these things?"

Lori replied, "I promise."

Soon after that promise, Lori's father returned. "Thanks for looking after Lori," he said. "The desk just wanted to know Lori's details, so the airline staff can meet the plane in Toronto and have a wheelchair ready for her."

Diane said, "Lori is a beautiful little girl and very bright and it has been a pleasure talking with her."

Turning to Lori, Diane then said, "Bye-bye, Lori. Have a good trip, we will be thinking of you."

As we made our way back to our seats, I turned my head and gave Lori a wink. She responded by giving me a cute little toothless smile.

Soon after we had sat down, Lori's mother returned clutching her toiletry bag. She then picked up a holdall, which was on one of the seats, placed it on the floor and opened it. Kneeling beside it, she started dragging its contents out; it was obvious she was looking for something as most of its contents were now strewn over the floor. Lori's dad had sat down on one of the seats going through what looked like their tickets and travel information. We could see Lori was being true to her word and was sitting quite still with the blanket still in position, covering her whole body up to her neck. Lori's mother then said something to her husband and he too knelt down; together, they were looking through the holdall's contents.

While this was happening, our boarding announcement was called and we got up and started to join the queue to go through the gate. As we steadily neared the door where boarding passes were being checked, we looked over in Lori's direction. Still busily sorting through their luggage, Lori's parents hadn't noticed her blanket had now fallen to the floor. Very slowly, Lori started to stand up clutching her Teddy bear tightly. She was now free of her chair and stood completely unassisted as her body was now that of any other normal little girl. We were nearly at the boarding pass checkpoint when we saw Lori steadily walk, then stand next to her parents. Her mother gave out a kind of joyous wail as she finally noticed her daughter standing in front of her, while her father just seemed to collapse in tears. Lori looked over and gave us one last smile as we passed through the gate to board our plane. I personally had never felt so inwardly touched, as the scene of emotional delight unfolded for Lori's parents. It was a picture that would be imprinted in my mind forever.

It was another long flight from New York to Las Vegas and you would have thought that during it we would have been wallowing in our achievement in curing Lori. But the truth was we never mentioned the incident. It seemed it wasn't the time to feel smug, as in the world there would be thousands of little children like Lori who we would never meet and would continue to suffer.

As we neared Vegas airport, the captain announced we were passing over the Grand Canyon and that the passengers on the left hand side of the plane would get a good view. Just our luck! We were sitting on the right, so we couldn't see it, but as we came into land, we had a fantastic view of the Las Vegas strip and because the airport was so close to everything and because the sun was just beginning to set, the strip stood out and sparkled, like a multi-coloured neon mirage.

Once we had landed, all we had to do was pick up our luggage and then find the car rental desk, which was located within the airport's grounds. By now the long journey from England was taking its toll and we were both feeling the effects, but I think excitement and adrenaline was still keeping us going when, after about thirty minutes, we finally managed to rescue our luggage from a temperamental conveyor belt. Our next task was to rent a car.

Eventually we found the car rental desk in the kind of airport's basement and with relief we dropped our heavy cases on the floor. Diane, with her half-closed eyes, sat on her case as I approached the counter. A tall, thin man in his thirties, wearing a smart blue waistcoat, greeted me by saying in a chirpy American accent, "Good evening, sir and how may I be of assistance to you today."

"I'd like to hire a car for a week," I replied.

In a mildly sarcastic tone, he responded by saying, "Well, you have come to the right place. All the way from Australia are we?"

He must have mistaken my mild cockney accent for the Australian drawl.

"No, we are British, from England," I replied.

"Well, what kind of car do you need?" he said.

I thought I would also use a little bit of sarcasm, not that I was really in the mood for it. "One that has four wheels on the ground and an engine to make it move," I replied.

He replied back, "No, sir, I mean do you want a compact, full size, or convertible?"

"I suppose the compact is going to be the cheapest, isn't it?" I said.

"Sure is" he said.

"Then I'll go with that one."

Although our venture was to make money out of this trip, there was no way I was going to splash out on non-essentials. I have never counted my chickens before and I knew there was no guarantee my little scheme was going to pay off.

Having done all the paperwork and handed over the payment, I went over to Diane, where I found her asleep, sitting on her case. Meanwhile the man lifted a flap on the counter and was heading toward me, holding a set of car keys and a folded piece of paper.

I woke Diane. "Come on sleepy head."

She awoke with a start and just stopped herself from toppling over. As we toted our cases, the man led us out of the office exit doors immediately into an underground car park. Handing me the keys and a street map of the Vegas area, he pointed along a row of cars to a red one, right at the end.

"Oh, by the way," he said, "the horn is on the indicator arm. Have a great vacation!"

After saying thanks to him, Diane and I made our way to the car he had indicated. The boot, or as the Americans call it, the trunk, was already open, so I heaved our cases into the spacious compartment and slammed the lid down. We then got into the car. After such a long flight, I think my brain was a bit frazzled and it took me a good ten seconds to realise that there was no steering wheel in front of me. Diane and I just looked at each other and laughed and without saying anything, we got out of the car to change seats. I had never driven an automatic car before, let alone a left hand drive, but after resetting the mirrors, I turned the ignition key to an almost silent purr of the engine.

This car was the cheapest rental I could get, yet it only had eight thousand or so miles on the clock and was kitted out with all kinds of things that only a really expensive car would have in England. It even had cup holders, which I'm sure back home would be frowned upon as being dangerous. I turned the ignition and turned on the headlights. The next step was to actually drive it and with no clutch to worry about, I kept my right foot firmly on the brake and told my left foot to stay still and not to move. It didn't take much to work out the gear controls, so I pushed the lever on the steering column to *R* for reverse. Releasing the footbrake, I began to move backward without any use of the accelerator. I then selected *D* for drive and off we slowly went to find the exit. Still within the rental garage, I noticed a car was coming toward me, flashing its lights. I then realised I was on the wrong side of the driveway and inwardly I told myself to wake up and think more about what I was doing. Eventually finding the exit, I pulled out sharply onto the road and slotted neatly into the stream of traffic, to a loud exhale of relief from Diane.

Cruising along, we came to a T-junction and the traffic lights were red. I first thought that the cars in front of me were all jumping the lights, till I realised that it was common practise to turn right on a red light, if it was safe to do so, that is. With this in mind, I followed suit and found myself heading directly toward the bright lights of the Vegas strip, passing the famous WELCOME TO FABULOUS LAS VEGAS sign.

I soon got used to driving on the right and I felt quite comfortable as we cruised at about twenty-five miles an hour on the four lanes of the Las Vegas Boulevard. Alternately, Diane and I were making sounds of "Ooo!" and "Wow!" as we passed the ornate themed buildings with their flashing neon lights. Caesars Palace was incredible, with its huge porcelain and gold statues at its entrance and after passing the famous Stardust, the Circus Circus casino looked like a massive red and white tent.

Eventually we came to Sahara Avenue, which, previously in England, I had researched for a reasonable motel to stay in, so I turned right and started down that road. It wasn't long before I saw a large neon billboard with flashing four ace cards on it and beneath it a sign that read, The Four Aces Motel, vacancies. I drove into its forecourt and stopped the car in a vacant parking bay; we then got out and went into the office.

It was quite a small office area with a counter in the corner. Behind the counter was a rather plump man of about fifty. He was sitting on a stool smoking a really smelly cigar and looking at a television set mounted on a high shelf on the wall opposite the counter. His eyes averted from the TV as we entered.

"Hey, guys, how can I help you this evening?" he said.

"We'd like a room with a double bed for the week," I said.

He replied, "No problem. How does a ground floor with a queen bed sound?"

"Sounds good to me, how much?" I enquired.

He said, "For you a special, a hundred bucks for the week."

That sounded like a lot of money initially, but with our exchange rate, I thought that was actually quite cheap.

"We'll take it," I said.

While I was sorting out the different denominations of dollar bills, the man said, "Just arrived from Australia have we?"

I answered, "Yes, we have just arrived, but we are from London, England."

"Oh, sorry, pal, but your accent sounds Australian."

"Yes, you're the second person to tell me that," I said.

After I handed over the cash, he thrust in front of me a large black ledger and attached to a piece of string and anchored to the counter with multiple layers of sticky tape, was a biro to write with.

He then said, "Just need you to sign and put your car's registration down."

I was feeling really tired by now and it felt like a real chore just to go out to the rental car to look at its registration number, so I said with a sigh, as I began to exit the office, "Won't be a minute"

Diane quickly asked me, "Where are you going?"

"To get the cars registration number," I replied.

"It's on the key fob," Diane said, raising her eyebrows and giving a little smile.

I looked at the fob and felt a little embarrassed. "So it is," I said.

After signing the book and jotting down the cars registration number, the man said, "That's it, all done. Room number four is just along a little ways to your right. You can park right outside. Have a great vacation."

I forced half a smile and thanked the man as we left the office.

Having parked the car directly outside, we got our luggage inside the room and shut the door. Both completely knackered, we flopped onto the massive queen-sized double bed.

"We're finally here," Diane said.

I just lay there with my eyes shut and replied, "Finally."

7

It was our first real day in Las Vegas. Diane woke up about 10:30 a.m. and gave me a shake to release me from my sublime slumber.

"Come on, Terry," she said, enthusiastically. "We've got a lot of exploring and investigating to do."

My brain was gradually starting to function as I began to realise exactly where I was in the world.

Full of beans, Diane continued. "I'll have a shower first, while you come back into the land of the living."

With a mighty yawn, I replied, "OK, then."

I was too tired to even care last night, but now, while Diane was having her shower, I started to look around our new domain for the coming week. The room was actually quite large and it was the biggest bed I had ever slept in. The main thing that struck me was how clean it was. It had bedside tables, each with their own lamps, a couple of chairs and a TV perched on a cabinet in the corner of the room. Oh yes and air conditioning. I thought that we had got a really good deal for our hundred dollars. I hadn't seen the bathroom yet and Diane had closed the door before she got in the shower. I was bursting for a pee and the sound of the shower running made it even worse.

"I'm coming in," I shouted.

I opened the unlocked door and dashed to the toilet directly in front of me and lifting the seat lid, I sighed loudly with relief. During mid-pee and with the desperation half-relieved, I noticed on the wall above the toilet a chromed wire shelf, with an assortment of various sized white, fluffy towels. Then to my left was the bath, with a shower curtain across the full length. On flushing the loo, Diane yelled out, "Don't use the water, it affects the shower temperature."

"Oops! Sorry," I replied.

Well, this was too good an opportunity to miss. I pulled the shower curtain half way across, got into the bath and stood behind her with my body touching hers.

It was almost as if she expected it as she turned toward me covered in soap suds. Lovingly our naked bodies began to intertwine. Sharing the soap, we lathered each other's body slowly and sensually and then in turn kissed intimate parts of the other's anatomy, while the shower rained warm water on us. I'll never forget that amazing feeling and after a quick dry off with those fluffy white towels, we made love on that huge bed.

After the passion had died down, we just lay there in each other's arms, contented and happy, until there was a knock on the door.

"Maid service," a voice called out.

"Give us ten minutes," I called back.

With that we jumped up from the bed and rummaged through our cases, which we hadn't unpacked, then we got dressed and into some clean casual clothes. Giving the room a quick tidy, we locked our cases and stood them in a corner to unpack at a later stage. We then emerged from our room to our first taste of the warm Nevada sun. The maid had now skipped our room and was next door in number five. I spoke to her through the open door.

"Sorry about that," I said. "We only arrived yesterday after a long flight."

"That's OK," she replied.

I was starving and I thought Diane must be too.

"Can you recommend a good place to have breakfast?" I asked the maid.

"There's a Denny's diner not far," she said. "Make a right onto Las Vegas Boulevard and it's about a thousand yards on your left. You can't miss it. It has a big yellow sign outside."

"Thanks a lot!" I replied.

Armed with those easy directions, Diane and I, getting into the correct sides of the car this time, drove off to find the diner. It must have taken less than three minutes before we had parked up again and entered the busy restaurant. There were food signs plastered all over the windows advertising their meals but mainly their breakfasts, which they served all day.

Once inside, we approached a waitress standing next to about a nine-inch square, waist height box; it had a sheet of paper on the sloping top, which contained a list of names pencilled in with some names struck through.

"Good morning," she said. "Party of two, and the name?"

"Seer," I replied.

"Be about five minutes, is that OK?" she asked.

"That's fine," I replied.

This diner was obviously popular as I realised there were people queuing inside and out, waiting to be seated. I doubted whether we would get seated in five minutes, but I was hungry and was going to wait no matter what. Sure enough, five minutes had passed when my name was called and another waitress led us to our booth by the window. The booth consisted of two fixed, green leather-padded bench seats facing each other, with an oblong table also fixed in the middle. It was spacious and comfortable and we sat opposite each other with a menu, each placed on the table in front of us.

"Coffee?" the waitress said.

"Yes, please," we both replied.

"Both with cream?" she asked.

Again we both replied, "Yes, please."

"Isn't this great?" Diane said.

"Yes," I replied. "And take a look at this menu. You can even have steak for breakfast."

It was only a few minutes before the waitress returned with two mugs of black coffee and a small jug of rich creamy milk. The sugar was in sachets, in a condiment rack on the table.

"Ready to order?" the waitress asked.

We had only briefly looked through the menu, but we had both decided we would try the Grand Slam. The Grand Slam was comprised of two sausages, two strips of bacon, two eggs and two fluffy pancakes.

"How do you want your eggs?" the waitress asked.

A bit bewildered, I replied, "What do you mean?"

"You can have them sunny-side up, over easy, well-done, scrambled, or poached," she said.

With so many choices confronting me, I just said the first thing that came to mind: "Over easy, please."

"Me, too," Diane added, also mind-boggled.

"I like it here, Terry," Diane said. "I'm even excited by the breakfast."

While we waited for our breakfast, we drank our coffees and talked about our excitement at being in Las Vegas and what new experiences we were probably going to encounter. Meanwhile another waitress came up to us and without saying anything, refilled our coffee mugs. Diane and I just looked at each other in amazement.

"That's good, buy one and get the rest free!" I said.

Soon after that, our breakfasts arrived. Again we looked at each other with dropped jaws.

"I'll never get through all that," Diane exclaimed.

"I'm going to have a good try though," I replied.

Together with the breakfasts, two small glass jars, about two and a half inches tall, were put on the table by the waitress. I smelled it to try to fathom out what it was.

"Smells sweet," I said.

So as not to look too ignorant, I looked around at the other diners to see if anyone else had a similar breakfast with the jar included.

Luckily I spotted a diner nearby who was just pouring this liquid all over his pancakes and fried food. I thought, *nothing ventured, nothing gained*, so I poured some of the contents of the jar over my food and started to eat.

Diane waited in anticipation to see what my reaction was when I tasted it, I then said.

"It's warm maple syrup and it tastes great."

Diane followed suit and poured some on her pancakes.

After a large mouthful she said, "I like it too."

We both must have been really hungry because we ate everything on our plates and as we gulped another mouthful of coffee, our waitress came over with the coffee pot again.

"No more coffee for me, thanks," I said.

"Me neither, thanks," Diane added.

"Did you guys enjoy your meal?" the waitress asked.

"Yes, great," I replied.

With that, the waitress put the bill for the breakfasts upturned on the table and said, "I'll take care of that for you when you're ready. Have a nice day." And then she promptly left.

Gingerly I picked up the bill to see how much the meals had cost us. It came to just over seven dollars.

"What's the damage?" Diane asked.

I replied, "In our money, it comes to about three pounds."

"For all that and the coffees, that's ridiculously cheap," she said.

"Yeah," I replied. "Even adding on a fifteen- to twenty-percent tip, it was well cheap."

"The Americans sure know how to live," Diane remarked.

We needed to let those breakfasts go down a bit and finish our coffees before we made a move, so I used that time to look at the street map that the car rental man had given me. Our next port of call was to be Fremont Street, which according to the map, wasn't that far away.

Having finally decided we should leave the diner, I left ten dollars and the odd cents on the table as payment of the bill and tip, and then as we went to open the exit door, another diner employee said, "Have a nice day. Come back and see us soon."

While we were in that air conditioned diner, the sun had rose high in the sky and as we came out into the open air, the heat hit us like a blast from the back of a jet engine. Quickly getting into our car, I started the engine and put the air conditioning on full blast. The steering wheel was so hot; I had to wait until the cooling system took effect. Our car was just a basic rental, yet it was equipped with air conditioning, something that I had never seen in a car back home. I suppose, though, we didn't really need it for English climate.

The famous Fremont Street was just a short ride away and as we turned left into it, the images I had seen on the TV in England became a reality. Full in view was The Golden Nugget, The Mint and The Pioneer casinos, with the cowboy and cowgirl animated signs set aloft on the vast buildings. At the very end of the street was the Union Plaza Hotel and Casino, the one that was being renovated and the one that I had used as a reason for our trip. I did feel a little bad at seeing it, as it reminded me that I had lied to our parents, something which I wasn't entirely happy about. I was glad though that the traffic was slow moving along Fremont, as it allowed us to take in the atmosphere of the flashy casinos and hordes of tourists frequenting them. As I reached the end of the street, I turned left again and soon found a car park.

"Come on Terry, hurry up," Diane said, as she literally jumped out of the car as I turned the ignition key off.

I think she was a little bit more excited than I was, having at last reached the hub of the town. As I got out of the car, looking at Diane I suddenly realised how much Diane looked the part, like a true American girl, in her tight jeans, checked blouse, white plimsolls and long blonde hair in a ponytail. Apart from her accent, she could have passed for an American quite easily. Holding hands, with Diane virtually dragging me, we turned the corner and mingled with the rest of the tourists on the wide pavement of Fremont Street, staying on the side which had the most shade from the sun. All the casinos were open-fronted, so anyone could just walk straight in off the street. The sounds of the one-armed bandits and the clinking of winning coins in their trays were prominent at every step we took on the pavement and depicted what the whole place was about: Gambling!

"Let's go in The Golden Nugget," Diane said, pulling my arm at full stretch, as she gripped my hand. Once inside, the noise of the machines was quite deafening as we strolled around looking at all the different types of fruit machines and the many different nationalities of gamblers. As we reached the inside rear of the casino, we came across all the card tables, roulette wheels and dice throwing tubs. This was where the serious gamblers hung out. Gambling chips that were purchased previously were used here, with no actual dollar bills changing hands. There seemed to be large well-built suited men at every table near all the croupiers, as if they were overseeing all that was going on. Although these men were saying nothing; it was obvious that they were there to keep everything in check and were making sure that there were no dodgy dealings going on, either by the punters or the croupiers. I had the feeling that the gamblers and staff didn't really want idle onlookers around, so I said to Diane, "Let's go back to the machines. We can check out the roulette tables later tonight."

She nodded in agreement.

Having ambled our way back to the plethora of machines, Diane said, "Can we play, Terry?"

"You can," I replied. "Remember I'm not old enough according to Nevada law."

I went over to the cashier's iron bar clad cage and produced a five dollar bill to be exchanged for two dollars' worth of nickels (five cent coins) and three dollars' worth of quarters (twenty-five cent coins). He gave me the coins in two large plastic cups—one for the quarters and one for the nickels. As Diane sat on a padded stool in front of a nickel machine, I handed her the cup of the appropriate coins. Dipping her hand into the cup, she placed a coin in the machine's slot and pulled the handle. After five or six attempts she hadn't won anything, so I decided I would give her a helping hand, without telling her, of course. At first I froze the spinning reels, so they stopped on minor prizes, which delighted her; she was at least winning something and the tinkling of the winning coins hitting the metal tray beneath excited her no end. Then I decided I would increase her winnings by stopping the reels on more major combinations of symbols. She clapped her hands with delight at winning so many coins, so much so, she needed another plastic cup to accommodate them. Lucky enough someone had left an empty cup at the side of the machine.

I said, "Why don't you cash them in and play on the quarter machines."

Having two full cups of nickels, she agreed and exchanged them for bills at the cashier counter.

"Fifteen dollars," she said on her return. "I only started with two. Let's find a good quarter machine."

I handed her the original cup that I got the three dollars in quarters in. Full of excitement, she led me to a machine she said, "Looks lucky." Having sat on the stool in front of this electronic machine, she inserted a coin.

This particular machine was Native American themed.

All its symbols were indigenously related with tepees, bows and arrows and that sort of thing; the jackpot symbols were three Indian chiefs. After the first pull of the handle, Diane won nothing and I decided that this time I would not intervene to show her that gambling was all about luck and that the odds were always on the side of the casino. She inserted her second coin and pulled the handle once again. Of course, the reels stopped on the three jackpot symbols and the machine went wild with flashing lights, bells and sirens. Everyone was looking in her direction as one of the casino staff came over and muted the machine, then he handed her a voucher to take to the cashier's desk and said, "Who's a lucky gal this day?"

With utter jubilance and handing me the cup with the remaining quarters in it, Diane went and presented the voucher to the cashier. The cashier asked to see her ID, just to make sure she was over twenty-one. Diane handed him her passport and he returned it along with a hundred dollars in ten dollar bills. With a smile, I said to Diane, "So, dinner is on you tonight. Come on let's check out some other places."

As we came out of the Golden Nugget, Diane stopped suddenly, turned to me and with a straight face, said, "Hang on! Did you freeze those reels so that I would win?"

"No, honestly," I replied. "I helped you a bit on the nickel machine but your winning on that last one was all your doing. I promise."

"Really?" she said.

"Really," I replied.

With her face returning again to a wide grin, she said, "That's all right then."

For the rest of the day, we stayed in the Fremont area, going into various casinos, having a good look around and spending minor amounts of dollars on different machines.

For the most part, I let Diane play without intervention until it came to a point where she was losing too heavily; then, I would manipulate her luck a bit. We also spent time just watching different street performers, acrobats, jugglers and celebrity impersonators, like Elvis.

All the while we were in the area, at random times, I would spot the face of a man who somehow didn't fit with the rest of the tourists. This man's face kept cropping up in our vicinity and his body language gave me cause to look around from time to time to see if I could spot him. He always seemed to be acting overly nonchalant when he saw me looking. I didn't tell Diane about the man because I didn't want to spoil her fun or make her feel uneasy.

It was getting late in the day and although that mammoth breakfast we had had kept us going, we were starting to feel as if our fuel tanks were running low and as the sun was setting, we found a nice restaurant to have a meal and relax, as we had literally been on our feet all day. We both ended up having the largest steaks we had ever seen and I insisted Diane pay for the meal out of her initial winnings and just before we intended to leave the restaurant, I asked her if she had enjoyed herself. Her reply with a chuckle was "More than you can possibly imagine."

I then said to her, "Good! Because we are probably going to do it all again tomorrow, but this time to find the casinos that I feel would suit our needs.

We left the restaurant to find a pitch black sky outside, with the most twinkling stars I had ever seen, something that you would never see in London because of the polluted atmosphere. On Fremont street itself though, it may as well been midday, as the multitude of illumination seemed to light every nook and cranny. I thought that the casinos must bolt down their electric meters; to stop them taking off like mini-helicopters because of the rate those gauges must have been spinning.

It was about 11:00 p.m., yet there was just as many people about as there was at 11:00 a.m., if not more. We made our way to the end of the street, dodging people all the time, as they were more interested in what was going on around them rather than where they were walking. As we turned the corner to head to where I had parked our car, it was a different story entirely. The street lights seemed very dim and there were very few people around; it now felt a little seedy. Although the evening was still pretty warm, I put my arm around Diane, as I'm sure she also felt the ambience had changed in the area we were now in. We entered the dark car park and walked arm in arm toward our vehicle. Suddenly, emerging from between two parked cars, a man pointed a gun at us and said, "Hold it right there."

In a flash and without thinking, I projected my mind at the man and he was literally propelled backward over three parked cars and landed on the bonnet of a fourth, dropping his gun somewhere in between. The force of the landing must have knocked him out cold, as he wasn't moving. We knew he wasn't dead, as we would have seen his portal open to take his life force, so we went over to see who had threatened us. It was the man who had been hanging around us since Diane had won that jackpot. Diane wanted to touch him, so he would heal from any injuries he had sustained, but I insisted she didn't and explained to her how he had been stalking us all day and that any injuries he had might deter him from threatening anyone else.

With a concerned look on her face, Diane said, "Did you know? When you propelled that man over those cars, your eyes changed to a milky white; there was no colour in them at all. Then for half a second, I swear I could see out of the corner of my eye, you and me looking on, standing to the side."

"That's weird, I didn't have any loss of vision and maybe you saw our reflection in that car's rear windscreen."I replied, pointing to a parked car.

"Yes," she said. "That's what it must have been."

"Well, I'm not going to worry about the bloke on the bonnet. All I care about is that your safe and I'm glad I reacted fast enough before either of us got hurt. I don't want anyone or anything to spoil our time here."

Leaving the man still sprawled out on the bonnet of that car; we went to our car and got in. I could see Diane was a little shaken by the incident, so I asked her if she was still worried about the unconscious man.

"No way," she said. "The bugger got what he deserved. No, I'm more worried about you. It's obvious your telekinetic power has evolved to a new level and I just hope there's not going to be any adverse side effects. I suppose it's just that I can't think of a medical explanation in my mind, why your eyes went like that."

I replied to her by saying, "Don't worry, Diane, I feel great. Remember that I self-heal, so any changes to my body can't be harmful in any way, can they?"

"I suppose you're right," she replied.

On the way back to our motel something made me think of when we were in London airport waiting for our flight out. The way I managed to put pressure on the light case the porter was lifting. Up until that point I was able to lift and move things about with my mind, but nothing with any great force. Even lifting Diane off the floor in our flat was a bit precarious. Now I was able to exert as much directed force as necessary and instantly, without any concentration. I realised that I now had a formidable power!

Although the events of last night had been a little disturbing, they didn't affect our sleep in any way and we both woke up feeling refreshed and eager to continue our mission and after both having a nice shower and donning some fresh casual clothes, I said, "Grand Slam?"

"Too right," Diane replied.

So off we drove for our second visit to Denny's.

This day I wanted to check out the casinos on the main Las Vegas strip, in particularly Caesars Palace. It had caught my eye seeing its exterior for the first time as the most affluent location; so from Denny's we headed south along the strip, in the direction of the airport.

Nearing the Circus, Circus casino, I thought it was far too interesting a shape to bypass, so I decided we would check it out first. After finding a space in its many car parking areas, we went in through the rear doors. From the outside it looked exactly like a huge red and white big top circus tent, but from the inside lower level, you would never have known that. It wasn't until we went up to the next level that the theme became apparent. There was a large area, exactly like a circus would be, with trapezes and a central performing stage. Stepped seating was on opposite sides to view the varied free performances. Apart from the circus acts, I would say the whole circular upper level was mainly dedicated to children, with various amusement booths located on the circumference of the outer and inner sides of the walkway. They were differently themed and provided a challenge for the player, much like you would find at a fair, like a coconut shy and sharp shooting. If you beat the challenge you would win different-sized cuddly toys—from the size you could hold in the palm of your hand to ones that were as large as a ten-year-old child.

Usually one win would get you the smaller prize and with more wins you would trade up for a larger one.

"Win me a Teddy, Terry," Diane said, with a false, pitiful voice and expression.

I gave a relenting smile and thought; *Surely it can't be that difficult to win something.* It seemed like every other person walking around had a huge cuddly toy under their arm. Because the different booths had different-shaped cuddly toys, I said to Diane, "Pick out the booth with the cuddly toy you want me to win."

After a few minutes walking around and inspecting the variety of toys hanging up vertically at the sides of each booth, Diane finally opted for the teddies at a basketball challenge. With three basketballs thrown into the net consecutively, you would bypass the smaller teddies and win a huge one straight off. I handed my dollar bill to the booth attendant, a man of about fifty, wearing a straw boater hat and a red and white striped waistcoat. For my dollar, he presented me with three basketballs, which were put on a low counter in front of me, lined up on dished indents. I picked up the first ball and after carefully working out the right pitch and distance I would need to throw it, I hurled it through the air at the net. The ball hit the metal ring that gave the net its circular shape and rebounded back hitting the other two balls on the counter. After picking the two balls up and replacing them back on the counter, the booth attendant said, "That's one down, two to go."

I could see Diane sniggering out of the corner of my eye as I lined myself up for the second shot. This time I planned to recalculate to rectify my first failure. With a skilful lob, I let the ball fly, only to hit the backboard high above the net, sending the ball rebounding back again. Dejectedly I picked up the third ball and the sniggering from Diane seemed to have gotten louder and I looked at her with a straight face for a few seconds until it cracked and I laughed with her.

"This isn't as easy as it looks you know!" I said, with a touch of seriousness in my voice.

"You're rubbish," Diane replied.

With the third ball poised ready for takeoff in my hands, I took a deep breath and let it fly. Boing! It hit the front of the metal ring again, but this time bounced upward and with its descent it fell squarely into the net.

"We have another winner!" the attendant exclaimed, handing me a white teddy bear about six inches tall, with a red bow around its neck. I handed the Teddy to Diane.

"Aaah! He's cute," she said. "I'm going to keep him and love him forever."

I knew there was no need to try to win any more cuddly toys. Diane was contented enough with the one she had and quite honestly, I didn't really want to embarrass myself any further, so I decided we should head down to the lower level of the building to the main casino.

On the ground floor, the main gambling area was huge and seemed to go on forever. Once we had passed the menagerie of one armed bandits, we came to the poker and black jack tables and then to the roulette tables and wheels. There seemed to be a fair amount of people around these tables all looking on at the luck of the players, with the occasional *oooo's* and *aaah's,* as the players almost won but not quite. There was a man about fifty years old at one roulette wheel who had a meagre amount of chips in front of him. He held his brow with the palm of his hand each time he gambled and then consistently lost. Diane was standing next to me with her arm around my waist and clutching her teddy bear close to her body with her other hand. I had one arm around her shoulders.

"I think it's time for a bit of practice," I whispered in her ear.

On the man's next attempt to win, he put four of his chips down on separate numbers—four black, seventeen black, fourteen red and thirty-two red. Other players put their chips all over the board, but I couldn't see if they had any kind of strategy. The croupier then spun the wheel, announced, "No more bets," and skilfully made the small wooden ball spin round the outer most edge of the wheel in the opposite direction.

I followed the ball with my eyes until it began to lose momentum. Having the man's numbers in my head, I began to determine where the ball was most likely to finally drop into the numbered pockets of the wheel. The ball was roughly going to land in the vicinity of thirty-two red but more likely in fifteen black, so with a little coaxing from me, it jumped out of fifteen black and into the thirty-two red.

"Yes!" the man said jubilantly, clenching his fist and swinging his bent elbow in front of him. I realised that the man had won $175 worth of chips, as he had used a five-dollar chip for the stake. I also realised that making that little wooden ball land in the correct numbered pocket was not as easy as I thought it might be, especially as I had to try to make it look as natural a resting place as possible. It wouldn't do for me to make a stationary ball suddenly jump up and go into another pocket.

The man, now with a big smile on his face, used the same technique as before for his next bet, only this time using different numbers. Just as before, I followed the spinning ball around the wheel but this time, I misdirected the ball and it ended up two pockets away from one of the man's numbers. Diane whispered in my ear.

"Did you mean to do that?"

"No," I replied. "It looks like I am going to need a good bit of practice before you play."

I gave Diane ten dollars from our kitty we had brought out with us for the day and said, "You go and play some of the machines while I stay here and practice. I've got to get my technique sorted out, or we will be going home with less than we started with."

Diane agreed, kissed me on the cheek and said, "You can do it, Terry," then went off to the bandit section.

I spent a good two hours trying different methods of making that ball land exactly where I wanted it to and finally I had achieved a way of doing it so that it looked as natural as possible.

The players also benefitted from my efforts as I made each one of them win at least something and with my technique mastered, I was feeling rather pleased with myself, so I left the roulette table to find Diane. I eventually found her playing a machine in the twenty-five cent section.

"How are you doing?" I asked.

"Not bad," she replied. "I've still got the ten dollars and I'm up about three."

I said, "Do you fancy going for a snack now?"

She replied, "Yes, why not. I'm feeling a bit peckish."

After collecting all her quarter coins from the machine's tray, we went to the cashier's cage to change them back into dollar bills.

"Where shall we go?" Diane asked.

"Let's just go with the flow of people, we are bound to find a place to eat in this maze somewhere," I replied.

Sure enough we soon found a snack bar along the wide corridor of shops toward the front of the casino. Hamburgers, hot dogs and soft drinks were on the menu and I was just about to ask Diane what she wanted when she said, "I'll have a hot dog and Coca-Cola, the same as you please."

I wasn't surprised. I was getting quite used to Diane reading my mind before I had the chance to open my mouth. Picking up our order immediately from the counter, we found a vacant booth like the ones in our breakfast diner. We then sat opposite each other at the table and in turn, used the plastic squeeze bottles on our table to put lashings of tomato ketchup and a streak of yellow mustard onto our hot dogs.

"Do you think you have mastered the roulette wheel then Terry?" Diane said as she sank her teeth into the frankfurter sausage that was sticking out of her ketchup-dripping, elongated bun.

"I think so," I replied. "But I really have to concentrate to make it look as smooth and as natural as possible."

Wiping the ketchup from around her mouth and the underside of her nose with a paper serviette; still chewing, she said, "I think I know you well enough by now Terry. You're rubbish at basketball, but dead accurate when it comes to your mind tricks. Look how you sorted that bloke out who pulled a gun on us."

"Yes," I said, "but that was instinctive and there wasn't much finesse about it. It's a bit trickier to make a little wooden ball fall into an inch-square slot and make it look as though momentum and gravity did all the work."

Winking one eye, Diane replied, "I know you can do it."

I could tell Diane wasn't just humouring me but did actually have complete faith in my abilities.

Swallowing a piece of hotdog myself, I said, "When we have finished our snack, we have to go to Caesars Palace. I have got to see the layout of the place and get the feel of it, to sort out our game plan."

Diane replied, "It sounds like we are casing the joint to commit a robbery."

"Oh blimey, I suppose you're right, but I've got to tell myself that we are not actually committing a crime. I'm just using my abilities to our advantage," I replied, not quite believing my justification.

"That's right," Diane said, also with a bit of false conviction.

After chomping through our huge hotdogs and forcibly drinking our oversized cardboard cups of cola, we decided it was time for our next port of call, Caesars Palace.

As we came out of the fast food bar, about fifteen feet in front of us was a little Down's syndrome girl. She was about nine years old, with hair in pigtails and smartly dressed in a little blue frock. She wore short white socks and shiny, black buckled shoes. She was dragging her mother by the hand in our direction.

"Come on, Mommy, hurry up," she said, as she drew closer.

"Jessica! Slow down," her mother said.

It was obvious this little girl had spotted Diane and wanted to meet her for some reason. It seemed that Diane had a kind of talent for attracting Down's kids. On reaching us, little Jessica spoke to Diane in that childish, cocky, know-it-all kind of way: "You know, 'Ner, Ner, N'Ner, Ner'" way.

Speaking rhythmically, she said, "I know who you are,-are."

With an American accent, Jessica's mother spoke. "I'm so sorry. She has never done anything like this before."

Diane replied, "Oh, that's all right. Jessica obviously thinks she knows me."

"I can't see how," the mother said. "This is the first time she has ever been outside of Virginia and you're from Australia, aren't you?"

Diane replied, "Well, actually we are from London, England, but I suppose our accents sound a bit like Australian."

Jessica then butted in, saying, "I *do* know who you are. You are Diane and you mend people." She said indignantly.

Startled, Diane replied, "Jessica, how on earth did you know my name?"

Jessica's mother then said, "Do you mean that Jessica is correct and that Diane is your name?"

"Yes," Diane replied. "And I'm near to qualifying as a doctor, so I suppose that's what Jessica meant when she said I mend people."

I and Diane both knew exactly what Jessica meant by "mend people."

Jessica's mother was amazed.

"I don't know how she could have possibly known that," she said.

Diane crouched down to Jessica's height and said, "Are you going to tell me how you know me?"

Jessica replied, "It's a secret, but I will whisper it to you."

The little girl whispered in Diane's ear, "David told me, but you mustn't tell anyone else."

Stunned by what Jessica had said, Diane felt in a predicament. The mother would obviously want to know Jessica's secret, which would only lead to more questions.

Diane asked Jessica's mother, "Do you have any connections with other Down's children from abroad, maybe?"

She replied, "No, not at all. We live in a quiet town and Jessica has never even met anyone like herself before."

Diane said, "Well, maybe Jessica has a psychic ability you never knew about because I can't explain how she knew of me."

"But what did Jessica whisper to you?" she asked.

Diane replied with a smile, "Oh, I couldn't possibly tell you that. I am sworn to secrecy."

Jessica began to tug at her mother's sleeve. "Come on, Mommy. We've got to see the clowns in the circus."

"Well, it was very nice meeting you Diane." The mother said. She then just smiled at me as she was dragged off by her daughter's hand in the direction of the ramp to the circus acts on the upper level.

After Jessica and her mother quickly vanished from sight, I asked Diane, "What did Jessica whisper to you?"

Diane replied, "She said that David had told her my name and how we helped his sister."

"But that's impossible," I said.

"I know," Diane replied. "The only explanation I can think of is that somehow, Down's children must be telepathic in some way and can communicate with each other no matter what the distance."

I replied, "But there must be hundreds of thousands of Down's kids in the world who have never met each other. That would mean that they would all know what the rest of them had experienced or done; it would require fantastic brainpower."

Diane then said, "Well, we've certainly experienced things that normally would seem impossible, but now know them to be fact. It seems there's a lot more to this world that meets the eye."

Still with my brain half pondering on the dynamic brainpower Down's children must have, I said to Diane, "Come on, we've got a date with Caesar."

It only took about ten minutes from the parking lot of Circus, Circus to get to the Caesars palace car park and from there, only a couple more minutes to enter the casino. Once through the doors we were transported back in time to ancient Rome, although it was a lot cleaner than the actual place I had seen in Theron's archival footage.

This place, or should I say palace, was vastly different from the casualness of the big top casino. Waitresses wore short, flimsy white togas, with leather sandals that were tied criss-crossed up around their calves and their hair was in a kind of platted beehive, high upon their heads. The main thing I noticed was the clientele. They seemed to be dressed just a tad more than casual, which said to me that Caesars attracted upmarket and more affluent people. Strolling through the vast halls of marble floors, pure white porcelain pillars and titanic statues with gold leaf highlights, I realised just how much money must have been spent to produce these settings. The elaborately painted ceilings of cherubs and Roman god-like scenes were in such detail that Michelangelo himself could have painted them.

As we strolled on, we came to a kind of courtyard with cobbled paving and the ceiling this time was painted like the sky on a bright, sunny day. It was so good you could not tell if you were inside or in the open air. Shops were on either side of the courtyard, but they were modern fashion places here, not in keeping with the Roman theme.

I wanted us to keep a low profile in this casino, so as when we returned to play the roulette wheel, we would look and sound a lot different. A common English cockney and a slightly Welsh accented lass would just not do. After looking round and getting the general feel of the place, we passed through one hall with what seemed like hundreds of fruit machines, lined in neat rows and then into another great hall where the gaming tables were. I explained to Diane that she should try and not make eye contact with any of the casino staff; she understood my reasons and agreed.

The entire casino was not overly full of people and for the most part they seemed to be favouring the machines. This was reflected by about half of the gaming tables being covered up and just a few people playing on the rest. I suspected that it was because it was now afternoon and everything would come to its full potential in the evenings. There were four roulette wheels in total, but one seemed to be set apart from the others. It was obvious to me that this was the high-stake table and the one that I was going to perform some magic on.

Diane said to me quietly, "When do we do it?"

I replied, "Tomorrow evening. For now we go to another casino and win some stake money. Are you up for it?"

"Too right," she replied.

Really, I was very nervous about the whole thing, but Diane seemed completely at ease and totally un-rattled.

We left Caesars Palace and drove to the Dunes Casino and Hotel not far away. After Diane had amassed a couple of hundred dollars on the machines with a lot of help from me, we decided, as it was evening time, to have our main meal in the hotel's buffet. Moderately priced tickets led us to a table by a smartly dressed and overly polite woman. She then put two sets of cutlery, wrapped in white cloth napkins and our tickets on a kind of toast rack in the centre of the table next to the condiments. Once seated, she asked us what we would like to drink—soft drinks, juices, tea, or coffee—and then pointed to a stack of clean plates at the beginning of the buffet selections. Diane and I then stood up again and went over to get our plates. We then took the food tour around the unbelievable amount of different dishes. By the time we had done the rounds and returned to our table, our plates were brimming over with every kind of food imaginable.

My particular plate consisted of roast beef, prawns, mashed potato, crabs legs, sticky spare ribs and many other things a dinner would not normally be mixed with. Diane's plate wasn't much better, only she had more vegetables than me. We looked at each other, quite disgusted with ourselves, but I said to Diane, "Well, if it's there, you've got to try it. Haven't you?"

"Of course," she replied, with a (*yes we are pigs*) false indignant look on her face.

While we were busy up-loading our plates with food, the smartly dressed usher had brought our order of two glasses of orange juice. The juices were freshly squeezed and about a pint in each plastic tumblers. As my family was not that well off when I was younger, I was always taught not to waste food. Because of this, I had always tried, even if I was full, to finish what was put on my plate. In this particular instance, there was no way I could eat all the food on my plate and I felt very guilty that there were leftovers. Diane didn't manage to eat all hers either, although, looking around at other people, we saw some were returning for second helpings.

"I'm not having a buffet again," I said to Diane.

"Me neither," she replied. "It makes you into a pig and there's so much waste, I feel I couldn't eat another thing"

"Me neither." I replied.

Downing about half of my orange juice, I looked at Diane and said, "Wonder what puddings they've got?"

"Let's go and see." Diane replied.

So off we went again to sample the desserts.

After about three different desserts were forcibly swallowed and our juices were finally drunk we both felt totally stuffed, I said, "I feel like an early night, do you?"

Diane replied, "Yes, if I can get up out of this chair that is."

We managed to stagger out of the Dunes and waddle to our car and by the time we got back to our motel, we both just wanted to go to bed and sleep the meal off.

The next day we woke up about 8:00 a.m. and casually got ourselves ready to go and have breakfast in our usual diner. By the time we had finished breakfast, the time was around 10:00 a.m. when we returned to our car ready to seek out more new experiences.

I said to Diane, "Right, I thought we'd take it easy today with no casinos till tonight, so shall we just have a leisurely drive around to see what else Las Vegas has to offer?"

"Yes, all right," Diane replied. "I need to go and get some make up for tonight anyway."

I said, "That's it then. We'll have a look around the shops."

We drove around some of the large roads that were off the main strip. There was every kind of store imaginable and it seemed like, at every major junction, there was a pharmacy. The great thing I found about driving in Las Vegas was in fact the parking. Every single store had its own parking lot directly outside, so there was never a need to try and find somewhere nearby to park. There didn't seem to be any small shops though, like Mr. Patel's. Stopping at one of the pharmacies, we went inside to discover they not only sold pharmaceuticals but almost everything from straw hats to cigarettes. Diane headed for the cosmetic aisles, while I generally scanned around the variety of goods that were for sale. Everything was so cheap compared to English prices, all except the actual pharmaceuticals, which seemed to be much more expensive for some reason. Systematically going down the aisles, I found there were lots of things I could have bought, but as I didn't really need them, I didn't bother. There was, however, a selection of Las Vegas novelties and I thought it was a good idea to get something for the folks back home.

I bought each of our parents a pack of playing cards, all printed with that famous "Welcome to Fabulous Las Vegas" sign and a couple of pairs of pink, fluffy dice to hang on the rear view mirrors of their cars. Fluffy dice hanging from the interior mirror of a car were a bit of a rage in the seventies, as well as nodding dogs on the rear parcel racks. By the time I had seen everything in every aisle, I came to the cosmetic section. Diane had not moved from that section once, yet she was still deciding what to buy.

"Look at all this stuff, Terry. We don't get this sort of selection in England, yet they are the same manufacturers. I've got too much choice, so I don't know what to get."

I replied sarcastically, "Well, then, it's lucky this store is open twenty-four hours a day so the store keeper can bring you a pillow and some blankets for the night."

"All right," she said. "I can take a hint. I won't be much longer."

I said, "I'll wait in the car" and left Diane to it.

As I came out of the store, I saw the sky had changed from clear blue to a very dark grey and it just started to rain as I got into the car. Within minutes it poured down the heaviest I had ever seen. Thunder cracked overhead, like a plane going through the sound barrier and lightning streaks lit up the sky with bursts of bright, jagged lines, both vertically and horizontally. I started the car's engine and put the wipers on at full speed, but the rain was so heavy they couldn't clear the windscreen quick enough for me to see out. Suddenly the passenger door opened and a soaked Diane got in.

She said, "Blimey! Where did that come from? I've never seen rain like it."

"Me neither," I replied. "I think we will have to sit it out until the rain stops. I'm not driving in this."

After about five minutes, as if by some magic, the rain completely stopped and the sun came out and although now bright and sunny again, the main road was awash with water the drains couldn't handle. As we were parked in a bay facing the junction, I thought I would wait and see the excess water subside before I decided to move off in the car. Just as the drains swallowed the last of the deluge, a man in his forties, wearing a denim shirt and shorts, started to cross the road while a white "Walk" sign was flashing in his favour. A front row of cars on this four-lane road had stopped at the red stop light, waiting for it to change to green, when a crash of metal resounded in the air: A large lorry had obviously not taken the road conditions into consideration and by breaking hard had skidded and smashed straight into the rear of one of the stationary cars. This had shunted the car forward, hitting the man on the crossing.

Instinctively Diane and I got out of our car and rushed over to see if we could help in any way. The man lay in the road on his back, with his legs underneath the front of the car. The lorry and car driver had gotten out of their vehicles to come to his aid, as we did. Although conscious and not bleeding from anywhere, the man was crying out in pain indicating that one of his legs hurt. I lay down on my stomach to get low enough to see the man's legs beneath the car. His left leg was badly broken and bent at an angle that a contortionist could never achieve. I looked at Diane and she read my mind as to what to do. The man had propped himself up onto his elbows by now, so Diane put one of her arms around his shoulders and whispered in his ear, "Trust me. You're going to feel a little pain and then you will be all right."

Still grimacing and with painful tears in his eyes, the man said, "But I can see my leg has broken in two."

"Trust me," Diane repeated with another whisper.

"Stand back. I'm a doctor," Diane proclaimed to the small crowd that had now gathered around the man. She then came over to me, lay flat on her stomach by my side and pushed herself forward beneath the car to reach the man's injured leg.

By grabbing his bare leg just above his sock, she managed to manoeuvre it into a more natural angle. Consequently the man gave out a loud, painful groan. Then while Diane pretended to be analysing the damaged leg with one hand, I touched her other hand which she was using to stabilise herself on the ground; the tingling lasted for about twenty seconds. During that time, his leg, as if by internal hydraulics, reshaped itself and mended. The man was now completely out of pain and said, "My leg feels fine now. What did you do?"

Diane replied, "Oh, it was just dislocated. You'll be all right now."

I went behind the man and put my hands underneath his armpits and pulled him out from beneath the car and then I hoisted him to his feet to a small round of applause from the crowd. In the meantime, someone must have called an ambulance, as it arrived on the scene just as I pulled the man to his feet. Two burly but smart men got out wearing green, boiler suit–type overalls, with white T-shirts showing through their unbuttoned tops. The man, who had been the victim of the accident, was still a bit dazed, but he intently and directly looked at Diane knowing full well that his injuries had been far worse than any dislocation.

"We'll leave you in the capable hands of the medics now," I said to the man.

Still a bit bewildered, he replied, "OK, thanks."

We then returned to our car and got in.

"That's our good deed done for the day," Diane said.

"Yes," I replied. "But look at the state of us. Getting down on the wet road to attend to that man, we've both got soaked and dirty. We'd better go back to our motel and change."

Diane replied, "We may as well and start getting prepared for tonight; I've got some ironing to do."

I hadn't realised how the time had flown by that day. We had only been in one store, but what with the accident it was now late afternoon. Diane wanted to iron some clothes that had gotten creased in our suitcases, so I went to the motel owner and for just a couple of dollars, hired an ironing board and iron. On my return to the room, Diane had lots of clothes lying on the bed, ready to iron.

"Tell you what," I said. "How about—"

Diane continued what I was about to say: "You going to that fried chicken place down the road and getting us chicken and chips. Yes, do that, but after that buffet blowout last night and this morning's breakfast, I couldn't face another big meal yet, so just get one portion for the two of us."

With that I didn't need to say anymore, so I jumped into the car and left Diane with the ironing.

I returned to our room about twenty minutes later, with our fried chicken meal and a couple of cardboard cups of cola with plastic lids. By that time Diane had managed to wade her way through a big stack of ironing. If I had attempted the task, I would still be on my first T-shirt and there would have been more creases in it than before I had started.

We thoroughly enjoyed sitting on the bed, sharing that chicken and chips and at least we had a bathroom to wash our greasy fingers. After we had eaten, I decided it was the right time to go over our game plan for the big event of the evening, so I said to Diane, "Now I know that you are reading my mind, but I am going to go through tonight's plan anyway."

Diane stood up from the bed to attention and saluted. "Yes, sir, three bags full, sir."

Squinting, I looked her in the eyes and with my mouth tightly closed, blew sharply through my nostrils before saying, "Come on. Stop mucking about. You know we have got to get this right."

Sitting back down on the bed and sounding half serious, she said, "OK, I'm all ears and mind."

She then proceeded to blow through her straw into her cup of cola.

After sighing, I began. "Right, tonight we become aristocrats, or at least the grown up children of them. From the time we enter Caesars Palace, I will call you Diana and you will call me Terrance. Now I know you can read my mind, but you will probably also have to do a bit of adlibbing, without going over the top. Got it?"

"Yep," she replied.

I continued. "You will need to dress as elegant and as sexy as you can and remember to take your passport and our bank details. At first, I will act as if I don't want you to play the roulette wheel, but you will insist you do play, as you feel exceptionally lucky tonight. Before you play, I will tell you how much to bet and what number or sections of the table to put your chips on. You will have to read my mind for that information though and make sure you are always reading my thoughts. Do you think you will be able to do it?"

Diane replied, "Of course I can. I used to love doing a bit of acting in our school plays till the other kids started to laugh at me because of the alien thing."

I knew Diane very well by now and also knew she was entirely confident and fearless. I wondered if it would be me that needed to keep my cool and think straight.

"Right, it's about 5:30 p.m. now and we need to leave here about 8:30 p.m. That gives us three hours to transform ourselves into believable Toffs."

To lighten the mood I then said—in a posh, English, Royal Air Force kind of voice. "OK, do your best, team Seer. Over and out."

It was about 7:45 p.m. when I could finally get into the bathroom. Diane had been in there for a good hour and a half. I was in there for just twenty minutes and when I came out, Diane was using curling tongs on her hair.

"Time's getting on," I said.

Diane replied, "I can't help that, Terry; my curling tongs have taken ages to warm up."

I remarked, "It must be the low voltage then because my shaver is only working at half speed, too. Don't worry: I'm not rushing you. The time we arrive at the casino is not cast in stone. It's just that I thought around 9:00 p.m. would be about the right time to get there."

We were both finally ready and Diane looked absolutely stunning.

"What do you think?" she said, as she turned full circle in front of me.

"Wow! Absolutely amazing," I said, in wonderment.

Diane's long, loosely curled; blonde hair flowed over her shoulders and down her back, like strands of gold. She was wearing delicate, dropped diamond earrings, which sparkled when they emerged from beneath her hair as she moved her head. Her necklace was of a similar design and hung equidistantly between the top of her low cut dress and the start of her neck and a matching bracelet hung loosely on her left wrist. Her dress was bright red and clung to her perfectly shaped body, ending well above her knees. Gold sparkling high-heeled shoes and matching clutch bag completed the ensemble, but her face, with her bright red lipstick and delicate green-eye shadow, made her look like a modern day goddess.

"You don't scrub up too badly, either," she said.

Well, I wasn't too sure about that, as I was wearing a black suit that I had bought off the peg a couple of years ago for a distant relation's funeral. It was a little tight, I suppose, but passable.

I had a white shirt, black patent shoes (also a little on the tight side) and a black bow tie, the tie-up kind that my sister had given me as a Christmas present one year. God knows why, but this would be the first time I'd ever worn it.

"You could pass for James Bond," Diane said.

"Yeah right," I replied, with disbelief.

Anyway the way Diane looked; there was no way anyone was going to take notice of my outfit.

I asked, "Have you got your passport and our bank details in that bag?"

"Sure have," Diane replied.

I took a deep breath, exhaled loudly and said, "Then away we go."

It only took about fifteen minutes to reach Caesars Palace, park up and arrive outside the main doors.

Before going in, I said, "Right, from here on, we are the posh Diana and Terrance."

Diane replied, "Have we got to synchronise our watches or something, only I'm not wearing a watch."

"Stop mucking about," I said. "You might be full of confidence, but I'm as nervous as hell."

"Sorry Terrance," she replied, looking at me with an overly cute smile.

I pushed my way through one of the huge double glass doors and held it open for Diane to enter the building. The casino was brimming with people and as I suspected, they were all dressed to the nines. A security guard stood just inside the door, wearing a gold badge on the chest of his grey shirt and he was also wearing a holstered gun on a leather belt, which held up his grey trousers.

As we entered, he took one of his hands that were clasped behind his back and with his index finger touched the side of his brow as a gesture of greeting. Because of Diane's high-heeled shoes, I held her hand as we carefully negotiated a small series of carpeted steps to lead her down to the casino floor. We then slowly walked through the bustling halls of the casino, I with one hand in my pocket and sporting a slight swagger and Diane holding my other hand with finishing-school elegance until we came to the gaming tables.

"Relax, Terry," Diane whispered. "It'll be all right."

She was obviously reading the uncomfortable state of my mind. As we approached the roulette table that Diane was to play at, I could see a heavily built suited man with his hands clasped in front of him, standing about five paces to the side of the croupier, overseeing the game. There was just one high-seated stool with a back support that was not occupied by any players. We took a few steps passed the stool when Diane let go of my hand and sat in the vacant seat. (We were now in Toff mode.)

I exclaimed, in a slightly louder-than-normal way, "Oh, come on, darling, we will be late for our dinner reservation."

Diane replied indignantly, also slightly louder than normal, "No, Terrance, I want to play. I'm feeling lucky."

I replied back, "Oh, all right then, but not for long, OK?"

She had already got the attention of all the players on the table and, in her tight dress with her legs crossed as she sat on that high stool, she was showing a great deal of thigh, which the men nearby were quick to zero in on. The croupier then addressed her, saying, "This table is a no-limit, twenty-dollar-minimum stake table, Miss, if you want to play I'll have to see your ID."

Not replying, Diane undid her clutch bag and produced her passport for the croupier to inspect. He then nodded and returned the document. After she had returned it to her bag, she then turned to me and with a bent elbow and the palm of her hand pointing upward, she singularly said, "Money."

Now getting into the role, I gave a loud "tut" and raised my eyebrows. I then got out my wallet from the rear pocket of my trousers and opened it so all could see its contents. Before we left our motel room, I made sure that I had a big wad of dollar bills in my wallet, mostly ones, but the first two were each for a hundred dollars, which gave the illusion, when I gave Diane a single hundred-dollar bill, that the rest were all hundreds.

She then gestured for the croupier to take the hundred dollar bill and said, "Twenty-dollar chips, then, please."

While the money conversion to chips was going on, I was looking around the rest of the five players just to get a bit of an insight as to who her fellow gamblers were. One man in his forties was wearing a white Stetson hat and was smoking a large cigar. His ornate shirt collar and pencil-thin bow tie, with long tail ends, told me he was probably some rich Texan tycoon, in oil or cattle. The second man was in his fifties, with a few strands of hair combed across the rest of his bald head. He was wearing small round glasses and had a little red notebook full of figures in front of him, which looked as if he was trying to work out or use some kind of betting system. The third player was a woman again, probably in her fifties. She had some sort of dead ferret around her neck and was dressed in a fashion that went out in the thirties. Next to her was another man who was dressed in a similar era to her. They may have been related, but there were no verbal signs to say that they were.

Last of all and next to Diane was a young man in his late twenties, wearing a flashy blue suit, with an undone double-breasted, large-lapelled jacket and black and white shoes, which were resting on the foot bar of his stool. I could see that he was swinging one of his knees closer and closer to Diane's legs and I thought to myself, *Just one more inch mate and I will floor you*. Diane must have read my mind and swung her legs further away from him.

"Place your bets," the croupier said.

I started my thought instructions. *Put a twenty-dollar chip on twenty-four black.*

Diane heard my thoughts and complied.

The croupier spun the wheel, then skilfully whizzed the ball in the opposite direction and announced, "No more bets, please."

As the wheel and ball began to slow, my ability came into effect and I neatly manoeuvred the ball into the slot of twenty-four black. None of the other players had chosen that number and the croupier proclaimed, "The lady wins."

At thirty-five-to-one odds, $700 was a very good start and the winning chips were pushed in front of Diane to the disdainful look of the other players.

"I told you I felt lucky, Terrance," Diane exclaimed.

"Place your bets," we heard the voice of the croupier say again.

Put all your winnings on the black section." I instructed Diane.

Diane complied.

Again, none of the other players copied her lead.

"No more bets," the croupier said, as the little wooden ball flashed round the higher rim of the wheel. I made sure that when the ball finally settled, it landed on a black number.

"The lady wins again," the croupier announced, as he pushed double the amount of chips she had staked in front of her.

"Oh, goody," Diane said aloud.

After two wins, her initial stake of twenty dollars was now $1,400.

Now everything on the red section, I told Dianne mentally.

Diane picked up my thoughts and pushed her chips to the red.

For the third time, "The lady wins again," rang out from the croupier.

By now the other players were taking notice and were intent to see what Diane's next bet would be before committing to theirs.

In my mind, I said. *This time we need to lose one, so put just $300 on any number you fancy and I won't interfere.*

Diane opted for the number seven red and the Texan and woman wearing the dead ferret followed suit. I relaxed my concentration and was scanning all around me while the wheel was spinning for this one.

"Seven red," the croupier announced. Diane had won yet again but without any help from me. Her $300 dollar stake had earned her $10,500. Four times in a row was just a little too much, so her next bet I would have to make sure she lost.

I then said aloud, in my posh voice, "Diana, darling, why don't you try a bet on a three-line section?"

I also said in my mind. *Just fifty dollars.*

A three-line section was three ascending numbers, like ten, eleven and twelve.

If the ball landed on any of those numbers, the winnings would be odds of eleven to one.

With a loud *humph*, Diane complied and on this spin I made sure she and two other players that copied her lost.

"That wasn't very clever, Terrance," Diane scowled. "You leave the bet placement to me."

This failure to win this time was good as the overseer had taken a step closer to the table, starting to suspect Diane's four in-a-row luck.

I projected my thoughts again,

Now pick three numbers that are side by side on the wheel and put a thousand dollars on each.

Diane turned her head slightly to glance at me, as if to say, "Are you sure?" but she still did exactly what I had asked. She picked numbers thirty-one, eighteen and six, as they ascended clockwise on the wheel. I manipulated the ball to end up on number six. The croupier didn't announce her win this time and I could see he was physically sweating as the overseer had taken another step closer. Although she lost two thousand dollars on numbers thirty one and eighteen, she had won $35,000 on number six. A gasp arose from a small crowd that had started to gather around the table as the croupier pushed thousand dollar and five-thousand dollar chips in front of Diane.

Knowing Diane would know it was a bluff, I said to her out loud, "Shall we go now, darling? We are already late for dinner and you know how your father hates us being late."

Diane replied in her themed acting voice, "Daddy can wait, Terrance. I'm not leaving now. Can you not see I'm on a winning streak?"

"Place your bets please," the croupier said.

I gave Diane her instructions: *Now the same again, but this time $2000 on five different ascending numbers in a row.*

Diane made her bets and I landed the ball on one of her numbers. She lost $8,000 but gained $70,000, as an even larger crowd gathered around the table gasping loudly as the ball landed on the winning number. The overseer whispered something in the croupier's ear and the croupier left the table.

Then the overseer announced, "I'm sorry, ladies and gentlemen, but there will be a small delay."

A short while after, another croupier attended the table, apologised for the break in play and said, "Place your bets, please, ladies and gentlemen."

I told Diane via my mind to make the same bet again but with different ascending numbers. Yet again she won another $70,000. The croupier looked at the overseer and shrugged his shoulders as if to say, "I don't know how she's doing it."

The next bet was the same again, but I let Diane know she would lose this time. A ten-thousand loss was nothing at this stage and it slightly reassured the overseer that there was no fiddling going on.

About an hour passed, with Diane winning a lot and losing relatively little; she had amassed $1.5 million. Now very suspicious and concerned about his failure to know what was going on, the overseer addressed Diane, saying, "Are you continuing to bet, miss?"

Diane replied, "This is a no limit table, is it not?"

He then said to Diane and the rest of the players, "I will first have to suspend play for a few minutes then. Would anyone care for a cocktail or something else while you wait?"

"That would be most acceptable," Diane replied.

With that he called a nearby waitress to come over and take her order and went off through a door marked Employees Only. Diane received her ordered Coca-Cola with ice at double quick speed and soon after that the overseer returned with a new roulette wheel.

After removing the old one, he got a small spirit level from his pocket and made intricately sure the new wheel was dead level. He then disappeared back through the employee's door with the old one. The croupier didn't restart the game and it was obvious he was waiting for the overseer to return. A few minutes later, the overseer did return but was accompanied by a very smartly dressed man. As the two drew closer to the table a bolt of panic ran through my body and Diane immediately sensed my agitation. With my thought waves, I said to Diane, *Look who's with the overseer.* Diane's eyes bulged as we were now both looking at the man who had his leg broken in the accident earlier on in the day. The man looked directly at me and Diane but did not show any sign that he recognised us.

The new wheel had been reset and the croupier looked toward the smart man for guidance and, with a nod from him the croupier, addressed the players once again and said, "Place your bets."

I could not read Diane's thoughts but as she could read mine, I said mentally: *There's no going back now, we need just one more win. Put all of the one and half million on black.*

Before Diane did what I asked, she feigned a yawn and, without showing any kind of emotion, said to me, with her posh, brat-like raised voice, "I'm getting bored now, Terrance; one last bet."

She then said to the croupier, "Everything on black" and pushed all her chips forward.

The wheel was spun and the eager-to-see crowd behind me surged forward and pushed me to one side, totally distracting my concentration. The ball had landed in its slot, which I couldn't see and had no mental contact with. Inwardly I started to panic, thinking it had all been for nothing. Even the crowd's loud gasp didn't give me a confirmation of the outcome and those few seconds felt like hours before the croupier finally announced, "Twenty-four black. The lady wins."

The crowd gave Diane a huge round of applause as I exhaled loudly with relief. Diane's sheer luck had completed our intended target.

Diane then said for all to hear, "Oh, goody, Daddy will be pleased."

The man whom we had helped earlier that day and the overseer came around the table to speak to Diane.

"Congratulations miss" he said calmly.

He then said to the overseer, "Have the lady's chips taken and counted at the cashiers."

"Yes, Mr. Stein," the overseer replied, as if complying to the order of a higher chain of command.

"Would you please follow me?" Mr. Stein said to Diane and me.

A little nervously we followed him through the Employees Only door, along a passageway to a large ornate, solid wooden door. He opened it and said, "Please come in." Because of this man's stern demeanour, my mind was working overtime, wondering what to expect. Was he going to call the police because he suspected us of cheating in some way? Or was there going to be a couple of heavies in the room, ready to duff us up, to tell them how we managed to accumulate so much money. His fixed expression did not reveal anything and I wasn't sure if he had even recognised us from earlier in the day.

The wooden door, once opened, revealed a spacious and elaborate office with a large wooden desk, inlaid with green leather. There were two comfy wooden chairs in front of the desk and a name plaque sitting on top, which read, "Mr. Stein, executive manager."

Mr. Stein beckoned us to sit down on the chairs, while he sat on his brown, leather high-backed swivel chair on the other side of his desk.. Quite calmly he started to speak, "You seemed to have had a great deal of luck out there. Now, I am thinking that if you two were on the level, why would you both be putting on an upper class English accent? The only reason I can think of is that you wanted people to believe that you were used to being around large sums of money; therefore, you expected to win a large sum of money." Before either of us could speak, there was a knock on the door.

"Enter," Mr. Stein said, with a raised voice.

A rather small man came in wearing a striped, black and white shirt, with those elasticised metal bracelets just above his elbows to keep his cuffs from dropping over his hands. He was also wearing glasses and a crownless green visor cap on his head. The man whispered something in Mr. Stein's ear and left the room, closing the door behind him.

Mr. Stein then said, "Apparently you have won a total of $3,445,000. That is no meagre sum. From time to time this casino has a winning client who bets large amounts and wins large amounts, but that is a very rare occasion indeed and would happen once in about ten years. You have won this money from a mere twenty-dollar stake, which is quite remarkable."

There was then a long silence, as if Mr. Stein was deciding what to do. Diane and I still hadn't spoken since we had entered the room and weren't about to until we could determine what kind of action this man was going to take. Mr. Stein then did a peculiar thing. He removed his left shoe and sock, stood up and then rolled his trouser leg up to his knee. He then sat back down and put his exposed leg onto the desk.

"Do you see my leg?" he asked.

My silence had to be broken to answer the question but no longer in an upper class voice. "Yes, of course, I do."

"When I had that accident earlier today, I could see that this leg had been completely snapped in two places below the knee. I can't see anything wrong with it now, can you?"

"No," I replied hesitantly.

"Now, can you see anything wrong with my foot?" he asked.

Puzzled, I replied, "No, nothing."

Wiggling his toes and continuing, he said, "When I was born, all my toes on this foot were malformed. In fact, they were so misshapen and useless that when I was three, surgeons had to break them just so I could walk. Since that time they have been rigid with no feeling in them. There's doesn't seem to be anything at all wrong with my toes or leg now, is there?"

"No," I replied, unsure of what this was leading to.

After rolling his trouser leg down and putting his sock and shoe back on, he then picked up his telephone receiver and asked for someone to come to his office. A minute later the small man in the striped shirt knocked on the door and again entered the room. Mr. Stein then said to the man, "Would you please see that this young lady is fully paid out, in whatever form she chooses."

Mr. Stein then stood up and came around the desk to us and said, "If you go with my clerk, he will see to your needs."

As we went to follow the clerk out of the room, Mr. Stein put his hand on my shoulder and whispered in my ear, "I don't want to see you in this casino ever again, am I clear?"

"Loud and clear," I replied.

We followed the clerk to a much smaller office where Diane gave him our bank details to telegram the money straight into our bank account, all except for ten-thousand, which we wanted in cash. After about twenty minutes, we had a verbal confirmation that the money was in our account and we left the casino with the ten-thousand neatly stuffed into my pockets.

On returning to our car, we finally relaxed our scared-stiff demeanour and threw our arms around each other.

"We did it! We're rich!" Diane exclaimed.

"We are, aren't we?" I said, still not quite believing it.

It had been an intense night and all we wanted to do was to go back to our motel and wallow in the glorious outcome. Once back, on entering our room, I took all the money from my pockets and threw it in the air and it landed randomly all over the bed and floor. We were laughing uncontrollably until our laughter turned to passion and, surrounded by dollar bills, we ended up intensively making love before finally falling asleep in each other's arms.

The next day, Diane was the first to wake up and as soon as she did, she shook my body violently. "Wake up, Terry, wake up."

Fearing something was terribly wrong, I said with alarm. "W-what's the matter?

She replied excitedly, "We're millionaires Terry, millionaires!"

Sighing with relief that there weren't ten-armed men trying to break into our motel room, I replied, "So it wasn't all just a dream then?"

"No, silly," she replied, waving a handful of hundred dollar bills in my face.

In that instant, I couldn't help thinking that our new found wealth was again a product of a contrived destiny and the money we had won was a necessary tool for our predetermined future. It was as if the entire events of yesterday were jigsaw pieces, all fitting perfectly together to justify the outcome.

"What are we going to do today then?" Diane asked.

I replied, "Well, first we are going to get ready and we'll go and have some breakfast. And then, we're going shopping."

"Ooo! I'm so excited," she said.

Luckily, I think that Diane was so excited that she couldn't concentrate enough to read my mind as to what we were going shopping for.

After we eventually got our acts together, got ready and went to breakfast at Denny's, we headed down the strip to a group of expensive-looking shops, near to the Stardust casino. These shops, or boutiques as they called themselves, were very upmarket and obviously catered for the more well-off visitors to Vegas. Most of the boutiques were selling clothes from Paris and Milan and that sort of thing. One was even selling luxurious fur coats and I'm sure I could see some dead-ferret stoles more toward the rear, like the one the woman was wearing at the roulette table last night.

Having parked the car in one of the spaces directly outside these upper class emporiums, we got out. I took Diane by the hand and led her to one particular shop. It was a jeweller's and looking through the window from the outside, we could see the most fantastic display of gold and diamond rings. I shuffled down onto one knee and still holding Diane's hand, I said, "This time I'm doing it properly. Diane Smith, will you marry me? You beautiful creature, you!"

Diane actually blushed, as she quickly glanced around to see if anyone was looking on. “Of course, I’ll marry you, Terry,” she replied.

As I got to my feet, Diane flung her arms around me and we locked lips for a fair old time. Finally being able to breathe again, I asked, pointing to the contents of the window, “Do you think you might be able to pick out an engagement and wedding ring from that lot?”

“Oh, I don’t know about that. I’ll have to go in and see if they are going to be up to my standard or not before I decide.” She said with a straight face.

As we entered the jewellers, a small man—with short, dark, greased-back hair, a pencil thin moustache and wearing a brown pin striped suit that looked as if he had forgotten to take the hanger out of the jacket, —came from behind a series of glass cabinet counters and said, “Bonjour, Madame et’ Monsieur. Ow may I elp you today?”

I could swear there was an American twang in his voice somewhere.

I said, “First we would like to see your engagement rings.”

“And your price range?” he replied.

“All price ranges,” I said.

The man returned behind the glass counters and opened the sliding door to one. He then put four trays of engagement rings on top of the counter.

“Wow!” Diane said, as she bent over the trays and meticulously examined all the rings.

She picked out a gold ring with four diamonds, set in a cluster on the top. “Can I try this one on?” she said to the jeweller.

“Certainmon, Madame,” he replied, then took it from the tray and handed it to her.

Putting it on her finger, she said, “Oh, yes, I like this one. It’s a little loose, though.”

The man replied, “No matter, Madame, we ave all zizes ere.”

He reached behind the counter and brought out a set of brass lettered rings, attached to a large thin metal hoop. After trying the various sizes of brass rings on Diane’s finger, he said.

“Yes, Madame, we ave your zize in stock.”

After fumbling about in a lower cabinet, he brought out the same ring in Diane's size and now trying on the perfect fit, Diane said, "What do you think, Terry? Do you like it?"

"It looks amazing," I replied.

"How much is it?" I said to the man.

"That one is eight undred dollars," he replied.

I instinctively swallowed with a gulp. Then I realised, with our new found wealth, $800 was nothing.

"Is that the one you want then?" I said to Diane.

"Yes, please," she replied.

"We'll take it," I said. "Now we need to look at your wedding rings."

Putting the trays of engagement rings back into the cabinet, the jeweller, with obvious delight that he had made a sale, then put another four trays of rings from another cabinet out in front of us.

"Zeese are our latest designs from Parie," he said.

As Diane peered at the rings and got to the third tray, her eyes lit up and she said, "**Oh,-- my,-- God.** This is the ring I saw in a magazine when I went to have a trim at the hairdressers the other week."

This particular ring was made of platinum and had a large sapphire in the middle with blue and white stones alternating around it.

"Try eet on Madame, eet is your zize" the man said, enthusiastically.

Diane put it on her finger and sharply inhaled. After a few seconds of holding her breath, she exclaimed, "I love it."

"How much is that one?" I asked the man.

"Two Zouzand and five undred dollars" he replied.

This time, without hesitation, I said, "We'll take that one too."

"A very good choice," the man said, letting his accent slip a bit.

The rings were separately put in little black boxes with mauve velvet interiors and then into a small cardboard bag, with red strings as handles. I paid cash for the rings and we left the jewellers to go to our car. Once in the car, I opened the box, which held the engagement ring, then I took the ring out of the box and put it on Diane's finger.

"Now we are officially engaged," I said.

Diane, with a tear in her eye, kissed me and said solemnly, "I'll love you forever, Terry, forever."

I replied, "I'll love you forever and I never want us to be apart."

After a long emotional hug, I started the car and off we drove.

"Where are we going?" she asked.

I replied, "We are celebrating and I know just the thing for us to remember this day always."

It was only about a ten-minute drive to get to the airport and driving past the main entrance terminals, we came to a small, vertically semi circular shaped, corrugated, metal, hangar.

I drove through between the large pair of crisscrossing wired gates and parked the car. I then led Diane through the main door and into the hangar's office.

"What's this?" she asked.

"You'll see," I replied.

The office belonged to a small company called Whirlybirds, who owned a fleet of four helicopters. I happened to see their advertisement on a billboard near to our motel the day after we arrived. The billboard said that they ran tours over the Grand Canyon and Hoover Dam. Our trip to Vegas was the first time Diane and I had ever flown, so I thought, *let's go the full hog and take a trip in a helicopter.*

"How do you feel about a helicopter ride?" I said to Diane.

"To be honest Terry, I don't know. Those things look a bit flimsy to me, but if you're going to do it, so am I."

I knew Diane would be game because I found her to be totally fearless in the past once she was into something. At first there wasn't anyone behind the office counter so while we waited I looked around. There was a family of three people—a man, a woman and a child—sitting on a wooden bench beneath the high, rather dirty front office windows. I hadn't noticed them when we came in, as my eyes were directed to the office counter. The man was rather large and in his thirties and looked as if he was one of those people who go back and have thirds at a buffet. The woman, about the same age, wasn't much slimmer. The child though was a thin, funny-looking boy of about ten years old, with bushy, ginger hair, a plate face that was covered in freckles and large, protruding ears. He reminded me of a comic strip boy I had seen once on the cover of the American magazine called *M.A.D.* This poor little fellow's feet didn't touch the floor, as he was cramped between his straight-faced parents.

"Morning," I said.

It was actually about a quarter to one in the afternoon.

"Morning," the man replied, while his wife just nodded and smiled.

Just then the rear door of the building opened and a man entered in brown overalls, wiping his greasy hands with a piece of rag.

"Can I help you?" he said.

I answered, "Yes, we would like to take your tour over the dam and canyon today, if you can fit us in?"

"Then you're in luck. There's a tour leaving in about ten minutes and only one party has shown up," he said.

"So we will have to share a 'copter then?" I asked.

"Fraid so, we can't afford to operate unless we have butts on all seats," he replied.

"That OK with you, Diane?" I asked.

"I don't mind," she replied.

The tour was thirty-five dollars each and would last about forty-five minutes, which I didn't feel was a bad price.

"Right, let's get you weighed," the man said.

"Weighed?" I replied.

"Yes, we have to weigh you for your seating positions, for equal distribution of weight," he explained.

He led us over to the corner of the room, to a set of old-fashioned scales, the ones where a pointer is slid along a metal bar and weights are added to the side until it is balanced. Having weighed us both individually, he jotted his findings onto a scrap of paper.

"Are you the pilot?" I asked.

"No, I'm the mechanic, come general dog's body here," he replied, as he returned behind the counter and gave us a pair of green tickets.

"You'll all be set to go in a little while," he announced.

Sure enough after a couple of minutes, the man poked his head outside the rear door, turned back round to us and said, "OK, we're all set if you would all like to follow me."

Diane and I followed the man through the rear door of the office, closely followed by the couple and their child. We only had to go a short distance before we came face to face with the pilot and his craft. The pilot was a very tall, thin man, about forty and smartly dressed. He was wearing a short-sleeved shirt with pilots stripes fixed to the epaulettes.

He spoke and said, "Tickets please. Red and blue ones first."

The couple both had red tickets, while their son had a blue one. He directed the couple to sit in the rear seats of the helicopter, with their child between them, just as they sat in the office hangar.

He then said to us, "You two must have green tickets. You sit in the front with me."

The pilot sat in the front on the right hand side, while Diane sat next to him in the middle and I sat next to her, by the window. The man in the brown overalls then shut the doors of the copter from the outside and tapped the glass window with his hand to indicate to the pilot that all was secure.

"Can everyone put their seat belts on please?" the pilot said.

The seatbelts were just straps around the waist, like you would find on any airplane, only the pilot's belt came over both his shoulders, which joined to a locking clasp between his legs. I thought this was a bit naff and wondered why we all didn't have full restraint belts. While putting my seat belt on I happened to look around at the family in the backseats.

I felt an uncontrollable chortle coming on because my vision was of these two overweight people virtually crushing this skinny, funny-looking little kid between them. Luckily I managed to subdue it.

The pilot then spoke again. "Above your heads you will each find a set of headphones. As you will not be able to hear much when we are in the air, you will need them to hear my voice."

We all followed the pilot's instructions and put the headphones on, all except the little boy. Just like a car, the pilot had a rear-view mirror and could see the little boy was not wearing his headphones.

"You, too, son," he said to the boy.

The mother then spoke. "Tommy doesn't need to wear the headphone as he is deaf and dumb."

"Oh, OK," the pilot replied.

Hearing those words from Tommy's mother, I squeezed my eyes tightly shut. It was one of those moments when you immediately hate yourself for saying or thinking something about the way someone looked and then you realise that, what was initially funny was actually quite tragic. This was not the first time that fate or destiny had put Diane and me in a situation where we could put right one of nature's defects and help a child and I somehow knew it wouldn't be the last. Although there was no way on board the craft we could get to touch Tommy, I was confident the opportunity would present itself.

"OK. Everyone comfortable?" the pilot said. "Then we're off."

The rotor blades began to turn and the helicopter started to shudder as the blades reached a spinning crescendo. The pilot pulled on what looked like a handbrake and we started to ascend. Whenever I had seen a helicopter in the sky before, I always thought it looked smooth and stable as it flew. This new experience enlightened me, as this flying craft was not smooth and stable at all; it seemed to be shaking all over the place. It was obvious that this was the norm though, as the pilot was completely unperturbed and totally relaxed. In fact, as we headed high above the ground to our destination, the pilot seemed to be reading a manual and was steering the copter with his knees and with the joystick between his legs. *Is this guy a trainee or something?* I thought. I would *have* to ask.

"What's that?" I said to the pilot, pointing to the book.

"Oh, this is a check list," he replied. "We have to go through a sequence of about thirty items when we take to the air, checking instruments and things. I actually teach other pilots and yet I can never remember in sequence all the checks." That reply made me feel a little easier and I'm sure it did the other passengers too.

It took about twenty minutes to reach the Hoover Dam and the pilot told us some of the history and about its construction. He also said that a lot of people still call it the Boulder Dam, as that is what the project was initially called. After about five minutes of circling, we started leaving this particular area of Lake Meade and we headed toward the Grand Canyon. Reaching that vicinity and hovering around certain parts, it became apparent how awesome the canyon really was. Sitting on the wrong side of the plane coming into Las Vegas airport when we arrived, we had no idea of what the canyon truly looked like, but now its sheer vastness and beauty would be imprinted in our minds forever.

Finally, after an amazing tour and commentary, the pilot headed back to Vegas and flew above the entire length of the strip, before a perfectly soft landing back at base. We waited until the rotor blades had come to a complete standstill before emerging from our glass bubble. As I alighted first, I helped Diane dismount the tricky footplate of the copter. I was also on hand to next help the woman in the rear seat onto the tarmac. She was closely followed by little Tommy.

Diane knew that this was our opportunity to help this little lad and she stepped forward to take his hand as he alighted. I discreetly held Diane's other hand, while the woman was busy straightening her clothes. Diane made a bit of a meal helping Tommy down, but it was necessary to allow enough time for our healing to work. After Tommy was down and safe and as her husband was getting out of the craft, the woman said,

"Thank you for helping, Tommy. My legs are still a bit wobbly after that trip."

To her and her husband's amazement, Tommy first made some inaudible sounds, but then he attempted to form some words. "Mm…Mom, I can hear you."

Rigid with amazement, followed by a burst of jubilation, Tommy's father lifted him into his arms and began to cry, uncontrollably.

I said, "Wow, something must have happened to Tommy on the trip. Maybe it had something to do with that mystical Canyon." I was trying to steer the reason for Tommy's miraculous healing away from Diane and me.

"But he has always been deaf and has never actually spoken before," Tommy's mother said, wiping tears of joy from her eyes.

Diane replied, "Well, who knows or cares what it was. I think this is a trip that we will all never forget."

Having left Tommy and his parents in utter euphoria, we returned to our car and drove back to our motel. It was late in the afternoon, so we decided we would relax for a while and then change our clothes to go out for a slap-up evening meal. Relaxing on the bed, Diane looked at the ring on her finger and said, "I've had a wonderful time, Terry and I'm going to remember my official engagement day forever."

During the remaining days in Las Vegas, we did some sightseeing and Diane played the machines in a few of casinos. We also took in a couple of shows before the day finally arrived that we had to leave Las Vegas and start the gruelling trip for home. That day, getting up really early, we stuffed all our clothes into our suitcases and left the motel to go to the airport. Arriving in good time, we returned our car to the rental firm and went to our check-in desk inside the airport. We still had a couple of thousand dollars left, so I said to Diane we could use it to upgrade the seats on our flights home to first class, to make our journey a bit more bearable. Of course Diane was in full agreement.

Our first flight was to New York and it departed Vegas on time and consequently arrived at New York on time. The seats on that flight were huge and very comfortable and the complimentary champagne and stewardess pandering to all our needs was also very nice indeed. After landing at the New York airport, we were directed to a transfer lounge to while away about three hours before our next flight to England. The transfer lounge was vast and had many boarding gates leading from its perimeter to various parked planes. Once a flight number was called, one of these gates would be manned by airline staff and then opened to lead us to the waiting plane. The lounge was very busy with people carrying hand luggage in all directions and as Diane and I headed for an area close to our boarding gate, I noticed something.

"Look, Diane," I said, pointing to the backs of two adults and a small girl walking about fifteen feet in front of us.

"What am I looking at?" Diane replied.

"The teddy bear that little girl is holding at the side of her," I said.

Diane remarked, "I recognise that; it's Lori's."

Looking closer at the backs of this family, we could tell it was indeed Lori and her parents.

I said, "They must be returning from Canada and getting a transfer flight home. How big a coincidence is that?"

Diane replied, "It's great that they are not pushing her in a wheelchair anymore, isn't it?"

"Absolutely," I said. "But we mustn't let Lori see us, so let's hang back a bit to see where they go."

Lori and her parents headed straight for a boarding gate that was already open, where a line of people were going through. We hung back until it was their turn to go through the gate. Lori's dad was holding their hand luggage, while her mum was holding one of Lori's hands. Lori's other hand was still holding her little teddy bear. Just as they were about to disappear through the gate, for some reason Lori turned her head around, looked straight at us and gave a little wave with the teddy's head going from side to side.

"She must have somehow sensed we were here," Diane said.

"Yes, because she certainly didn't turn her head round when we were behind her," I replied.

It was so nice to see that little girl walking along holding her mother's hand, just like any other normal little child and it was another image that we would always remember.

Our flight to London airport seemed endless, but being in first class at least made it tolerable. On arriving at the airport, we collected our luggage and went to an exchange bureau to exchange what dollars we had left for British sterling. I was surprised to received roughly £150 for the notes, but they wouldn't take the multitude of shrapnel (American coins) I had in my pockets. Luckily on the way out of the airport, I offloaded the coins into a glass charity cabinet for overseas aid, so at least they weren't going to be stuck in a drawer at home for all eternity.

Instead of getting a coach to transport us home like the one we had to get us here, I hailed a taxi to take us all the way to our flat. As we finally walked through the door of the flat and hurled ourselves onto the sofa, it felt as if we had been away for months, not for just a week. It had been a very long day and after a nice cup of instant coffee, we dragged ourselves to bed and we both quickly fell asleep.

The next day I woke up about 11:30 a.m. and still felt completely zonked. The jet lag had really gotten to me, although not to Diane, it seemed. As I came bleary-eyed from the bedroom to the lounge, she was already busying herself, sorting out the dirty washing from the cases and generally multitasking.

"How long have you been up?" I asked, barely being able to open my eyes.

"Oh, about an hour. Do you want a coffee?" she asked.

"Yes, please," I replied.

"Well, make it yourself. I'm busy. On second thoughts, I'll make it. You'll only get in my way."

Diane made me a coffee and brought it to me, putting it on the coffee table next to the sofa. She then kissed me on the cheek and said, "Drink up. We've got lots of things to do today."

"What things?" I asked.

"First thing is to go to the bank because I need to see in writing that the money we won is actually in our account."

"Blimey, yes, you're right. Now you've got me worrying."

"Second thing is I want to buy a vase and some flowers. I had to chuck your Wellington boot out; the flowers were dead and the water stank to high heaven."

Diane made me think that there was a possibility that all that money we had won might not actually be in our account. If that was the case, it meant that the whole trip to Vegas was for nothing and we would be in a worse financial situation than we were before the trip. I soon got my act together and within half an hour, we were both ready to go out.

With a little more haste than usual, Diane and I went to the local branch of our bank. After nervously waiting in a queue of about five people, we eventually arrived at the teller's window.

"Could we have a statement of our account, please?" I said, after showing the teller our account number.

"One moment, I'll look it up," she said and went into a room behind her. A few minutes later she returned and said, "Mr. Dobson, the manager would like to see you. Would you mind coming through to his office?"

The teller went to a locked side door, opened it from the inside, poked her head out and said, "Would you both like to come through?"

Oh, dear, I thought, *something must be wrong.*

We went to the door and followed the teller through another door into a small office where a portly, well-dressed man of about fifty was sitting at his desk. As soon as we entered the room, he jumped to his feet and greeted us, shaking my hand exuberantly.

"Come in, come in. Take a seat," he said.

"What's this all about?" I said.

He replied, "Oh, I just wanted to meet you both in person."

Then, maintaining his delighted, eager-to-please grin, he said, "It isn't every day that such a large sum of money is deposited into my bank and I wanted you to know that if I can help you invest it in any way, my door is always open to you."

Instantly relieved, I thought, *Great! The money is in our account,* so I replied to the manager by saying, "For now we just want a statement of our account, please."

"Oh yes, of course," he said. "I have it here in front of me."

Mr. Dobson handed me a printed paper with the balance of our account on it. Our last balance showed we had £410 -24p on it. The new balance, including that sum, was £1,435,826- 90p.

With a smile that almost split my cheeks, I handed Diane the piece of paper. She looked at me with the same huge grin. I just wanted to shout for joy at the top of my voice but, containing my jubilation, I just said to Mr. Dobson in a business-like demeanour;

"Well, thank you for your time. We'll probably be in touch."

"Anytime, anytime, my door is always open," he replied, enthusiastically.

We emerged from the bank onto the street and I gave out a sigh of relief.

"It's confirmed, Terry; we really are rich," said Diane. She then added, "Right, where's that florist?"

8

We waited until the next day to contact our parents to say we had arrived home safely. I had to ring my sister to find out our parent's new phone number, as they had now moved to Hastings, but Diane managed to contact hers OK. We had decided our new found wealth was not something we would tell our families over the phone, so we made arrangements first to go and see Diane's parents and then mine.

The following day we arrived at Diane's parent's house about ten in the morning. Diane opened the front door as usual with her key.

"Hi, Mam, it's me and Terry," she called out.

There was no answer, so we went through the kitchen where the door to the back garden was open. Lottie, Diane's mum, was hanging some washing on the line, while her father Jim was doing a bit of weeding of the flower bed at the end of the garden. Diane and I stood in the kitchen by the opened door and quietly watched her parents. They were totally unaware that we were there until Lottie had finished hanging out the clothes and started making her way back to the kitchen. Lottie jumped back with a start and dropped the empty washing basket as she saw the two of us quietly sniggering in the doorway.

"You nearly gave me a heart attack," she said. "Jim! Look who's here!" she shouted.

Then she said to us, "Come into the lounge, I'll put the kettle on and you can tell us all about your trip."

We went into the lounge and soon after, Lottie appeared with the usually tray of tea. Jim entered the room and sat in his favourite chair after washing the dirt off his hands from the garden..

"How are things?" I said to Jim.

"Oh, not bad Terry, still haven't got another job yet, though."

"Don't worry about us," Lottie said, as she poured the tea. "I want to hear all about your trip."

"It was great, Mam" Diane said. "A trip of a lifetime we will never forget. We had a helicopter ride, saw the Grand Canyon and Hoover Dam, saw some shows and loads of other things, too."

"What's that on your finger?" Lottie remarked.

"Oh yes, me and Terry got officially engaged," Diane replied.

Jim said to me, "I thought you were going out there to get a job?"

I replied, "Well, it didn't quite work out that way."

"So you're no better off then," Jim said with a stern face.

"Well, I wouldn't exactly say that," I replied.

Butting in quickly, Diane said, "We brought you back some presents."

She then picked up the plastic bag she had put by the side of the sofa, when we came into the lounge. Diane pulled from the bag the pair of pink fluffy dice on a string, the pack of playing cards and a white envelope.

"The dice are yours, Dad. The cards are for you Mam and the envelope is for both of you."

"What am I supposed to do with those dice?" Jim said.

I replied, "Oh, there just a bit of fun. That's all. Put them on the parcel rack of your car."

Diane remarked, "There wasn't exactly anything decent we could buy you both. The things there were either cheap and nasty or very expensive. The dice and cards are just a little memento. That's all."

Jim said, "Well, I suppose, like me, you'll have to find a job here then, Terry."

Diane reached for the envelope she had put on the coffee table and handed it to her father.

"What's this then?" Jim said.

"Open it and see," Diane said, forcefully urging her father.

Jim picked up a teaspoon from his cup and saucer and with the handle slit the envelope at the top. He then pulled out the contents. Eagerly expectant of what the envelope contained, Lottie said, "What is it Jim?"

Jim was very quiet, as he tried to take in what was now in his hand and after about twenty seconds, he said, "It's a cheque."

"**A cheque**" Lottie said.

"Yes, a cheque from Terry and Diane's bank account," he said hesitantly.

Lottie said, "You two can't afford to give us money."

Jim then remarked to Lottie, "It's not the cheque that concerns me. It's the amount."

Diane and I were grinning like Cheshire cats, but silent in expectation of Jim telling Lottie the amount. Jim's inability to reveal the amount to Lottie was too much for Diane to bear and she said, "For God's sake, Dad, tell her."

Jim uttered the amount, "It's for a hundred thousand pounds."

Nearly swooning, Lottie said, "Oh, my goodness! Where on earth did you get all that money from?"

I replied, "Diane won it on the roulette wheel."

Coming to his senses, Jim said, "If you can afford to give us this amount, how much did you win?"

I replied a little smugly, "Well, in our money, it works out to be; One million, four hundred and thirty five thousand, four hundred and sixteen pounds."

There was total silence in the room while Lottie and Jim were trying to take the figure in. The silence seemed to be going on forever, so Diane said, "Are you pleased for us then?"

Lottie came out of her stupor first. "Pleased! We're over the moon for you. You'll never have any money troubles ever again and now you can afford to get married properly."

Also now coming down to earth, Jim said, "Thanks to you two, we won't have any money troubles either. We were finding it pretty tough with me being out of work and all. You must have had a hell of an amount of luck to win that amount."

I replied, "Well, we're not going to go into details, but yes, we did."

Our teas in the cups had not been touched and as I drank some of mine, I found it had become lukewarm and a stain had formed in a ring around the inside lip.

"Well, we are going to be shooting off now. We are going to my parents' to tell them the news," I said.

Lottie replied, "Oh yes, they live in Hastings now. Don't they?"

"Yes," I replied. "So I've got a bit of driving to do."

We all stood up and Diane and I started to make our way to the front door. In the passageway, in turn, Diane gave her parents a hug and said, "We'll see you again soon. Take it easy."

"You too," Jim said. "And thanks for the, you-know-what."

It was a great feeling that we knew Diane's parents wouldn't have any money troubles ever again and they could now look to us if they had any financial problems, instead of us going to them, although I doubted they would need any more funds.

It took the usual hour-and-a-half drive to get down to Hastings and eventually we arrived at my parent's new house. The street, Grange Avenue, was about a mile or so up from the coastline and all the houses were bungalows. As we parked the car at the side of the road outside, I could see my mother looking through the window with the curtain pulled back. She opened the front door, as we came up the path and Diane went in front of me, carrying a similar plastic bag she had given her parents.

"Hello, you two. I thought you had got lost," my mother said, ushering us inside.

"Well, what do you think of the place?" she said excitedly, addressing us both.

"Very nice," Diane replied.

The property looked as if it had been well maintained by its previous owner and the front garden was neatly set out with a central patch of lawn and an earth border, with dwarf rose bushes evenly spaced all around.

As we entered the hall, my father emerged from one of the rooms and we were then given a guided tour by both my mum and dad, with me and my father ending up in the rear garden. The rear garden seemed huge, with a large lawn, vegetable patch and patio area that formed a square directly outside the sliding doors of their lounge.

My father then said, "What do you think son?" as he put one hand on his hip and rubbed his back with the other.

I replied, "It all looks great, Dad and everything seems to be in very good condition."

He replied, "You're right there, son. I haven't even got to give it a lick of paint."

"What's wrong with your back?" I asked.

"Oh, I pulled it last week when we were moving in and it hasn't healed up yet."

Diane and my mother were lagging behind in the tour and were now just stepping out of the kitchen door into the garden.

"Give me a hug then," my father said to Diane holding out his hand to take hers. Diane took his hand, then hugged him and kissed him on the cheek.

My mother then said, "Let's go inside. I've made us some sandwiches and you can tell us all about your trip, while we have something to eat."

We all filed into the large, bright lounge and Diane and I sat on the sofa facing the patio doors, with a nice view of the garden. My mother entered the room with two plates of sandwiches that had tin foil covering them, which she must have prepared well before we arrived. My father sat down in his chair and said, "Do you know? My back is starting to feel a lot better all of a sudden. It usually hurts whenever I go to sit down."

As she also sat down, my mother said, "Never mind about your back. I want to know all about their trip."

"Hang on. What's that on your finger, Diane?" my mum asked; homing in on Diane's ring as it sparkled from the light flooding in from the garden.

Diane replied, "We are now officially engaged and Terry got me this ring in Las Vegas."

My dad then said to me, "Looks expensive. You didn't get the job you were after then, so how did you manage to afford that?"

I replied, "You're right, Dad. I didn't get the job, but we still came back with a little bit more money than we went with."

"By gambling, I suppose," he said with a disapproving tone.

I replied, "Well, yes and no. I didn't gamble. I'm not old enough, but Diane won some money."

He then said, "You're going to have to look for another job then."

"No," I said abruptly.

"Well, you can't live on thin air can you?" he replied.

The conversation was taking a slightly aggressive tone and my mother quickly changed the mood by directing a question to Diane, saying, "Tell us what Las Vegas was like?"

Diane told my parents all about our helicopter trip and the glamour of Caesars Palace and the other casinos.

She even told them about the place we went for breakfast each day and the amount of food that was offered in the casino buffets. The mood of the conversation did lighten a little when Diane brought out the playing cards and fluffy dice from her plastic bag and said, "There wasn't anything half decent for us to buy you out there, but we got you these just for a laugh really. We did want to give you this though, as a treat, out of our winnings."

Diane then produced the other white envelope.

"What is it?" my mother said, taking the envelope from Diane.

"Open it and see," I said.

Without hesitation my mother opened the envelope and looked at the cheque.

"This is a joke, isn't it?" she said, smiling.

"No joke, Mum," I said.

"Look at this," my mother said, handing the cheque to my father.

His eyes bulged wide as he said, "How much did you bloody win then? Excuse my French."

I replied, "In dollars, $3,445,000, or in our money, £1,435,416."

He then said, "No wonder you didn't seem bothered about getting another job."

I replied, "No, I don't have to now and Diane can finish her doctor training without us having to scrimp and scrape. So, are you pleased with the little treat we have given you?"

He replied, “Of course we are, but you didn’t have to give us anything. We’re just pleased that you two are going to be all right from now on.”

“Rose, where is that bottle of sparkling white wine we was saving for a special occasion?” he said, asking my mum enthusiastically.

“Underneath the bureau” she replied. “I’ll get the glasses.”

My father found the wine and opened the bottle. There was less of a pop than was expected, but nevertheless, it tasted like champagne.

My mum then said, “I suppose you will want to go out and buy yourselves a nice little house somewhere.”

Diane replied, “Do you know? We haven’t even thought about that yet.”

Diane and I spent another forty-five minutes or so with my parents joking about what we could afford and how we might spend the money and my mother also raised the question of when Diane and I were thinking of getting married. I replied to this by saying that Diane needed to finish her training before we would set a date.

We finally said good-bye to my parents and left them in a very joyous mood as we headed down to the Hastings shoreline to give the news to Diane’s aunt and uncle in their restaurant. We noticed, as we passed by the front of the restaurant, heading for the rear, that the council had finally started work on installing a pedestrian crossing where that young man was killed a few months ago.

Having told Bob and Sally of our good fortune and, giving them a cheque for twenty-thousand pounds, we eventually made our way back home to our flat.

“What a day,” I said to Diane.

She replied, “Yeah and I’m glad it’s over in a way. At least we didn’t have to answer any awkward questions. Everyone was so wrapped up in the amount we won they didn’t ask how we actually won it.”

She then said, “I don’t feel much like eating anything tonight. Those sandwiches your Mam made have filled me right up.”

“Me, too,” I replied.

We ended up watching the television that evening, then talked about going to see some estate agents in the morning, to see what kind of property we might be interested in.

The next day we decided we would go to Wimbledon to check out some estate agents windows. We decided Wimbledon would be a good area for our search, as it was only just out of town but close enough to keep in touch with what was familiar to us. I particularly didn't want us to move anywhere I might feel isolated and out of my class comfort zone. Diane seemed to agree and said that when she qualified, she wanted to work in a London hospital and therefore didn't want to have to spend hours commuting each day.

After looking at what was on offer in a couple of estate agents, we finally came across a property that seemed to tick all the boxes. It was a detached house built in the early thirties with an attached double garage, large front drive and huge rear garden. Inside on the ground floor, it had a large-fitted kitchen, two reception rooms and a lounge. Upstairs was a modern bathroom, with separate shower, three reasonably sized bedrooms and a small room that could be used as an office or even a nursery. The house also had central heating, something that I had never been used to before. The asking price was £450,000 and Diane totally fell in love with it and I must admit, I did, too. Apparently, according to the estate agent, the property was owned by some sort of government envoy who had been reassigned abroad and had to move there with his family and because of this, he needed a quick sale. Diane and I both wholeheartedly agreed we wanted to buy this property and I offered the agent £430,000 for it. He took our details and said he would be in touch once he had relayed this offer to the owner.

Excitedly Diane and I returned to our flat, talking about all the things that we could do with the house and possibly how we could furnish it, but it was going to be an anxious wait to see if our offer was to be accepted.

A week passed before the estate agent finally phoned us and said the owner was prepared to accept £440,000, but not £430,000. Diane and I readily agreed to the new price as we were prepared to pay the full price if our offer was rejected anyway.

It was mid-December now and Diane's twenty-second birthday coincided with the day we moved into our new abode and she said that it was the best birthday present she had ever had. I was a bit sad to leave my flat though, as it had become home and had a lot of happy memories attached to it, Diane and me sealing our love for each other being the foremost.

The removal men did a good job of moving all my acquired junk from the flat, much of which was swallowed up by the size of the rooms in the new house, but a lot of it I put in the garage for sorting out and probably discarding at a later date. Diane didn't really have anything except books, lots of clothes and a million pairs of shoes.

With the move now complete, we realised how sparse the new place was and because the last owner had only left the curtains and fitted carpets behind, we knew we had a lot of shopping to do, much to the delight of Diane.

When we first viewed the property, it was a nice sunny day, which made all the rooms look bright and airy. Although we had the opportunity to look at the sizes and general layout of the rooms, we hadn't actually looked in detail at anything, because the estate agent seemed to be flitting from room to room quite rapidly. With the removal men finally gone, we were now truly alone in our very own house, so we decided to meticulously look around to give us some idea of how we might furnish individual rooms. The most obvious place to start was the upstairs. We had already picked out the master bedroom, in which we got the removal men to put our double bed and second hand wardrobe.

The first thing Diane did once the bed was in place was to put the bed linen on it and sit her little white bear, with the red ribbon, the same one I had won in Vegas, in the centre up against the pillows. From that point on, that little teddy would sit in that position on our bed no matter where we were in the world.

Apart from our room, there was another bedroom front facing, the third bedroom, bathroom and box room were all facing the rear. Generally the house looked as if it had been decorated not too long ago as the wallpapers we could see were fairly modern. Starting our own private tour in our bedroom, Diane came up with lots of ideas for a new colour scheme and obviously a new bedroom suite. I hadn't got a clue about colour schemes, so I basically agreed with everything she was suggesting.

She said, "Right, I can see that you are not going to be much help with this, Terry, so you just keep nodding unless I say something you totally object to, OK?"

"OK," I replied.

She continued. "Now, let's look at the other front bedroom. It will be the guest room for our parents when they come to visit."

"Nod," she said, putting her hand on the top of my head and physically rocking it back and forth. Coming out of our room, we went onto the landing and then to the door of the other front bedroom.

"That's funny," I said. "It's locked."

I hadn't noticed beforehand, but this door had a lock and key, when all of the other rooms just had catches.

Diane said, "I suppose the last owner kept files and work stuff in there that he didn't want anyone to have access to."

"Yeah, suppose so," I replied.

I turned the key of the lock, opened the door and we went in. Somehow this room was out of character with the rest of the house. Although it had no furniture or carpet in it, the wallpaper and curtains didn't quite seem right. There was a chimney breast on the far side wall, which had an old-fashioned fireplace with a wooden shelf and an elliptically shaped mirror on a chain hanging above it.

Diane remarked, "It's like this room is from another era, thirties maybe."

I replied, "I think you're right. It's like this room has not been decorated from the time this house was built."

On our first viewing, we had only really looked at the room from the door opening and hadn't actually gone inside.

Diane said with shimmying shoulders, "This room gives me the creeps, Terry."

"I know what you mean," I replied.

In the centre of the ceiling was a single light-bulb, hanging without a shade and as the afternoon sun was very weak, I switched the light on to make the room brighter. Having switched the light on, it wasn't much better.

"Blimey, that must be a twenty-five watt bulb," I said.

Diane replied, "It is a bit dim."

I said, "I'll see if I can find a hundred or 150 watt bulb in the cupboard under the stairs," and I went off to look.

Sure enough next to the fuse box was a cardboard box with an assortment of light-bulbs. I selected a 150 watt bulb, returned to the room upstairs and switched off the light.

I could just barely reach the bulb standing on tiptoe but managed to remove it. The bulb was still a bit warm, but I managed to see what wattage was printed on it.

I remarked, "That's strange, this is a hundred watt bulb. It should have been giving off more light than it did."

Putting the old bulb on the floor by the skirting, I, again on tiptoe, managed to put the 150 watt bulb into the bayonet fitting. I returned to the switch and flicked it on. The amount of light this new bulb was giving off was no better than the last and the room still had its dim, creepy qualities.

"There must be something wrong with the electrics in here," I said.

Diane replied, "Well, I'm not staying in this room until it's a lot brighter than this. It's making the hairs on the back of my neck stand up."

"I'll check the electrics out tomorrow."

We left the room, shut the door and continued our tour and decorating assessment of all the other rooms in the house. Of course Diane had a lot of ideas.

After getting a takeaway pizza and discussing several colour schemes, we finally went to bed that night about 11:30 p.m. and because of the move, we were pretty tired and soon fell asleep. Just after midnight, I was awoken by Diane shaking me.

"Terry, wake up! There's someone moving about in the room next door," she said, alarmed.

"What makes you think that?" I replied.

"I can hear footsteps on the floorboards," she said.

I replied, "That's probably just the central heating pipes cooling down and making the floorboards creak."

"No, it sounds like footsteps. Go and have a look." She said, pushing me out of the bed.

Tired, stark naked and reluctant, I went to the room next door, turned the key, opened the door and switched on the light. The light was still only giving off a very dim glow, but from the doorway I was able to see there was nobody in the room. I turned the light off, shut the door and instinctively locked it. I then returned to Diane who was now sitting up in our bed with her knees under her chin and the blankets tightly pulled up around her neck and also a very worried look on her face.

"Well, what was it?" she said.

"Nothing, there's no one there," I replied.

"Are you sure?" she said.

"Of course I am," I replied, as I got back into the warm bed.

I managed to persuade Diane that we didn't have any unwelcomed guests and she finally went off to sleep, closely followed by me.

The next day we awoke about 9:30 a.m. got dressed and had some cereal for breakfast in the kitchen. Luckily for us we did have the foresight to bring some fresh milk with us yesterday. After breakfast Diane said she was going to clean out the kitchen cupboards, because although the house had been cleaned before we moved in, she said they were not clean enough for her. I said I was going to try and sort out the electrics in that bedroom.

Although I was a plasterer by trade, you tend to learn a few things about other trades when you work on building sites and I knew what I needed to do to check out the lighting circuit in that room. I thought, for some reason, that particular room can't be connected to the rest of the upstairs lighting circuit, but as it turned out, it was. That didn't really make sense as all the rest of the lights upstairs were fine.

The only logical answer was that the box of light-bulbs under the stairs must be a faulty batch. With this in mind, I took a perfectly good hundred watt light-bulb from the bayonet fitting on the landing and swapped it with the one in that room. The result was the same. The landing was bright and the room very dim. I knew in my mind that there was nothing wrong with the wiring to that room, but I thought that my knowledge of electrics might not be as good as I thought it was, so maybe a qualified electrician would have to be brought in to sort out the problem.

I had now given up on the room's lighting and decided I would just check out the room in general. The floorboards seemed in good condition, although they did creak when I walked over a certain area—between where a bed would have been sited and the window. As the central heating radiator was beneath the window, I naturally assumed the pipe-work for it must be fixed to the joists (wooden floor support beams), in that creaking area, so I thought no more about it and continued over to the chimney breast. The fire surround was made of a hard wood but wasn't very ornate and the mantelpiece shelf that sat on top seemed to be made of a different type of wood, which didn't exactly match. For some reason, I gripped each end of the shelf to check if it was secure, but I found it came away and separated from the surround. Beneath where the shelf had sat, was a hollow that formed a kind of void; it was stuffed full of what looked like letters, each in their envelopes with old stamps on them. I removed the contents of the void and placed all the letters on the floor.

"Diane! Come up here," I shouted.

Within a couple of minutes, Diane came into the room.

"What's up?" she said.

"Look at all these letters," I said, as I knelt on the floor sorting them through.

"What are they?" Diane said, kneeling beside me.

I replied, "They're letters from an army captain to his wife by the look of it, from World War II."

Sorting through the letters, I came across one letter from the Ministry of Defence and read it out to Diane. It was to the captain's wife, informing her that he was missing in action.

"Oh, that's sad," Diane said.

All the rest of the letters were from the soldier. Some were love letters, dating back to what would have been the couple's teens and others were from his tour of duty on the front line.

After a few minutes, Diane, dismissing the letters, stood up, made her way to the door and said, "I have got a lot of rubbish in the kitchen that the previous owners have left behind, so can you give me a hand to throw it into the dustbin?"

I replied, "OK, but what shall I do with all these letters?"

"Put them back where you found them for now and we'll decide what to do with them later," she replied.

With that she made her way downstairs to the kitchen.

I picked up all the letters from the floor and put them back into the void of the fire surround. I then fitted the shelf on top. Just as I slotted the shelf in place, I felt a cold breath on the back of my neck. Instinctively, I glanced into the mirror that was directly above the shelf. There behind me was the ghostly face of an old woman. Her face was ashen and her staring, bloodshot eyes were surrounded by darkened skin, as if she had not slept for a long time. Her shoulder-length hair was grey, frizzy and unkempt and although I could only see her from her shoulders up, it looked like she was wearing a dirty white nightdress. I turned around quickly in fright, but in that split second, the woman had disappeared.

I could feel there was an eerie presence all around me then, so I backed out of the room trying to look in all areas but at the same time hoping she would not reappear. Although physically shaken by the vision of this woman, I decided I wouldn't say anything to Diane, as she had been freaked out by the creaking floorboards the previous night. Making sure I closed the door behind me and that the lock was fully engaged, I made my way down to the kitchen. Diane wasn't in the kitchen, so I figured she must be outside putting rubbish in the bins. There were a couple of cardboard boxes filled with out-of-date packets of food and old cleaning materials, which the previous owner had left behind, so I picked them up from the work surface and headed for our dustbins out front. Our two dustbins were located on four paving slabs, laid at the side of a flower bed, next to a picket fence, which separated our front garden from next door. As I carried the boxes out of the house, I saw Diane near to the fence, crouching down and stroking a young Jack Russell terrier dog. The dog's owner, who was standing on the other side of the fence talking to Diane, was a woman probably in her late sixties. She was wearing a floral pinafore tied round her waist and with folded arms; the sleeves of her green cardigan were rolled up to her elbows. As I approached, Diane said to the woman, "This is Terry, my other half."

The woman then said, "Pleased to meet you, Terry, I'm Ethel, your next door neighbour."

I put the boxes next to the dustbins and replied, "It's nice to meet you, too, Ethel."

I suppose because of the location and size of our properties, I expected the woman to be middle class and posh speaking, but her accent was similar to my South London cockney drawl.

Looking at me Diane said, "Ethel has been telling me that she has lived here since the house was built in the thirties and also about what the previous owners of our house were like."

"Yes, ducks," Ethel said. "Didn't care much for the last owners, they were really snooty and ignored me every time they saw me. But the original owners were a nice couple, Edward and Alice Brady. He was a captain in the army. Tragic though, he never came home from the war. Missing in action, they said. His poor wife just went downhill after that. She didn't eat and by all accounts never left her bedroom. I had a Jack Russell named Alfie then and every time I passed the house to take him for a walk, Alice would have her bedroom curtains pulled back, looking out for her husband to come home. Of course he never did and eventually she just wasted away and died in that bedroom. They reckon she died of a broken heart. Oh! Sorry ducks, you probably didn't know that she died in the house. I hope I haven't spooked you."

With Ethel's dog contentedly and quietly sitting at her feet, Diane said, "Well, I think the estate agent should have told us that, but he didn't. We thought it was a bit eerie in that room, didn't we Terry?"

"Yes, we certainly did," I replied.

Ethel, changing the subject, said, "I can't believe little Benji there has taken to you both. He usually doesn't get on with anyone and the postman absolutely hates him. I'll try and get the hole in the fence fixed, which he got through though."

"Don't worry about that; I'll sort it out," I replied.

Ethel then said, "Oh, all right, then; that'll save me a job. Ooo, it's getting a bit nippy out here. Well, it has been very nice to meet you both, must go, there's a radio programme I want to listen to, all about the supernatural.

I like all that kind of stuff, the unexplained, ghosts and aliens and that type of thing. Come on Benji. Come and get a biscuit." She said, as she made her way to her front door.

You could see Benji was actually thinking about whether to go with Ethel or stay at Diane's side, but in those brief few seconds, the biscuit took precedence and off he went in a flash, back through the hole in the fence and then through Ethel's front door.

Back in our kitchen, Diane said, "Ethel is a nice lady. I'm glad we've got someone like her as a neighbour, although I didn't much appreciate her telling us about the woman dying in that bedroom."

I replied, "Let's have a coffee and a sit down, there's something I want to tell you."

Diane replied, "Now you're freaking me out, what is it?"

"Nothing to be freaked out about, you make the coffee and I'll tell you," I said.

Diane made the coffees and we sat down at my old table and chairs we had brought from the move.

"Right, go for it, I'm all ears," Diane said.

I began, saying, "Remember I told you that Theron enlightened me on a lot of things to do with this world that most people think are myths."

"Yes," Diane replied.

"Well, one of the things he told me was that ghosts do actually exist. He said that sometimes if a person dies tragically in some way, their spirit doesn't fully go through to his dimension. It gets trapped in a void between the dimensions. That spirit can be seen by a living person who can receive its brain waves or psychic energy and can manifest itself at will."

After a few seconds, Diane shut her open mouth, swallowed and then said, "So what you are telling me is that we have a ghost in the house."

I replied, "Well, yes. But there's nothing to be frightened about."

"You've seen it, haven't you?" Diane said.

I replied, "Yes, I've seen Alice, but only briefly. It's obvious from Ethel's story about her that she believes that her husband will return home to her one day and she refuses to accept he's dead. And that's why she is still here."

Diane then said, "I can't live in a house where I know a ghost can pop up at any given moment, Terry. It would make me a bundle of nerves."

I replied, "That's why we must help her to cross over fully."

"How do we do that?" Diane said.

I answered, "It seems going by the creaking floorboards last night that she manifests herself around midnight. We must be in the room at that time and try to persuade her to cross over."

Diane said, "But how do you know that we can even speak to a ghost and if so, that a portal will appear for her to go through?"

"Truth is I don't, but I've got a strong feeling it will work."

Although I could see Diane was very scared at the thought of confronting a ghost, I also knew that she had a very strong mind to overcome that fear and true to form, she said, "OK, we'll do it tonight, but if it doesn't work you know I won't be able to live here, Terry."

I replied, "Deal. If it doesn't work, we'll move again."

About ten minutes to midnight that evening, Diane and I, not knowing what to expect, entered that room. I switched the light on and it gave off that dim, dingy glow, making both our hearts beat faster. Diane stood behind me, clutching one of my arms with both her hands; the pressure she was exerting felt like a tourniquet. As the minutes and seconds neared midnight, I was breathing deeper and swallowing every few seconds in anticipation of what was to come. Around midnight, the room seemed to cool down rapidly and each breath we exhaled was now visible. At first there was a distortion in front of the chimney breast, making the fire surround shimmer and look hazy. Then like a neon light that was flickering to come on, a figure started to form. A few seconds later the ghost of Alice was in full view and she was gliding toward the curtains of the window. I could feel Diane's heart thumping as she pressed herself close to my back, peering over my shoulder. Alice pulled the net curtains to one side and looked out of the window into the dark street and we could hear a feint sobbing sound coming from her direction. With a last deep intake of breath and gulp, I spoke to the spectre to get its attention.

"Alice, Alice," I said forcibly.

The ghostly figure turned to look in our direction. Diane's grip on my arm became even tighter and the fingers of my hand began to tingle with the restricted circulation.

Again I spoke to Alice. "Edward is not coming home, Alice."

"He will return to me," Alice replied, in a slow, soft whimpering voice before turning her gaze back to the window.

I continued. "He's waiting for you on the other side."

Alice turned her head toward us again.

From the corner of my mouth, I whispered to Diane, "I could do with a little help here."

Almost instantly, Diane let go of my arm and stood at my side and with bold courage, she exclaimed, "Edward has passed over and has been waiting for you to join him. You must go to him, Alice."

Alice's ghostly, pallid face changed from a frown to half a smile. It was as if she had been waiting for guidance to end her eternal doubt of Edward's demise. Diane's forceful voice had made Alice consider her words.

At about half the usual brightness, a portal began to open near the chimney breast.

"Edward awaits you, Alice," Diane repeated.

Alice's face changed to a full smile as her head turned away from us and looked toward the light. Slowly, her frail body began to glide toward the portal and as she entered, she and the portal were gone in a flash. Almost immediately the room's temperature lifted and the ceiling light lit up the whole room, reaching its full capacity of a hundred watt bulb.

"She's gone," I exclaimed.

After that night, the room and the rest of house truly felt like home, although the floorboards still creaked of an evening, when the central heating was cooling down.

Christmas was soon upon us and Diane and I had bought chairs and a dining room table that, when fully extended, sat ten people. Needless to say we had all our close relatives over for Christmas dinner and because we had the resources, we made sure everyone got a really good present. We had always existed on takeaway and ready meals in the flat, so I didn't really know if Diane could actually cook. It turned out that she was a brilliant cook and the quantities to feed our lot didn't faze her one bit. A good time was had by everyone and our first Christmas together as a couple was a big success.

My twentieth birthday came along in January and it was another excuse for a family get-together. It was also a chance to announce to all the family that Diane and I were going to get married in July, although we hadn't settled on a specific date.

During the next few months, I had made one of our downstairs rooms into an office for Diane. We bought a nice desk and I covered one of the walls with shelves to take Diane's vast collection of medical books. She spent most of her days in that office, while I continued to decorate the rest of the house. We also got to know Ethel, our next door neighbour, quite well and Benji was a frequent visitor. Ethel's husband, Joe, had died of a heart attack about five years ago; apparently, he was a bookkeeper for a big importer company and he left Ethel very secure financially. She turned out to be a real asset to us as she would keep an eye on the house when Diane and I decided to go out for the odd day. She was also a mind of information about the area we now lived in and the local people, who, she said, some were real oddballs.

It was one fine day in April around about lunch time, when Diane and I were busy doing our daily routines, when there was a ring at our doorbell. I shouted out to Diane that I would go to the front door to see who it was. When I opened the door, there stood an elderly gentleman, who must have been in his eighties. He was about six feet tall and stood perfectly upright—not what you would expect from someone of his years. His full head of hair was pure white and smartly combed with a side parting. He also had a well-trimmed white moustache and his general semblance was immaculate. The only thing that was out of place in his appearance was a long scar from the centre of his temple around his left eye and half way down his cheek. The man looked a little surprised when I opened the door.

He said, "Oh! I'm sorry to bother you. I was expecting someone else."

I replied, "Are you sure you have the right address?"

"Oh yes!" he said. "I most certainly have the right address. I used to live here. My name is Edward Brady."

My mind seemed to freeze up as it tried to take in what the man had said; then, all at once past events relating to this man flooded my brain. After a few long seconds, I said, "I think you had better come inside."

I showed the gentleman into our lounge, asked him if he would like a cup of tea, which he graciously accepted. I then invited him to sit down, while I went to the kitchen to make it. My next step was to tell Diane who the caller was.

"Oh, my God, it can't be," she said.

"It is," I replied with trepidation. "Go next door and get Ethel; she used to know him. We could do with her support."

Diane immediately went next door to get Ethel, while I put the kettle on, returned to the lounge and sat down.

"Tea won't be long," I said, nervously tapping my foot up and down and hoping Diane would get back quickly with Ethel. After a pregnant pause, I then said, "I know a little bit about you, but only what my neighbour has told me."

Luckily just then, I heard our front close; the cavalry had arrived and Diane and Ethel entered the room. "Edward, where have you been?" Ethel said, with part joy and part condemnation.

"Hello, Ethel. It's very nice to see you again after all these years and who is this with you?" he asked.

I replied, "This is my fiancée, Diane. We live here together."

"Pleased to meet you Diane, what beautiful green eyes you have," he remarked.

Directing his speech back to Ethel, he said, "I suppose Alice has departed, hasn't she?"

"I'm afraid so dear," Ethel said. "Alice died a good few years ago now and people thought, including me, that she died of a broken heart because you never returned after the war. How is it you've returned now?"

"It's a long story," Edward said.

I butted in, saying, "Well, before you tell it, I am going to make the tea. Does everyone want one?"

Ethel and Diane answered, "Yes, please," and Edward looked at me and gave a secondary nod of confirmation. The kettle had already boiled once, so I made the four teas in double quick time. Putting the pre-poured teas on a tray with the sugar bowl, I added a recently opened packet of digestive biscuits to the mix before carrying the tray into the lounge.

We were all now sitting down, with our teas within easy reach and Ethel, Diane and I were poised with baited breath in anticipation of what was to come, when Edward said, "I suppose I'd better begin then."

"As you all probably know I was an army captain in the war. I was sent to the front line trenches in France to replace a commanding officer who had been badly injured. I suppose I was there about three weeks before the Germans brought in heavy artillery to speed their advance. We were taking heavy casualties throughout and one of their shells had a direct hit on my location. From that point on I remembered nothing except waking up behind enemy lines in one of their camps. My uniform had been replaced with tatty civilian clothes and my head was bandaged. I knew nothing of my rank, or who I was. I was then transported with other English soldiers and some French civilians to a prisoner of war camp, somewhere in Germany.

"The Germans knew I was a soldier, but with my loss of memory and no uniform, they had no way of knowing who I was, either. I must admit the camp guards treated us quite well really as long as we conformed to their rules and didn't try to escape, that is. Anyway that is where I spent the rest of the war until we were liberated. After we were all repatriated, I ended up in a Ministry of Defence hostel in Dover. You would be surprised how many more injured soldiers were there, just like me. I still couldn't remember who I was, or anything at all about my previous life before my injury and the hostel has been my home ever since. It was only a couple of weeks ago I woke up one morning and remembered everything. Not knowing what to expect, I've spent the past two weeks trying to rationalise the situation, knowing full well that what I once called my life didn't really exist anymore and that my eternal love, Alice, must have either remarried, moved away, or, worse, passed on. I had to mentally prepare myself to accept what I would find if I returned."

Diane said, "Oh, you poor man. The war has taken your whole life away."

Edward replied, "It's strange. When my memory fully returned, I knew somehow that Alice was no longer with us. She was always and will always be my one and only love and before, I had always felt her presence anywhere I was. That presence is no longer with me. I'm OK, though; I know someday I'll see her again and until that day comes at least, I will have my memories of her. For now I still have a life. I've even got a job, at my age, in a cold fish shop in Dover, far removed from the accountancy job I had before the war. I enjoy it and it brings in a little bit of money to help with my pension."

Ethel spoke up and said, "I'm sorry Edward. When Alice died, they couldn't find a will and this house was put to probate. The new owner had something to do with the government and I'm sure he got it through some ministry dodgy dealings. He moved abroad a few months ago and this nice couple have now bought it."

Edward said, "Oh, I'm not here to contest the ownership of the house, or anything like that, but I would ask a favour of you good people."

He was directing his words to Diane and me.

"What's that?" I asked.

He said, "Before I left for service, I put some personal belongings, papers and photographs, in a small leather case behind the water tank in the loft. I don't know why, but I thought they would be safe there. I wonder if you would permit me to recover them."

I said, "Well, give me five minutes and I will go up there and if it's still there I'll bring it down."

"Wonderful," Edward replied.

Leaving Ethel and Edward talking in the lounge, Diane followed me up the stairs to see if she could help. I hadn't been into the loft before and the hatch and attached ladder were a bit creaky and in need of some oil on the springs. Having got the hatch fully open and the ladder firmly seated on the floor of the landing, I climbed to the top. Scanning around the loft hatch entrance, I said to Diane, "I can't see a light switch, so can you get me a torch from my tool box?"

I tried to adjust my eyes to the darkness of the roof space, while I waited for the torch and saw the water tank neatly sitting on the joists, about six feet to my right. Climbing up a few steps of the ladder, Diane handed me my torch. The loft hadn't been boarded out, but Edward must have previously put some temporary boards on the joists in order to make a pathway to the tank. I soon found the dusty brown leather case behind it and carried it back to the landing.

"I've just thought," Diane said. "Did you throw away those letters and things you found in the fire surround shelf?"

"No, they are still there," I replied.

"Well, we had better give Edward those, too," she said.

Diane took the case down to the kitchen to clean it of dust, while I recovered the letters from the fireplace and then met her back in the kitchen.

Diane said, "You do realise Terry, we inadvertently lied to Alice's ghost. We told her Edward was dead and because of that, we coerced her spirit to enter the portal."

I replied, "I'm glad we did. I couldn't imagine what would have happened, if after all this time Alice's ghost finally saw a living Edward coming down the front path and then leaving again because we now live here. I mean, what would the outcome have been?

"She was a troubled spirit and who knows? That spirit might have turned malevolent. No, we did the right thing; she is at peace now."

"Yes, I suppose you're right," Diane replied.

I then said, "Don't you think it's strange though, that Edward only got his memory back around the time Alice's spirit finally entered the portal. It's as if the Nature entity wouldn't allow Edward's memory to return until Alice's spirit wasn't around. Also how come it was us that bought this house and were able to deal with Alice's spirit the way we did. I don't think that was a coincidence either."

Back in the lounge Diane gave the case to Edward and I handed him Alice's letters from the fireplace.

"I found these when I was doing a bit of renovation," I said.

Recognizing the letters, Edward said, "Oh, my word, I had no idea Alice had kept these."

There was a short pause as Edward swallowed and tried to fight back a tear.

"Thank you *so* much. You have no idea what these mean to me," he said.

After composing himself, Edward announced, "Well, I really must be going now and with a bit of luck, I'll catch the 3:30 p.m. train home."

I said, "I'll get my car out of the garage and drive you to the station."

"Oh, thank you," Edward replied.

As I left the lounge, Edward stood up and started saying his good-byes to Ethel. I went and got my car out of the garage and was back in the lounge in a very short space of time.

Ethel said to Edward, "Now you've got my phone number, ducks and I've got yours, so let's keep in touch."

"I certainly will," Edward replied.

Diane then said to Edward, "It has been very nice to meet you and if you are in the area any time, please come and visit us. It will be lovely to see you again."

Edward moved toward Diane, took one of her hands and kissed the back of it. He then said, "How very gracious of you and thank you both for your hospitality."

I took Edward to the station in my old banger of a car and he had plenty of time to catch his train. Shaking my hand with a firm grip, he repeated his thanks and marched off.

I couldn't help thinking on the way back home that Diane and I were somehow destined to be cogs in Nature's machinery—by putting right, not only human growth failings but also the enigmas of its equilibrium as well.

Who knows? There were probably many others in the world like us also playing a similar role to maintain the balance of Nature. I also thought it was about time I got a new car.

About a week after Edward's visit, Ethel came knocking at our door with urgency. I opened the door and Diane came out of her office to find out why

Ethel was calling. Slightly out of breath from her short trip from her house to our front door, Ethel said, “I’ve just had a phone call from Edward.”

“I hope he’s all right?” Diane asked.

“Well, that’s the thing I want to tell you. He’s more than all right,” Ethel said, inhaling deeply and gulping to slow her heart rate down.

She continued. “You know that horrific scar on his face; well it’s vanished. Edward told me that every day for the past week in the mornings when he looked in the mirror to shave, he noticed the scar was becoming less visible, until this morning he looked and it had completely gone. How spooky is that?”

“That’s incredible,” I said.

Ethel spoke on, saying, “Yes, but come on: scars don’t just vanish, at least not to the point where they are totally invisible. Somehow I know it has something to do with you two.”

“What do you mean?” I replied.

She said, “Well, I can’t explain it, but I know there’s something different about you two. For a start, Benji doesn’t like most people, but the first time he saw you both, he was completely at ease.”

Ethel then seemed to analyse her words and thoughts for a few moments, with her hand across her mouth. Removing her hand and stepping back a pace, she said, “You’re aliens!”

Just as Ethel started to take another step backward, she caught her heel on the raised threshold of the door and fell backward onto the stone step. In this instance I couldn’t react quickly enough to freeze her. As she fell, she flung her arms out instinctively and hit the empty milk bottles that our milkman had not yet taken. Her arm had been badly cut from the broken glass and without thinking Diane and I responded by getting either side of her, grabbing an arm each and lifting her to her feet. The dress she was wearing was sleeveless, so both our hands had direct contact with her skin. The effect of this was the same as if Diane was touching someone and I was holding her hand for virtual instant healing. We all three were looking at the gash on Ethel’s arm when, as if by magic, the blood stopped flowing and the wound healed. Still holding

Ethel's arm, I said to her, "We are not aliens, Ethel. Look you've had a shock. Come inside and sit down. We'll make you a nice cup of sweet tea and we will explain."

Ethel came to her senses a bit and realised she was in no danger from us, so she agreed. We sat Ethel down in the lounge, while Diane and I went in the kitchen to make the tea.

"We can't get out of this one Terry," Diane said.

"I know," I replied. "We have got to tell her the truth, but not all of it. Leave it to me."

In the lounge Diane gave Ethel her tea; she immediately took a couple of sips from the steaming cup.

I said, "Right, Ethel, let me explain."

"Both Diane and I knew there was something different about us, but we didn't know what it was until we met purely by chance. We discovered Diane could heal people when she touched them, but it took a week or so for it to work. That's why her gift wasn't apparent.

"Again, purely by chance, we found if I was touching Diane at the same time she touched someone else, a cure would be almost instantaneous. I sort of boosted her powers. Now there is a "*But* "to this.

"We also discovered that it will only work on unnatural ailments, imperfections that humans shouldn't have, like a deformity or an injury. Other stuff that relates to old age or the natural wearing out of the body, we cannot cure, such as an age-related heart attack. Because most of the things we can cure are imperfections from birth, we mostly concentrate our efforts on curing children. Edward's scar was not a natural occurrence of his age, that is why when he kissed Diane's hand last week, it began the process of his facial reconstruction. Also your cut today did not naturally occur, so when we both lifted you from the ground, our touch instantly healed your arm and possibly cured you of some other ailments you may have had that weren't age related."

Ethel sat quiet for a moment, obviously trying to take in and make sense of what I had told her. "You must be angels then," she said.

With a slight chuckle, Diane replied, "No, Ethel, we are just ordinary people with an ability to help others."

I then said, "Ethel, Diane and I have only been together for less than a year, yet in that time we have helped a lot of children who without our help would either be in a lot of pain or dead. If anyone knew that we could cure people, there would be a stampede to get to us and we wouldn't be able to continue helping people, especially the children. It is vital that you do not tell a soul about what we can do. Even our own parents don't know, so we are asking you to promise to keep our secret. Not even your best friend in the world can know."

Ethel drank the rest of her tea in one go and sat thinking for a few minutes. Diane and I looked at each other in anticipation of Ethel's thoughtful response.

"Does it work on animals?" Ethel said.

I replied, "We don't think so, but Diane once diagnosed a stomach ailment in an aggressive dog."

Ethel sat quiet and thought for a little while longer before saying, "You have my word. I will never tell anyone what you can do or what you have told me."

"Thank you, Ethel," Diane said, with relief. "Now, do you want another cup of tea?"

Ethel replied, "No, thanks. I had better get back. Benji will be wondering where I am."

With that she stood up and made her way back to her house next door.

Diane then said to me, "Do you think our secret is safe with Ethel?"

I replied, "I certainly hope so."

9

At the end of May Diane finally finished her studies and completed her training to become a doctor. A month later her qualifications were confirmed and she was now able to get a proper post as a paediatrician. I teased her quite a bit by calling her Dr. Diane at every opportunity, but aside from the joking, I was so very proud of her. Because her full time studying was now over, we set a date in July to get married. I finally bought a new BMW car, but I also kept the old one for Diane to use for driving lessons—and anyway I was too sentimentally attached to sell it.

Diane's mother completely took over all Diane's related wedding arrangements, which Diane was pleased about, since for ages, she hadn't had the chance to have quality time with her. But both our parents were absolutely overjoyed that we were finally going to tie the knot.

The big day had arrived. Diane had spent the night in her parent's house so she could get ready for the day without me seeing her in her wedding dress. Later I had arranged for a white Rolls Royce to pick her and her parents up to take them to the church. I got myself ready in our house and my sister's husband Martin was to take me to the church in his car. Martin had accepted my invitation to be my best man, so when he arrived I gave him the ring that I bought in Las Vegas to hand to me at the altar. All our other relatives were coming in their own cars and my mum and dad were bringing Linda and Steven. I had made all the arrangements to make sure everything went to plan and on time.

Martin was a big stocky man who worked in a warehouse, driving a forklift truck. I got on with him OK but found him to be one of those people that weren't quite precise in what they did.

In his home his decorating wasn't up to scratch and things never seemed to be finished off. I, on the other hand, had always planned and executed what I did to a high degree and would never leave anything half done or substandard. I suppose that is why he was all right as a relative, but I couldn't really call him a mate. Anyway although he arrived about ten minutes late to pick me up, knowing what he was like, I had already allowed for the eventuality of him being late. After handing him the ring, which he put in the small pocket of his waistcoat, we set off for the church. The church was a large building, with a massive round-stained glass window in the front. Diane had chosen it because when the sun shone through that window, it projected coloured aspects all around the altar and it was reasonably central for most of our relatives. There was plenty of parking in its grounds and it was only about three miles away from where we lived.

About a mile into our short journey, Martin's car started to get a bit bumpy and it turned out he had a rear flat tyre. A certain panic whizzed around in my head, like a fly trapped in a bottle.

"You have got a spare," I said to Martin, as I looked at my watch.

"Oh yeah," he said. "It won't take long to fix."

We pulled into a small council estate, got out of the car and lifted the boot lid. The boot was full of all sorts of stuff, greasy rags, jump start leads and various things that were not quite intact. Among all the rubbish was a car jack, which I picked up because we were going to need it to change the wheel. This item was also broken.

"Martin," I said. "Tell me that this isn't the only jack you've got."

"Oh blimey, I forgot that it was broken. I intended to get a new one about a week ago," he said.

This can't be happening, I thought! *I'm never late for anything and I certainly don't want to be late for my own wedding.* If it came to it, I would have to try to distract Martin and levitate the car to change the wheel.

"Get the spare wheel out anyway," I said. "I might be able to find someone who has a jack."

While Martin pushed the junk aside to lift the spare wheel out of the boot, I kind of prayed that the spare wasn't flat also; luckily it wasn't and at least amid the junk, I saw that Martin did have a wheel brace. While I looked around in vain for someone in another car, I spotted something that might just solve our problem and that would keep my levitation powers to a minimum.

"Have you got a flat-headed screwdriver?" I asked.

Martin handed me one from the boot.

I then said, "Right you loosen the wheel nuts, just a bit."

As Martin started to loosen the nuts, I went about fifteen feet up the road to a manhole. I used the screwdriver to pry the lid off. When I came back, I said, "Right, you push and steer the car and I'll push from the back, so that the flat tyre is over the manhole."

Martin replied, "Right, I see what you're thinking."

As Martin pushed and steered the car with the door open, I pushed the car from the rear, with a little bit of force from my mind. As soon as the wheel was over the manhole, I said, "Right I'll hold down the opposite front wing to keep the car level and you change the wheel."

Martin didn't realise how much strength you would need to do that and thankfully he couldn't see that I did it without any physical effort. Anyway it worked and Martin did his best to do the job quickly. After throwing the wheel with the flat back in the boot and replacing the manhole lid, we set off as fast as we could to the church.

We arrived at the church to find all our relatives sitting in the pews waiting for us. My dad gave me a stern look, as Martin and I made our way to the altar. Literally a few seconds later the organ started up, playing the wedding march and I and everyone else turned our heads to look down the aisle and toward the church entrance. Diane entered, holding her father's hand. She was wearing a high waist, pure white dress, with a round low cut neck and laced sleeves. Her veil lightly obscured her face, but her loosely curled, long blonde hair draped her shoulders like thick strands of gold. Like a mythical fairy princess, she looked breathtakingly beautiful and my mouth fell open and dried up instantly. As she came toward me, I tried desperately to salivate and swallow and in that brief moment my stomach knotted and a tear ran down my cheek. I somehow questioned myself as to whether I was worthy to marry such a goddess and I didn't know that so many emotions could be felt all at the same time. Her father was holding her hand up at shoulder height until she reached my side; then she whispered in my ear, "Where have you been? I had the chauffeur go round the block twice."

That little remark brought me back to my senses somewhat and I realised I was marrying the love of my life, not a fairy tale illusion. I whispered back, "Sorry, Martin." She knew exactly what I meant without having to read my mind.

The rest of the service went off without a hitch and when the vicar finally pronounced us man and wife, we kissed. I felt like I was the happiest and luckiest man on the planet. Then we turned to face the multitude of family and guests and I noticed most of the women were using tissues and handkerchiefs, carefully trying to mop their tears without spoiling their makeup. I heard a loud mucosa blow coming from one of the rear pews and saw Ethel with a hanky in hand, wiping her nose from side to side. There seemed to be huge grins all round from the men and only a small amount of the children, including Steven, looked as if they were bored silly.

After going into a back room and signing the register, we eventually emerged and walked back down the aisle to the entrance door and out into the sun-drenched church lawns. We were closely followed by an orderly but grateful assemblage that could now stretch their legs, and I saw at least half of them lighting up cigarettes in desperation.

The photographer I had arranged had already set up his tripod in a position where a side-stained glass window and rose flower bed would be visible in the background of his shots and after he could see the exodus from the church was complete, he started to call people over. With Diane and me occupying centre stage, relatives were placed at our sides in order of closest relations and the rest were ushered together in a couple of tiers behind. After that, there were endless combinations of relatives photographed with us and children sat on the grass, cross-legged in the foreground. Diane looked amazing with her veil lifted. Her golden hair was shining in the sunlight and her pure white dress ballooned from her waist to the ground and hugged the shape of her upper torso. I was wearing a light brown three-piece suit, with feint cream stripes.

It consisted of a single breasted jacket, flared trousers and waistcoat, which felt a little bit tight and my brown platform shoes made me look taller than I actually was. It was unfortunate that Diane didn't have bridesmaids, as there wasn't really anyone I or she knew to be suitable, because they were either too old or too young, or not closely related enough, but that didn't detract from the ambience of the event.

Finally, after about half an hour, the photographer thanked everyone, detached his camera and folded up his tripod. Most of the unattached women who were present and some of the married ones gathered together, to try to catch Diane's bouquet as she threw it high into the air behind her. Some jostling occurred, but it was Ethel who ended up the victor, holding it at arm's length above her head with a huge victorious smile on her face. The vicar came out of the church soon after and had a word in my ear. He said that there was another wedding going to take place soon, so could we all begin to leave. Diane and I made our way, showered in confetti to our white Rolls Royce and got into the rear seats and after another hand held chorus of clicks from the pro and amateur's cameras, we were driven off to the reception venue.

I had hired a moderately sized hall for our reception, which everyone was given directions to with their invitations. We had decided on a buffet to cater for our guests and when we arrived, all the food, tables, chairs and disco were all set up ready and waiting. As people began to arrive, we met them at the main door and shook everyone's hand, thanking them for their attendance. Little did they know that they were all receiving a gift from Diane, a cure of all their ailments, which would start to take effect during the following week. The gathering lasted the rest of the day and well into the night and then gradually people started to leave, although there were still some diehards bopping away to the disco tunes. Diane and I left the venue about 10:30 p.m. with her parents who drove us back to our house. It had been a long memorable day, but we had to be up again quite early in the morning, as we were off to sunny Spain for our honeymoon. That isn't to say we didn't consummate our marriage adequately!

The next day, after leaving the security of our house to Ethel, we boarded our plane for Spain. The flight seemed to be quite short, but I suppose I was just comparing it to our very first flight to America. On arriving at the Spanish airport, getting through passport control was a breeze (again nothing like America), but picking up our luggage was a different matter. It was about an hour before our cases emerged onto the carousel, so we could finally make our way outside to where our transfer coach would be waiting. As we exited the airport building, the sun hit us like a fireball and the hot air, mixed with diesel fumes, rapidly filled our lungs. The coach park was teeming with people, both with arrivals and a vast majority that were homebound. It was easy to tell the difference between them, as large straw sombreros and two-foot high stuffed toy donkeys and bulls were being carried by suntanned or burnt red people everywhere. I suppose there were a greater amount of leavers because they all had to vacate their hotel rooms from different resorts all at the same time and then all congregate at the airport to await their differently timed flights home.

I think I got lucky when I happened to spot one of our holiday reps, dressed in a dark blue skirt suit, with her name and the company's logo badge pinned to her white blouse. She was talking to someone by one of the hundreds of coaches in the area, most of which had their engines running. As we made our way to her, her conversation finished with that person and she noticed us approaching. With her clipboard firmly gripped by her left hand and supported by her arm, her right hand was poised with a Biro, which was capped at the end by a miniature troll with green hair. Hazel, which was the name on her badge, then said in a northern English accent, "Names?"

I replied, "Mr. and Mrs. Seer."

I kind of felt a little proud as I announced the title *Mr.* and *Mrs.*, but Hazel then said as she crossed our names off her list, "OK and your first names?"

Diane replied, "Terry and Diane."

Hazel then told us to put our luggage next to a line of cases waiting to be loaded into the bottom side compartments of the coach and then, to get on board and find a seat. As we boarded the coach, closely followed by Hazel, I noticed a shallow wicker tray on the dashboard. In the tray it had a piece of card reading, "Your driver is Ernesto. Gracias. (Thank you)." Obviously the tray was for Ernesto's tips. Looking for a pair of seats, there were only a couple left untaken and as we made our way to one pair, Hazel announced, "Say hi to Terry and Diane, everyone!"

I suppose it's my typically reserved English upbringing, but I hate it when people put you in a situation where you are forced to communicate with total strangers and the round of half-hearted responses told me I wasn't the only one. Diane sat in the window seat and as I started to sit next to her, I noticed that sitting behind us was a couple of girls, probably in their early twenties. One of them was holding a folded, articulated white cane. Diane and I had already accepted that a major part of our destinies was that we were frequently going to encounter people that were going to need our help, so a blind person in our vicinity was no surprise.

Ernesto, smartly dressed in black trousers and a crisp, white short-sleeved pilot's shirt, boarded the coach, sat in the driver's seat and closed the hydraulic door with a whoosh, much like the sound of the door in Theron's craft. At last everyone could stop fiddling with their air conditioning jets and finally set them to cool themselves down. Hazel stood next to the driver, picked up a microphone and tapped it a couple of times as we started to drive off.

"Right, is everybody ready to have a good time?" she exclaimed.

Again a half-hearted response rang out. "Yeah."

She continued. "We will be travelling for about an hour and when we reach the resort, we'll be dropping you off at your respective hotels, six in all. I will call out your names at each hotel. Till then, sit back and enjoy the scenery and I will be pointing out places of interest on the way."

I hated coach trips and the prospect of sitting with a numb bum for an hour didn't exactly enthuse, but it was our honeymoon after all, so I told myself that I must make the effort. I turned to face Diane and said, with an exaggerated smile, "Sun, sea and Sangria for a week then!"

She replied, "Don't forget I can read your mind, Terry. I know that this holiday setup isn't really your thing, but loosen up and you'll enjoy it."

I kissed her and said, "Sorry, I just don't like long coach trips. Especially with total strangers, that's all. I'll be OK when we get there."

Holding each other's hand, we sat back in our seats and looked out at the unfamiliar scenery, as the coach whizzed along. After about fifteen minutes, I noticed the expression on Diane's face seemed very pensive.

"What's the matter?" I said.

Diane replied, "Shush, Terry. I'm talking to someone."

I replayed her reply in my mind: *Talking to someone.*

I knew Diane could read my mind and possibly others, but I didn't know she could actually have a psychic conversation with someone. I even wondered if she knew she could herself.

The journey continued and for the next fifteen minutes, we sat in silence because I could see by her facial expressions, Diane was really into this psychic chinwag. Finally, a smile on Diane's face, as if by signing off, told me her conversation was over.

In a low voice, I said, "What was all that about?"

Diane replied, "I've been talking to a savant. She saw us getting on the coach and knew that we were different."

"What's a savant?" I asked.

Diane replied, "A savant is someone who knows things, someone who has a greater intelligence and understanding of...well, things."

I said, "Did you know you could talk to someone with your mind?"

"No," Diane said. "This is the first time I've met someone with that ability."

"Well, who is she?" I asked.

Diane replied, "Her name is Emma and she is sitting behind us with her sister, Laura."

I said, "Oh, the one sitting next to the blind girl"

Diane answered, "No, Emma is the blind girl."

I remarked, a bit mystified, "But you said that she saw us getting on the coach."

Diane replied, "She did. That's what we have been talking about. Apparently Emma has been blind from birth, but from an early age, she discovered she could see with her mind. She said it's a bit like sonar; her brain sort of sends out waves that give her a mental picture of what's in front of her. It is so sophisticated that although she sees the images in black and white, the degrees of grey in between the images shows her infinite colours and shades. She can also sense what people are like by scanning their brains. It's not that she can tell what people are thinking, just what sort of person they are."

I said, "Wow, that's some ability, but we could give her sight."

Diane said, "I've been down that road with her and she said she really doesn't need it and it probably wouldn't work with her anyway. She said she's fine just the way she is."

I turned my head round to glance at Emma and sure enough, she saw me somehow and smiled.

Still keeping her voice low, Diane said, "I think that this is one of those occasions where Nature, or should I say evolution, is experimenting with the basic human design. Emma was born blind but has adapted or evolved to have more abilities than ordinary people—greater intelligence, personality insight and a very sophisticated form of vision. Emma is probably right; our healing would have no effect on her, as she is how she was intended to be."

Surprisingly the long, boring journey I dreaded from the airport went quite quickly, with Diane and I talking about Emma and the occasional tapping of the microphone, followed by a rendition by Hazel, pointing out chemical installations and hardly recognisable ruins from the fourteenth century, which also broke the arduous road trek up.. But at last the coach entered the built-up areas of the Costa Brava resort.

Diane had chosen Spain for our honeymoon as she had always believed that Spanish was a romantic language, also a holiday brochure once had given her the idea that Lloret de Mar depicted Spain's classical charm.

The coach's first stop was the Miramar hotel and with one broken *A* of the neon sign above the main entrance, it looked a little bit tatty, but it wasn't our hotel anyway. Hazel called out Emma and Laura's name while Ernesto got out of the coach to retrieve their luggage from the hold. As Emma stood, then stepped into the gangway, her folded white cane sprang open from her hand to form a rigid stick that touched the floor.

"Have a nice honeymoon," Emma said as she put her other hand on my shoulder for stability and to show we weren't total strangers anymore.

"I hope you two have a great time, too," I replied.

"Yes, enjoy it," Diane reiterated.

As Emma and Laura made their way along the aisle to the open coach door, I heard Laura say to Emma, "How did you know they were on their honeymoon?"

I didn't hear the reply but something told me Laura wasn't aware of her sister's abilities.

Four more stops were made at different hotels until we reached ours, which, of course, was the very last one.

Hazel then announced, "Right, Terry and Diane, Maggie and Les, this one's yours, the Oasis Park."

Looking through the coach window, I thought, *At least this hotel isn't showing signs of neglect.*

There were only a few coins in Ernesto's wicker tray, so as the last of us got off the coach; I put a ten pesetas note in it. He didn't see me do it as he was busy getting our luggage from the coach and putting it on the pavement, but at least he may have thought on his return that not all Brits were stingy buggers.

"Don't forget: I'm holding a welcome meeting in the hotel restaurant at 10:00 a.m. tomorrow morning," Hazel said, as she walked off down the road, leaving Ernesto to drive off with an empty coach.

When we finally arrived at the resort, I noticed all the surrounding areas seemed to have building work going on, with half-built hotels in every vacant location. So the tourist trade was really booming here, mainly because of us Brits. Even the shops and restaurants we passed, as we peered from the coach windows, were all geared up for the British. Restaurants were advertising fish and chips, and English beer could be bought anywhere.

Our hotel was a four star and at the reception desk, Diane had her little red Spanish phrase book at the ready, only to be disappointed, as the Spaniard behind the desk spoke very passable English.

"Number 404 with balcony overlooking the pool," he said, as he handed me a large cork fob, with the numbered key attached. We lugged our cases into the cramped lift and made our way to the fourth floor, eventually finding the door to our room opposite a vending machine on the concrete landing. I had a little bit of trouble opening the door as the large key fob kept getting in the way, but finally, after dragging our cases inside the room, Diane and I dived side by side onto the double bed.

"*At last*, we're here," I said, sighing with exhaustion.

After taking a few minutes to relax while scanning the room décor, Diane said with gusto, "Come on, let's get unpacked, places to go and things to see."

She then kissed me on the cheek and jumped up from the bed. Secretly I could have just fallen asleep, but Diane was so full of enthusiasm, I couldn't very well disappoint her.

After unpacking our clothes, with Diane commandeering 95 percent of the wardrobe and drawer space, we went onto the balcony to inspect the view. It was early afternoon and the sun, yet again, hit us with a vengeance as we stepped out onto the light blue-tiled balcony with rust-spotted railings, obligatory white plastic table and two chairs, which had brown burn marks from cigarettes. Although the room didn't have air conditioning and was quite stuffy, it was nothing compared to the heat of the outdoors. I looked down at the pool and could hardly see any water as it was packed with so many people—mainly children with their rubber rings, animal-shaped water beds and oversized plastic balls, which seemed to be flying about everywhere. There was no way anyone could swim in that pool.

Although our hotel was only a hundred yards or so from the beach, the rest of the hotel complex obscured our view, so in terms of vistas, the balcony did absolutely nothing.

"Come on. Let's go walkabout and explore," Diane said, as sweat trickled onto her nose from her forehead. I, too, started to melt with the excessive heat. We went back into the room and Diane put her little teddy bear from Vegas on the bed, in front of the pillows. Then with Diane's boundless energy and with me trying not to show my fatigue, off we went to familiarise ourselves with the locality.

A couple of hours passed while we looked around the local shops, mainly to get a bit of respite from the searing sun, and outside when we crossed the streets, it was a challenge not to get run down by the busy traffic that didn't respect Zebra crossings in the slightest.

After a light meal that evening, I was glad to get to bed and after we had made love, I soon dropped off to sleep.

The next day, at about 8:30 a.m., Diane woke me from my slumbering bliss and said, "After we've had breakfast, we can go down to the beach."

Bleary eyed and yawning, I replied, "OK then, but what about the welcome meeting?"

Diane replied, "Oh, I'm not bothered about that. It will only be booking excursions and things. We can do those ourselves if we want."

We had breakfast in a nearby restaurant, which was adorned with the *Union* Jack painted over nearly every bit of wall space. The set breakfast consisted of eggs, bacon and toast and a rubbery tasting coffee. I suppose the locals assumed all English people consumed this kind of meal at the beginning of each day. After breakfast, we went back to our room to don our swimming costumes. I put on my blue Speedo trunks and Diane wore her tight yellow bikini, which left hardly anything to the imagination. I was so glad when she also put on a white linen smock, as I had already noticed the local lads giving her a bit more than just a passing glance.

Armed with a coconut smelling sun oil, brush, comb, different toiletries and other items Diane had packed into a rope tied plastic bag, we rolled up our towels and put on our flip-flops for our trek to the nearby beach.

It was only about 9:30 a.m. when we arrived and the beach was still fairly empty, so Diane designated our sunbathing spot on the soft yellow sand, about fifteen feet from the water's edge. We carefully rolled out our towels side by side, then Diane removed her smock and then we lay down to soak up the warm Spanish sun. After about ten minutes, Diane decided that we had better put some sun oil on our bodies for protection, so after smearing it all over her front, she handed me the plastic bottle to cover her back. After that, she then rubbed that greasy smelly stuff all over my back. I don't believe that in the early seventies, sun lotions came with a factor number and I'm sure instead of protecting our bodies from the sun, it actually helped to fry us, but whatever the outcome, Diane was determined to get a tan. Even though Diane had finished her training, she still took a medical reference book with her to read at every opportunity.

A few hours passed and by now the Sun's heat grew in strength and with it the beach became quite crowded. It seemed that most of the people in the resort were young, between the ages of eighteen and thirty and most of the women on the beach were topless, so as any young man would do, I scanned the area to check out the female forms. Caught red handed, Diane lifted her eyes from her book and saw me looking around.

"Hey, stop looking at all the girls," she said, a little indignantly.

With a straight face, I replied, "I'll have you know I'm doing a very important survey."

"Oh yes, what's that then?" she asked.

I replied, "I'm making sure that I married the girl with the best boobs."

"And did you?" she said.

I replied, "I can't remember; you'll have to remind me."

With that Diane put her book down and took off her bikini top.

"Do these jog your memory at all?" she said.

"Oh yes, I can tell now. You have got the best boobs, but I'll have to give them further inspection later."

Diane gave me a gentle whack on the top of my arm, as she stood up and said, "Come on let's go for a swim to cool off."

I stood up and put my towel over our things and briefly wondered if the sea was going to be cold, but then Diane ran off toward it, so I was quickly in hot pursuit. With plenty of white foam caused by our feet and legs, we raced through the shallow water up to waist height and ended up diving forward at exactly the same time. On surfacing and standing upright with the salty sea water up to the height of Diane's boobs, we laughed, hugged and kissed and there was a brief moment I think that we both felt that, not only was our marriage the final act of commitment to each other but we also knew the love we had would last forever, no matter what.

We spent about fifteen minutes just larking around and constantly touching, hugging and kissing before we finally returned breathlessly back to the beach. I repositioned my towel next to Diane's and we both just lay on our sides, facing each other, silent and smiling, until the hot sun had completely dried us off. Eventually Diane sat up and applied more oil to her body and I could feel my skin tighten as the sun dried it out, so we went through the same greasy ritual as before.

The salt water had left a nasty taste in my mouth and had made me feel thirsty and as luck would have it, there was someone going around the basking sunbathers selling cold soft drinks.

The vendor was a local Spanish lad of about ten or twelve years old. He was carrying a polystyrene cooler box, which looked far too big and heavy for his small frame and the makeshift leather strap over his shoulder didn't seem to help much in easing the weight on his arms, as his little legs trudged with effort through the sand. Although his natural pigmentation of the skin was darkened by his constant exposure to the sun, a large red birthmark was visible on his right cheek. After asking Diane if she would like a cold drink (which she replied "Yes please" to the question), I pointed out the small boy who was selling them and made particular reference to the feature on his face.

"Do you think that the lad's birthmark would disappear if we did our magic on him?" I asked.

"I don't think so. I would say that Nature wouldn't regard the birthmark as an imperfection," she replied.

"But surely it is an imperfection if the rest of his skin is a different colour," I said.

"Well, I'm not one hundred percent sure, but I don't think it will work," she said.

"Well, there's nothing to lose if we tried, is there? And if the lad has any other ailments, at least we can put them right?" I iterated.

"OK. If you really want to try, we'll do it," she said.

As the lad neared our position, Diane called him over. "What drinks have you got, little man?" she asked.

The boy put his cooler box onto the sand, tilted it toward us and opened the lid. The box had various bottles of soft drinks in it, all surrounded by cubes of half-melted ice. Diane said to the lad that she would have an orange, fizzy drink and I opted for a Coca-Cola, which the boy handed to us, dripping with cold water from the melting ice.

I can't remember how much the lad wanted for the drinks, but I know after sifting through Diane's plastic bag, I gave him well in excess of the cost. Diane then said to the boy, as she outstretched one hand in his direction, "I can see that you must be very strong carrying that box around all day. Can you pull me to my feet?"

The boy grabbed her hand with both of his and started to pull; while I touched Diane's other hand, which she had placed behind her back. The boy was obviously struggling to perform his task as Diane held back long enough for any healing process to happen. Finally when she thought ample seconds had passed, she made the effort to stand, disconnecting her hand from mine.

Diane then said to the boy, "Mucho gracias, I'm heavier than I look, aren't I?"

The boy, although fatigued by his effort, smiled at Diane and put the lid back onto his box. In the time it took for him to compose himself and lift the heavy box strap back onto his shoulder, I was eagerly peering at his face to see if there had been any change. There wasn't any. Diane was right once again, as she was when I thought that David, the Downs syndrome boy, should have benefitted from her touch.

"Told you," she said.

I replied, "All right, I concede, Dr. Diane."

Most of the rest of our one week honeymoon basically consisted of lying on the beach during the day and going to different disco clubs in the evenings, which there were in abundance. There wasn't really any major incidents that occurred, not like the last time we were abroad, like being held up by a man with a gun, but one particular evening, I did have cause—at least I thought I had cause—to use my, let's say, persuasive powers.

We dressed up as usual that evening in our fashionable seventies garb and made our way to a particular disco place called the Jumping Frog. Like all the other discos, it was packed with people all taking advantage of the cheap, large measures of booze. Diane wore a white miniskirt and white boob tube with no bra that night and on the dance floor, her clothes glowed under the ultraviolet lights. Due to the rest of her body being now deeply tanned, it looked like her clothes were dancing on their own most of the time, but she still drew a lot of attention from other revellers, mainly young men.

On one of the tables close to the dance floor, five men in their early twenties were drinking quite a lot and being overly boisterous and ogling Diane at every opportunity. They hadn't attempted to approach her, I suppose because I was close to her all of the time, but they were all looking at her whispering and sniggering among themselves. I didn't really think much of it, as Diane seemed to unintentionally attract the attention of other men all of the time. Anyway, we had had a good night and at about 1:30 a.m., we decided it was time to leave and make our way back to our hotel. During the half-mile stroll back, the same five men ran passed us and were about twenty-five feet ahead when they decided to stop, face us and spread out to bar our way. They then each folded their arms, not in a threatening way but in an adamant, solid stance. And then one of them said to Diane in a demanding manner, "Show us your tits."

I said, "Come on, lads. That's my wife you are talking to."

Another of the five said, "Can't help that mate. We want to see her tits."

I looked at Diane in the face, sighed and raised my eyebrows. She knew exactly what I was going to do. Like a machine gun firing boxing gloves instead of bullets, in turn I hit them with the power of my mind, from right to left. Bam! Bam! Bam! Bam! Bam!

They hadn't a clue what had hit them. Two sprawled out on the pavement and three in the road. Funny, but they didn't say any more after that; they just gave us a look of disbelief as we continued our stroll arm in arm back to our hotel.

Our honeymoon was now over, but it was another memory that would be treasured forever. We both returned home with a deep bronze tan and Ethel, having spotted us arriving by taxi, came out to greet us, asking if we had had a good time and to tell us all was well with the property. It was a good feeling returning to our marital home and the small pile of letters addressed to Mr. and Mrs. Seer that we trod on as we came through our front door confirmed it for me.

Good old Ethel had put our ordered pint of milk left by the milkman in the fridge, so Diane set to making us a decent cup of coffee; at last, I could savour what I was used to instead of that rubbery stuff we drank in Spain. While she made the coffee, I picked up those letters from the hall floor. They must have only arrived that day because there was also a pile on the kitchen table that Ethel had picked up on previous days. Sifting through the circulars and junk mail, I came across one that was addressed to Diane. I could just make out a hospital frank mark on it, although it was too faint to read the hospital name. I handed the letter to Diane saying, "This one looks important."

We sat next to the table, sipped our long-awaited coffees and Diane opened the letter. She then told me its contents. "It's from Mr. Williams, the consultant who treated your nephew, Steven. He's head hunted me and wants me to join his staff at the Great Ormond Street Hospital as a junior paediatrician."

I remarked, "That's great news, but how did he even know that you had qualified?"

She replied, "Oh, that's easy. New doctors are put on a list and are circulated through the internal hospital post. The list goes out to different hospitals, according to your qualifications."

"You've got to accept," I said. "Think of the prestige, working in the best children's hospital in England, if not the world."

She replied, "Well, I think I do know my stuff, even if I'm still not happy about the way Mr. Williams initially heard about me."

I said, "That was just fate. I think you were destined for the post."

Diane replied, "In that case, yes. I'm going to accept!"

10

Five years passed by and Diane had made her way up from junior doctor to Mr. William's right hand man; or should I say woman. She was now a senior and highly respected for her expertise, and the fact that she was in a position to help sick children, day in and day out made it all the more rewarding. Diane had promised herself that she would only use her healing powers if she knew a child would not get better reasonably quickly with medication; this was so any unwanted attention would not come her way. She was not always in a position to help all the children though and there were a few cases that had either not been brought to her attention, or due to her work load, she could not treat them quickly enough.

Diane came home from the hospital very distressed one day, so I asked her what was wrong. She told me that a little girl about six years old had been brought in from another hospital, located in the north of England. The girl had been treated there since birth, as she was born with a disfigured spine. Because she was growing naturally, her bones were putting pressure on her major organs and it had got to the point where the hospital could do no more for her. Diane said as soon as she heard the girl had been brought in, she went up to the ward where she had been taken, but as she got there, the little girl's portal opened and it was too late. Diane said she would have risked everything to save this girl, but somehow she knew that fate, or Nature's force, had prevented her getting to the girl in time. She believed this was done purposely, so that her abilities wouldn't be discovered and she could continue to help other children.

I tried to pacify Diane by reminding her that she knew she could never save all the children, but she said that it wasn't fair, because when the child's spirit came out of her body, she wasn't disfigured in any way and it made it worse to see the little girl's image of how she would have been if she had reached her in time.

Although this was a tragic story, the fact remained that since Diane started working at Great Ormond Street, the survival rate of the children had gone up from 77 percent to 93 percent and as a result, the hospital and staff were recognised to be the best paediatric facility of its kind.

During those five years I wasn't idle either. I got a job for a couple of days a week as a plastering tutor, teaching young people the basics of plastering and how to use various tools. It seemed that doing a proper four-to-six-year apprenticeship was no longer necessary in the changing world of the building industry, as it had now been reduced to a six-week course. Although there were a few talented pupils in the classes, most of them I would never employ as qualified tradesman.

The rest of my time was occupied by making sure our investments kept us financially secure, keeping the house in good working order and doing general housework that Diane would never have time for. Not working full time also gave me the opportunity to sort out everyday things, like taking the car in for an M.O.T. (Ministry of Transport) roadworthy test. Yes, I still had my old banger, but I found out that wouldn't be for much longer.

A couple of years back I had taught Diane to drive and she now used the BMW to go to and from work, while I used my trusty old steed to get me about in our locality. I knew that in the past, my old car was barely scraping through the test, but I was devastated when the mechanic told me that this time it had failed miserably. His words were, "Well, the tyres are good, but I'm afraid there isn't enough metal left for the rust to cling to."

It was like being told an old friend had died. It had been the first thing that I had ever owned outright. It waited faithfully for my return from the Terran' world and was there all through my courtship to Diane. I'm sure I was not the only one ever to get emotional about a chunk of metal, but when the low loader came to take it to the scrap yard, there was a little tear in my eye.

I bought a moderately priced run-around after that and resented it for at least a month, but afterward, once I had gotten used to it, I suppose it became my new best friend.

A few more years passed and Diane hit her twenty-ninth birthday. She began to realise that her body clock was ticking and it might be time for us to have some children of our own. We must have tried for six months without success when finally Diane said that there must be something wrong and that she was going to get us an appointment through a work colleague to see a fertility consultant. After going through embarrassing tests and a traumatic wait for the results, we were told that we were both infertile and we could never have children. That news was devastatingly ironic because it seemed that we could give life to other people's children but not give life to our own. We came to the conclusion that it was just another cruel act of Nature to stop us creating an ever expanding tree of healers and that we were only given our powers to cure a selected few. Our parents, when told of our bad news, were also very upset but supportive none-the-less, although Diane never really got over it.

Soon after my thirtieth birthday, Diane and I realised that there was something, well, not quite right about me. Madri had told me the day my death portal closed for good that there could be side effects. The one side effect we originally found out about was that I could self-heal. That was a plus, but now over ten years later, it was becoming apparent that there was another side effect which wasn't so good. My initial reaction to disguise this newly discovered abnormality was to grow a full-faced beard. Not that I or Diane liked it much, but it was a kind of solution to my problem. This period in our lives was turning very grey, with Diane feeling robbed of motherhood and an issue with me that we knew could never be resolved. Finally one day, Diane came to the conclusion that she must stop feeling sorry for herself and suggested that we should expand our horizons and go and help less fortunate people somewhere else in the world. She said this would also help me as I would be away from family and friends who would eventually notice my abnormality.

Diane took indefinite leave from her job and we made arrangements for our house to be maintained and managed by an agency here in England who could do our bidding when and if we contacted them from abroad. A solicitor was engaged to deal with our personal and financial details, so we could then concentrate on the arrangements that were required for our mercy trip to Uganda in Africa. There was a civil war in Uganda at that time and the media was constantly giving out reports of thousands of people fleeing to the borders to escape the tyranny there. Militia factions considered these refugees fleeing the capital cities to be guerrilla sympathisers and they were constantly being abused, attacked and killed by them, but the truth was they just wanted to escape the inner city chaos and bloodshed. Diane believed that, as these people had no means of medical support, she could at least provide some, even if it meant putting her own life at risk. I didn't like the idea much, but I knew if Diane had it in her mind to do something, she inevitably would do it, but at least with my abilities I knew she would have the best defensive protection there was.

Firstly, to embark on our new mission, we had to renew our ten-year passports, so that meant new photos. Diane's new photo still reminded me of a Disney princess, whereas my image looked more like Fidel Castro, as I was now sporting a full-faced beard. We tried to plan for every eventuality and bought tents, medical supplies and other equipment. We also contacted the Canadian Red Cross, as they had established a network to get supplies of food and medicines over the Sudan border to the refugees. The Red Cross agreed to get us into Uganda and if we got established, they would continue to support us, but we were warned that there had been predecessors who had not returned and that many militia factions were constantly raiding the refugee camps to steal their supplies. In full awareness of these facts, our decision was made and with all the arrangements in place and I hoped, done with military precision, we flew out of England and were heading for our first port of call, Cairo Egypt.

It would have been nice to have had a tour of Cairo when we landed, as I had seen actual footage of some of its grand construction that Theron had showed me with his gizmo, but we had to be content seeing the pyramids and sphinx of Giza from the aircraft just before we landed. Diane seemed very enthusiastic and was excited about the mission we were about to embark on, but I was apprehensive; about everything.

At Cairo airport we and the rest of the flight's passengers, were corralled into a shabby white building, which turned out to be the passport control lounge. When it came to our turn in the queue, the military-dressed man that peered down on us from an elevated desk looked over our passports. He then turned his head to two men that were standing next to an office door and nodded, as if to say, "These are the two you are looking for." The two men then approached us. One of the men, who was about fifty years old, was short and portly with a dark complexion and even darker rings around his eyes. He also had a grey wiry moustache and was wearing a brown, tight fitting three-piece suit. With his jacket unbuttoned, we could see a gold chain hooked on a button hole, which was attached to a pocket watch tucked inside his waistcoat pocket. He was obviously some kind of Egyptian official.

"Welcome, welcome, Mr. and Dr. Seer. I am very honoured to meet you both." He said as he ceremonially stood with his feet together. With one arm behind his back, he bowed slightly as he offered his hand for me to shake.

"Oh, thank you," I said, appreciatively.

This procedure was then repeated in its entirety for Diane. The other man was in his mid-forties—white, tall and European looking. He was dressed in a more casual manner. This man then spoke to us with an American accent.

"It's good to meet you both at last. My name is Bob Davenport, Canadian Red Cross. I'm the guy who is going to fill you in on all the details we have arranged for you. That's if you still wish to go ahead with everything."

"Of course we do," Diane replied. "There's no way we are backing down now, are we, Terry?"

"No way," I replied.

"OK, then, please follow me," Bob said.

Bob led us into the room that he and the other man had been standing next to; the Egyptian man went off somewhere else. The room was quite stark with only a tubular metal table and four chairs in it. We sat at the table with Bob sitting opposite us. Referring to a few sheets of A4 paper, Bob began to explain our itinerary.

"As we speak, your luggage and equipment are being taken to a hangar at the far side of the airport. It will be loaded into one of our planes together with basic food stuffs for the refugees, medicines and other equipment we think you're gonna need. Our pilot is then gonna fly you to a remote airstrip this side of the Sudan border. You'll be safe there to spend the night. The next day we have arranged a truck with two guys who are familiar with the terrain to get you over the border into Uganda. They will load the truck from the plane and then take you to a place which the Ugandan militia hasn't found out about yet. Then they will unload the truck and leave you. From that point on, you are basically on your own. The journey there is not going to be without risk, so the truck guys will be armed. Let's hope they'll have no need to use their weapons. If everything goes according to plan and you manage to get established there, we will from time to time get more supplies to you. Because of the terrain we cannot air drop the supplies, so it will be done by using the same method with the truck. You will be issued with a couple of short wave radios, but don't use them unless you really have to, as the militia can tune into your signal. Also the pilot will give you a hand pistol for your personal protection or as you may feel the cause to use it, if you get my meaning.

"We commend what you are doing. The people out there could really do with your help, but it's at great risk to your personal safety and no one will think anything less of you if you decline. Do you understand what I have told you and have you got any questions?"

Diane replied, "I think you have made everything very clear, Bob and yes, we know exactly what we are letting ourselves in for."

Bob replied, "Well, the best of luck then and God's speed."

With the briefing over, we finally realised the enormity of the mission we were about to undertake and we followed Bob to a car just outside the passport control building. As we got in Bob said, "The driver will take you to your plane. Good luck, you guys: you're gonna need it."

The driver of the car took us to a hangar on a remote part of the airport and as we got out, a stocky, six-foot or so tall character in his late fifties and wearing a red baseball cap, came over to greet us. He was also wearing a well-worn, fur lined leather flying jacket and had a grey handlebar moustache. With a half-smoked unlit cigar in his mouth. I thought, *you have got to be kidding me. This pilot is straight out of a comic strip.*

"Hiya, guys. I'm Jack," he said, with I suppose a Canadian accent. "You and I are gonna spend a bit of time together."

"Pleased to meet you, Jack," I replied.

"Me, too," Diane said.

"What's first then?" I asked Jack.

"All-righty, let's get this show on the road, or should I say in the air," Jack replied.

He then continued. "Right, my old bus is in the hangar loaded to the gills; you can help me get her out. I'll get the tow truck and you open the hangar doors."

The doors to the hangar were very large and heavy but were on rollers, so with Diane's help and a bit of telekinetic influence, I managed to slide each door open. Jack had gone around the side of the hangar, then came back driving a small, funny-looking vehicle, like a tractor with solid tyres, which kicked out black smoke from the upright exhaust of the exposed diesel engine. He then attached a long metal bar from the rear of the tow tractor to rear of the airplane, just above the tail wheel.

Jack shouted, "Take the chocks away from the wheels, will you?"

We could just about hear his voice above the noise of the tractor, so I went to the front of the plane and pulled the wooden wedges from either side of both front wheels.

"Now you two stand well clear," he bellowed.

Gradually as Jack drove slowly forward, the airplane started to roll and this metallic monster emerged backward from its snug-fitting hangar. The first thing I noticed was the red maple leaf insignia on the tail of the plane and then as it emerged further, I saw a red cross had been painted on the single passenger door, near the rear. The aircraft was an old DC3 cargo plane that was probably built in the thirties. It was definitely showing signs of age and looked as if it should be in a museum somewhere. Diane and I just looked at each other as if we both wanted to say, "Bloody hell, I hope this thing still flies OK," but we didn't say it.

Having towed the plane well clear of the hangar, Jack stopped and unhooked the metal bar from the plane and tractor. Then he drove it back around the side of the building. On his return he said, "C'mon then, what are you waiting for?"

He opened the door near the rear of the plane and got in, with us following close behind. He then shut the door behind us and switched on the interior lights.

As it was a cargo plane, there were no windows in the fuselage and all the equipment, our luggage and gear had been neatly stacked and tied down in the centre leaving a walking space all around it. The inside walls of the fuselage were covered in a large gauge, loose netting, with some wooden boxes bolted to the floor below them. To get to the cockpit, Jack had to walk up the steep ramp of the fuselage floor; again, we followed close behind. There was no door to the cockpit, only an opening in the bulkhead. Now sitting in his cockpit seat, Jack said, "Fraid we only got one more seat up front here. One of you will have to sit on one of those boxes and hang on to the netting for takeoff."

Obviously, that was going to be me. Diane sat in the co-pilot's seat and buckled up and Jack started the two propeller type engines, while I sat on a box and braced myself as best I could. The plane started to shake violently as the propellers rotated faster and faster, but I could only feel what was happening as I had no windows to see out of. I felt the plane turn on the spot a full 180 degrees and then with another burst of the throttle, we started to move slowly forward. After a minute or two, the plane stopped and I heard Jack speaking on his radio. After another few minutes I could just make out the words "Good to go" above the noise of the plane's engines. The propellers increased in speed and before long we were hurtling along the runway with the fuselage now level. Then up we went at what seemed a very steep angle, so much so I had trouble stopping myself from sliding to the rear of the plane. My stomach ended up in my mouth as the cargo ropes stretched and creaked as they were put under the heavy strain of the climb. It seemed quite a time before the plane finally levelled out to the relief of my fingers, which were red raw after holding on for dear life. Eventually, I decided it was safe enough to make my way to the cockpit.

"There he is. You survived then," Jack said and chuckled.

Diane said, "Wasn't that amazing?"

I replied, "Not from where I was sitting, it wasn't."

Changing the subject and leaning on the back of Diane's seat, I said, "How long is it going to take us, Jack?"

"About four hours. There are some blankets under the seat there." He said, indicating beneath Diane's seat with his eyes. "You're probably going to need them."

"Why is that Jack?" Diane said.

"Cause the heater doesn't kick out much and it's going to get mighty cold up here quite soon."

Sure enough, the temperature seemed to plummet rapidly and as we were only dressed in casual clothes, we soon needed those blankets.

Jack said, "Why don't you two go in the hold and try to get some sleep; there's nothing you can do here and you must have been up real early this morning?"

Come to think of it, both Diane and I had been yawning intermittently, so we decided to take Jack's advice. We managed to cuddle up in the hold with a couple of blankets, between two boxes on the aircraft's hard floor and even though the plane was noisy and rattling, we soon fell fast asleep.

It only seemed we had been asleep for about ten minutes when Jack's raised voice woke us. "Hey you guys, we will be landing soon; you'd better get up here."

We had slept through the whole trip and with a blanket each wrapped around us, both of us made our way to the cockpit.

As we peered out of the small, scratched-up, oblong-shaped windows, we could see a large herd of what looked like wildebeest way below us on the vast African plain; further on in front, there was a large jungle area. As we started to pass over this dense green wilderness, Jack said, "Do you see that dry grassy strip a couple of miles ahead us?"

"Yes," I replied.

"Well, that's where we're gonna land. You'd better get buckled up."

I was dreading the landing, as the tarmac runway in Cairo on take-off was bumpy enough. So, I wondered, what was it going to be like on grass?

I felt my stomach rise to my chest, as I went to sit on my wooden box seat, then I clung on for dear life, again. I'm sure Jack put the plane into a steep dive purposely, just to thrill Diane and give me a raw flying experience. At least I knew after landing the bruises on my posterior would heal up almost immediately, but, to say the least, I was relieved when the plane finally came to a halt on the ground.

We were now in northern Sudan, just across the border of Uganda. It was early evening when we landed on the makeshift airfield and I could tell that there wasn't going to be a lot of daylight left. Jack was obviously no stranger to this place, which meant we were probably not the first civilians he had brought here.

"Sausages," Jack said. "I hope you like sausages."

"Yeah, we like sausages," I replied.

"Good, because that's what we are gonna be eating tonight. Now let's get out of our hotel room and find some wood for the fire," he said.

When we all got out of the plane, Jack showed us the place where a camp fire had been lit in the past. It had two sawed-off tree trunks, set at right angles to each other and a pile of old ashes in front. About fifty yards away was a clump of trees that looked as if they were just about clinging to life from lack of water.

"Right, you two go and get the wood and I'll sort out the rest," Jack said, pointing to the trees.

"Oh and be careful where you walk; snakes don't like to be trod on," he added, with a playful smile.

This was an entirely new ball game for Diane and me as the closest we had ever come to the wilds was the images we had seen on our television back home; now these kind of surroundings were going to be our new home for God knows how long.

Between us, Diane and I managed to gather a fair bit of dry burnable wood and by the time we returned with our second armful, Jack had got the fire started. On top of one of the seating logs, Jack had put three tin plates, three forks and a large carrier bag. He also put a metal tripod over the fire, with a hook dangling from the centre.

It wasn't long after the fire got blazing that the sun started to disappear on the horizon. It was getting really dark and I could feel the temperature dropping dramatically. Soon, all around us was pitch black; it was the darkest night I had ever experienced. The crescent moon and millions of stars in the night sky lit up nothing on the ground and if it wasn't for our fire, I couldn't have seen my hand in front of my face. For Diane this was a great adventure and I was glad that her past depression had now gone, but I was still apprehensive about what or whom we may encounter on this trip.

We cooked our sausages on sticks over the fire and the pot which hung on the hook of the tripod, provided us with boiling water to make our coffee. We both quite enjoyed eating the sausages, sitting on a log with blankets wrapped around us and during that evening we got to know Jack quite well. He was a real character and had us looking at him in awe and laughing at the many exploits and stories he told us about his past.

Near the end of the evening, as we put the last of the wood on the fire, Jack became a bit more serious.

"You know you're not the first people to attempt what you are gonna do," he said.

"Six months ago I brought an older doctor and his wife here to do the exact same thing as you and they haven't been heard of since. You're still young. Why would you put your lives at risk like this?"

Diane replied, "I've been a doctor for about ten years now mainly working with children. I came to realise how fortunate people are in England to have access to medicines and treatment and how doctors are well paid for their efforts. Not that they shouldn't be well paid and that people shouldn't get the best treatment possible, but it made me think about how much good one doctor could do for the less fortunate people of this world, especially the oppressed ones. What chance do they stand getting any sort of medical treatment? I felt as if I have got to at least try to help no matter what the risks."

Jack looked to the ground, sighed and gently shook his head from side to side.

"Don't worry about us, Jack," I said. "We may be quite young, but we are not stupid. If anyone can pull this off, it's us. We have got a few tricks up our sleeves. Believe me."

Jack lifted his head, smiled and said, "Do you know what? I do believe you have. C'mon, I think it's time to hit the sack; you've got a big day tomorrow."

We gathered up our things, left the fire to burn out and headed back to the plane, with Jack leading the way with a torch. Having boarded the plane again, Jack found himself another blanket and bedded down on one side of the cargo, while we lay on the floor on the other side. The temperature had really dropped and as Diane and I cuddled together under our blankets, our bodies gradually ceased to shiver.

Apart from the faint animal noises now and again, the silence was nothing like I had ever experienced before. It was as if cotton wool had been rammed into both my ears. I was actually already missing the reassuring sound of traffic from the London streets.

Jack woke us about 8:00 a.m. the next morning. He had already got up, built another small fire and had some coffee ready and waiting for us. We also noticed a towel draped over one of the aircraft's wheels, a toilet roll, a bar of cheap soap and a five-gallon can full of water, which sat on the ground next to it.

He said, "Toilets are wherever you want them to be, but be careful where you put your asses, though, guys."

After pouring the coffees, Jack gave us a kind of muesli bar each.

"Breakfast," he said.

"Thanks, Jack," we both replied.

We had our coffees and breakfast, singled out our personal latrines and had a bit of a wash. Then we changed our smelly T-shirts, which we had slept in and worn the day before. I rooted around one of our cases to find a pair of scissors I had packed and gave my beard a good trim, as I was sure some kind of insect was trying to make a home in it.

Jack remarked, "Wow, there is a face under that fuzz. You look a lot younger now."

"Very funny," I replied.

I noticed a whirling sound that seemed to be getting closer and looking in its direction, I could see a large truck heading to our location.

"They're here," Jack said.

On arrival, I could see the truck had a double-rear axle and was an old American World War II army truck.

The olive-green colour and the thinly painted over single white star on each door was an obvious give away. Two black men got out of the truck and with American accents greeted Jack, warmly.

"Hiya, guys," Jack said.

"How are you doing old friend?" one of the men said.

"Introduce us to our passengers," the other man said.

Through the introductions we found out that the two black guys, Yomi and Jasper, who were both in their forties, were African-Americans and were ex-GI's who wanted to keep an element of danger in their lives; being around conflict was like a drug to them. These were the men who were going to be our escorts and bodyguards and who would get us and our equipment to our final destination.

The first thing, though, was to load all our gear from the plane to the truck.

It took about two and a half hours for all five of us to load up and secure the equipment inside the rear of the truck. The canvas roof was then tied down to shield the contents from the sun and any prying eyes. We were now all set to go, so we all said our good-byes and Diane and I thanked Jack for all he had done for us, and as Diane got into the truck, Jack called me over to him. He handed me an automatic pistol, with a spare clip of bullets.

"Be safe, Terry and look after that gorgeous doctor wife of yours," he said, in a serious way.

I replied, "Thanks, Jack, but you will be seeing us again and that's a promise. Have a safe flight back."

Jack smiled then headed for his plane and I went and squeezed into the truck next to Diane. Four people compressed onto the bench seat of an old truck with a couple of hundred miles to do over rough terrain. This was going to be fun!

With a violent shake and a burst of black smoke from the exhaust, Yomi started up the truck.

He seemed to struggle with the gear stick at first, as a grinding noise and clunk established first gear and by doubling the clutch at each gear change, we headed off along a dry, grassy track, which was only just visible by faint indentations left from previous vehicles. A couple of miles into the journey, Jack flew his plane directly overhead, as a kind of salute before heading off in the other direction and vanishing into the bright blue sky.

After approximately half an hour, we reached the border between the Sudan and Uganda and once the border guard's palms were greased with a wad of American dollars, we were quickly on our way again.

The journey was very arduous, as it was just a dirt track all the way and sometimes the road became much rougher ground to drive on. We occasionally saw wild animals and as we passed close to a small herd of elephants, they didn't seem to bat an eyelid to our presence. About half way to our destination, we stopped to stretch our legs. That was a very welcomed respite, as I'm sure Diane's bum was as numb as mine and because of the heat of the midday sun, the truck's cab reeked of everyone's sweaty bodies, even with both windows wide open. After about fifteen minutes, we were on our way again, with Jasper now sitting next to the passenger door with a rifle between his legs. I surmised we were entering into dubious territory. On a couple of occasions I'm sure I could hear gunfire in the distance, but I think that our luck was in this day as we didn't encounter any of the militia groups. After driving for another three hours or so, we finally came within reach of our destination and for the last half mile; we drove along a single tight track, with huge jungle type plants brushing the sides of the truck. As we continued through to the end, it opened out into a large dry grassy area with jungle one side and a wide, fast flowing river the other. There were a hundred or so people in this area that scattered and ran to take cover in the undergrowth as we drove in. The elderly and disabled, quaking in fear, stayed in their places, sitting on green-leaf woven mats on the dry, dusty ground.

I could see that there were makeshift shelters, dotted about everywhere; all were made of large leaves and branches from trees and shrubs. As we came to a halt and got out of the truck, we could hear screaming babies from within the undergrowth, where their mothers hid, startled and alarmed by everyone's sudden exodus. I looked around this shanty site, took a deep breath and thought, *You had better get used to this, Terry, because this was now going to be your new home.*

Gradually after five minutes or so, realising we were not their enemies, the refugees began to emerge and one by one they formed a crowd in front of us. Diane started to address them, saying, "I am Dr. Diane Seer and this is my husband Terry. We are here to give you medical assistance and food rations."

The crowd started to surge forward and I quickly stood in front of Diane.

"Stand back," I shouted forcibly. "First we need to get this truck unloaded and our tents and equipment set up. I need as many able-bodied volunteers as possible. The rest of you clear this immediate area."

The people seemed to immediately comply and sort themselves out and we were left with about twenty able-bodied men and some women.

Diane whispered in my ear, "Wow, Terry, I'm impressed. I didn't know you could be so commanding."

"Nor did I," I whispered back.

Luckily for us, most of the refugees spoke English, as it was their primary language and they also took my directions subserviently during the unloading. I was more surprised than anyone with my new found ability to command and also the decisions I made for setting up order in the camp and within about an hour and a half, our main tents were up and the truck completely unloaded.

We had got to know Yomi and Jasper quite well on our journey and they had become good friends. They had also given us a sense of security just by being there, but it was now time for them to leave. After our final farewells, we saw the truck disappear back along that narrow track. I then knew that we were completely on our own and totally separated from the rest of the world.

Soon after the truck's departure, I organised the rationing of the food we had brought and a long orderly queue quickly formed. While I did the dispensing of the food, Diane organized our personal stuff in our tent, then the medical supplies and equipment in another tent. By the end of the day, Diane and I were completely zonked and it didn't take long after dusk before we fell asleep on our single camp beds in our new canvas home.

We awoke the next day to the sound of unfamiliar animal noises, just as the sun rose on the horizon. This day was the onset of our task in defending and keeping the people of the camp safe and in good health. After having a meagre breakfast of butter-less bread, singed as toast on an open fire, Diane went to her medical tent and started to prepare for examining and treating as many people as possible, while I went around the refugees makeshift shelters to gather people who were bilingual, people who could relate to the others what I was going to say to them. Diane and I desperately needed assistants who we could rely on, so I first asked if there were any medically trained people in the camp. Fortunately there was a second-year student doctor and a couple of nurses who volunteered their help. I sent the English-speaking trio to Diane, so she could recruit and organise their services. I then asked others if they knew of anyone in the camp who needed urgent medical attention; there seemed to be quite a few, so I told them to take them to our newly established medical tent. Lastly I needed a kind of man Friday, someone who could help me with distribution of rations. One fairly healthy young man about twenty-five stepped forward; his name was Ade. Ade could speak English and Swahili and seemed eager to help in any way possible.

Sorting through the provisions and equipment the Canadian's had put together for us, I found a box of fly fishing lines. The Red Cross obviously knew the terrain of our location and realised that the fast flowing river could be fished. Rods were not needed as the lines could be thrown into the river by hand. I gave Ade about a dozen of these lines and told him to distribute them to men who had the aptitude to use them; also, I said that all fish caught must be handed over, so they could be distributed to the rest of the people evenly and fairly.

Having set Ade that task, I returned to the medical tent where a long queue was already beginning to form. One of the nurses was outside the tent assessing the patient's ailments, while the other nurse was helping Diane inside. The student doctor was put in charge of the medicines to save Diane's time in finding the right ones.

On entering the medical tent, I saw a young boy, about twelve years old, sitting on our one and only examination couch, with his mother standing near him. The boy was missing his left hand and with an infected stump, it looked very gruesome. Diane was sitting at a flimsy table made of tubular aluminium with a Formica top, she was writing the boy's name on a card before any treatment, as she was going to document everyone for future reference. She looked up at me with a stern expression and said,

"This boy's mother tells me that this was done by the militia at another camp. Apparently the militia came to forcibly recruit the men and anyone that resisted they killed. And for sheer spite, they maimed children and raped the women."

"Bastards," I angrily replied.

"Well, that isn't going to happen in this camp," I remarked, determinedly.

Diane got up from her chair and inspected the boy's stump. She asked the student doctor to hand her some solution which she then put on his wound. Diane knew by touching him that the healing process had already started, but she bandaged his wound to keep it clean.

Diane and I both knew that our healing abilities didn't stretch to the re-growth of limbs, but at least we knew the boy wouldn't die through infection. There seemed to be quite a few similar cases like this in the camp, mainly children, women and older people; somehow the few able bodied younger men had escaped capture, but I'm sure it was only by sheer luck.

It had been a tiring first day for both of us, with Diane treating as many people as possible and with me using some of my building knowledge to improve the makeshift shelters. During that day, Diane had sent someone to fetch me a couple of times when she knew without both our combined healing abilities, someone was going to die. So from that very first day, rumours spread around the camp that we were angels sent by God to perform miracles and protect them from their oppressors.

On day two, we awoke to some sort of commotion. We heard people screaming and thought that the militia had found the camp. As we hurriedly came out of our tent, we saw a young lion that had wandered into the camp area and had caused the panic. He was standing midway between our tents and the undergrowth. The lion looked confused and was roaring at people scurrying about in all directions. I went back into our tent for the gun I had been given, which I kept under my pillow. When I came back outside, Diane was already heading in the direction of the lion.

"What are you doing?" I said loudly, with concern.

"It's OK, Terry. I'll be all right," she replied.

I would not have accepted that answer from anyone else except Diane and I knew she would somehow be safe. She slowly moved toward the lion, which was holding his ground, bearing his teeth and still roaring.

"What's all the fuss about?" Diane said to the beast, in a reassuringly gentle voice. She then stood at its side, crouched down and put her arm around its full mane. The lion then sat down, whimpered like a pet dog and immediately calmed down.

"Now come on, you know you shouldn't be here," she said. "Go back the way you came."

A few seconds passed and as if the lion had thought about what Diane had said, it then contentedly trotted off away from the camp. While all this was going on, the wide-eyed onlookers were cowering behind anything they could find, but after they saw the entire event and the lion leave, they came out and fell to their knees in front of Diane, as if to pay homage to a god. Diane just walked back to the tent, smugly smiling at me and said, "I told you I'd be all right, Terry."

I just sighed with relief and smiled back at her.

Of course that incident just fuelled the rumours that Diane must be an angel and by now it seemed everyone in the camp believed it.

A few weeks went by and so far we had not been found or bothered by any militia. Diane always had queues of people to treat, even when there was nothing really wrong with them. The fit ones just wanted to seek her reverence because even by this short time, everyone in the camp was now fairly healthy. The only real thing we could not heal was muscle tissue and bone weakness due to malnutrition; Nature, it appeared, didn't accept those ailments to be a natural flaw in its design, so we could do nothing for them. But on the whole, the people of the camp were not doing too badly for food, now that the men had quickly got the hang of catching fish.

A month or so passed since we arrived and there hadn't been any new arrivals until one day a group of about ten people emerged from the narrow entrance track. They were very distraught and were glad to finally find more of their own people. Diane immediately took them to her medical tent to assess their well-being.

"**Kunambi**!" One newcomer woman exclaimed, with fear.

"He's coming," she continued, breathlessly.

I had heard that name around the camp from time to time. Apparently it was General Kunambi, one of the most notorious and infamous militia leaders that were in Uganda. Rumour had it that he was a self-made general who had conscripted lots of men for his own private little army. He's always decamping to seek out fleeing refugees, to steal everything they have, rape the women and force the men to join him. He is known for carrying a pistol in one hand and a machete in the other and he met any resistance by cutting limbs off women and children. Any man that retaliated would be shot. After calming down the fraught group, we managed to find out that this General Kunambi had raided them two days ago about ten miles away. He had looted their camp and killed most of the people there. Some did get lucky though and managed to run and hide in the dense jungle. Apparently he knew where they had hidden themselves but because of the undergrowth's density, Kunambi couldn't find them, so he shouted that he would track them down and kill them no matter what. This fugitive group of ten had been fleeing nonstop until they came upon our community.

I asked Ade, my man Friday, to take the group to some other members of our camp to get them familiarised with how we operate and to find them a place where they could settle. I also told him from now on, we would need someone to watch over the entrance track to the camp, so we had prior warning of any unwelcome visitors.

When the newcomers left the medical tent, I said to Diane, "If what those people say is true, then this Kunambi character is not going to be far behind. If he does show up, I want you to stay in the tent and let me handle things."

Diane knew I was very adamant and serious about what I had said, so she just nodded with agreement.

Around noon the next day, while Diane and I were talking in the medical tent, a male member of our camp burst in. Quite flustered and gulping for air as he spoke, he said, "I have just heard a vehicle coming along the track."

The track had lots of twists and turns, so although vehicles could be heard they could not be seen until the last fifty yards.

"Get everyone as far away from the track as possible," I said to him.

I then told Diane to stay in the tent as I left to get the pistol from beneath my pillow. After retrieving the gun, I tucked it into my belt behind my back and quickly made my way to the mouth of the track. I could hear this vehicle getting louder as it got nearer, until it finally appeared. It was a truck with a couple of familiar faces sitting in the cab. Yomi and Jasper had returned with a fresh load of supplies for us. This was a very welcome sight as our food rations and medical supplies were beginning to get very low.

"Hey Terry, how are you doing?" Yomi said, as the sweat-soaked pair got out of their truck.

"OK," I answered. "I see that old bus of yours is still going strong."

"Nothing wrong with this old girl," Jasper said, hitting the high wheel arch with the palm of his hand.

I hugged them both in turn and shook their hands.

"Did you have any trouble on the way here?" I asked.

Yomi replied, "No, but we have heard some gunfire, which didn't seem that far away."

I then said, "We think that this general Kunambi is in the area, so we had better get your truck unloaded, so you two can be on your way as quick as possible."

Having realised the familiar faces of the pair, quite a few of the men of the camp came near to the truck, knowing its cargo had to be unloaded. Diane also came out to greet and hug the welcomed duo.

"Have you brought more medical supplies? I'm running low on a lot of essentials," Diane said.

Jasper replied, "There is one sealed crate in the back, but I've no idea what's in it."

From the first batch of supplies, Diane knew that whoever put the medical stock together had a great insight as to what was needed and we were grateful for whatever the load consisted of anyway.

There was no time to waste; it seemed that it was inevitable that sometime soon we were going to get a visit from the infamous Kunambi and I didn't want Yomi and Jasper to be involved in any way, especially as they were our only lifeline to the outside world. With a multitude of able-bodied men and women, we had the truck unloaded in double quick time and after a few light refreshments in our tent; I urged Yomi and Jasper to leave the camp for their own safety. To the refugees, these men were now heroes and a long single line formed to shake their hands and thank them as they made their way back to their truck. It was sad to see them leave, especially as there wasn't the time to ask them what was going on in the rest of the world, but hopefully it wasn't going to be the last time we would see them.

About half an hour after our intrepid truckers left, the sound of gunfire could be heard all over the camp; it was obvious from the clarity of sound that it wasn't that far away. I could only hope that Yomi and Jasper wasn't the reason for it. Once again I told Ade to get the people as far away from the camp entrance as possible and Diane to stay in the tent, while I made my way to the track. Having reached our camp entrance, I could hear a faint whirling of a single vehicle. This time, it was highly unlikely it wasn't going to be a friendly visit.

The vehicle, an open Jeep, finally emerged and stopped about twenty-five feet ahead of me. I was standing in the middle of the track to let the hostiles know I wasn't going to let anyone pass. The black driver, who was wearing green army fatigues and a black beret, got out of the Jeep first, faced me and held a rifle diagonally across his chest; then the passenger got out.

This man had almost jet black skin, which glistened as the sun reflected on the beads of sweat that covered his face; he too was wearing fatigues, and a black beret. Built like a brick latrine, this man stood about six-foot-three inches tall and seemed about three feet wide. He wore sunglasses and held a pistol in one hand and a machete in the other. This man's ugly face would terrify an elephant. Obviously no introductions were necessary.

"Stand aside, white man. This war has nothing to do with you," he said.

I replied, "You call this a war. I always thought a war was between two armies, not unarmed civilians."

"These people are traitors, what would you know about it?" he said.

I replied firmly, "Enough to know that you have killed and maimed helpless women and children. You're a bit of a coward really, aren't you?"

Kunambi was beginning to boil with rage, like a bull with steam pouring from its nostrils. "Stand aside or be shot," he said.

I pulled my pistol out from behind my back, stood sideways to him and aimed like an old-fashioned, duelling participant, so that I would be as slim a target as possible. His driver quickly pointed his rifle in my direction.

I said calmly, "I suspect I have a better chance at shooting you, rather than either of you have at hitting me. Don't you think?"

It was obvious that Kunambi was enraged by my observation, but he remained cool enough to way up my claim. After a bit of consideration, Kunambi gestured for his driver to get back in the Jeep.

"OK, white man, you win this round, but you know I will be back," he said, as he sat next to his driver.

His driver started the engine and reversed back the way he drove in and as they disappeared down the track, I lowered my weapon and breathed a heavy sigh of relief. I had won this time, but I knew it wasn't going to be that easy the next.

Diane, seeing that Kunambi had left, rushed out from the cover of her tent and met me as I walked back. "My god, Terry, that man was a monster. Are you OK?"

"Yes," I replied. "It's lucky he didn't see or hear my knees knocking together, though."

"He's going to come back, isn't he?" Diane said.

"Yes," I replied, "but it won't be today. There's not much daylight left and he wouldn't try to attack in the dark seeing as there is only one way into the camp. I'll get Ade to put someone on guard for tonight, though."

As Diane and I walked back and neared our tent, a cheer rang out from some of the refugees brave enough to be in the immediate area.

Diane said, "I think they look on you as a bit of a god now, Terry. You must be the only one ever to stand up to that menacing giant. But what are we going to do when he returns? He's bound to have a lot more men with him next time."

"**We** are going to do nothing. I will handle him on my own by doing what I can do best."

Diane knew exactly what I meant.

It was an uneventful night in the camp as predicted, but I somehow knew the next day wasn't going to be as calm.

Morning came and at about 8:30 a.m. life in the camp was bustling with people doing their daily chores, including Diane setting herself up for any medical eventualities. I was doing my rounds, checking on construction progress of a community house we had started to build and seeing if I could help with any other problems.

As I talked to different people I realised there were two definite reactions to yesterday's event. The superstitious ones, of which there were quite a few, seemed to revere me as their protector, while others thought the end of their world was imminent and that there was no way I could stand up to Kunambi's monstrous might. All I could do was to try and pacify and convince them to carry on as usual. I told them no matter what, they would always be safe within the camp.

Around 10:30 a.m. the inevitable happened. The sentry guarding the track came running over to say that he could hear vehicle sounds nearing the camp. I told him to get everyone as far away from entrance track as possible. Hearing the sudden panicked voices and realising what was happening, Diane came out of the medical tent.

"He's back, isn't he?" she said.

I replied, "Looks that way."

Giving Diane my gun that I now kept in my belt, I said, "You take this just in case everything goes pear shaped."

Diane replied, "But you might need it?"

I answered, "I don't think the gun will help me in any way this time; now I've got to depend on my wits."

After insisting Diane go back in the tent, I quickly made my way to the mouth of the track. About a minute later, Kunambi's Jeep pulled up, again about twenty-five feet away from me.

This time it was followed by a troop carrier vehicle, with another eight men, all fully armed with rifles. Kunambi and his armed driver got out of their Jeep and quickly after, the rest of his troop formed a human barrier in front of him, with their rifles all pointing in one direction—mine.

"Well, well, if it isn't the return of the big brave Kunambi, this time hiding behind a wall of armed men and here I am not even armed," I said, slowly turning a complete circle with my arms raised in the air.

"I am not stupid white man. You would not be standing alone unarmed against me." He said, peering from side to side into the undergrowth.

"Oh, but I would," I replied. "Because the gods are here to protect me and all the people in the camp."

I had noticed before how a great many people in this country believed in God, the gods, voodoo and other superstitious nonsense, so I thought I might try and convince Kunambi that he was dealing with a power much greater than his. So I said to him, "If you come any closer, I will rain the wrath of the gods upon you and your men."

I think I must have sounded very convincing, as I noticed some of his troops look at one another as if to say, "I hope he's not telling the truth."

"Step aside or be shot," Kunambi bellowed out.

With those words, his men straightened their wavering rifles and took aim. I folded my arms and stood full faced at the firing squad. Although a little unnerved by my resolute stance, the men kept their aim.

"Don't say I didn't warn you," I said sternly.

My defiance was far too much for Kunambi to bear and with rage he shouted, "Shoot him!"

Literally all eight men pulled their triggers simultaneously and my brain-power sprang into action. I dropped my arms and as if in slow motion I saw the bullets heading toward my chest. When the bullets reached about a foot away from me, I froze them in mid-air. Then holding them with my thoughts for a few seconds until the thrust behind them had diminished, I let them go.

With a random split second between them, they all fell to the ground and I heard one of Kunambi's men shout, "Look at his eyes."

Although to me my eyes were normal, I did remember Diane saying in Las Vegas that my eyes changed to a milky white colour when I reacted to the gunman there. I can only assume that when this change happens, I am able to see things in slow motion, a process which allows me enough time to respond to a situation. The firing squad was very rattled at what they had seen, but Kunambi just got even madder.

"Shoot him!" he shouted again, as he raised his own pistol and fired.

As before I managed to stop all their bullets, but what I didn't see was his driver shooting his rifle a few seconds later from the side of his Jeep. The timing and the angle were different and his bullet hit me at full velocity high on the right side of my chest. I felt a searing pain, like being stabbed with a red hot poker, as a spurt of blood splashed out from the wound. The rage on Kunambi's face had turned to a big beaming grin as he watched my khaki-coloured shirt darken to the redness of my blood. Having seen that I had finally been shot, Kunambi and his men had stopped firing to watch me finally collapse to the ground; the only thing was, I didn't. Although my shirt was soaked in blood, the wound had actually stopped bleeding and I ripped my shirt open to reveal my bare chest and the mini-crater the bullet had made there. As everyone watched, including me, my body slowly pushed the mangled bullet painlessly out of my chest, then it dropped to the ground and my wound healed up without a trace. The soldiers stood there wide eyed and open mouthed and Kunambi's face changed from a grin to the same expression as his men. I could not take the chance that the soldiers and Kunambi might shoot again though, so with the power of my thoughts, I wrenched all their weapons out of their hands and hurled them high into the jungle's dense vegetation.

While the soldiers panicked to get back into their vehicle, my directed thoughts ripped Kunambi's trousers down around his ankles, spun him half round and with a force of a size fourteen boot, kicked his arse and propelled him face down onto the ground. The troop carrier's wheels caused a mighty cloud of dust as they spun in reverse. Even Kunambi's driver jumped aboard the troop carrier, which left the self-styled general all alone with the jeep. Kunambi had been beaten and humiliated and it didn't take long for him to pull up his trousers, start up the jeep and reverse in hot pursuit of his men.

I had ordered everyone to stay as far away from the track as possible, but there was still a few of the refugees that were in sight of what had happened. Although they could not see what I had done with the bullets, they still witnessed the weapons being flung and Kunambi biting the dust. A cheer went up from some of the onlookers as the threat disappeared back the way it came, but some of the women flung themselves to the ground, chanting something about how their salvation had been due to the two angels who had been sent to them by God. As I walked back to the heart of the camp, minus my shirt, Diane rushed up, flung her arms around me and planted a big wet kiss full on my lips.

"You did it, Terry, you did it!" she said excitedly.

I replied, "Yeah, I don't think we will hear from him again. The only thing is they ruined one of my best shirts!"

For the following few weeks, I still had a sentry keeping his ear to the ground by the track, just to be on the safe side, but after that incident I really couldn't see that Kunambi, despite his humiliation, would return.

Life in the camp returned to normal from then on. We had a few deaths in the camp, but they were all age related and Diane and I watched their body forms enter their respective portals, but always their visible spirits gave us a glance and a smile before they left.

All in all, we probably had the healthiest collection of refugees that ever existed and now Diane's work consisted mainly of midwifery. I managed to finish a secret little project that Diane knew nothing about, a wooden double bed with a canvas mattress stuffed with dried vegetation. Making love on a ground sheet, then having to return to a single camp bed, wasn't exactly ideal and those friction burns were uncomfortable, even if it was only for a few minutes before they healed.

Over the next couple of years, our camp turned into a proper village. We were growing our own food and a small body of men would go out into the nearby bush to kill an animal or two, which could feed a lot of people and allow more variety to their diets. We were also building permanent living quarters, large enough to house families and our community hall was great for social events and weddings. Occasionally a few new refugees would arrive who had found us by sheer luck, but I had no doubt Kunambi and his men were still terrorising whomever they came into contact with.

We hadn't heard from Yomi and Jasper and I'm afraid that I thought the worst had happened to them after we had heard the gunfire soon after they had left the camp. Although Diane and I believed that the Red Cross hadn't abandoned us, we also knew that getting any aid to us must have been impossible due to what was happening outside the realm of our now established village.

In the autumn of 1986, one of the village children, playing not far from the track, ran into Diane's medical tent to say that she could hear the sound of a vehicle coming. Diane immediately sent someone to find me. Luckily I wasn't far away and I went to the track to investigate. It turned out to be Yomi and Jasper in that old American cart horse of theirs. I must admit the sight of them brought a tear to my eye. Diane, seeing who it was, rushed over to greet the pair as they parked up; she also had tears of sheer joy in her eyes. After a few words of greetings, I said, "We thought that was the last time we would see you two. After you left the camp that day, we heard a lot of gunfire going on."

Jasper said,

"Yes, that was Kunambi and his men. Lucky for us his lead vehicle hit a big pothole and we managed to outrun them." He pointed to the bullet holes in the rear of the truck.

I asked, "Where have you been these last few years? And how come you have managed to get back now?"

Yomi replied, "Kunambi set up a new base a few miles from where we cross the border. He must have worked out that any aid to you and the refugees must come via that route. There was no way possible that we could get through."

I asked, "So how come you're here now?"

Yomi said, "There has been another coup in Kampala and now the Uganda People's Defence Force seems to be running the show. Militia groups are being rounded up and disbanded and there is a report that Kunambi is dead."

I said, "Does that mean the war is over?"

Jasper replied, "I wouldn't say that yet, but it looks promising. At least it's much safer for the refugees now. Anyway we've got a cargo to unload, but by the looks of things, there's not much you need."

Diane said, "Oh yes, there is. I hope you've brought me more medicines."

"Certainly have," he replied.

Diane then said, "With things how they are now, can you stay the night?"

"Sure can," Jasper said enthusiastically.

"Then you are now our official guests of honour," she said.

With the sun setting and their truck unloaded and parked up securely for the night, Yomi and Jasper joined us for a meal in our community building together with a good few of our closest and trusted villagers. The news about the coup quickly spread and that evening, celebrations went on all around the village. In our community building and sitting around a central fire, we were all tucking into a fish and sweet corn dinner when Yomi said,

"How come you have lasted this long and Kunambi didn't take over this camp?"

I replied, "He did visit the camp, but I asked him if he would kindly leave."

"Yeah, right," Jasper said. "C'mon, what's the story?"

"No story," I replied. "I just managed to block his way in. You know how narrow that track is."

Jasper looked at Diane for her reaction to my claim.

Diane just shrugged her shoulders and smiled as if to say, "That's what happened." Fortunately I didn't have to elaborate on my explanation and the rest of the evening was filled with laughter and information as to what was happening in the rest of the world. The party atmosphere went on into the small hours of the morning.

The next day Diane and I got up a little later than usual due to the two crates of beers Yomi and Jasper had brought. They also brought some sausages, eggs and bacon, which they had cooking when we joined them for breakfast.

"Wow, sausages, eggs **and** bacon. Haven't had those in a while," Diane said.

Jasper replied, "Thought you might appreciate them. We also brought you a transmitter, receiver and battery, so you can be in contact. Those radios you had when you first got here must be useless by now. Bob Davenport said he will be getting in touch with you in the near future, to arrange for you to go home back to England. It looks to me as if you've both done a great job and I'm sure the people here are pretty much self-sufficient now."

I smiled, but Diane began to frown. "Home, I've forgotten what home is. This has been my home for such a long time now." She said pensively.

I said, "You must want to see your mum and dad and the rest of the family?"

She replied, "Of course I do; it's just that! Well, it's all a bit sudden; that's all."

Jasper then said, "Well, it's not going to be right away, you'll have time to get your head around it."

I spoke. "Well, I can't wait to have a decent cup of coffee and drink some ice cold milk."

Yomi replied, "Whatever floats your boat. Anyway, we had better make tracks, so we are going to leave you good people to it."

It was sad to see our good friends leave, but as we saw the back of their truck disappear down the track, my mind started to think about going home and then the realisation set in that my facial appearance would now probably be more noticeable to our family.

About a month passed when we finally received a communication via our new radio from Mr. Davenport, the Red Cross man. He told us to start to get our things together for transportation home in two days' time. He also congratulated us on a job well done and asked for our permission to take our story to the world's press. We flatly refused, as there was no way we wanted to be in the public eye, so he gave us his assurance our return would be kept as quiet as possible.

I had prepared for Davenport's call by making Ade and a few trusted men managers and peace keepers of the village. I entrusted my pistol to Ade on the specific instructions that it could only be used if and when an extreme case arose and never on any of the villagers. I also had been letting my beard grow long and full faced again. Diane came to terms with going home and had started to actually look forward to it. During her time in the camp, she had trained up the student doctor to a high standard, along with a couple of dedicated nurses to manage the well-being of the people, so altogether our job was now done and had been a real success.

The two days passed quickly and Yomi and Jasper must have travelled through the night to arrive early on that morning, not in their usual truck but in a covered Jeep.

Basically we were only going home with the belongings we had brought with us. Minus a good few clothes that had perished through sweat or wear and tear, we didn't have much else. The hardest thing though was leaving behind all the good friends we had made.

We were all loaded up and ready to go and all the villagers came to see us off. On emerging for the last time from our tent, we came out to a uniformed line of people, all wanting to say good-bye individually. It was like a guard of honour for a head of state.

The first person we came to was Ade. He stood to attention and saluted and I chuckled and pulled his saluting hand down, gave him a hug and with tears in both our eyes, I said, "I'm going to miss you, dear friend. Look after the place for me, won't you?"

Still snivelling, he just nodded. In turn, we hugged and kissed everyone that had been close to us, until we came to the end of the long line. At the very end of the line, there were a group of crying women rocking on their knees on the dusty ground, lamenting that their angels were leaving and wailing about what they would do now if they didn't have us to protect them.

Yomi commented, "Wow, you certainly made an impression on them."

With our meagre luggage loaded, Diane and I sat in the rear seats of the jeep. Jasper then started to drive off.

Stop!" "Diane shouted.

She got out of the jeep, ran to our tent and entered. A few seconds later, she emerged, clutching her little white teddy bear. On returning to the jeep, she said, "I would never have forgiven myself if I had left him behind."

Finally as Jasper drove down the track, Diane and I peered from the rear of the jeep and saw the villagers waving until they had disappeared from our view. Yomi, sitting up front riding shotgun, said, "Sit back folks; we've got a long ride ahead."

That wasn't an understatement. I had forgotten how long the journey was and by the time we reached the familiar little airstrip over the Sudan border, Diane and I ached all over.

"We're on schedule and it shouldn't be too long for your next ride to appear," Yomi said as he started unloading our luggage. Sure enough the sound of a plane was getting louder and louder and all of a sudden from the low lying cloud cover, an aircraft emerged. As it came into land, we recognised it to be Jack's DC3. My only thought at that time was if Jack was still the pilot; after all, we hadn't seen him for five years and he must have been approaching sixty then. Not that I thought he might have died or anything like that, but I just thought that he was probably retired by now.

The aircraft came to a halt about thirty yards away from us and a few minutes later the rear side door opened and the pilot got out. It was Jack and he was chewing on a cigar butt. Diane raced ahead of me and flung her arms around him.

"Hello, little lady," he said. "I see you're still saddled with old bushy beard."

Eventually reaching the pair and then shaking Jack's hand warmly, I said, "How have you been Biggles? I told you we'd see you again, didn't I?"

"You sure did, but God knows how you managed to pull it off," he replied. "Now less of the chat let's get your things on board and get out of here."

We had left Yomi and Jasper back at the Jeep with our luggage because we were so eager to see Jack again, but just as we looked around, they pulled up in the Jeep.

Sarcastically but with a smile, Yomi said to Jack, "I suppose it's too much trouble to land and come to a stop where you're supposed to. We had to put Diane's and Terry's luggage back in the Jeep to get it here, silly old coot."

Jack jokingly replied, "You guys, always complaining."

These three men had known each other for quite a few years and it seemed each time they met they would always enter into this kind of playful banter.

Jack continued. "No time to lose. Some of us have a schedule to keep. Now let's get this stuff on board, so we can get out of here."

We all said our good-byes to Yomi and Jasper and Diane and I especially thanked them for all they did for us. As we got on board the plane and Jack closed the door behind us, it was a sad thought that we would probably never see Yomi and Jasper ever again. Once we made our way to the front of the plane, I noticed a subtle change to the cockpit.

Jack had got another seat welded behind the co-pilot's seat, so I wouldn't have to sit on a wooden box during the flight. "Snazzy, eh," Jack said, with a grin, brushing some cigar ash off the seat.

I replied, "Absolutely wonderful"

I wasn't kidding; the last flight I had in this old bucket on that wooden box was horrendous, especially on landing. We strapped in and after a bumpy take off, we soon reached our cruising height. Jack said because we didn't have much of a payload and had a tailwind, we could make the journey to Cairo airport a lot faster than we did coming out. With the same old smelly blankets around us, the ride to Egypt literally flew by, with us telling Jack about what it was like in the camp and about different events that took place over the past five years. We obviously left out our encounter with general Kunambi, though.

On arrival at Cairo airport, we were met by Bob Davenport and after we said another tearful good-bye to Jack, Bob drove us to a hotel in the heart of the city. It was very late in the evening when we arrived at the hotel and Bob told us to get a good night sleep as we were booked on a flight to England at 11:00 a.m. the next day and that he would pick us up at 9:00 a.m. to take us back to the airport.

What luxury! We now had room service, an evening meal and a proper bed to sleep in, all funded by Bob's agency. We had forgotten what normal living was all about and it didn't take us long to fall asleep in that comfortable bed after the long, tiring day we had had.

The next day we were woken up at 7:00 a.m. with an early morning wake-up call, which Bob had arranged just in case we overslept. It was quite alarming having someone rap on the door to wake us, especially as our unconscious minds were still in camp mode, but we soon came to our senses and realised we were finally going home. I phoned our solicitors in London to expect us later on that day and to make certain arrangements for our arrival.

On arriving back in England and seemingly breezing through passport control and customs, we got a taxi to take us to our solicitor's office to pick up all our personal papers, some ready money and a set of our house keys. I had given the solicitor instructions before we left to engage a firm to clean the house at regular intervals, so it wouldn't look like the haunted mansion on our return. Also with my phone call from Cairo, I asked the solicitor to arrange a stock up of our larder with a few bare essentials. At his office he sorted out our cab fare and after I signed a few papers we got another cab to take us home to our house in Wimbledon.

Before we left for Uganda, we only told Ethel that we would be away for an unspecified time and didn't go into any more detail than that and as the taxi pulled up outside our house, we saw that familiar sight. Ethel was in her front garden, with her back to us, tending to her flowers. The taxi driver kindly helped me get our not very heavy cases across our drive and onto the doorstep. Of course I gave him what I thought was a good tip, but I was a little shocked how much the fare was. My initial thought was that inflation must have really escalated in the past five years. After I opened our front door and put our cases in the hall, we looked back in Ethel's direction.

"Hello, Ethel," Diane said, with a raised voice.

Ethel didn't answer and just carried on with her weeding.

I said to Diane, "Do you think Ethel has turned funny with us because we've been away for so long?"

Diane replied, "No, she's not like that."

I then tried calling her, this time with a much louder voice.

"Ethel," I shouted.

The poor woman nearly jumped out of her skin as she turned around and finally spotted us. Heaving her slightly overweight and elderly body off her knees, we all then met at the party picket fence.

"Hello, you two," Ethel said. "I didn't expect to see you again and with that beard Terry I can only just about recognise you. I thought you must have emigrated or something."

Diane replied, "No, we've been working abroad for the past five years."

Ethel repeated, "You've been onboard a boat for five years."

I answered in a loud voice, "No, Ethel. We've been working abroad for the past five years."

"Oh! Sorry ducks, my hearing aid is on the blink and I didn't hear what you said properly. I bet you're tired from your journey, though. We'll have to catch up in a few days and you can tell me all about it."

"Where's Benji?" I asked.

Ethel replied, "Oh, he's at the vets. He's got something wrong with his stomach. I suppose he's eaten something he shouldn't have. They were going to x-ray him today and I've got to pick him up in the morning."

Diane said, "Well, I hope he's all right. Let us know how he gets on."

Ethel then said, "Hang on! You'll want a cup of tea or something. I've got a spare pint of milk in my fridge. I'll get it for you."

Kind old Ethel went into her house and brought us out a bottle of milk.

"Thanks Ethel, you're a star," I said.

After finally getting inside our house and into the kitchen, Diane said, "The place smells nice and fresh."

"Yes," I replied. "I think our solicitor seems to have done a good job arranging the cleaners and everything. I'll put the kettle on."

I made us a couple of well-appreciated coffees and we began to talk about being back in England and what that would mean.

I said, "I think we should put off phoning the family until tomorrow. I couldn't face getting into long conversations over the phone today."

Diane agreed and then said, "What do you think about the situation with you, though? You can't hide behind that beard forever."

I replied, "I know, you're right and it looks as if we've got no alternative but to come clean, at least with both our parents. I think we owe it to them to tell them the whole story. I did promise Theron that I wouldn't tell anyone about him and his world, but what else can I do now?"

Diane said, "We've just got to trust our parents that they will keep it to themselves and explain that if it was to become public knowledge, it would ruin our lives forever. I don't think they would risk that, do you?"

"No, they wouldn't," I replied.

After a decent night's sleep we both woke up feeling more refreshed and Diane was looking positively perky, as she made us our caffeine fix that we had missed in the mornings for such a long time.

When we had finished our breakfast, I decided I should try to see if one of our garaged cars would start, so that I could go to our local shops to get a few more supplies in and replace the pint of milk that Ethel had given us. One of the solicitor's instructions was to keep our cars in running order with the tax, M.O.T. and up-to-date insurance, so they would be usable when we got home. Diane said she wanted to sort out our clothes and wash the ones she thought were worth keeping.

My car started first time and on my return from the shops, I knocked on Ethel's door to give her the milk. She answered the door with puffy eyes.

"What's wrong Ethel?" I said.

"Oh, I'll be all right ducks," she said. "It's only that the vet phoned to say Benji has cancer and that the kindest thing to do is to put him down. I told them I wanted to see him first before they did it, so I'm just mustering myself up to go there."

"Oh, Ethel, you poor thing, you're not going there on your own, though. I'll take you in the car. Give me ten minutes to unload this shopping and we'll go there together."

I told Diane what Ethel had told me and she said it was worth a try for us both to go with Ethel. I knew what she meant.

It only took about ten minutes to drive to the local vet and on the way Ethel tried hard to disguise her sorrow. Although Ethel knew we could, as a pair, cure people, she also knew that when it came to animals, we didn't know if it would work.

The three of us entered the vets and were immediately taken by the receptionist past the waiting pets with their owners and to the rear of the building. We were then led into a room where all kinds of animals, mainly cats and dogs, were stacked in metal cages, like oversized pigeon holes, only with wire fronts. Benji was in the third row from the bottom and looking very sorry for himself.

A woman of about fifty, who was wearing a green uniform and a clear plastic apron, entered the room; presumably, she was the surgery nurse. She opened Benji's cage and put him on the cold stainless steel table. She then said, "I'll leave you alone with Benji; take as long as you need" and left the room.

Benji's body was trembling with fear, as he looked up with his sad frightened eyes and gave Ethel a quick lick on the cheek as she stooped to cuddle him. Diane along with Ethel had tears in her eyes.

"Right let's see what we can do," I said, hoping in my heart a cure would work.

Realising we were going to attempt to cure Benji, Ethel said, "You mean—"

I interrupted, saying, "We don't really know, Ethel. We've never really tried it on animals before so don't get your hopes up, will you?"

Ethel replied, "I understand. But at least it's worth a try, isn't it?"

"Of course it is," Diane said.

Ethel stood back while Diane and I laid our hands on Benji from both sides. Benji's shuddering body vibrated through our hands as we held the stance for at least a full minute. Finally I said, "You take him now, Ethel; that's about as much as we can do."

I went out of the room to get the nurse, who was in an adjoining room doing some paperwork.

"Have you finished in there?" she asked.

I replied, "Yes, but we want the vet to do another x-ray on Benji before any decision is made."

The nurse then said, "I'll go and get him then; it will take a lot to convince him to do it, though."

I went back into the room with Diane, Ethel and Benji and soon after, the vet came in. He said, "I understand you want me to repeat the x-ray on Benji, but you do realise that it will be very expensive to perform another x-ray. And to be frank, I cannot see that it would make any difference."

I then replied, "Don't worry about the money, I'll pay whatever it costs as long as you do the x-ray and study the results."

The vet said, "I think it will be a waste of time, but if that's what you really want, I'll x-ray Benji again this afternoon."

Addressing Ethel, the vet said, "I'll give you a call this afternoon as soon as I have the results, but if they are the same as before, you really shouldn't let Benji suffer."

"I understand," Ethel tearfully replied.

Nobody said a word in the car on the way back home; it was like none of us wanted to presume the outcome either way.

After seeing Ethel safely indoors, Diane and I went into our house.

"We really must phone our parents," Diane said.

I replied, "I know and we had better arrange to get them round here for our big confession meeting. Shall we try to make it for this Sunday? At least that will give us a couple of days to get some proper food in and sort things out."

Diane replied, "OK, Sunday it is."

As far as they knew, we had told our parents that we were going to Africa to help out a few underprivileged villagers there. What we didn't tell them was that we were going to a part of the country that was in civil conflict. At the time we didn't see any reason to tell them anything different because they would have tried to stop us.

Diane and I both manage to speak to our respective parents on the phone and of course, because they hadn't seen us for such a long time, they both said that they would come to our house on the coming Sunday. We had also asked them not to tell any other relatives we were back as we wanted to speak to them alone first about something important.

After we had some lunch, Diane said she was going to see Ethel since she was all alone next door and must be worrying about Benji. About three quarters of an hour passed when Diane returned, trying to hide a crafty smile.

"What's going on?" I said.

"Well, let me tell you," she replied.

"About ten minutes ago, Ethel's phone rang. She knew it was the vet calling and couldn't face hearing the outcome of Benji's x-ray, so she asked me to take the call."

"And…" I said.

"Well, when I picked up the receiver and told the vet I was taking the call for Ethel, I could hear a dog barking loudly in the background. The vet said he couldn't understand it, but the second x-ray showed there was no trace of cancer in Benji whatsoever. He also said he performed a blood test and still nothing. The last thing he said was to please hurry and pick up the little monster as he is barking the place down and trying to chew his way out of his cage."

I said, "Well, what are we waiting for? I'll start the car and you get Ethel."

It was a far cry from that quivering little dog with the sad brown eyes we saw in the morning, to this over-lively little terror we picked up in the afternoon. Ethel was so overjoyed that she was not going to lose her little companion that she must have thanked us at least fifty times in the car going back home. We were only glad that it worked and realised that it was probable that our healing powers would work on all mammals and not just humans. I didn't tell Diane this, but I would have been devastated if Benji had to be put down.

Our first full day back had already been eventful and after dinner that evening, we decided to watch the nine o'clock news on the television to try to catch up with what was happening in the rest of the world. As the TV set warmed up, the female newscaster had just started an item on Uganda:

"Uganda conflict update.

It has been reported that a British doctor and her husband arrived home yesterday from Uganda. They have been giving medical aid and assistance to refugees for the past five years in a camp a few hundred miles from the Sudan border, where militia groups have killed and maimed thousands of people.

British and Canadian Red Cross workers, who have just officially been allowed into the country, said the doctor and her husband had somehow managed to keep the refugees safe and healthy during their time in the camp. Some of the refugees interviewed said that the couple had been sent by God, because the doctor could instantly cure the dying and that single handed, her husband had fought off fifty armed militia without the use of weapons. The Red Cross would not comment as to who the couple are.

Other news;

Margaret Thatcher the prime minister said today"…"

Diane remarked, "Terry, they're talking about us."

I replied, "Yes, I realised that, but at least they didn't give out our names."

Diane then said, "Our parents are going to put two and two together, though if they've seen that news item."

I replied, "Well, there's not much can be done about it now, is there? It just goes to show, though, how rumours and legends start. I mean come on, fifty men. There were at least a hundred of them."

"Oh, funny, ha, ha," Diane replied.

I said, "No, but seriously, I bet by the time those people tell the story about us a few times, you will have walked around with wings on your back, sporting a halo with glowing hands and I will be fifteen feet tall, breathing fire. By the end of it, there will be people starting a new religion, Seerism."

Diane replied, "Don't forget, though, Terry, we are not normal people and without our powers, those out of context, escalating stories about us wouldn't have started. So maybe there are some basis of truth in all religions and legends; there must have been something very unusual happening in the first place to create them."

I replied, "I agree and if those people want to believe the stories and even make them into a religion that's fine, but it's the stupid things that they tag on that I don't understand.

"Like you must cover your head or face in a certain direction or even make a sacrifice with blood to uphold and keep each particular god happy. Also why is it people seem to think that a god must have a recognisable human or animal form, come to that? I don't get why people can't realise the creation of life itself couldn't have been by a man, woman or beast, those forms came way after this world was created. **No !** Nature, if you want to give it a name, is the true creator, through trial and error until an acceptable balance was reached to support and maintain all living things. There's your true god, and it doesn't tell you to go out and kill people because they don't pray to it. Let's face it: religions have been the cause of more deaths than nature ever has."

Diane replied, "Well, remind me never to bring up religion as a subject with you again."

I said, "Sorry, I do go on a bit, don't I? It's just that human beings seem to have a knack of turning the seed of something good into something that ends up hurting or killing thousands and I just don't understand it."

Diane finally managed to get me off the subject of religion and the rest of the evening we spent talking about how we were going to handle our confessions with our parents on Sunday.

The dreaded day had arrived and around 11:00 a.m. Lottie and Jim, Diane's parents, turned up. It was quite emotional for Diane and her mother, as they had always been close and five years apart produced a good many tears from them both. Jim commented on the fullness of my beard and said he hardly recognised me. About ten minutes later, my parents pulled into the drive and through the window, I saw my dad get a big bunch of flowers out of the boot of his car and give them to my mum to give to Diane. We greeted them at the front door and my dad said, as he smiled at Diane, "Hello, Diane. Have you remarried?"

I said, giving him a hug, "Very funny, Dad."

Diane then said to my mum, "Thanks for the flowers, Rose. I'll just put them in water while you go with Terry into the lounge; my mum and dad are already in there."

Diane put some water into the kitchen sink, and laid the flowers so the water covered their cut stems. Then she came into the lounge and sat on the sofa between her mum and dad. My parents each sat in the armchairs facing the sofa, with the coffee table in the middle. I got a chair from the kitchen and sat next to my mum.

"Would anyone like a drink?" I said, opening the cabinet where we kept our booze.

My mum replied, "I'd love a cup of tea."

"Me, too," Lottie said.

"What about you two?" I said to Jim and my dad.

Looking at each other, they both said, "Tea's fine with us."

It was a good thing really that they all wanted tea. That booze was left over from when Diane and I got married. Neither of us were drinkers, so who knows whether it was off or not.

I went into the kitchen to make the tea and left Diane to answer all the initial questions about our time abroad. Apparently my parents had seen the news item the previous day and had realised it was about us and was in the middle of asking Diane about it when I came into the room with the teas.

"We didn't see that news item," Jim said. "Uganda! That must have been bloody dangerous."

Diane said, "Dad, you can see we're back no worse for wear, can't you?"

Jim replied, "Suppose so, but anything could have happened."

The conversation seemed to be getting a little heated, but I suppose Jim was only concerned about the safety of his only daughter.

I then said firmly, "Look! There is a reason why we have asked you all here today and hopefully when you have heard what we have to say, you will understand and realise why we did what we did."

I then had to go over my words again in my head to see if they sounded right, while the room went quiet with expectant ears.

I then started to speak again. "Right, this might be difficult for you all to take in, but please try to bear with me until I've finished."

Everyone seemed to take a gulp of tea at the same time and I drank some of mine also to stave off a dry mouth.

"It all started when I was at nursery school…blah!…seeing shapes… blah!…hazy opaque figures…blah!…plastering ceiling…fell off scaffold…

blah!...struck by lightning...bright light...another dimension...blah!... not aliens...blah...survived...froze in midair...blah!...blah!...Hastings... Diane...fell in love...portal...saved me...blah!...brain waves...Madri...side effects...cured Mum's cancer...saved kids...Las Vegas...powerful telekinesis...*blah!*...another side effect and that's why we have asked you here today, so you can see for yourself and accept us for how we are now, especially me."

After a good thirty seconds or so of complete silence, everyone was sitting with bewildered expressions except for Diane, of course. My father said solemnly, "You're serious, aren't you?"

"Yes, Dad, deadly serious," I replied.

He then said, "So let me get this straight. You've visited another dimension. Diane can cure people, but with you she can do it almost immediately and she has an affinity with all living things. You can both see the images of people after they die, then they go into a bright light. Your body can heal itself if you get injured and you can move things or freeze them in mid-air with your mind."

I said, "Yes, Dad, that's exactly right."

"It's a bit much to take in though son," he said.

I said, "Well, watch this then."

With my mind I raised the coffee table, together with its cups and saucers, about three feet into the air. Our startled parents all pushed hard back in their seats. I then turned the table 180 degrees and gently lowered it back down to the floor.

"Bloody hell," Jim said.

Finally accepting what I had told them to be the truth, my dad said, "And you two have been like this for the past fifteen years. Why didn't you tell us before?"

Addressing both our parents, I said, "Because I made a promise to Theron that I wouldn't tell anyone. Can you imagine what would happen if everyone knew what we can do? Not only that, millions of people would be freaked out if they knew what happens to them when they die. The world isn't ready for that yet Dad and none of you can ever tell anyone."

My mother then said, "So why are you telling us now, son?"

I replied, "Because I have another side effect that you would eventually find out about."

Joining the conversation, Lottie said, "What is that then?"

I replied, "I will have to show you. I'm just going up to the bathroom but I will be down again in about ten minutes. Then you'll be able to see for yourselves."

I left Diane answering more questions, while I went up to the bathroom to shave off my beard. About ten minutes later, I finally came down and entered the lounge to a look of amazement from our parents.

With astonishment my father said, "Oh, my God, Terry. Your face, it's..."

Interrupting him I said, "I know, Dad. Now you can see why I grew the beard and why you would have eventually found out."

My mother then said, "How do you feel about this Diane?"

"I've just got to accept it," she replied.

I said firmly, "Now, we are going to need your solemn oaths that you will tell no one about any of this, ever."

I didn't expect it, but one by one each member of our family said, "I promise."

Diane said, "Good! Now let me clear these cups away, so I can go and prepare the dinner. We're having roast turkey."

Her mum then said, "Ooo, it's a bit like Christmas."

How Lottie likened the day to be like Christmas, I'll never know.

The rest of the day and evening went surprisingly well. Our parents just seemed to now accept all they had learned about us; only Lottie and my mum did go on a bit about being violated just before they gave birth to Diane and me. It was actually a weight off our minds knowing that we didn't have to lie to our parents anymore and after they had gone and we went to bed that night, we made love in a very satisfying way. If you know what I mean!

A few weeks passed and Diane started to get very bored being around the house all day. She also felt that she should be out there curing people. I suggested that she should try to get her old job back at Great Ormond Street Hospital. After thinking about it for a couple of days, she started making inquiries. Now I've said this to Diane before, coincidences happen but not on the scale they happen to us. I'm sure this unseen force was somehow still guiding our destiny through life, because when she finally rang Mr. Williams, the consultant at Ormond Street, he said that the post of head of department had just come up and he would be over the moon if Diane would take the job. He also said that since she left, the survival rate had gone down in the hospital and he was sure it was Diane's expertise that kept the rate up previously.

Of course Diane accepted the position and within a week she was back working in the hospital, back to her normal self and actually enjoying putting in a fourteen-hour day. It didn't leave much of a home life, though, but at least she was happy.

One evening around 7:00 p.m., I got a call from Diane wanting me to come and meet her in the hospital. She couldn't explain why over the phone, but said she would tell me all about it when I arrived. I managed to get there in about thirty-five minutes and went straight up to the ward where Diane had asked me to meet her.

"What's going on?" I said.

Diane replied, "There's a twelve-year-old boy who was admitted yesterday who has been in a traffic accident. The machines here can only do the breathing for him, but his organs have sustained such trauma that he should have died by now. The thing is, I believe if he could just get through a week or two, his organs will be able to heal enough for him to survive."

I said, "Do you mean your healing powers are not working on him and you need me to help?"

Diane said, "To be honest, Terry, I don't know. I have seen his portal open and close six times now. It's as if he's fighting to stay alive and every time the portal opens, he refuses to enter it. One minute I think he can be saved; the next I think it's too late."

"Well, it's worth giving it a try, isn't it?" I said.

Luckily for us, the boy was in a room of his own and we shut all the window blinds so no curious eyes could see what was going on. We gave it our best shot and applied our hands for well over a minute. With anyone else, they would have jumped up and skipped along the corridor, but there was no change in this lad's condition.

Diane said, "You see what I mean Terry. He's kind of not dead but not alive either."

Just at that moment a portal appeared, but it wasn't the boy's; this one was blue tinged and Theron walked through the portal into the room.

"Theron, what are you doing here?" I said, startled.

He replied, "You know it's my job to investigate anomalies and this boy's portal has not performed its task in many openings, but I was surprised to learn you and Diane were with this boy when I scanned from the other side."

I said, "We have developed the power to heal Theron, but it does not seem to be working on this lad."

Theron said, "It does not surprise me that you have developed unusual powers. Madri had told me that you both should be capable of them."

Diane then said to Theron, "Do you know of anything that we can do to help this boy?"

"I'm afraid I do not," Theron replied. "Very rarely these cases crop up when a living body fights internally to survive and the balance between life and death is so equal that a state of limbo occurs. The balance usually shifts one way or the other within a twenty-four hour period, but in this case it has exceeded that. I should not think it could go on for much longer."

"So it's just a waiting game, then?" Diane said.

"I think so," Theron replied.

There was nothing more we could do for the boy except wait for the outcome. I could tell Theron wanted to leave, so I said to him, "Is it a possibility I could talk to you and Madri about some developments that have occurred? To do with the side effects Madri said I might experience."

Theron replied, "I must leave now, but I will ask the permission of the council if it would be possible. But what would be your location for this meeting?"

I said, "About fifteen years ago, a women named Alice Brady passed through a portal that was years overdue. She remained as a ghost in the house we now occupy."

Theron answered, "Such an event does fall into categories I investigate. I will check my data base to find the location."

I suggested, "Then if the meeting is approved, shall we say in forty-eight hours' time at that location, 8:00 p.m.?"

Theron replied, "I will do my utmost to accommodate you, Terry."

Theron then entered his portal and it zapped shut without a trace.

Diane then said to me, "Do you think it will make any difference to that side effect of yours?"

I replied, "I really don't know, but it's worth a try."

Unfortunately about six hours after we tried to cure the lad, his body gave up and he died. His portal had finally claimed his spirit. Diane was a bit upset about the boy, but she had hardened over the years and knew that she had done all she could for him.

Two days passed and about five minutes to 8:00 p.m., Diane and I were in Alice's old room, with the curtains drawn, expectantly waiting for Theron's arrival. He did not let us down. Precisely at 8:00 p.m. the flash of light from a blue-tinged portal opened exactly where Alice's portal appeared years ago and Theron and Madri stepped through into the room.

Madri spoke. "It's very nice to see you both again, although I hardly recognised you, Terry, with that facial hair."

I replied, "It's good to see you too. I hope you didn't have any problems with the council letting you meet us again?"

Theron replied, "No, the council agreed that we had already met you once before in your world and **that** meeting proved to be no risk to our species. Now what was it you wanted to speak to us about?"

I began, saying, "Well, first I have a confession to make and I hope you will understand and accept my apology in advance."

"That sounds very ominous," Theron replied. "What is your confession?"

I continued. "I once promised you that I would never tell anyone about your existence, but due to the circumstances of a side effect caused by closing my death portal, I found I had no other option."

Theron asked, "Whom have you told?"

Apologetically I said, "I told both mine and Diane's parents. It was the only way I could explain the way I looked."

Theron replied, “Through your facial hair, I think I know what you mean, but nevertheless you may have put my species in danger.”

Madri spoke up. “Oh, Theron, can’t you see the man had no option; he obviously believes he can trust the people he told.”

Addressing me, she continued. “Thank you for being honest Terry. Now, is the way you look the reason you wanted to see me?”

I replied, “Well, yes, but I also wanted to tell you about other things we are now capable of and I would like to know if you think these abilities might affect our bodies in any adverse ways.”

After I had run through what Diane and I were capable of, Madri gave us her scientifically based opinions. “I am afraid there is nothing that can be done about your appearance, Terry. If we hadn’t closed the portal somehow, you would certainly have been swallowed by it, so unfortunately the side effects are the price you had to pay. Now, the marvellous brain potential I said you had. This is good news indeed. It is what Terrans have been striving for every time we enhanced the foetal brain in humans. You both are the forerunners of what humans brains can be capable of.” She said excitedly.

I then said, “That may be so Madri, but we have found that we are both sterile and cannot have children of our own.”

Madri replied, “Those dysfunctions I would like to investigate by fully scanning both your brains and maybe then I can give you some answers.”

I said, “Well, we obviously can’t come to your world, but could you maybe bring your equipment and come back here tomorrow at the same time?”

Madri looked at Theron for an answer and he gave a gentle nod.

“Tomorrow evening at 8:00 p.m. it is, then,” she said enthusiastically.

As Theron reopened the portal with his gizmo, we said our good-byes until tomorrow, before the blinding light zapped shut and disappeared.

Madri was a scientist through and through and relished the opportunity to scan any human brain, whereas Theron was a diplomat and bookkeeper at heart, but I think he enjoyed his high status and making decisions, even though Madri was the equivalent of a human wife to him.

Diane hardly said a word through the brief meeting with the Terrans and I could see that she looked a bit despondent.

"What's the matter?" I said.

She replied, "Oh, nothing really, Terry; it's just that, well I've sort of come to terms with the fact that we can never have children and I can't see how Madri can help just by scanning our brains."

I said, "Well, what harm can it do, then?"

She sighed. "I suppose your right."

The next evening again a couple of minutes before 8:00 p.m., we were back in that room with the curtains drawn, ready for Madri's arrival. Once again bang on eight, Madri and Theron stepped through their artificial portal and this time Theron was carrying the familiar scanning helmet, while Madri carried a couple of her small gadgets. As I had turned the room into a guest bedroom many years ago, I had to bring up a couple of chairs from the kitchen. The room already had a small armchair and a bed.

After twiddling the dials on her gadgets for a bit, Madri said, "Who is going first then?"

"I think I'd better go first," I replied.

I sat on one of the kitchen chairs and Madri put the helmet on my head. Diane sat on the bed to watch, while Theron sat on another chair. I felt a slight vibration as I did when I had my first scan, but it wasn't uncomfortable in any way. A few minutes later, after she had looked and assessed the readings on one of her gadgets, Madri said, "OK, Terry, I have all the data I need from you. Now it's your turn Diane."

Less than enthusiastically, Diane swapped places with me and Madri adjusted then put the helmet on Diane's head. Not knowing what to expect, Diane closed her eyes tight.

"Don't worry, relax, it doesn't hurt," Madri said to her.

A few minutes later it was all over and Madri removed the helmet from Diane's head.

Madri then said apologetically, "It will take me a few minutes to analyse this data."

Diane said, "Oh, there's no rush."

Addressing Madri and Theron, Diane added, "Can I get you both anything?"

Theron replied, "Some water would be very nice."

Madri didn't answer, as she was too engrossed reading the dials on her gadgets.

"I'll bring up a jug and glasses," Diane said, as she left the room.

You could literally hear Madri's brain ticking as she analysed the data and periodically said "aha, aha" to herself. Before Madri had finished, Diane returned, carrying a tray with four glasses and a pitcher of cold tap water. She put the tray on the spare chair, poured out the water into each glass and handed me and Theron one each.

"Thank you," Theron said.

Just then Madri said, without any giveaway expression, "I have finished my findings."

I said impatiently, "Well, what are your conclusions?"

Madri answered, "It appears that both of you at one time have been in close proximity or contact with a natural portal. The time Terry nearly died because of the lightning strike and the time Diane touched Terry's portal to close it. Both your brains instigated a kind of failsafe to your bodies to preserve any organs being damaged. This meant that a hormone was produced, which literally shut down your reproductive systems to protect them. Because the effects of the portal were completely alien to you, your brain has not recognised the threat has passed. Basically all we need to do is stimulate both your brains to produce their own antidote to that hormone."

With newfound enthusiasm, Diane said, "You mean the condition is reversible?"

Madri replied, "Oh yes. If you give me a few minutes I can recalibrate the scanner to stimulate the areas of your brains to unlock the failsafe hormone, so to speak."

Diane and I looked at each other with a massive smile across both our faces.

"Will you do that for us now Madri?" I asked, almost begging.

Madri replied, "Certainly Terry, may I have a drink of water first, though?"

Diane poured Madri a glass of water but was shaking so much with excitement she was spilling the overfull glass all over the carpet. Madri took a few sips of water from the glass then started to turn a few dials on the helmet and gadgets.

She then said, "OK, that should do it. Who is going first?"

"Me. I'll go first again," I said.

If there were going to be any instant side effects from this process, I didn't want Diane to suffer them. I felt the helmet warm up a little as I wore it for a couple more minutes and after the experience I didn't feel any difference. But to be honest why would I feel any different. Eagerly Diane went through the same process and when it was finished, she said to Madri, "Do you think there will be a time period for the stimulation to work?"

Madri replied, "I can't really answer that. I suppose it depends on the cycle time your body would normally ovulate, but for Terry it would probably be a matter of hours. Now is there anything more we can help you with?"

I replied, "No, Madri, we are so grateful for what you have already done. It means so much to us."

She then said, "Then, my human friends, I think it is time for Theron and me to leave."

I felt like I wanted to hug Madri and Theron but due to their slender body frames, I feared I might crush them with my exuberance. But, as they reinitiated their portal and we said our good-byes, I said, "Now you know where we live. Come and visit us sometime."

On reflection, I thought it was a stupid thing to say to beings from another dimension, but I was so wrapped up in the thought that Diane and I might now be able to have children, I'm surprised total gibberish didn't come from my mouth. I had also forgotten that I was still stuck with the dilemma of my side effect, which nothing could be done about. After the portal had closed and my Terran friends had gone, Diane said to me.

"Oh, Terry, do you think what Madri did to us will work? I'm not as young now to be a mother."

I said to Diane reassuringly, "You're only thirty-seven. You know better than anyone that you're not too old to have kids."

"I hope you're right," she replied.

It probably isn't difficult to guess that, from that point on, we were at it like rabbits and that, six weeks later, Diane discovered she was pregnant. Of course both our families were overjoyed at the news and when we had told them it was only due to Madri and her technology, they were even more convinced that the Terrans were a benevolent species.

We decided that Diane should have the baby in St. Gregory's Hospital in Tooting, the one in which she worked during the final years of her training. She had a normal pregnancy and even worked in Great Ormond Street right up until a week or so before she was due.

The day finally arrived and Diane's labour pains were scaring me silly. Having first put the passenger seat of our old Beamer all the way back to accommodate her huge bump, I managed to manoeuvre her into the seat. Partly the reason we chose St. Gregory's was that it was only ten minutes down the road, but I'm sure I got her there in five. Having stopped directly outside the accident and emergency entrance, we got a couple of nurses to get her inside in a wheel chair. Then, I rapidly drove to the car park and ran all the way back. By the time I got there, the nurses had already taken Diane to a room in the maternity wing, and as I entered the room, she was in a hospital gown, in a birthing position, giving out forced blows from her mouth at one second intervals. There was a midwife at the foot of the bed, poised with a white towel encouraging Diane to push, while a nurse stood at the side of the bed, ready for every eventuality. I went to Diane's side and held her hand and inadvertently found myself blowing in unison to her puffs. With one great instruction to "push" from the midwife and with a straining screech reaching a crescendo from Diane's larynx, it was all over.

"It's a boy," the midwife said, as she cradled the baby in the white towel and started to wipe off the birth gunk. My huge, beaming smile and tears of joy wouldn't let me speak for a moment; all I could do was kiss Diane's sweaty forehead.

After the midwife had done her stuff, she placed our wailing son into Diane's arms and he immediately stopped crying. Both of us had tears trickling down either side of our noses.

"Well, done, Mum," I whispered, as I ran my hand gently over our son's tiny head and as I did so, the little fellow briefly opened his eyes twice. The first time I could have sworn his eyes were blue, but the second time they were a vivid green, like Diane's. I thought that I must have been mistaken and my own watery eyes must have blurred my vision in some way, so I thought no more about it. After making sure Diane and son were OK and comfortable, I said to Diane I had better telephone our parents to give them the news. Very contentedly, she nodded in agreement, without removing her gaze from our wondrous little bundle.

I rang our parents and gave them the news and both said that they were going to come to the hospital immediately. Lottie and Jim were there within half an hour, but my parents took a couple of hours, seeing as they had to come from Hastings. It's amazing, though, how time just goes when you're wrapped up in something so special, because it didn't seem like those two hours had passed before my parents entered the ward room. The smiles of happiness on their faces as each parent in turn held the baby's hand and made silly noises at him.

Jim said to us, "What are you going to call him?"

I replied, "To be honest, Jim, we haven't really thought about a name because we didn't know if it was going to be a boy or a girl."

"I have," Diane said, looking straight at me. "Radim."

"Radim," I said. "What made you come up with that name?"

She replied, "Well, I wanted a name that was different and we owe the birth of our baby to Madri. Radim is an anagram of Madri. Don't you like it?"

"I think it's great," I replied.

Diane then asked our parents, "What do you think?"

Everyone agreed it was a nice, unusual name, a name they had never heard of before.

Another hour passed, with everyone talking to Radim with words from the baby language dictionary: "da da and goo, goo, goo,"but it looked like Diane was getting tired, so I suggested to our parents we had better let her get some rest. The four overjoyed grandparents reluctantly agreed to go home and said they would come and visit us over the weekend. I called the nurse in and told her Diane was tired, so the nurse went to get a wheeled, walk-about cot for Radim to be put in. When she came back with the cot, she put the sound asleep little lad into it, next to Diane's bed and then said to me, "We'll keep your wife in overnight, just to make sure everything is all right and you can come back tomorrow morning to pick them up."

I didn't really want to leave Diane, but I realised she was very tired, so I gave her a massive thank-you kiss and said I would be back around 9:00 a.m. in the morning. Diane smiled and with her eyes half shut, said, "See you tomorrow then, Daddy."

The next day I was back at that hospital bang on 9:00 a.m. and when I entered Diane's room, she was dressed and ready to go. As we began to leave, I looked around the rest of the ward to see if I could see the midwife and nurse that helped with the birth to thank them, but neither of them was on duty, so I just thanked the nurse who was there and asked her to relay my thank-you wishes when they came back on their next shift.

Once Diane and son was safely in the front seat of the car, I drove home extra carefully to avoid any sharp braking or pot holes in the roads.

Ethel was in her front garden when we finally arrived and as I helped Diane out of the car, Ethel had positioned herself by our adjoining fence.

"Let me see the baby then," she called, excitedly.

Diane walked over to the fence, cradling Radim in a thick, light blue woollen shawl her mother had brought into the hospital the day before.

"Oh, he's beautiful. And what lovely blue eyes he's got," Ethel said, as Radim briefly opened his eyes and yawned.

"Yes, he takes after his father," I said, jokingly. "Come on Diane; let's get you inside so you can put your feet up." I said quickly, before Ethel could start a Spanish inquisition of all the aspects of how the birth went. Once inside Diane sat down on the sofa in the lounge and put our baby beside her in a kind of carry cot we had bought a couple of months ago.

"I'll make us a nice cup of coffee," I said.

"That will be nice," Diane answered.

I went to the kitchen to make the coffees and when I brought them into the lounge, Diane was crying.

"What's the matter?" I said with concern, as I put the drinks on the coffee table.

Diane replied, "Oh, nothing, Terry, it's just that ten years ago I was so depressed and convinced I could never have children. I am so happy now that my emotions don't know whether to make me laugh or cry."

"Listen darling," I said. "There is no one more deserving than you to be happy, so when you've finished crying, let's have a good laugh, because come the night times, one of us will have to get up to see to Rad when he's crying his eyes out to be fed or needs changing."

Diane began to smile and then said, "That will be you, Terry."

"Not likely," I replied. "He won't get much out of my breasts."

Diane began to laugh, probably at the vision of me breast feeding, but at least her mood had lifted and I think her emotions had finally sorted themselves out.

11

Rad, which is what we mainly called him, was a good baby. He hardly cried and always smiled at any time, anyone approached or talked to him and for the first six months, he slept in a cot in our bedroom and hardly ever woke us up for anything. During those six months, I converted our box room into his nursery and kitted it out with everything we thought he would need. I had papered the walls in a pastel blue-base colour, with comic cars and airplanes in little scenes all over. We situated his large, high-sided cot in the middle of the room, with one of those things you hang from the ceiling light shade. He would lie there quietly for hours, looking at the moving shapes of the stars, moon, sun and other planets.

One afternoon when Rad was about eight months old, I went into his room to check on him. As I entered, the thing dangling from the ceiling was whizzing round at a fair old speed and I immediately thought there must be a hell of a draught to cause that, but when I looked at Rad in his cot, his eyes were bright green and he was giggling to himself. It didn't take much to put two and two together and realise Rad was moving the shapes above his cot with his mind, but as he saw me and became distracted, I noticed his eye colour change from green, back to blue. I wasn't really surprised. Even before Rad was born, Diane and I discussed the possibility, indeed the probability, that our child would inherit certain traits from us. I lifted Rad from his cot and took him downstairs to Diane, who was busy in the kitchen ironing some of his clothes.

"I think we may have a problem," I said.

"Problem! What problem? Rad's all right, isn't he?" she said, with panic in her voice.

I replied, "It's OK. He's absolutely fine. It's just that he has just moved that dangly thing above his cot with his mind and when he did it, his eyes changed from blue to green."

"You mean he's showing signs of your abilities already?" she asked.

I replied, "Yes, but that can't be a good thing. He's far too young to understand the consequences of what he's doing. We are going to have to keep a keen eye on him from now on, but at least his eyes are a tell-tale sign that he might be up to mischief."

Diane agreed and realised that a baby who could move things about with his mind could potentially put himself and others in danger.

Another thought did cross my mind, but I didn't share this one with Diane. All those years ago, when I was talking to Theron in his special place in his world, he said that the elders of his race believed that one day a human would be able to walk among them. Having a supernatural power at such an early age I did wonder: Could Rad turn out to be that human?

Luckily enough over the next few years, Rad only used his ability with his toys and by the time he was four, he was talking and understanding most of the things we were telling and teaching him. But at that age, how do you tell a child he's not like other children and mustn't use his gift in front of anyone except his parents?

Diane had returned to work about a year after Rad was born, which left me solely responsible for him during the weekdays. He was quite easy to look after but it makes you realise that keeping a child happy and amused every minute of the day can be very hard work. Although we were apprehensive about Rad being in other people's company for fear he might use his inherent talent, we decided that he should mix with other children of his own age, so we managed to get him a place at a local pre-school nursery.

I remembered back to my first day at nursery school. The thought that my mother was going to leave me there and never return haunts me to this day. Rad, on the other hand, didn't bat an eyelid when I told him I would come back in a couple of hours to pick him up, so my reluctance to leave him with someone unknown to him and nine other unfamiliar little faces really had no basis.

Mrs. Grant was the thirty-something lady that was looking after the ten kids in the group. According to the pre-school literature, she had four children of her own and was fully versed in tending to and assessing children who would go on to prospective primary schools. Her assessments were apparently recognised by the heads of schools over a local but wide area. I just hoped Rad would behave himself.

On that first day, I left Rad at the nursery at 11:00 a.m., then I went back to pick him up at 3:00 p.m. Just before I entered this large one-room building, I crossed my fingers, hoping Rad hadn't done something out of the ordinary. Once through the door, Mrs. Grant saw me and asked me to hang around until the other parents had left with their children, so she could have a chat with me about Rad. *Oh, God! What has he done?* I thought. When the last parent left, Mrs. Grant sat on a low table with her handbag at the side of her and beckoned me over.

"Is there a problem?" I said nervously.

She replied, "Oh no, not at all. It's just that I wondered whether you or your wife had any engineering background."

"Why do you ask?" I said.

She replied, "Well, look at those building blocks on the floor. Your son did that."

Although slightly crude, Rad had built a bridge structure, which had a moveable span with a counter lever, a bit like Tower Bridge but with only one lift-up section.

Mrs. Grant then said, "I tried to watch Rad as he built that and I could see he was thinking about what he was doing all the time. Most children his age will just put one block on top of another and then knock them down again, but Rad has preserved his creation and shielded it from the other children. I believe your son has the makings of an engineer, or something similar, because he certainly seems to be far in advance of his years, whatever the case."

I replied, "I am a plasterer by trade and his mother a medical doctor, so no: we don't have engineering backgrounds, but thanks for your observations. We'll see you tomorrow then."

"Yes, you certainly will," she replied, as she started to collect her things together.

Looking all around the immediate area, Mrs. Grant, mystified, said, "Where's my bag? I had it by the side of me just now."

Noticing that her bag was now sitting on the top of a stack of shelves, I said, "Is that it up there?"

She replied, "How odd? It was at the side of me. How did it get up there?"

"No idea," I replied, knowing full well that while we were talking, Rad must have levitated the bag onto the shelf.

"Good-bye, then," I said.

With that I put Rad in his buggy and started to walk home. It occurred to me while I was walking that when I was in the Terran world, Theron had told me that, just before I was born, I had been enhanced with the thoughts of a renowned mechanical technician. As I had never shown any real interest in that sort of thing, I wondered if my enhancement had somehow skipped me but had surfaced in Rad. I knew Diane hadn't passed out during her labour with him, so no enhancement had occurred at that point. So maybe through me, he would grow up to be an engineer.

Rad got through his time in nursery school thankfully, without any more unexplained incidents—at least, during that time, I hadn't heard of any. On Mrs. Grant's recommendation, he then went on to a good local primary school and after that, a top grammar school. During his school days, we discovered he was a self-healer, just like me, after cutting himself a good few times, playing rough games and doing general stupid things that young boys get up to. He also told us that he had cured a friend of his when his friend fell out of a tree and dislocated his thumb. Helping his friend to his feet the dislocation was somehow put right. So that was yet another ability he possessed.

From an age when Diane and I knew Rad would understand, we told him all about ourselves—absolutely everything. We also told him about the importance of keeping his abilities secret, or we would all end up as guinea pigs because people would exploit us for what we could do. He was intelligent and level headed enough to realise what we had told him must be upheld at all times, for all our sakes.

Also, Rad and I became very close as he grew up. We would go on fishing trips and exploring days together, usually to a place where no one was around. This kind of trip we used as an opportunity to hone his abilities. I found out a couple of important things on those trips. For instance, together we'd try to see who could lift the heaviest rock with our minds. Of course I always beat him hands down, a fact which led me to believe that maturity of mind somehow reflected the power that could be exerted and I found that as he got older, the more powerful he became. When Rad was fourteen I discovered that he could actually levitate himself, something that I had never achieved. To me it was like standing in a bucket, then trying to lift myself up with the handle: my mind couldn't get past that. It made me think of my childhood days, though, when I and all the kids were reading comics, such as Superman.

When I really thought about it, I realised that my son was probably better equipped than Superman. If Rad could levitate himself, then with practise he could make himself fly. He was already impervious to body damage, so that made him invulnerable and as far as Kryptonite was concerned, there wasn't a known substance that could affect him. His only give-away was that when he exerted his powers, his eyes turned green, which Diane and I thought to be a good thing because it would make him aware that he couldn't use his abilities without people noticing the source. But we didn't need to drum protocols into Rad because he was wise enough to comprehend the importance of our words, things like he must never use his abilities to seek revenge and must never use them to hurt another human in any way. It wasn't only me bonding with Rad though; the three of us would go out quite often on trips. He especially enjoyed Hastings beach and pier, and visiting his grandparents and great uncle and aunt. He was also quite partial to Rock Salmon and chips, funny that.

Rad's main passion as he grew up was electronics and mechanics. Anytime he was given a device of some kind, the first thing he would do was dissect it. Then he would put it back together as if it had never been touched. After I told him about the Terran world and their kind of transportation, everything he did with the subject, centred on finding the secret of their propulsion system.

At sixteen, Rad went into a technical college to expand his love of mechanics and at twenty, because of his creative talents; he was offered a high-level job by an international aerodynamics company. I myself got into buying, renovating and re-selling properties, which was quite a lucrative business then and it helped keep our bank balance well up. It also gave me something to do. Diane, now fifty-nine, had been a consultant for quite a few years, but to my mind she was still putting in too many hours at the hospital.

At home sometimes, I would walk into the lounge and find Diane and Rad sitting in total silence. Then I'd realised they were having a conversation by reading each other's minds, although they didn't do it if I was in the room. At least, I think they didn't! Although Diane didn't show it, she was devastated when Rad left home soon after his twenty-second birthday. He was earning such good wages that he bought a real posh flat, overlooking the Thames near Tower Bridge. Times, technology and wages had really changed since we were his age.

My son was all about his career, but he did have girlfriends from time to time, nothing really serious though. At thirty he announced that he had been offered a high position in the corporation he worked for, but it meant that he would have to move to Florida in the United States. Although devastated for a second time, his mother and I agreed that he should follow his own destiny in life and after Rad left the country, Diane finally retired and I decided it was my time to stop working also.

It was sad, but a few years previous, Diane's parents, Lottie and Jim, both died within a month of each other. Jim died first, of course from natural causes—or we could have saved him—but Lottie's death was sudden, which other relatives believed was due to a broken heart at losing Jim. A year or so after Lottie and Jim died, my mum also passed away and a year after that my dad. Although our parent's deaths affected us badly, at least we knew that they had lived out their lives fully as Nature intended and not been taken by some mad disease the modern world had inflicted upon them.

Cuddled up on the sofa one night in the year 2024, Diane and I were watching the global news on our television when this item came up:

It has been announced today that Radim Seer of the Global Aerodynamics Corporation has invented and produced a new propulsion system that will eliminate the use of fossil fuels completely by the year 2035. The system has been called the Magnetic Aerodynamic Dispersion Relay Isolator or MADRI for short. This new system is set to replace all existing powered means of travel.

"He's done it; Rads done it," I said with jubilation.

"That's my boy," Diane replied.

Soon after that TV announcement, our Skypecom phone bleeped and by my verbal command to answer the call, Rad appeared in the top quarter section of our TV screen.

"Hiya, Mum. Hiya, Dad. Did you hear the announcement?" he said excitedly, but in a pushed-for-time kind of way.

I replied, "Yes, we have just seen it on the television."

He then said apologetically, "Sorry I couldn't let you know about it first, but everyone in the company was sworn to secrecy until it was simultaneously announced around the world. Anyway I've got some other news: I'm coming home for a bit and I'm bringing someone with me. Is that OK?"

Diane replied, "Of course it is. When can we expect you?"

"Tomorrow afternoon," Rad replied.

I said, "We'll look forward to it then. See you tomorrow."

"Love you!" Diane said.

"You too, Mum," he replied.

Rad switched off at his end, which reinstated the full TV screen.

Full of smiles, Diane said, "Great, he's coming home. I've missed him so much. I wonder who he's bringing with him, though."

I replied, "I hope it's not his boss. I wouldn't know how to entertain a mega executive, would you?"

Diane said, "Well, we will just have to wait to see who it is when he arrives."

We worked hard the next morning to make sure the house was clean and the guest room was ready. The sofa converted into a bed and we knew Rad wouldn't mind sleeping on that. Diane was so happy Rad was coming home, but he did indicate it was only going to be a brief visit.

At about 2:30 p.m., a taxi drew up outside our house. I missed Rad as much as Diane, so I couldn't stop myself hurrying to greet him as he got out of the cab.

"Hiya, Dad," he said, with a slight American twang to his voice.

Just as I returned the greeting, a long, high-heeled leg emerged out of the taxi.

"This is Emily, my fiancée," Rad said.

I was quite taken back as this beautiful, tall, long-haired brunette woman of about thirty years of age stood before me. She was wearing a white blouse, short black skirt and shiny black high-heeled shoes.

"Hello, Mr. Seer. It's very nice to finally meet you," she said, with a sophisticated American accent, if there is one.

Emily then did the non-touching false kiss to both sides of my bearded cheeks.

I replied, "Well, it's very nice to meet you, too."

"C'mon," I said. "Let me help you with your bags."

As Rad and I carried their overnight bags up the drive heading to the front door where Diane was waiting, I noticed the curtains move from next door.

Poor old Ethel died years ago and Benji lived till he was seventeen, but the replacement neighbour we now had was a right, nosey old biddy. Arriving at Diane by the front door, Rad dropped his bag to the ground and flung his arms around her.

"I've missed you so much, Mum," he said.

With a tear in her eye, Diane replied, "I missed you too, Rad."

He then introduced his companion. "Mum, this is my fiancée, Emily. We only got engaged yesterday."

"Hello, Mrs. Seer. At last I get to meet the lady Rad talks about all the time," Emily said, doing the double-kiss thing again.

I piped up, saying, "Come on in you two. I'm sure you've got lots to tell us."

We left the bags in the hall and all went into the lounge. Rad and Emily sat on the sofa, while Diane sat in her armchair.

Still standing, I said, "Coffee anyone?"

Rad replied, "I wouldn't mind a cup of tea, Dad. You don't seem to get a decent cup in the States."

Emily spoke up. "I wouldn't mind tea also, milk with no sweetener, please."

I knew Diane would want a coffee the same as me, but how strange it is that an Americanised couple wanted tea and an English couple wanted coffee. While I was in the kitchen, I noted something very odd: I couldn't hear any voices. It turned out that Rad and Emily had arranged between them a special way to introduce Emily to Diane.

They were both talking to Diane with their minds and Diane was reciprocating. As I brought the drinks into the room, Diane said to me," Emily is one of us."

"What do you mean?" I said.

"Emily has psychic abilities," Diane replied. "She's telepathic."

I was a little miffed about their mind talking abilities, but only because I couldn't join in. I suppose though, I wasn't overly surprised that Rad had found a partner who wasn't the run of the mill. I was sure it must have been that pre-determined destiny at work again, just as it was for Diane and me.

Diane soon accepted Emily into the fold, especially as Rad had told her all about us and we knew our secret would be safe with Emily as it would involve her too.

I said to Rad, "So you finally perfected that propulsion system you have been working on all these years."

Rad replied, "Yes, Dad, finally."

I said, "It sounds similar to the Terran form of transport."

Rad replied, "It's probably very similar. It's a pity they couldn't have steered me in the right direction though. I would have got there a hell of a lot quicker, but it was your description of their crafts that encouraged me to work out how it was done in the first place. The domestic versions, which will replace cars, will be OK, but for supersonic travel, we have still got to create an artificial atmosphere inside the vehicle. At the moment our test pilots can only fly at a fraction of the craft's potential speed because their bodies just can't take the g-forces."

I replied, "I'm sure you'll eventually get your head around it."

Rad said, "Well, I've got the best there is to help me. Emily is a technician on the project. That's where I met her."

After chatting for quite some time, Diane and I felt very at ease with Emily; it seemed as if we had known her for years and she explained that the no-contact kiss nonsense when we first met was just a totally nervous reaction to us.

Toward the end of our chat, Rad said, "Sorry you two, you know this is only a flying visit. We have got to get back to the States tomorrow. We've got press releases and board room meetings to attend to."

"Board room meetings?" I repeated, with surprise.

Rad replied, "Oh yes, I haven't told you. I have been made a partner in the company and now I own twenty percent of the shares."

"That must be worth millions," I said, with astonishment.

"Er, yes, I suppose you're right," he replied. "I've been very lucky though. If Lori hadn't had faith in me and taken me under her wing, I would never have got where I am today."

"Lori?" Diane said.

Rad replied, "Yes. Lori Clark. Her married name is Lori Stein, though. She was the founder of the company and has just retired from the CEO position. Because there's now a new CEO, a position on the board was offered to me, which she nominated me for. Apparently she started out with a small company and after a few years, she married this Mr. Stein. He is mega-rich because his father has shares in umpteen casinos in Las Vegas. Everyone seems to still call her Lori Clark though, because the company started out as Lori Clark Aerodynamics."

Diane and I were dumbfounded.

It was far too much of a coincidence that the little Lori Clark we met at New York airport and the son of Mr. Stein, the casino executive, were not relative to the people we encountered back in the seventies.

The predetermined destiny hypothesis really hit its mark this time, but we didn't let on to Rad and Emily.

Diane cooked a meal that evening and after looking through old photos and telling embarrassing stories about Rad as he was growing up, we probed into Emily's Californian background. Then, we all decided it was time for bed. Needless to say, the sofa bed didn't need to be used.

In bed Diane and I cuddled up as we always did and started to talk about Rad.

Diane said in a low voice, "Emily is perfect for Rad."

I replied, "I know. They remind me of us when we first met, totally smitten with each other."

"I wish I was that age again," Diane said.

Replying, I said "You're as beautiful now as you were then."

"Who are you kidding?" she said.

I replied indignantly, "I mean it, Diane. When I look at you, I see the girl I fell in love with and that will never change."

Diane replied, "I'm nearly seventy-five years old, Terry. I'm a wrinkled old woman."

Again I replied indignantly, "You're not. Not to me."

She then said, "I was lucky to have met you."

I replied, "I don't think luck had anything to do with it, like Rad and Emily and Lori and her husband, we were destined for each other."

Diane faced me and smiled. "Good night then, darling," she said.

"Good night, gorgeous," I replied.

We then looked at each other, lovingly kissed, then turned our bedside lights off and went to sleep.

The next day we woke up about 9:00 a.m. to the smell of bacon cooking from the kitchen. When we came downstairs to investigate, Rad and Emily was preparing a cooked breakfast.

"Hi, Mum. Hi, Dad," said Rad. "Sit yourselves down. Breakfast won't be long. Coffee ?"

"Yes, please," we both replied.

Going by Rad and Emily's track-suit trousers and sweat-soaked T-shirts, It looked as if they had gotten up early and gone for a run before returning to cook breakfast. Emily put our cooked breakfasts in front of us on the table and then our coffees.

"Where's yours?" Diane said to her.

"Oh, we've had ours," she replied.

Rad then said, "We're gonna have a shower while you're having breakfast. Is that ok ?"

"Of course it is," I replied.

While chomping our way through the sausage, eggs and bacon, Diane said, "Oh, I wish Rad and Emily lived in London. They seem to bring a breath of fresh air when they're around."

I replied, "Yes, I know what you mean. It's a pity they're going back to the States today."

After breakfast Diane and I did the washing up and as we were finishing Rad and Emily came into the kitchen, both smartly dressed.

Rad then said, "Sorry it's been such a short visit, but we've got to leave soon to catch our flight."

I said, "Well, let me get dressed and I'll run you to the airport."

Rad replied, "No, no need for that. We've already ordered a cab."

No sooner had he finished his sentence when a toot- toot sound came from the entrance to our drive.

Diane said disappointedly, "Oh, Rad, when are we going to see you again?"

Rad replied in an effort to appease her, "Soon, Mum, soon. Sorry, we've got to go."

Rad gave his mum a big hug and kissed her on the cheek and as he was a lot taller, gave me a one-armed hug around my shoulders. I really felt dwarfed by my six-foot-two-inch son but also felt very proud.

"Love you both," he said.

Emily also gave Diane a hug and kiss on the cheek and later I found out she also said telepathically to Diane. *Don't worry. I'll make sure he's all right and get him to take time off work to come back here again soon.*

"Bye," they both said and in an instant they were gone.

I thought that Rad's whirlwind visit would depress Diane, but actually it gave her a new lease of life. After that visit she seemed to want to go out more and we'd go to different places around the English countryside, just to explore and amble around. One area we went to was Ludlow in Shropshire, the place where her childhood began. She took me to the actual spot in the field where she was abducted by the Terrans. Although at the time it was quite traumatic for her, she now realised that if it had never happened, her life would have been completely different. We sat in that field for hours and talked and laughed about all the things she and I had experienced during our lives together. She certainly hadn't lost her affinity with animals as while we sat talking, butterflies flew around us and a couple of wild rabbits came to sit by her side. During our talk though, I couldn't help wishing for her sake that she was that young girl again who raced me from Hastings beach to the promenade.

A few more years passed and Rad and Emily did in fact visit fairly often—at least within three or four monthly intervals—and on one visit, they announced that they were getting married, much to the delight of Diane. The only thing was, the wedding was going to take place in Florida. It wasn't really a problem going to Florida, but I was a bit concerned as Diane's health had begun to deteriorate a bit and this was obviously due to age.

We flew out to Florida the day before the wedding and stayed in Rad and Emily's house, which they had bought soon after their engagement. What a pad that was! The house was huge, with a large swimming pool and every conceivable mod con that was on the market. We finally got to meet Emily's parents and because they came from California, they were also staying in one of the numerous bedrooms the house had to offer.

Emily had warned us ahead of time that her parents didn't have abilities and also didn't know she had them, as her telepathy hadn't developed until she was twenty years old. By that time, Emily thought it best to tell no one, in case they thought her to be a freak or something. That was until she met Rad, because she somehow knew he was like her in some ways.

The wedding was spectacular and of course Diane and Emily's mother shed many tears. There must have been at least a hundred guests at the reception that was held in the garden of the house. I say garden, but to be honest it was more like a botanical reserve. Not really knowing anybody and not wanting anyone looking too closely at my true appearance beneath my bushy beard, I sat alone on the veranda, with a bottle of beer in my hand. It was a good opportunity to sit down, loosen my tie, slouch and relax. I had never liked putting a suit and tie on before and I would have felt much more comfortable if I had been casually dressed. It was nice though looking out over the grounds and pool areas with the ambience of guests, chatting and laughing as they drank their champagne in tall, fluted glasses. The background music was good too, playing melodies from all eras with no vocals whatsoever. It was also just at the right volume, so as the guests didn't have to shout to make themselves heard. I hadn't got a clue where the music was coming from as I couldn't see any speakers around anywhere. I had only sat there for about ten minutes when Rad came over to join me, also with his tie loosened, shirt unbuttoned at the neck and with a beer bottle in his hand. I think he had just finished going around to all the guests to thank them for coming and now he wanted a little time with me alone. As he sat down, he said, "Well, what do you think of the place, Dad?"

I replied, "It's amazing, son."

The veranda looked out onto a huge patio and further on from the swimming pool, the garden stretched hundreds of feet back, with flower beds dotted everywhere. Then as I looked to my right, there was an outbuilding that looked like stables.

"You've got horses too?" I asked.

He replied, "Yep, one each. We've got a groom who looks after them for us."

"Blimey, how the other half live" I said jokingly.

After a short lull in the conversation as we sat back sipping our beers, I said, "Have you seen your mum? I haven't seen her for ages."

"Yeah," he replied. "She's with Emily looking at her flowers. Emily's hobby is growing exotic flowers from all over the world. There she is."

Rad pointed to a spot about eighty yards away. I could just make them out. Emily was still in her cream-coloured wedding dress as she took Diane around all the flower beds.

Out of my earshot, Diane said to Emily, "You've got some amazing flowers, Emily."

She replied, "Yes, I love flowers, but it's funny. I read all the data on what soil any particular species needs to provide them with all their nutrients, but the only one that isn't responding that well is my English rose."

"Can I see it?" Diane said.

"Sure, it's just over here," Emily replied.

Emily led Diane a few yards further on to a droopy-looking rose bush. After inspecting it, Diane said, "You're right. It does look a bit sad. Let's see what we can do."

Diane crouched down and stroked the main stem of the plant, being careful not to be pricked by its thorns. Within thirty seconds or so, the rose bush's branches went from limp to erect and flowers bloomed all over the bush.

"Wow! I wish I had that sort of power," Emily said.

"Horse manure," Diane replied.

"Excuse me," Emily said, stunned by Diane's words.

Diane replied, "You need to dig some horse manure into the soil around the bush. I may have given it a bit of a boost for now, but it won't last."

Emily then said, "It doesn't tell you that in the data slabs, but we have got plenty of that stuff."

Diane explained, "It's an old fashion method my father used and his roses always came up a treat."

At around midnight, the last of the guests left. Emily's parents had decided to go to bed because of an early flight home the next morning, which left Rad, Emily, Diane and me still sipping drinks, as we sat around the table on the veranda.

Emily said, "We've had a wonderful wedding. Thanks for making it here."

I replied, "We wouldn't have missed it for the world."

After about thirty minutes of general chitchat about the wedding ceremony and reception, I could see Diane looked very tired. It had been a long day for us both, so I said, "Well, I suppose it's time to hit the sack. We've got an afternoon flight back to London tomorrow."

Noticing how tired his mum looked, Rad said, "Yeah but have a lie in tomorrow. I'll be taking you to the airport."

As we stood up to head for our bedroom, Diane exclaimed, "Well, Mr. and Mrs. Seer, I hope you have as long, happy and healthy a marriage as we have and don't leave it too long before you know what."

I suspected Diane transmitted the word *grandchildren* to Rad and Emily.

Although Rad and Emily visited us quite often, it was four more years before we got that important Skypecom call from our son. Diane was now eighty one.

In his call he said, "Hiya you two, got some great news for you. We've finally solved the g-force problem for the propulsion system and get this: Emily is pregnant. We can't come over yet because we have things to finalise at work and that sort of stuff, but Emily and I have agreed we want the baby to be born in England. We were hoping that we could stay with you nearer to the baby's birth."

I replied, "Of course you can, son. Just let us know when you're coming."

As the Skypecom was a visual two-way devise, Rad could see that his mum wasn't looking too good, so he asked, "How are you, Mum? Are you OK?"

Diane replied, "Oh, I'm all right. Just a bit of a cold that's all."

Accepting his mother's answer, he said, "OK then, I'll be in touch with you nearer the time. Love to you both."

The communication was then ended. Diane didn't have a cold. In fact I was quite concerned about her general health because she didn't seem to have much energy of late. Immediately after Rad had signed off, Diane said to me, "At last I'm going to get a grandchild. I thought it might never happen."

I said, "Yes, they have left it a bit late, but Emily is the same age as you when you had Rad."

Diane replied, "Yes, but that was because of different circumstances."

The months quickly passed and we finally got the call that Rad and Emily were on their way over to stay with us prior to the birth. They had already made arrangements to have the baby in St. Gregory's Hospital, where Rad was born.

On arrival and getting out of the taxi, a totally different Emily emerged from the car than I saw the first time I met her. Instead of being slim and elegant, she now had a huge belly and was very ungainly, but I expected nothing less seeing as she was almost to term.

"Hi Dad. How's Mum?" Rad said.

"Not that good, son," I answered.

He said, "I suppose she hasn't been to see a doctor?"

I replied, "No, you know her; she always diagnoses herself."

I carried their luggage into the house, while Rad helped his waddling partner to a seat in the lounge, where Diane sat in her armchair.

"Well, look at you," Diane said to Emily.

"Yes, not long now," she replied.

Diane then replied back, it seemed, with an element of thought, "You're right. It isn't long to go now."

For a moment, I somehow felt that there was another meaning to what Diane had just said, but to be honest I just dismissed it.

Emily then said, "Now, how are you, though? I hear you haven't been too well."

Diane replied, "Oh, I'm all right; I think they call it old age. That's all."

While the three of us were in the lounge, Rad had taken their cases up to the guest bedroom and was generally preparing for their stay. As he finally entered the lounge, he said, "Right, that's all sorted."

I said ignorantly, "What happens now?"

Diane said, "Now we just carry on as normal till Emily feels she needs to go to the hospital."

"Right then," I replied. "Tea or coffee?"

It was a week later when Emily felt her first contractions and Rad immediately went into a panic. *Like father like son*, I thought. He grabbed a holdall that they had prepared previously with all the things that Emily might need; then, he helped her outside and into the passenger seat of our car. Diane was feeling particularly out of salts that day and decided she would stay in bed, so before he drove Emily to the hospital, he ran back upstairs to our bedroom where I was sitting on the side of the bed next to Diane. Rad entered the room with our portable Skypecom and put it on one of the bedside tables.

He then said breathlessly, "Right, we're all set for the off. I've set the com to automatic and there is a direct link to me at the hospital. Now, are you sure you are all right, Mum?"

"Of course I am. Stop fussing and get Emily to the hospital," she replied.

Rad came over to his mum, gave her a hug and kissed her on the cheek. "Love you both. Speak to you soon," he said, as he rushed out of the door.

I somehow knew Diane was not all right and a wave of emotion hit me like a brick. Instinctively I knew my beautiful wife was dying and there wasn't much time left.

After Rad left for the hospital, Diane was falling in and out of sleep and her breathing was becoming more and more laboured. I felt there was something I must do before I lost her completely. I hurriedly went to the bathroom and with uncontrollable sobbing and shaking hands, shaved off the beard that I had had for so long and when I looked in the mirror at my shaven face, the truth of my second side effect was clearly visible. My reflection revealed the boyish look of a nineteen-year-old man. Yes, although I was seventy-nine, I hadn't aged a minute in sixty years. Over the past twenty-five years or so, I dyed my hair greyer and greyer and Diane would help me during that time with make-up to help me seem much older than I actually looked.

Knowing that there wasn't much time left, I rushed back into the bedroom accidentally knocking the skypecom screen away from the direction of the bed.

I was now at Diane's side holding her hand. Although my hair was dyed grey, I wanted Diane to see my face as it truly was, so she could remember the time when we first met and fell in love.

Diane briefly opened her eyes.

"Terry, my lovely Terry," she said with a breathless voice.

"I'm here, gorgeous," I replied, trying not to break down with emotion.

Diane's eyes then closed and her little white teddy bear with the red bow tie, which she had been clutching with her other hand, fell from her grip and rolled to the centre of the bed. Then her breathing stopped and she slipped away.

With floods of tears, I cradled her head and kissed her brow and then I stepped back and went to the foot of the bed. A beautiful multi--coloured portal appeared in the bedroom and Diane's spirit started to rise from her body. In the past, I had seen a person's spirit enter their portal looking the way they were when they died, but I suppose that people, who can see the spirit of a loved one, see them how they would want to remember them. To me, Diane's spirit was that of a twenty-one-year-old. She looked exactly how she was when we first met.

As Diane's spirit moved toward the light, she briefly stopped and looked directly at me with a loving smile, then continued toward the portal. It was too much for me to bear. I couldn't live in a world without my Diane and as she approached the entrance to the portal, I made a dash to be at her side.

The next thing I knew I was standing in the Terran world. Diane's spirit had vanished and the intense light all around me was blinding my eyes. I fell to my knees still sobbing as I realised I would never see her again, but I thought at least the Terran atmosphere would kill me off quickly and put me out of my terrible misery.

In the other dimension, Diane's lifeless body lay alone on the bed as Rad's smiling face appeared on the Skypecom. With delight and then bewilderment, he exclaimed,

"It's a girl…Mum, Dad…where are you?"

His daughter had been born at the exact same moment of Diane's death!

After a few minutes, I could feel the burning Terran atmosphere affecting my body and I thought my suffering would soon be over, but then a shadow appeared over me, shielding my face and body from the searing sun. Squinting, I looked up and saw a figure. It was Theron and somehow my eyes were becoming accustomed to the brightness. A dark, dome-like opaque skin was rapidly growing over each of my eyes and the sun's rays ceased to burn my body.

Theron then spoke, "It appears that the elder's prophecy has been fulfilled, Terry! You are the human that would walk among us!"

* * *

Three days had passed since Diane's death and I was now residing in Theron's and Madri's home. Word had gotten around the immediate Terran community that their legendary human, who could tolerate and survive their atmosphere, now existed, and according to Theron, the news was met by the Terran populous with varying opinions as to whether it was a good thing or not, As for me, I just didn't care. The loss of Diane and the failure for me to be with her in death, had just left me in total despair,

But it was in the afternoon of the third day of my melancholy that Madri told me that she had discovered something about Diane's transition through the portal. She said that she could find no record of her brain power entering the Terran world. Madri also said that, this could only mean one thing; Diane's spirit was trapped between the dimensions and it was probably due to me entering her portal at the exact same time. I said to Madri, "Does that mean Diane is in a ghost like state?"

Madri replied, "Yes, in spirit form."

"Then no-matter what it takes, I'm going to find her!" I exclaimed.

The End

Printed in Great Britain
by Amazon